rescue you

ELYSIA WHISLER

rescue you

mira

ISBN-13: 978-0-7783-1008-2

Rescue You

Recycling programs
for this product may
not exist in your area.

This edition published by arrangement with Harlequin Books S.A.

For questions and comments about the quality of this book, please contact us at
CustomerService@Harlequin.com.

Mira
22 Adelaide St. West, 40th Floor
Toronto, Ontario M5H 4E3, Canada
BookClubbish.com

Printed in U.S.A.

For Magdalena—
and all those who fight for the ones who can't

rescue you

one

Constance slammed on her brakes. Steam rose from the street as rain gurgled through the ditches. She killed the engine, stepped into the pattering droplets and scanned the shoulder of the road. Nothing there but the remains of a goose carcass. "Where are you, boy?" Constance gave a low whistle.

It hadn't been her imagination. The picked-over goose only made her more certain she'd seen a dog, weaving through the foggy afternoon air like a phantom. A lost dog, with his head bent against the rain as he loped along the muddy ditch.

Constance whistled again. Silence, but for the sound of rain hitting the trees that lined the road. "Maybe I'm just tired." She'd done a lot of massages today, which made her feel wrung out. Constance almost ducked back into the van, but halted.

There he was: a white face with brown patches, peeking at her from behind a bush. "Hey, boy." Constance squatted down, making herself smaller, less threatening. The dog watched, motionless. Constance drew a biscuit from her coat, briefly recalling the cashier's amusement at the grocery store today when she'd emptied her pockets on the counter, searching for her keys. Five dog biscuits had been in the pile with her phone, a used tissue and the grocery list.

"Dog mom, huh?" the elderly cashier had said.

"Something like that." More like dog aunt, to all of the rescues at Pittie Place. Her sister, Sunny, had quite the brood.

Constance laid the biscuit near her foot and waited. A moment later, the bush rustled and the dog approached. He had short hair and big shoulders. He got only as close as he needed to, then stretched his neck out for the prize. As he gingerly took the biscuit, Constance noted a droopy abdomen and swollen nipples, like a miniature cow.

So. He was a she. Constance inched toward her. The dog held on to the biscuit, but reared back. Constance extended her fist, slowly, so the mom could smell her. "You got puppies somewhere?"

The dog whimpered, but crunched up the biscuit.

"Where are your puppies?"

The dog whimpered again. Her legs shook. Her fur was muddy, feet caked with dirt. She had blood on her muzzle—probably from the dead goose. By her size and coloring, Constance decided she was a pit bull.

Constance rose up, patted her thigh and headed toward her van. She slid open the side door, grabbed a blanket and spread it out, but when she turned around, the dog was several yards away. Her brown-and-white head was low as she wandered beneath a streetlamp, the embodiment of despair in the drizzle that danced through the light.

Constance followed, slipping on the leaves that clogged the drainage ditch. The dog glanced once over her shoulder, but her pace didn't quicken. Constance decided her calm demeanor was working, keeping the dog from fleeing. And let's be honest: the biscuit hadn't hurt. Chances were, the dog would be happy to have more as soon as she got wherever she was going. "Let's see where you're headed, then. Show me if you've got a home."

Constance followed her across the road, around the curve and down the narrow lane. Frogs popped like happy corn all over the slick street, but the chill of the oncoming winter slithered through Constance's blood.

She followed the dog for a good quarter mile. Even before she hooked a left down the unpaved road hidden behind the trees, Constance had figured out that the mama was headed to one of the handful of empty places that sat decomposing on the hundred or so acres the Matteri family owned. Constance paused only long enough to squelch the sizzle of anger that bubbled up inside before she pressed on, determined to know if the dog was a stray or a neglected mother from Janice Matteri's puppy mill.

Constance took the same turn and watched as the dog neared the abandoned house up ahead. Nobody had lived there in years. It was only a matter of time before it became condemned. The dog bypassed the crumbling porch of the old colonial and went around back. Constance knew little daylight was left, and she hadn't brought a flashlight. She broke into a trot, clutched her coat tighter around her and didn't slow until the dog came back into view. Constance followed her, her heart thumping harder with each step.

The dog passed the rusted chain-link fence and disappeared over a rise in the property, near an old shed so overgrown with trees it was only recognizable by a pale red door. Just as she reached the hill, Constance heard a squeak. The sort of high-pitched noise that echoes from everywhere and nowhere all at once. Another squeak came. And another. She crested the hill and saw the dog slink inside the shed door. Constance got to the shed and pushed inside. The dog had reached her destination: a battered old mattress, three shades of brown, lying a few feet inside. The mewls, now loud and hungry, came from a shredded section of the mattress.

Constance narrowed her eyes. At first, she counted only two bobbing, brown heads, but as she drew closer there was a third. Then a fourth. The last one didn't move nearly as much, just sort of waded on his stomach. The puppies had cocoa-colored fur and black muzzles. Eyes open. The ones that moved didn't really walk, just stumbled into each other, like drunks. Mama dog curled around them and they all wiggled toward her abdomen.

Constance knelt down next to the mattress and watched the suckling puppies. She decided they were about two weeks old. The air in the shed smelled of sour milk, poop and urine. She dug out another biscuit and reached, slowly, her hand in a fist to protect her fingers, her gaze on the mama for any sign she was upset, such as pinned ears, bared teeth or a raised ridge of fur down the back. The energy around the mom and her pups was calm, to the point of exhausted. Constance had certainly helped with enough of Sunny's dogs over the years to know. She offered the biscuit and the mom took it. With her mouth busy, Constance carefully touched the smallest puppy, who shook so hard the tremble came from deep inside, beneath his skin and fur, straight from his bones.

Constance rose slowly and did a quick search of the vicinity for more puppies, which turned up nothing but trash, vermin and an old orange crate, which she brought over to the mattress.

Now to see if Mom was going to accept help.

Though daylight was precious, Constance waited until the pups were done suckling before she offered a third treat. "Let's go back to my place," Constance said as Mom accepted the biscuit. "My sister has a rescue for critters, just like you. And I help her all the time. You'll be safe there. Does that sound okay?"

While Mama crunched, Constance reached for the two pups closest to her and, keeping an eye on Mom the whole time, she lifted them and settled them in the crate. Mom's chewing quickened, so Constance acted fast, lifting the last two pups swiftly but carefully. She rose to her feet, crate in her arms. The mother dog was on her feet almost ahead of her, pointing her muzzle at the crate and whining.

Constance knew the mom would follow her anywhere she took those pups, but she also lacked any signs of aggression, almost as though she knew that this was their only chance. Or as Pete, owner of Canine Warriors and Constance's longtime childhood friend, would put it, "You just got something about you, Cici. Everybody trusts you. People. Dogs. The damn Devil himself."

Constance headed back to her van, chasing the sunset. As expected, the mother followed. Once to the vehicle, Constance opened the van and set the crate full of pups next to the blanket she'd spread out earlier. The mama dog leaped in after them.

Constance slid the door closed, settled behind the steering wheel and let out a great sigh. Mission accomplished. She edged down the long, lonely road. The rain pattered on the windshield and the scent of dirty puppies hit her nose. She'd take them home tonight and get them settled in, see how they reacted to a new environment, then text Sunny in the morning. Constance had worked with enough dogs, and people, to know that introducing another new person this evening was bad news. Let Mama get used to Constance first, and get some good food and rest, before she was moved to Pittie Place.

Tonight, at least, this girl and her babies belonged with Constance.

★ ★ ★

By the time Constance pulled into her garage, the dogs were silent, like they'd fallen asleep. She used the opportunity to dash inside and get the whelping box ready. Pete had made it years ago, and Constance had used it plenty while helping Sunny. Made of corrugated plastic, the box was over a foot high, had guardrails and a low entry for the mom. It collapsed to fit under the couch when not in use. Constance pulled it out and got it ready next to the gas fireplace. In went the heated whelping pad, with the liner over top. The last thing she needed to do was get Fezziwig situated before she brought in the newcomers. He wouldn't be any trouble, but Constance had a good idea how a protective mom would react to a strange, male pit bull.

"Fezzi." Constance led him into the kitchen and pointed to his dog bed, by the window. "Place."

Fezzi climbed on and waited.

"Stay."

He settled down on the bed, as used to the commands Pete had taught him years ago as he was to his feeding and walking routine. Constance collected a leash and went back outside for the mama and her pups. Mama blinked her eyes open when Constance slid open the rear door of the van. Constance let her sniff the leash and feel it against her fur, then slipped it over her head. She lifted the orange crate in one arm, took the leash in the other hand and led them inside.

Constance transferred the pups to the whelping box first, which prompted the mom to climb right in after. Once they were settled, Constance left to collect food, water and a wet, warm cloth. Fezzi snorted at her as she went by, but Constance only held up a finger. "Stay."

As always, Fezzi obeyed.

While the mom ate from the bowl of food, Constance used

the wet towel to wash away what she could of the grime. "Life has not been kind to you," she murmured as she toweled off the pittie. There were several old scars that ran over the dog's face, including a chunk missing from her ear. Most likely, this had been a bait dog for one of the Matteri thugs, years ago, back when they ran a dogfighting ring. Over time, all of those Matteris had ended up in jail, with the exception of Janice, who'd turned instead to running a puppy mill.

Who knew how many fights this mama had been used for or how often she'd been bred. Whatever damage was left, Constance would have to leave for Dr. Winters, the mobile vet who worked on Sunny's dogs.

Other than massage, of course.

That was Constance's milieu.

The pittie's energy was low, which was no surprise. But as Constance ran her hands gently over the dog's shoulders and back—white with brindle patches, like puddles and pebbles—she could feel the life inside, the ember that remained, even after all she'd been through. Despite probably being used as a bait dog, this girl was a fighter. Constance maintained light pressure and rhythmic breathing to loosen the mom's muscles and get her deeply relaxed. Her abdomen was smooth and cool, indicating clear milk ducts. Soon, her eyes fluttered closed.

"That's it."

The pittie's eyes opened again, drooped, opened and drooped, like the dog was used to having to fight sleep to stay alive. Constance raked her fingertips down the dog's sides and over her rib cage, loosening her tight intercostal muscles. Her ribs expanded more fully, and her next exhale came in a great sigh. Finally, the dog's eyes closed for good, the orangey light of the fireplace washing over her and the puppies like a blanket.

Constance left her hand at rest on the mama for a few more

minutes. Everyone was asleep and seemed stable. The small, weak pup who'd shook so hard beneath Constance's touch didn't look as good as the others, though. His fur was duller and his breathing more shallow. Constance said a little prayer, knowing the vet would check them all tomorrow.

She quietly rose and went to take a shower, washing away the fur and dirt and smell, then settled on the couch for the night, to stay close to the brood. It wasn't much of a sacrifice. Even after six months, Constance didn't like sleeping alone in her bedroom. Josh's side of the bed remained cold and untouched, even though Constance could've sprawled out and taken up the entire mattress.

She snapped her fingers, and a few seconds later Fezziwig came padding into the room. He leaped on the couch, curled up behind her knees, settled his chin on her legs and puffed out a great sigh. He knew the mom and puppies were there, but he wouldn't go near them until Constance allowed it.

"That's my boy." Constance rubbed his head. Five years old, he was Sunny's first rescue. She'd found him in the street, lying in a pool of his own blood, his foot so mangled it looked like hamburger. He'd been thrown there, not far from the same house where Constance had just found Mama and her pups. He'd been left to bleed out, since he couldn't be fought anymore. Sunny took him home and Dr. Winters had him on IVs for days. When she finally gave him back she'd said, "Don't get your hopes up."

Fezzi had lost his leg, but not his life. And despite the odds, Pete had turned Fezzi into his first Canine Warrior.

As Constance's eyes closed and her mind drifted into dreams, she felt the tiniest bit guilty at how much comfort she got from the warmth and glow of the fire, and the presence of so many heartbeats to match her own.

two

The scarecrow's grin hadn't changed in decades. Sunny's first memory was from age four, tripping on her witch costume and falling headfirst into the dummy's knees. Back then, it was the jack-o'-lantern smile that made her freeze. Was he happy? Angry? Sad? She couldn't look away, trapped by what she kind of liked and kind of hated, until a sneeze broke the spell, the hay in her nose saving her from drowning in the thing's eyes.

Back then, Sunny wondered how Daddy managed to carve the same grin, Halloween after Halloween, into that stupid scarecrow's pumpkin head. The jack-o'-lantern's eyes changed, sometimes round, sometimes triangular, the whole bit. Noses were worse, sometimes didn't even exist. But not that grin. He always had that same secret, spooky smile. Every. Single. Year.

Sunny pulled her jacket tighter around her, suppressing the fickle Virginia November air, which was warm yesterday and had gone frigid today. She made her way toward the front porch, where fake spiderwebs covered the meticulously clipped hedges. The house, a forty-year-old colonial, sat as a well-cared-for backdrop to the old-fashioned decorations. In addition to the scarecrow, Constance had put out hay bales, pumpkins, a tractor with a flat tire, the trailer filled with ghosts that popped against the sky and some coffins containing skeletons and undead creatures. Sunny had never understood the quiet diligence with which her father had reserved for Halloween, when every other holiday mostly passed unnoticed. She understood less her big sister's insistence on carrying on his ghoulish traditions since he'd passed and she'd inherited the house.

Halloween had come and gone, but Constance had left the decorations up, claiming they were just as good for Thanksgiving.

Sunny let herself in, like she always did. "Cici!" She hung her coat in the foyer and peeked into the kitchen. It was warm and smelled like sweet bread. Constance had set the table with coffee and muffins. She sat near the window, wearing baggy sweatpants and a sweatshirt, leafing through the *Washington Post*. Sunny sighed. She couldn't quite get used to the sight of her big sister in those old, oversize clothes. Cici had never been fashionable, but up until last year, she'd worn cute running shorts or leggings and colorful tech tees. Ever since she'd completely given up running her attire had consisted of cheap fare from the men's department. Her strawberry blond hair, once full of feminine waves, was several different lengths of bad hack job. She'd chopped it off after Josh left, kept chopping it, and ever since then it'd grown out like an awkward teenager, gangly and all different lengths.

Sunny's perusal settled on Constance's cheek. "Where'd you get that bruise?"

"Fell off a stair-stepper. Have you ever tried one of those things? It's just wrong."

"Those machines are wrong," Sunny agreed. "In any form. You should get back to running again. Outside. Like you used to."

"Nah." Constance waved a careless hand. "I don't want to run. But I had to do something. It's hard to explain. I—"

"You saw Josh, didn't you?"

Constance picked up a muffin and peeled away the paper. "I ran into him at the grocery store yesterday. Didn't want to tell you because you would've made it a thing." She took a huge bite and worked around the muffin as she spoke. "He told me I looked good, which is impossible. I was wearing...well—" Cici gestured at her lap "—this. And I hadn't washed my hair in three days. I even had it in a scrunchie." She touched the back. "What's left of it. He felt sorry for me. I could see it in his eyes."

"That was guilt you saw in his eyes. The jerk feels guilty for dumping you."

"Can't really blame him." Constance's voice dropped. "I'm not exactly the same girl he started dating once upon a time."

"No, you're not. You've changed with your life. Grown wiser. Better. Like a fine wine."

Constance stuffed the rest of the muffin in her mouth. "Do I look like a fine wine?" She chewed quietly, then said, "You can't bullshit someone who practically raised you."

"I'm not. You're amazing, and Josh is a douchebag." Sunny peeled back a piece of her muffin paper and took a small bite. Constance's muffins were deadly good. If you ate too much, you just wanted more. "You should try my spin class. I don't think you'd fall off the bike."

"Yeah?" Constance's voice had an edge. "So fake bikes are okay but all other machines aren't?"

Sunny knew she'd walked into that one, but she ignored it. "I dare you to try it. Just once. I swear I'll go easy on you."

"Maybe. But even if I do, I'm not going when you're teaching."

Sunny rolled her eyes. "Where's the bitch?"

A tiny smile hooked the corner of Constance's mouth and her lips parted.

Sunny cut her off. "Don't." She shook her head. "That would be too easy, even for you."

Constance giggled and sipped her coffee. "She's in the living room." She tilted her chin in that direction.

"And you just found them? Last night?"

"Was on my way home from working, after about six travel-to massages. Right there on Bright Valley Road."

"This wasn't a dog you'd been scoping out? For the rescue?" Even though Constance wouldn't take part in the "liberating" of abused and neglected dogs—from both Janice Matteri's puppy mill, and anywhere else they might find—she was constantly giving Sunny tips on this or that dog she'd seen somewhere, or updates on when Janice got a new batch of dogs, which meant the older ones were farmed out to the back, forgotten and neglected.

"Nope." Constance shook her head. "This dog appeared, literally, out of nowhere. I think she's a leftover from the pit bull fighting. I was so tired last night I thought I was seeing things."

Sunny pushed away the remains of her muffin, her stomach turning at the memories of Janice's brothers' and cousins' illegal cruelty, and went to investigate. She saw Fezzi first, sitting up tall like a soldier on his one good front leg, across the room from the mother and her nursing babies. He was a merle—a rare coloring that on Fezzi presented as a striking solid white head and a body of icy gray patched with stark black. She couldn't imagine why anyone would ever abuse such a beautiful creature.

The mama lay on her side inside the box. Four babies—who didn't look like purebred pit bulls, which suggested the mother had mated with a stray—suckled away. That was a small litter for a pit bull, but the numbers made sense. Either the mother had more and had lost them or her poor health had kept the numbers low. Plus, she was no spring chicken. Her age could be a factor. "The runt doesn't look so good," Sunny said. He was considerably smaller than the other three, skinny, and his suckling wasn't as active.

"I know." Constance leaned against the entryway that separated the living and dining rooms. She looked tired and sad. "I had to attach him myself this morning. He wasn't nursing like the others."

"Dr. Winters will be at my place in an hour." Sunny glanced at the clock over the mantel. "She can check them all over. I'll get them loaded up soon."

"You should call Pete, too. These pups will be good candidates for Canine Warriors."

"You've only known them for one night."

Constance shrugged. She looked just like Daddy when she did that—a lift of the shoulder so slight you almost missed it. Unlike most people's shrugs, there was no uncertainty in the movement. *I'm just telling you how it is. You can believe me or not, but I'm right.* "They're smart and have good dispositions. They'll train easy. They're going to be perfect for rehab dogs. Either vets with disabilities or PTSD. Pete's going to love them."

"You got that just from touching them, huh?" Sunny wouldn't believe it if she hadn't seen Constance do it a million times. She could read a dog, or a person, within a matter of minutes of assessing posture, gait, the way they carried themselves and, of course, how they felt to the touch.

"Chevy's a fighter," Constance said. "She's been through hell and back, but she'll hang on, no matter what."

"Chevy?" Leave it to Constance to have already named the mother. She might've even named the pups.

Constance crossed the room, stooped down and ran her palm lightly over the dog's head. The mother didn't even flinch, which indicated that Constance had already "whispered" her into trust. "Chevy can come back here, if nobody wants her. After the pups are weaned, I mean." She glanced at Fezzi, who sat nearby. "Fez is in love."

"Good thing he's such a gentleman." Sunny stroked Fezziwig behind the ears. "She'd take him out in a heartbeat."

"Yeah." Constance rose up and ran her hands through her messy hair. "C'mon. Let's get her loaded up."

By the time the mother and pups were in Sunny's van, Constance was yawning. Even though the dogs might've kept her up last night, the sight made Sunny's insides sink. She had a momentary vision of her big sister, years back, dressed in running clothes and a pair of one of the several sets of Nike shoes she kept in rotation, her strawberry hair back in a ponytail and a GPS watch on her wrist. She'd streak by the dog rescue on her morning runs, wave to Sunny and the dogs as her feet pounded over the trail that ran behind the house. She ran all those winding, long trails that connected Constance to Sunny, to Pete, and even to Janice Matteri—all of them out here on this rural acreage, separated by miles but connected by dogs, both the good and the bad of it. Then Daddy got sick, and Constance's routine changed and slowed, her mornings filled with hospital visits and caring for an elderly man sick on chemo and radiation. By the time Daddy died, Constance rarely ran at all anymore. And then, of course, came the day Constance stopped running for good.

"Remember to come try my spin class," Sunny said. Who knows? Maybe Cici would fall in love with spin like she had the open road, way back in her cross-country days in high school. "Evenings at the shopping center and mornings at Spin City."

"Maybe."

"Chicken."

"That hasn't worked on me since I was twelve."

"Bullshit."

Constance lips parted in retort, then closed as her attention was diverted to the police cruiser that was pulling smoothly up to the house.

Sunny's heart did a little flip inside her chest. The sight took her back two decades, to the first dog she, Pete and Constance had rescued. They passed by the Potter place almost every day, either playing in the woods or walking home from the bus stop. As the old Potter couple had gotten older and older, their coonhound had gotten more and more neglected. A dog that was once let inside during the cold or heat was now being left out to shiver or sweat, with no water or shelter in sight. Sunny, at the tender age of nine, had declared one day that she was going to save him, if none of the adults had enough balls—*balls* being a word she'd proudly learned from Daddy. Pete had been game to help and Constance, always the mother, had been the lookout; she could neither bring herself to break the rules nor leave the poor creature to suffer.

The old coonhound, Bert, had followed them home willingly and had lived in secret in the basement for three days until Daddy found him. Sunny had boldly pleaded her case, Constance had apologized, and Daddy had let the hound live out his last months there under the care of both girls, "long as he didn't have to lie to nobody or clean up any shit." The only thing that had saved Bert was that when the police cruiser drove up, investigating the missing dog and Mrs. Potter's insistence that she'd seen the Morrigan girls making off with him, was that Daddy had not been home to lie and Sunny had discovered that she was quite good at it.

Constance eyed the police cruiser today the same way she had back then. She squinted, then leveled Sunny with a cautious gaze.

Sunny raised her hands, palms spread. "Not me. You found Chevy wandering down the road, right?"

"Yes. The pups were on Matteri land, but at the abandoned house. There's no way Janice could know I was there."

"Are you sure?"

"Of course I'm sure. You sure this isn't about you? Because it sure looks like you raided Janice Matteri's puppy mill again. Or got caught rescuing another dog somewhere?"

"I swear," Sunny said. "Not recently. Plus, Janice has never called the cops before."

"Looks like she's stepping up her game." Constance tore her gaze from the cruiser. "Don't worry about it. Get those pups home. Dr. Winters will be at your place soon." Constance tapped her watch.

Cool as ice. Exactly how Daddy had raised her. Sunny often told her big sister she'd have been right at home inside his foxholes in Vietnam.

Sunny hopped to, getting behind the wheel and starting the engine before the policeman could even get out of the cruiser.

Constance sat on a scratchy green couch and leafed through the pictures, passing one beneath the other like a woman might her wedding photos, pausing at some, holding others up to the light. A German shepherd. Maltese. Pomeranian. Greyhound.

Adopted. Adopted. Adopted. Adopted.

Detective Callahan, as he'd introduced himself when Constance arrived at the station, bumped her arm with a Styrofoam cup of steaming black coffee.

"Thanks." Constance accepted the cup. "Nope." She slid the stack of photos to the desk. "I haven't seen any of these dogs." Constance's eyes locked into the detective's, which were a pale gray like the sky after a morning rain.

The detective's brow furrowed. "You sure?" He rubbed the back of his neck.

"As sure as I can be. I see a lot of dogs, Detective."

Detective Callahan settled into his desk chair and sighed. "Okay. Well." He raked his thick fingers through his light brown hair. "Janice Matteri claims that your sister's been regularly raiding her kennel for years. We're talking to her, of course, but your name also came up. Janice says you two work together."

"I do help my sister with her legitimately run animal rescue." Constance inhaled the steam of the coffee. She could tell it came from the bottom of a pot that had been cooking for hours. "But I don't steal them. Janice Matteri has never proven that Sunny has stolen any of her dogs, either. All of our dogs are microchipped, proving where they come from. If Janice bothered to chip hers, she might not have this problem."

"This is just what she's saying. That this has been going on for some time. That you typically handle it among yourselves, but things went too far this time." After a heartbeat, the detective pursed his lips. "She also said that her newly installed security camera was coated in black spray paint. Any idea who might've done that? Someone who works for your sister's dog rescue, maybe?" Detective Callahan rubbed the back of his neck again.

"No idea whatsoever. Pittie Place is nonprofit. Everyone's a volunteer and my sister gets a lot of her volunteers from the County Youth Corrections Program. So." Constance shrugged. "You're a cop. You connect the dots."

The detective squared his hands behind his head and leaned

back. His sharp features settled into resignation. "Anything at all you can tell me, Constance?"

Constance drew a deep breath, suddenly able to smell that dirty backyard kennel. "There is absolutely nothing I can tell you about Janice Matteri's overcrowded and filthy puppy mill. Perhaps she needs to check the locks on her gates. Better yet, perhaps she needs to stop running an inhumane and illegal operation. Then she wouldn't have these sorts of problems."

A heartbeat of silence passed. "We've been out there. Everything was clean, and though her dogs were to capacity, Ms. Matteri's numbers weren't over the limit. On paper, her business is legit and in order."

"Because she knew you were coming. You should set up a sting. Catch her by surprise."

A smile played around the corner of the detective's mouth. "Are you...?" He cleared his throat. The ghost smile vanished. "You're not joking. Well, maybe I should do that. Maybe we should pay a surprise visit to your sister's rescue, as well."

A tremor ran through her, but Constance held her breath, squelching it. Daddy had taught her how to play poker when she was only five years old. She'd had nearly thirty years to perfect her face. "You won't find any of Janice's dogs at Pittie Place." That, at least, wasn't a lie.

"I know." Detective Callahan shrugged. "The officer who visited you this morning paid a visit to your sister's afterward. She gave him a grand tour. He said it was the cleanest setup he'd ever seen for animals. Said he saw a new litter of pups, too."

Constance made sure nothing was written on her face before she spoke. If she showed emotion, it would come out in her voice. "Those aren't Janice Matteri's dogs, either. She doesn't sell pit bulls. Claims they're a 'dangerous breed.'" Constance made air quotes with her fingers. "Which is ironic, since her brothers used to fight them. But those pups are going to be Canine Warriors, not bait dogs. So Janice Matteri can suck it."

Detective Callahan suppressed a laugh by pretending he coughed. "Canine Warriors," he mused. "That's the guy who trains dogs for service members." A new light ran through the detective's eyes. "Does it for free. Right?"

"That's right." Constance seized the opportunity to make the most of Callahan's interest. "Pete Clark. My sister, Sunny, works with him. She donates pups who are good candidates to be trained as service dogs to Pete, and Pete trains them for service members who need them. It's a good partnership. Dog gets a home, service member gets help. Win-win."

"That's awesome."

Constance could tell he meant it.

"I have a buddy who could use one of those dogs."

"I'll leave one of my friend's cards with you."

Detective Callahan shook his head. "He'd never admit he needed one."

"All right, then." Constance rose from the couch, set the untouched coffee on the desk and smoothed out her clothing. She wished she'd worn a clean shirt. She looked like hell. Not that she was trying to impress anyone. Detective Callahan was hard, handsome and no-nonsense. Just her type. But ever since Josh, she only looked at men with cool detachment.

Detective Callahan followed her lead. "Thanks for coming in and looking at the photos."

Constance shrugged. "I knew the request wasn't really a request."

He gave a short laugh. "So your sister rescues the dogs. Pete trains them. What's your part in all that, Constance? Other than raiding the Matteri puppy mill, perhaps?" He rubbed the back of his neck.

Another thing Daddy had taught her was that diversion was often the best tactic to avoid a trap. "How long have you had that neck pain?"

His eyebrows rose. Then he shrugged. "Months, on and off."

"Anything specific happen before you first felt it?"

He shrugged again. "Not that I remember. But on this job, who knows?" He shook his head from side to side. "Feels better when I do this, though."

Constance came around the desk and stood behind him. "May I?"

"What are you going to do?"

"You asked my part," she said. "I'm a massage therapist. I work the dogs. Help them heal. Don't worry, I won't hurt you, Detective."

He laughed, but then took a seat. "Knock yourself out."

Constance hovered over his neck before she touched his skin. The air around him was warm and a little fizzy. "Lean your head forward." After he obeyed, she palpated his upper neck, allowing her fingertips to sink in along the spine. Detective Callahan drew a deep breath and expelled it slowly. She spent a couple of minutes there, working soft and slow, starting with fascia and only gradually moving into muscle tissue. After a while, she spoke softly. "Have you been saying yes to something—" Constance gave him some light traction "—that you really want to say no to?"

The detective's body froze. "What?"

"Not a small thing, like saying yes to meat loaf when you want steak. But a big thing?"

He chuckled softly. "Maybe."

Constance released him and came around to the front of the desk. "You need to come clean. Until you do, that pain in your neck won't go away."

"Come again?" His eyes sparkled with curiosity.

"You're saying no inside, while saying yes with your mouth," Constance explained. "Yes—" she nodded "—and no—" she shook her head "—occur at different joints. When you're thinking no, your neurons are already firing for no." Constance shook her head again. "But you're thinking no, and saying yes." She nodded. "The muscles you primed to say no are fired but don't get to move. And you're in pain because of it."

Detective Callahan rubbed his neck and cracked a smile. "So lying is literally a pain in the neck?"

"Sure." Constance had a better sense of him, now that she'd touched him. He was crisp and tidy as the mint gum he chewed. Hard-nosed and insightful but could list to the lazy side if not kept in check. "Your body tells you everything you need to know. If you pay attention."

Detective Callahan took his cup of coffee and sipped. "You massage humans? Or just the dogs?"

"Both." These days, Constance preferred the dogs, but kept that to herself.

"You work at one of those big chains? Massage Glory or whatever?"

Constance collected her purse. "No," she said. "They can't afford me."

He smiled, then handed her a business card. "Here. Call me if you think of anything. That'll get you straight to me."

"Thanks."

"Oh, and—" he kept his hand outstretched "—I will take that card of yours. Just in case my buddy needs it."

Constance dug out one of Pete's business cards and handed it over. She pointed toward the detective's neck. "Come clean if you want to feel better."

As she left, she resisted the urge to rub the back of her

own neck. Once she was safely out of the police station, she called Sunny.

"Are you in jail?" Sunny said as soon as she answered.

"No. All good. On my way home."

"Better stay off the Matteri property for a while. Even the abandoned lots, like where you found Chevy."

"You give yourself that lecture?" Constance's voice was terse. "You're the one who went too far last time you hit Janice's mill. You took too many at once."

"I couldn't help it." Sunny's voice went soft. "I wanted to grab them all. In fact, there's a beagle I want to go back for. He was too afraid to come with me last time—"

"No. You have to lie low with Janice. But that reminds me." Constance paused and bit her lip. She really shouldn't egg Sunny on. "Thirteen White Fern Road."

There was a pause at the other end. "You spotted a new dog?"

"Yes. While I was out working yesterday. I had a travel-to on that road. This was a distant neighbor I drove by. Large, black dog. Maybe a rottweiler? He was outside both before and after the massage. Just seemed thin. Something's off. But needs further investigation to know for sure." Constance had never liked the fact that her sister stole dogs. On the other hand, she couldn't stop herself from letting Sunny know when she saw one that was neglected. It was a dual-edged sword she'd yet to learn how to wield.

"I'll check it out for sure."

"All right. But be careful. They might be watching you now."

"You know I will."

three

In his dreams, they were still alive. At least for a little while. Devon, with his big grin and the dance moves that won him the ladies' attention, and Masters, tall and droopy like a willow tree, smiling half as often as Devon and couldn't dance a lick. Rhett rushed all his men into the bunker as soon as warning sirens blared. Only Devon and Masters were missing. In his dreams, Rhett knew about the rockets before they hit. He'd call out, searching for Devon and Masters, but his voice came out silent.

The explosions happened, no matter what, no matter how many times Rhett's slumbering brain tried to rewrite the story. About ninety percent of the time, the explosion was his alarm going off. Most people dreaded the alarm, but not him.

The alarm was a relief.

He reached, and a few empty beer bottles hit the floor. One smashed into sharp chunks. They were old, had been there for days, but Rhett wasn't much into cleaning lately. He wasn't going to lie—those beer bottles would be fresh every night, just enough to dull the dreams, if his physical well-being weren't so important to his job. He fumbled with his cell phone and rubbed his bleary eyes just enough to see so he could turn the damn thing off.

He got up. Pissed. Took a shower. Cleaned up the glass. Ate.

Did the stuff everybody else did. The fog began to lift, the memories to recede. The nightmares retreated to their corners, shied by the sunlight.

It was one bright, sunny fucking day.

Despite being ten miles away, the booms from the Quantico marine base shook Rhett's town house enough to make the glass rattle in the cupboards. The shadow box containing his Purple Heart, propped on an end table with old magazines, shuddered against the wall. A gift from his mother. Rhett sank to the couch, covered his ears and waited. He willed the shadow box to fall over, the glass to shatter. But it settled at an angle, teetering but safe.

"The beer bottles break and the shadow box doesn't." Rhett shook his head and glanced at the ceiling. "Shut up," he said. "I got it under control."

His cell vibrated in his pocket. *Melinda*. "Hey, fatso." Even though she weighed about a hundred pounds.

"Worst brother ever."

"Yep. Got the award to prove it."

"You awake?"

"Um. Duh." Rhett tossed his dishes in the sink, next to the others.

"You at work?"

"Going now." He found his car keys, buried in a pile of unopened mail.

Melinda made some kind of growling noise. "Beast," she said. "Do you think you could bench-press your little sister's fat ass?"

Rhett tripped over his sneakers, then grabbed them. "Two of you in each hand." He sank down on the top step and shoved in his left foot, then his right. "Hey. Why're you bothering me so early?" He cradled the phone against his ear and laced up his sneakers.

"Mama's making me ask about Thanksgiving. Again. You coming down?"

Driving down to North Carolina, in holiday traffic. Papa, making enough food to feed a small army. Turkey, yes. But also Papa's "secret recipe" hot sauce, homemade corn tortillas and, the next day, chilaquiles with leftover turkey thrown in— Papa loved mixing up the cuisine. Lazing in front of football all day with Mama, moving from the couch only long enough to eat. All sounded great, except for the traffic. "Nah," Rhett said, even though he wouldn't mind seeing his baby sister and little nieces. And getting the leftover food. Mama would stuff his car full and he'd be in hog heaven for a week. "Too busy. I told Mama that weeks ago. She only hears what she wants to hear."

"That sucks. Just be forewarned, Mama may do something stupid if you don't come."

"Like what?"

"I don't know. You know Mama."

"It's fine. I want to work." He'd much rather train the bulky powerlifters, the soccer moms who wanted to be "toned," the rich girls with all the money to spend but not a speck of intensity or even the little old ladies cheating death by lifting their very first barbells than do the Happy Family Holiday Thing. Anything was better than the Happy Family Holiday Thing. That was a pill he just couldn't swallow right now. "And hey. I'll save you another call, Mel. Tell Mama I'm not coming for Christmas, either."

A long silence followed. "You really want me to tell her that?"

"Yep. Might as well."

"Why not, Rhett? Surely you can get away for a few days—"

"Not—" Rhett stood up and tested his leg "—coming." His quad was worse today than yesterday. But he should be fine once he got warmed up.

"All right." Melinda gave a resigned sigh. "Go sweat it all out. But call me later. Tonight, maybe, just to check in."

"What if I have a hot date?"

"You don't."

"Shut up."

"You shut up."

Click.

Rhett braced himself for the cold, which he felt in both knees and his left shoulder. He ran his hand over the right thigh, which took the drop in barometric pressure hardest. He didn't need a weather report to know a cold front had moved in overnight. His battered body told him everything.

Just as he cracked the front door, the booms shook the house again. Rhett leaned in the door frame, closed his eyes and waited. Once it passed, he cleared his throat, opened his eyes and watched his breath turn to steam. All good.

No big deal. He was all good.

Rhett grabbed the headphone cord near Samuel's ear and yanked the bud out. "Hey."

Samuel took out the other side and let it dangle down his chest. "What'd you say?"

"I said, don't wear this shit in my class. This isn't open gym."

"All right, man." Samuel spread open his big hands and took a step back. "Chill."

"Don't tell me to chill." Rhett pointed a finger at Samuel's chest. "You came to me, remember? You want me to get you ready for your next meet. You want to increase your jerk by fifty pounds. You have all these goals. None of which are going to happen if you're not serious."

"I am serious, man. Shit. Sorry." Samuel's pale face went ruddy from ears to chin. He pulled his phone, attached to the earbuds, from his pocket and set it down on the jerk blocks. "Let's go. I'll do whatever you say."

"Good." Rhett pointed at the phone. "Get that shit off my jerk blocks. This ain't your living room. Grab a barbell. That's what's supposed to go there."

"Yes, sir." Samuel stripped off his hoodie and tossed it on the bench. He thought better of it, grabbed the hoodie, folded it up neatly and laid it on his gym bag.

As he went to grab a barbell, Rhett saw Hobbs in the corner, laughing. "What's your problem?" Rhett shot at him.

"Just glad I'm not one of your PT clients, Santos." Hobbs walked over, iPad in hand, his chuckles dying down as he watched Samuel put on his wrist wraps, his face solemn.

"People need to get in here ready to work. Don't waste my time." Rhett's voice rose at the end, to ensure Samuel could hear him.

Samuel sniffed, his teeth holding the strap while he wound the fabric around his wrist. He was a good guy actually. Just young. Late twenties, college-educated, never had to care about anything but himself. He was strong and worked steady, but lacked that edge Rhett desired in a client. Old or young, man or woman, Rhett didn't care. But give him a client with fire in the soul and a hungry heart and he was a happy man.

"Just leave the customer relations to me, man," Hobbs said. "You're a bit abrasive."

"The gym is thriving," Rhett shot back. "I'll run my gym my way."

"Settle down." Hobbs spread his hands open. "I'm not here

to fight. I'm here to talk holidays. So, you're going to be around all Thanksgiving weekend?" Hobbs let his humor die away, reluctantly, and tapped on his iPad.

"All Thanksgiving *week*," Rhett corrected. "And Christmas, too."

"Even better." Hobbs tapped the screen with his stylus, a lazy smile on his square jaw the only remnant of his mirth. "I guess. Kind of lame actually. You're not going home?"

"No." Rhett watched Samuel warm up his jerk, using the racks for what they were meant for. "But that doesn't mean I want to cover everything." He gave Hobbs a sidelong glance. If he hadn't known Hobbs since basic training, he doubted he could put up with that easy-rider attitude. Then again, Hobbs was right, about Rhett staying out of the customer relations. He turned back to Samuel. "More speed under the bar!"

"Liar." Hobbs flashed that easy smile again, the one all the ladies went crazy for. It was genuine, but not special. Any woman with a pulse was treated to that grin. "You'd happily cover every single class if I fired every last coach and turned in my key. Anything to keep your heartbeat up."

"Go home to Nebraska," Rhett said. "I'll be here for the holidays."

Hobbs was quiet a second while they both watched Samuel, who was adding weight too quickly, load up his bar. Rhett let it happen. Experience was the best teacher.

"You know what you need?" Hobbs's grin was back.

Rhett waited for the usual. *You need to get laid.*

"You need fresh blood. A new project to sink your teeth into. A superstar teenager who could make the Olympics. Something like that."

"You know what you need?"

Hobbs's smile didn't fade while he waited for the punch line.

"A kick in the ass."

Hobbs bent over and stuck his rock-hard butt in the air. He puckered his lips. "Only if you do it, big boy."

"Get away from me."

As Hobbs burst into laughter and headed for the office, Samuel failed his third warm-up jerk. The barbell slammed into the jerk blocks so hard everyone in the gym—which was about twenty stay-at-home moms doing boot camp—gasped and snapped their heads toward the weight-lifting area.

"I think I warmed up too quick," Samuel said, his long face sheepish.

"Ya think?" Rhett sighed. His leg ached. He was going to need more coffee to get through this day.

"Hey, Rhett." One of the boot camp ladies strolled by, her ass hanging out of a pair of booty shorts that were a size too small. "When can I get a private lesson?" She sipped from her water bottle, which left a ring of pink lipstick around the nozzle.

Rhett nodded toward Zoe, his most reliable coach, high-fiving the rest of the ladies who had just finished their workout. She was young, fit, stronger than most of the men and had an infectious personality. "Check with Zoe."

The woman—Candy? Caty? Corey?—thrust out her chest. Her cleavage sported a sheen of sweat. "I was hoping you could do it. I like the boot camp but I'm really interested in learning the barbell. I want to learn it right."

"Zoe's USAW certified," Rhett said. "You go through her Level 1 before you move on to Levels 2 and 3. I do mostly Level 3, some Level 2 on a case-by-case basis."

"Okay." The woman twirled a piece of her dark hair around her finger. "I'll check with Zoe, then." She turned with a little huff and grabbed her baby backpack from the floor.

"Jeez, dude." Hobbs hadn't quite made it to the office yet. "Can't you tell when a chick is hitting on you?" He watched the woman walk with determined strides toward the exit.

"Yes." Rhett followed Hobbs's gaze. Kitty. That was her name. "I can."

"You're made of stone."

"I'm particular," Rhett countered. "She gives fifty percent every workout. She's here more for the social hour than the exercise. She's got those fake nails." Rhett gave a creeped-out shiver. "And, most important, she's a client."

"And you take everything too seriously. You don't have to fall in love with her. Just go on a date and have some fun."

Rhett stiffened. He glared at Hobbs, who knew he'd gone too far. "You got somewhere to be?"

"I sure do. Like, right now. Far, far away from you." Hobbs shook his head. "Man of steel," he repeated as he walked away.

Rhett ran his fist over the scarring on his right leg and winced. If only that were true.

"Leg still being a pain in the ass?"

Rhett knew that voice. He hadn't heard it in months. He turned around and his mouth spread into a slow smile. "Callahan. You lazy SOB. How long's it been?"

Sean offered a sheepish grin. "Two months?"

"Try four." Rhett knew exactly how long it had been since Sean had been in for a workout. "And you're getting the soft belly to prove it." Rhett couldn't actually see Sean's abs at the moment. He was wearing a winter jacket over his shorts and Semper Fit T-shirt. But he'd known Sean long enough to know there was a soft spot for the doughnuts that stereotyped the police world.

Sean rubbed his middle. "I'm not gonna lie. I'm carrying a little extra. But—" he dropped his gym bag on the floor and peeled off his coat "—I'm here."

"Guess you've been too busy catching thieves to keep in shape, huh?" Rhett nodded toward the main area of the gym, where the first evening class was starting to gather. "We've missed you."

"I've texted so many times. Invited you out with the guys. You never come."

Rhett felt a wave of guilt, followed by fatigue. Just the thought of hanging out in a noisy bar made him want to burrow under the covers. "I'm a busy man." He faked a casual voice. "You know where I'm at."

"Hey, I'm a busy man, too." Sean beat his chest with a grin. "People will steal anything that's not nailed down. Money, groceries…dogs."

"Dogs?" Rhett laughed. "Now that's a good story, I bet."

"Had this woman in today. Works with rescues and service dogs. In fact, I've got the contact info. You might be interested." Sean's voice trailed off as his gaze went from the spot Rhett kept working on his quad, to his gym bag, now on the floor by his feet. "Eh, never mind." Sean waved a hand. "We'll talk about it later. I'm going to go get warmed up."

"Good idea." Rhett kneeled down, against the wall, and did the couch stretch for his bad leg. Sometimes it helped. At least for a little while. As he leaned there, breathing deeply into the pit of his stomach and exhaling slowly against the pain, he realized he was both glad and uncomfortable that Sean was here. He'd missed his best buddy and USMC brother, there was no denying that. But Sean was also the only person that could see right through him. Rhett got away with exactly zero bullshit with Sean Callahan, and the same was true the other way around.

"C'mon, Santos!" Sean called from across the gym. "Quit babying your leg and get over here."

Rhett rose up with a groan and laughed. Yeah, it was good to have Sean back. But his leg still hurt like a son of a bitch. Time to see how well he could hide it.

four

White Fern Road wasn't even paved. The long gravel lane was dotted with a half dozen houses, set far apart and well back from the road that crunched beneath Sunny's tires. Number 13 turned out to be several acres of old farmland, overgrown with grass and trees that hadn't been trimmed in years. A small house sat nestled in a grove of pin oaks that looked like zombies, slowly bending toward the home that they tried to consume. Even from this distance, Sunny could see that the wood siding was chipped and the wraparound porch rotting. If it hadn't been for the car parked out front, she might've thought the place was abandoned. Way out, in the middle of what might've been tobacco fields once upon a time, sat a faded, red barn.

Sunny typically liked old barns, big farms, rotting silos in the middle of Civil War–era battlefields. But not this one. That barn gave her the creeps.

She narrowed her eyes at the house. Was anyone home? She

pictured a white-haired old lady sitting on a moldy couch, staring at the TV.

Something black, out by the barn, popped up. Once it reared on its hind legs, Sunny could see that it was a dog. So, Constance had been right.

The dog looked like he sniffed the air. Maybe he barked. Sunny wished she'd brought binoculars. It was impossible to tell from this distance if the dog was neglected or just outside doing his business.

The curtain covering one of the front windows of the house shifted. A face appeared behind the glass. Sunny cursed under her breath, got one more look at the dog, who had frozen, before she put her foot to the gas and drove away. She'd have to come back later to get a better look. Pete was expected at the house in ten minutes.

By the time Sunny got home, Pete's battered blue pickup was already parked in the long, rustic driveway that led to her Queen Anne–style dwelling. Even though the house was proudly excessive, the passing of the elderly Potters and subsequent sale five years ago had been a sign to Sunny that it was time to make a serious go of Pittie Place. The Potter home had been the site of her first rescue: Bert, the coonhound. Daddy was already sick of her bringing home more dogs than his modest property could handle, so it hadn't taken much to convince him to front her the money on her vision: to restore the house into a home for herself and into a headquarters for Pittie Place, which sat on a sprawling twenty acres.

Sunny still remembered Daddy's expression when she'd told him of her plans and proudly announced, "It's a Queen Anne." When he was silent, his forehead wrinkled, Sunny had pressed on. "Do you know why this style bears that name?"

"Because it's hoity-toity?" Daddy snapped back.

"No." Sunny had faked a laugh. "It's actually an inaccurate

term, Daddy. The architectural expression is based more on the Elizabethan era than during Queen Anne's reign. We're talking a one-hundred-and-fifty-year difference. Isn't that fascinating?"

"What's fascinating is how much work this sumbitch is going to take," Daddy grumped, arms crossed over his chest. "The Potters haven't done anything to this house for years. And I'm guessing I'm the poor sumbitch who's gonna do most of it."

He hadn't been wrong. The three-story home had been a serious task of restoration, but with Daddy's help Sunny had completed it within a year to impeccable classic style. The intricate scrollwork had been cleaned and patched, the Williamsburg-blue fish-scale siding redone, the rotting boards of the wraparound porch replaced and the towers and turrets, flanked by two small balconies, revived to their former glory. Sunny's bedroom was inside one of the towers, an octagon-shaped master suite that had one hundred and eighty degrees of light from the long, single-paned, double-hung windows. The other tower held a smaller but no less glorious bedroom.

When Sunny walked by Pete's truck she saw that, despite the cold, the windows were rolled down. The interior was worn and muddy and smelled like dogs. Typical Pete. He was not, however, behind the wheel.

She went behind the house and spied him through the window of one of the several outbuildings Daddy had restored for the dogs. He was talking to Roger. Though not long into adulthood, Roger was Sunny's longest-standing and most trusted employee. Off in the distance, Sunny could see one of the couples who had rented out one of her cottages, walking through the woods. Rather than tear down the vast array of structures the Potters had neglected, Sunny had turned them all into either vacation cabins or buildings for the rescue.

Everything went hand in hand: the people who rented here wanted a rustic getaway and loved being exposed to the rescue.

Sunny went inside. Roger was closing up the feed bin. Pete was nearby, arms crossed over his chest, flannel shirtsleeves rolled to the elbows and ankles crossed in his tan work boots while the two laughed about something one or the other had said.

"Hey, Ms. Morrigan." Roger offered his wide grin. "How's it going?"

"Hey, Rog. Hey, Pete." She did a head count of the current brood. Twelve. Not counting the cats that came and went. Many were pitties, but not all. There was a German shepherd from the kill shelter, a dalmatian someone had tied to her front door with a length of rope and a retired greyhound she'd found in a metal cage in someone's backyard. He was healthy now, but at the time he was so starved each and every bone had shown through his skin.

"Hey, girl." Pete winked at her. His light brown eyes, the color of honey, always looked like they were sparkling. "Where are those pups?"

Sunny smiled. "In the house." She gestured with a tilt of her head and headed that way, knowing Pete would follow. She'd put the whelping box in the nook off the kitchen, which was warm and safe.

It didn't take long for Pete to appraise Chevy and her brood with a look of satisfaction. "Constance says they're good candidates, huh?"

"She did. Though I guess only time will tell."

"Cici's word is good as gold, far as I'm concerned."

Sunny gave him a nudge. "You just have a thing for her."

"A little bit."

"Like, since we were kids."

Pete shrugged. "She saw me as the pesky boy next door. Pesky Petie."

"Well, the pesky boy a mile over, anyway." Sunny laughed.

"I sure put in a lot of travel time to meet up with the Morrigan sisters." Pete shook his head. His voice dropped an octave. "How's she doing? Haven't seen her this week."

"She's okay," Sunny said. "Still not herself."

Pete tucked in the corner of his lip.

"She's getting by," Sunny amended.

"And how's my boy Fezzi?" The warm, smooth quality returned to Pete's voice when he spoke about the dog he'd trained for Daddy.

"Fezzi's good. He really liked this bunch." Sunny nodded at Chevy and her pups.

"He's a smart old guy." Pete gave the pups one last appraisal. "Thought you said there were four, though."

Sunny sighed. "Dr. Winters has the runt. She's feeding him because he's not latching by himself anymore. I don't think he's going to make it." Sunny nodded toward the kitchen, where she planned to fix them both some coffee.

Pete rubbed her shoulder. "Sorry, girl. You know that happens sometimes."

Sunny stiffened. "If the pup was born weak he'd have died within hours or days after birth. No. This wouldn't have happened if Chevy'd had somewhere decent to live. All because of that rotten Janice Matteri."

Someone pounded on the front door. Pete paused his strides on the way to the kitchen. "Expecting company?" He scratched the back of his head, ruffling his sandy hair. "Speak of the devil."

Sunny followed his gaze out the window and spied a tall, skinny figure with sickly pale skin and bleached blond hair.

Pete crossed his eyes and choked himself.

Sunny steeled herself as she headed down the hallway.

"Stay off my land." Janice's words erupted like vomit as soon as Sunny opened the door. She pointed a bony finger in Sunny's face.

"The hell you say." Sunny crossed her arms over her chest and tipped on her toes, making herself taller. In the back of her mind she heard Constance's voice, telling her to keep calm, not get confrontational.

"Don't you play dumb with me, Sunny Morrigan." Janice had saliva wadded in the corners of her mouth. It looked thick and white, like foam. "The police pay you a visit recently?"

Sunny tilted her chin in the air. "Maybe."

"Uh-huh." Janice took a step closer. "Consider this my follow-up warning. I see you anywhere near my dogs or my property—if I even *think* you're on my property—you and I are going to settle this the old-fashioned way." She sneered enough to reveal orange lipstick across her front teeth.

Sunny sputtered a laugh. "Do you think that scares me? You're nothing but a broomstick on legs, with smoker's lungs to boot."

"The great equalizer don't need strength, Little Miss Fit." Janice made a gun with her thumb and forefinger, pointed it toward Sunny's head and dropped the trigger.

"You threatening me?" Sunny wanted to step closer, but in order to do so she'd have to step down, onto the porch, and she'd lose the equal height she now enjoyed with the tall woman in front of her.

"You better believe I am." Janice nodded her head rapidly. "I let it slide all those other times. What with you always taking those used-up dogs nobody wanted, anyway. Damn near doing me a favor. But last time you snagged a wheaten terrier somebody came looking to buy. They'd picked her out online and everything."

"They'd have changed their mind when they saw her." Sunny's voice dropped as anger filled her to choking. *Keep calm. Don't get confrontational.* "Your online picture probably showed a healthy wheatie. You and I both know the one in your back kennel was shy ten pounds, and hadn't been fed in days."

Janice's cheeks went red beneath her clown rouge. "You." She stammered a bunch of words that never proved up. "You lost me money," she finally hissed. "And I'm here telling you, in no uncertain terms, to stay off my land! And you, too!"

Sunny sensed Pete's presence behind her shoulder.

"Stop smiling," Janice spat.

Yep, he was back there, all right.

Janice turned to go, but halted. Her expression changed. She smirked. "Oh, my God. Is that you, Stella? Dumb bitch. You ain't dead yet?"

Sunny turned to look and couldn't contain a gasp. Chevy had left the whelping box and pattered her way into the foyer. She peeked out from behind Pete's legs. When she saw Janice, she loosed a high-pitched whine from the back of her throat.

"Tossed her ass out after Tommy went to jail," Janice said, her voice oily with satisfaction. "Bait bitch was no use to me once all the fighting dogs were gone."

Sunny didn't realize she'd lunged at Janice until the firm grab of Pete's hands on her shoulders snapped her backward, against his chest. His grip slid down to her wrists, where he stilled her struggle.

Janice laughed, showing off her lipsticked teeth. "Bye." She waggled her fingers. "Remember what I said." She made a gun with her fingers again before she turned and strode away on her grasshopper legs.

"Pete." Sunny turned to face him, once his grip slackened. "I want to hurt her. Bad."

"I know." Pete spoke with a deep calm. "But you already

got the upper hand. You got her abused dogs." He nodded at Chevy, who whined up at them. "And you got Chevy."

"I got everyone but the beagle," Sunny murmured, thinking back to the scared creature who she couldn't get out on her last raid. "But I will." She stooped down and cradled Chevy's torso in her arms while she petted her head. She didn't let go until Chevy stopped shaking.

"You need to be careful." Pete closed the door and edged Sunny down the hall. "C'mon. Chevy is hungry. That's why she's begging. She's eating for four, y'know."

"I know that." Sunny was about to tell him he sounded like Constance when her cell rang. It was Dr. Winters. After a quick conversation, Sunny faced Pete, whose eyes told her he already knew what she was going to say. "The runt didn't make it."

"I'm sorry, Sunny."

"You know who's going to be sorry?" Sunny clutched the phone tight in her hand. "Janice Matteri."

five

A cold front had moved in overnight, the kind that made the sheets hard to touch in any spot. Constance had been lying in one place all night, curled in a ball like a cat. Fezzi was curved around the arch of her back, a welcome weight and warmth. She petted his head and glanced at the half-empty bottle of wine on the floor by the bed. She didn't particularly like wine, but had wanted to dull her senses last night after Sunny called to tell her the runt had died. Constance had no idea why that made her feel empty inside—like a complete failure. They'd known the pup wasn't going to make it. But even a year after Daddy's death, Constance didn't handle bad news well. Especially not that kind.

Just don't get up today. If she didn't get out of bed, nothing bad could happen.

But Fezzi had other ideas. He stretched, made a satisfied yawning sound, then plopped down on the floor, his nails tapping over the hardwood as he headed for the door.

Constance slid from the sheets, the warmth leaving her so fast she shivered. She tripped over her running sneakers, which had been in the same place on her floor since her birthday. Sunny had bought them for her, a not-so-subtle hint that it was time Constance start to regain her old self.

"What the hell." Like a snake you give a wide berth, the new shoes were on her radar. Constance had put them there the day they were unwrapped, to motivate her when she got out of bed. Instead of motivating her, she walked around them. Not once had she forgotten they were there and tripped over them.

Until today.

A chill ran through her body. Today, Sunny would say, would be a good day to dare dump trucks. That was the analogy she used for being at rock bottom and not giving a flying leap. Just step out in the middle of the street and dare the dump trucks to hit you. Which was easy for Sunny to say. With Mom's bright yellow hair, big blue eyes, sweet smile and secret fear of the dark, Sunny thought she could get through life by exposing a little leg and sweet-talking her way out of whatever trouble her impulsive personality got her into.

And that's the way it usually worked.

Constance hugged her arms around herself and pulled open the blinds. It might be cold, but it was bright and sunny as summer. Across the street, the Old Commonwealth Disposal truck went in reverse, *beep beep beep*, as it sidled up to her neighbor's house. Constance watched the men collect the trash and move off down the road.

From downstairs, Fezzi whined to get outside.

Like a tide, life was moving her, even if all she wanted to do was float.

After she let Fezzi into the backyard, she caught sight of her reflection in the sliding glass doors. One hand ran over her middle and the other down her thigh. Only then did Constance realize she'd been avoiding mirrors for a long time. She looked like a pudgy version of Daddy, before he got sick and frail, with the same red hair, pale skin, tiny nose.

"Well," Constance murmured as she watched Fezzi run around the yard, collecting sticks and putting them in a pile. He'd done that ever since Daddy died and he no longer needed to fetch the old man's socks. "Maybe spin class wouldn't be so bad."

What was it Sunny had said, about when and where she taught? *Evenings at the shopping center and mornings at Spin City.*

Great. Morning at the shopping center, it was.

Constance stood outside the gym and watched through the glass walls. Spin class had just ended, and the women were now falling off their bikes in pools of sweat. Most of them were adorable soccer moms who spun their hearts out to the house music booming out the doorway.

They chatted while they stripped their seats of the gel covers they'd brought with them. The seriously hard-core even had special shoes, with some kind of clips on the bottom. Were those cleats? Constance stifled a giggle—cleats on shoes that would never touch grass! She couldn't wait to tease Sunny about that: *Hey, baby sister. Do you wear cleats to ride a bike that goes nowhere?*

The ladies' towels were even more adorable than their owners, brightly colored and slung over their shoulders after they mopped away the happy shine from their foreheads. As they came out, they said things to each other like, "Ooh, girlfriend, that was serious!" and "My butt's gonna be sore tomorrow!"

"I feel soooooo tired," one lady said, rubbing her flat stomach. "That workout actually had me breathing heavy! I should not have had that bacon for breakfast!"

Constance closed her eyes and let her head sink to the glass. As the giggles and chatter moved away, Constance felt a wave of nausea roll through her. She needed to eat. She pushed off the building and headed toward a bakery that was three doors down in the strip mall. A man got there first and held the door. Constance went to go inside, enticed by the buttery aroma of warm eggs, sugar and flour, but paused.

The building across the street had caught her eye. Large and ugly, it used to be a tire factory, Constance was pretty sure. Now it read Semper Fit. She'd probably passed it a million times. She'd never been inside but she'd seen people going in and out with gym bags, or jogging around the perimeter, puffing in the cold, sloshing in the rain. It was supposed to be the kind of gym that attracted the types who liked to jump out of airplanes.

"Miss?"

Constance blinked at the man who held the door. "Sorry," she mumbled.

Chicken. Sunny's taunt ran through her head. As if on autopilot, Constance crossed the road. Something deep inside her pushed forward, making her feet go, one in front of the other, until she was right at the entrance.

The gym's bay doors were wide open, despite the chill. Inside, a large group of people stood in a circle, near metal rigging, which had bars and rings and racks. Constance stepped in and stood in the back, unnoticed.

She'd never seen a gym like this. Racks of barbells and stacks of weights lined the north wall, along with a shelf of kettlebells, dumbbells and mats. Boxes were stacked in the corner, a dozen or more deep. Ropes hung from the ceiling, but were secured behind the rig, out of the way of the large, open work space. A huge tire was tucked in the corner. *A tire?*

What the hell would they do with a tire? Rap music played softly from the speakers.

A muscular woman stood at the head of the circle, speaking to the group as she gestured toward a large whiteboard. She had her hair in a ponytail and her eyebrows looked recently plucked and shaped. Nothing else fancy about her, though—no makeup or jewelry, just one small hoop earring at the top curve of her ear.

Even from a distance, Constance could read the bold, black writing on the board.

1 Rope Climb.
10 Front Rack Lunges, per leg, 75/55.
2 Rope Climbs.
25 Kettlebell Swings, 53/36.
15 Sumo Deadlift High Pulls, 75/55.
20 Goblet Squats.
3 Rope Climbs.
20 Front Squats.
15 Kettlebell Sumo Deadlift High Pulls.
4 Rope Climbs.
10 Kettlebell Snatches.

Whatever all that meant.

Constance glanced around the room. The crowd was mixed. About twenty people, male and female, some with seriously muscled physiques, some not. All ages. There was a young couple who kept whispering and glancing at two small kids, plopped behind a baby gate with an assortment of toys. A tall lady wearing a WOD Now, Wine Later tank top. A man with more tattoos than bare skin. An elderly gentleman with a potbelly and big pecs.

"Everybody start the warm-up." The coach pointed at the

whiteboard. "Right here. Then we'll go over the movements for the workout."

Constance knew she should introduce herself, but that auto-pilot feeling hadn't gone away. She read the warm-up, then peeled off her coat. A second later, she found herself doing jumping jacks. Constance ran through the movements on the warm-up list, most self-explanatory. When she started to struggle through push-ups, a tap came on her shoulder.

"Hi," the coach said. "I'm Zoe. Are you new?"

"Um. Yes." Constance was keenly aware of her outdated fitness clothes. Capri tights from college, a sports bra that cut into her back and an old T-shirt that, alas, had a unicorn on the front. None of her old running clothes fit anymore and these had been the only passable things in her closet.

Oh, hell, who was she kidding? She'd never intended to go to spin class or anywhere else and hadn't cared what she put on this morning. Yet, here she was, doing push-ups without permission in a strange gym for people who played with tractor tires.

Had she gone insane?

"Okay. I'll get you a waiver. Keep warming up, but go ahead and do those push-ups on your knees."

Constance was a sweaty mess when the warm-up was over. Part of her felt like she'd already done her workout, but the really fit people hadn't even broken a sweat. She glanced at the entrance. The door was only a few steps away and it was so crowded nobody would notice if she slipped out, just like nobody had noticed when she'd slipped in. Through the window she spied the bakery.

Zoe turned down the music and clapped her hands together. "All right, guys, let's start going over this workout." She looked toward the rear of the gym and called out, "Rhett, you joining us?"

Everyone turned in that direction. Constance, two steps from the exit, froze. This was the first time she'd noticed the man on the far left of the gym. He worked alone, on a raised platform, his body deep in a squat with a loaded barbell on his shoulders. He stood up, rolled the bar off his back with a *clang!* and shook his head.

"C'mon," Zoe goaded. "This one's right up your alley."

"Yeah, Rhett," someone else yelled. "Come kick our asses!"

Rhett—tall, dark-haired and built like a brick house—shrugged. "Fine."

Constance tilted her head and stared up at the rope, attached to the twenty-foot-high ceiling. People really climbed that. Grown adults, not little kids in a gymnastics class. She wouldn't have believed it, except many of the people around her were already doing it. Quickly.

Everything was supposed to be done quickly, Zoe had said. The goal was to complete the workout as fast as possible. Everybody started at the same time, and everybody did the same thing. Except if you couldn't do something, like climb a rope fifteen feet, then you scaled the movement to your ability. Constance grasped the hemp and tried to remember what her scale was.

"Lower yourself to the ground—" Zoe raised her voice over Lil Wayne, booming from the speakers "—then back up." She pantomimed, her biceps flexing.

Constance gave it a go, but the rope slipped in her hands and she fell hard, on her ass. She paused a second before standing up and grasping the rope again, refusing to look around to see if anyone had noticed her spill. Why the hell had she come here? The last thing she needed in her life was another reason to feel weak.

"Tighten." Zoe was by her side, one hand on her midsection and the other on her lower back. "Tighten your core as you lower yourself down."

Tighten your core? Oh. Okay. Tighten rectus abdominis and quadratus lumborum. Glutes. Quads. *Now you're speaking my language.* Constance gritted her teeth and rappelled her way to the floor. Zoe helped guide her until she was flat on her back.

"Yep," Zoe said. "Nice. Now pull back up."

Constance sucked in her breath and hauled her way back to her feet. Her biceps, triceps and delts screamed. Functional fitness, Zoe had said. Everything about Semper Fit was supposed to be functional—fitness you could translate to real life. *When the hell am I ever going to need to climb a rope?* A middle-aged woman, off in the corner, was doing the same scaling option with the rope. She slipped and struggled, too. Feeling a little less helpless, Constance started in on the next movement on the list: lunges.

By the time she was done with the lunges and started in on two more rope climbs, sweat was dripping down her face.

"You can do it," Zoe said, smiling big and baring her dimples.

Constance took a deep breath, now completely unable to dwell on why she'd left her warm bed this morning. Why she'd bothered to dare dump trucks in the first place. All that mattered was getting through this. She lowered herself to the ground, much more gracefully this time, then braced to pull back up. The guy next to her—Rhett—caught her eye. He jumped on his rope, stuck out his legs and, without even using his feet, ascended to a piece of blue duct tape, which he tapped before he sailed down the rope, quicker than he'd climbed it. Without pause, he jumped and did a second rope climb, zipped down and picked up his kettlebell and began swinging it from between his legs to overhead.

Just like that.

Zoe, who'd moved off to help others, reappeared and loomed above her. "C'mon, Constance. You're doing great! Let's go!" She waved a hand in Rhett's direction. "Don't worry about him. C'mon!"

Constance watched Rhett a second longer. A powerhouse of energy, his traps and pecs bumped out beneath a T-shirt that read Westside Barbell. Each kettlebell swing was so controlled and well executed he made it look easy. And he was using a bigger kettlebell than the other men.

Maybe it was easy—at least for him. Constance grabbed the baby kettlebell at her feet, the smallest one in the gym.

"Pop the hips," Zoe said, pantomiming the practice they'd had with the bell before the workout began.

Constance's heart pounded in her throat. All her nerve endings were on fire and her lungs were tight, her throat dry. But she saw Rhett, from the corner of her eye, doing one swing after another, without pause. There were supposed to be twenty-five in a row, according to that whiteboard. Holy mother, Constance thought as she attempted to swing the bell over her head. It flashed up near her brow, then swung back down, pulling her forward and making her stumble.

"Keep tight," Zoe said. "And use those hips to get it up there." She lifted an unmanned kettlebell, much larger than what Constance was using, and held it between her thighs. She pushed her butt back, kept her back flat, then popped her hips forward as she swung. The bell rose without much visible effort. "Keep it right here," Zoe said as the bell rose to about eye level. "I want you to do Russian swings. When you come down, use the momentum to swing it up again."

Constance sucked in her breath and gave it another go. The bell swung a little smoother, a little higher. She felt a surge of accomplishment creep inside the bundle of screaming nerves and rivulets of sweat trickling down her back, chest, face and stomach.

"Ten," Zoe said, holding both hands open. "Not twenty-five. We're scaling your load. Just do ten. You're doing great!"

Time was a blur. The seconds and minutes crushed in on themselves and became nothing but sweat and heartbeats, fear and excitement. Once Constance completed everything on the whiteboard, she fell flat on her back and stared at the ceiling, the rope dangling between her legs as she sucked wind.

Physically, she was in just as bad shape as when she started. Something was different, though. Constance gasped for air and tried to make sense of her scrambled brain.

"Good job." Zoe beamed above her, her hand outstretched for a high five.

Constance smacked it, but laughed at herself. Zoe was a good coach, acting like Constance had done something awesome, even though she was the very last person to finish, despite all her scaling, and was now lying there, unable to move.

She figured she'd stay there, until everybody left, unwilling to face the aftermath—the giggling and the chatter and the discourse on the evils of bacon. But then another person showed up, the other lady who'd scaled her rope climbs, and she, too, gave Constance a high five. One after another, it seemed like the entire class was there, smiling down on her, slapping her palm, giving her praise.

What the hell?

Constance returned all the high fives, incapable of fleeing, even if she wanted to. The timer on the wall, with its bright red numbers, caught her eye. The clock had stopped at just after fifteen minutes, which would've been close to Constance's time. Just fifteen short minutes. A fraction of the time she used to spend training for marathons. Half of your standard sitcom on TV. The amount of time you give someone when you just need a few moments to get your shit together.

Yet, those were some of the longest fifteen minutes of Constance's life.

"Nice work, My Pretty Pony."

Constance blinked the sweat—tears?—from her eyes and looked up. A man loomed above her, hand outstretched. He was mostly a blur. Sweat dripped from his forehead, landing on Constance's chest. She went to give him the high five that apparently was expected, but he clasped her fingers and hauled her to her feet.

Rhett, she realized, once her vision cleared. The guy who had climbed that rope like he could fly. "Thanks." Constance hoped he'd been too focused on his own workout to see any of hers. Then again, he'd finished way ahead of her. In fact, Constance was pretty sure he'd finished before everybody.

"First time?" He glanced at her shirt. His eyes had a bit of a sparkle to them. Amusement, maybe.

"Yeah." Constance remembered what she was wearing. Her cheeks burned. Then she realized she still clasped his fingertips. She released him, her cheeks burning hotter.

"Nice."

"Thanks."

And then he was gone, off high-fiving others and gathering his bag in what seemed like a rush to get out as quickly as possible. "Zoe, I'll be back in an hour."

"Sure."

Constance noted a slight hitch in his gate. It was nothing anyone else would see, but Constance's eye was trained. If she had to guess, he'd injured his right quad. He stopped in front of the whiteboard, wrote down his name and then some numbers beside it. Sweaty people queued up, taking their turns with the dry-erase pen.

"Name and time on the board," Zoe said, once Constance was through mopping her face with the hem of her T-shirt. "Promotes community. Measures progress."

"Right." Her mind was still on Rhett. There was something about him that she couldn't quite shake. He'd touched her right after he'd spoken to her, so she'd gotten the full thrust of his energy right up front. It was overwhelming, but not in a bad way. Kind of like getting smacked by a wave that was bigger than you expected. It stung, but you were so impressed you couldn't be mad about it. He reminded her of that old adage: *Never turn your back on the ocean.*

Constance pressed the tip of the marker to the board and wrote her name, beneath all the others, as neatly as she could. Most of the times were between twelve and fifteen minutes, but Constance was dead last at 15:14. Most people had scaled the workout in some way, even if it was just lower weight for the lunges and front squats. Rhett was at the top, his time 8:01, with Rx written after. *As prescribed*, Constance thought. He hadn't scaled at all and he'd still beaten everyone.

"I don't remember seeing you before." The middle-aged woman who'd also scaled her rope climbs stood before her, with a foam roller in either hand. "I'm Sally." She offered a foam roller, which Constance took. Sally plopped down on the floor and shoved the roller beneath her butt. "You did great today." Her dark hair was stuck to her cheeks as she braced her weight on her hands and rolled out her glutes and hamstrings.

Constance lowered herself to the floor and joined in. Nothing was sore yet, but she figured by tomorrow she might have a tough time walking. "Thanks. I'm Constance."

"That's not a name you hear every day."

"It was my grandma's."

"Do you go by Connie?"

"No."

Sally chuckled. "Okay." A little pause passed, as though Sally expected her to say more. When she didn't, Sally changed the subject. "I remember my first day—" Sally leaned into the foam roller "—and it was nothing like today. Just some air squats and push-ups. Pull-ups with a band. If I'd have been faced with that—" she gestured to the whiteboard "—I'd have left. You're brave."

Constance wanted to laugh, but bit down on her lower lip. "I used to be a runner. Cross-country in high school. A few marathons. Tough. But this was hard in a different way. I haven't run in a while. I guess that's obvious." She gestured at her sweaty, old clothes, and was suddenly back to that day, when she'd gone out to surprise Josh. Wednesday morning, which meant a trail run in the park. Cumberland Trail. Constance hadn't joined him in longer than she could remember, which was probably why he hadn't been expecting her. Neither had the woman next to him—blonde, slender and stretching out her hamstrings on a tree stump.

Constance blinked, and the image of Josh with his new running partner vanished.

She turned to the whiteboard, avoiding Sally's curious gaze. "In my dreams I'll do this workout in eight minutes." She thought back to Rhett's figure as he flew up that rope.

Sally followed her gaze, then shrugged. "Don't measure yourself by Rhett. Or go ahead…reach for the stars." She grunted as she wedged the foam roller deep into her hamstrings. "He owns this place. He's a war veteran. Marines. Always on top." Sally laughed, her heavy bosom shaking. "But Rhett's not into these workouts as much as the other coaches. He coaches the weight lifting and prefers to spend his time over there." Sally waved at the corner with the platforms.

A combat vet. She knew that. She'd known it before she

knew it. That's why he seemed familiar. "Nice guy?" Constance peered out the doorway, but Rhett had disappeared.

"Eh, I don't know about nice," Sally said. "Great athlete. Great coach. Doesn't take any shit. But motivating." She lowered her voice and leaned closer, even though nobody else was within earshot. "I heard he was hurt in Afghanistan. Or Iraq. Or…maybe both. Hell, I don't know. He's got a Purple Heart." She touched her chest. "Who knows what he went through."

Constance rolled her hamstrings slowly over the foam tube and realized that not once, in that brief yet grueling workout, had her mind been anywhere but in the moment. She hadn't thought about the past year at all. Not about Josh. Or Daddy's long battle with cancer. Nothing. That workout had forced her brain to be put on hold. Her body had suffered terribly, but her brain had gotten some rare respite.

She glanced over and saw that Sally was wrapping up her cooldown.

"Well," Sally said, rising. "You coming back tomorrow?"

Coming back? Constance hadn't even considered it. "Maybe," she said. "Thanks for the encouragement."

"Hey," Sally said. "We need all we can get."

Sally wasn't gone long before Zoe appeared. "Yeah? You loved it, right?" She beamed from ear to ear.

"You and I—" Constance got to her feet with a groan "—have very different definitions of love."

Zoe laughed. "But seriously," she said. "You did great. You've got heart." She tapped her fist against her chest. "That was a tough workout for anyone, let alone a first-timer."

"Thanks." Constance grabbed her water bottle, which was empty.

"You can try out the week for free," Zoe pressed.

"Thanks. We'll see." Constance headed to her car.

At home, she found Fezzi snoozing on the couch, his

tummy fat with the biscuits she always overfed him while she sipped her coffee. Constance took a shower, then joined him. She got tired quickly these days. This morning was no exception, but as her lids drooped, Constance noted that her fatigue felt different. Rather than thick and lethargic, she felt wrung out. Rather than foggy, her head was clear, her muscles spent. She had enough time for a quick snooze before she met Sunny for lunch, so she gave in to the intoxicating pull of sleep.

Just before she nodded off, Constance saw in her mind again Rhett's eyes—an unusual mixture of amusement, interest, resignation and pain—and heard his voice, deep and honest: *Nice work, My Pretty Pony.*

six

"How are my babies?" Constance asked before Sunny had even had a chance to sit down. "The ones who didn't die, anyway."

Sunny held up a hand and frowned. "Too soon."

"Tell me about it."

"The rest are doing really good." Sunny peeled off her coat. "Dr. Winters says it's a miracle Chevy's so sweet, considering the life she's led. And Pete came by. He's excited about the pups. He says hi."

Constance waved, as if Pete were in the room.

"Oh, and—" Sunny tossed her coat in the booth and slid inside "—Janice Matteri has issued a warning. Stay off her land, or else."

"Or else what?" Constance opened her menu. "I won't let her touch a hair on your head."

"I know."

"But—" Constance wagged a finger "—you better pay attention to me now. You need to watch your step. I know your heart's in the right place, but you're playing with fire."

"Janice Matteri is the one who better watch out." Sunny peered at her own menu. Constance had always thought her reckless, and wasn't shy about saying so. Sunny's typical retort was that Cici was cautious enough for the both of them. "She's going to be sorry she ever darkened my doorstep."

Constance snorted. "Famous last words. I'm not bailing your ass out like I did when you were in high school."

Sunny snorted back, though she suspected Cici might not be kidding. Back then, Cici was following Daddy's orders to "take care of your little sister—no matter what," a directive Constance had followed to the letter since Mom's death. But Mom had been gone since Sunny was five years old, and now Daddy was gone, too. At some point, Constance might just decide she was done taking care of her impulsive baby sister.

Sunny's gaze went between the salad and pizza menus, which were adjacent to each other. The pancetta and ricotta pizza sounded crazy good, but the Mean Green Salad would sit so much better in her stomach.

Right then, the waitress showed up, pad and pencil in hand. She had puffy hair, colored yellow when it should have been white and a name tag that read Dolores. "What can I get you girls?"

"I'll have the Mean Green Salad," Sunny piped up. "With the dressing on the side."

Dolores scratched on her pad.

"I'll have the pancetta and ricotta pizza," Constance said. "Can you do that with extra pancetta?"

"Sure, honey." Dolores scratched on her pad again. "Nice choice." She collected the menus.

Once she was gone, Sunny pressed her lips together and shook her head. Constance had always been able to eat anything she wanted without an ounce of discomfort. Sunny once watched her down sausage links and a stack of pancakes with butter and syrup directly before a twenty-mile training run. After, she reported having the best run of her life.

"What?" Constance rubbed her belly. "I'm hungry. You wouldn't believe the workout I did this morning."

Sunny narrowed her brow. "Workout?" She reared back and studied her sister. "Hey. Did you go to my spin class? When I wasn't coaching? On purpose?"

"No. Well, sort of." Constance smiled at whatever look was on Sunny's face. Confusion? Irritation? Probably both. "I went over to your spin class—yes, on purpose, because you weren't coaching—but I never made it inside. All the giggling and brightly colored towels were just too much."

"I see." Sunny dug out the mini tape roller she kept in her purse and ran it over her chest, grabbing up the dog hair she'd missed before she left the house. "And?"

"I just stood outside and watched. Was getting ready to leave." Constance waved the spin class away. "But then I saw the place across the street and…well, first I saw the bakery, let's be honest, but then I saw the place across the street and I… I don't know. I went in. I actually went in and just started doing the workout. It was kind of surreal."

"Wait a minute, wait a minute." Sunny unwrapped her straw and plunked it into her water. "You went into the place across the street? Semper Fit? The place with the crazy people who run in the rain and flip tires down the street? On *impulse*?"

"Ah." A light flickered over Constance's face. "So that's what the tire is for."

"You're kidding me, right?" Then again, why was she surprised? Leave it to Cici to want to punish herself in the worst way possible.

"I learned some new moves." Constance did a bunch of

things with her arms, including what looked like rappelling a mountain.

"You climbed a mountain?"

"People were climbing ropes, Sunny. Ropes, hung from the ceiling. And they didn't have the knots in them. You know, ones you could use to step on to climb up?" She snapped her fingers. "None of that. These people were climbing knotless ropes."

"You climbed a rope?"

"Of course not. I rappelled myself to the floor and climbed back up again. With a rope in my hands. It was hard." She held up her hands and showed off what looked like rug burn on her palms.

Sunny eyed her sister's baggy sweatpants and basketball sweatshirt that dated back to when the Washington Wizards were still named the Bullets. It was thin with age and had a tear at the collar. "What did you wear?"

Constance considered that in silence. "The new shoes you bought me."

Carefully chosen words and emotions neatly contained. Typical Cici. "And? What else did you wear? Please tell me you didn't wear that." Sunny pictured Constance struggling with a rope in her oversize sweats and bit back a grin.

Constance mumbled something around her straw.

"What?"

"I might've—" she set the water down "—worn a T-shirt with a unicorn on it."

"Oh, good Lord. Not—" Sunny traced a horse figure on her chest "—the one from when you were a teenager?"

Constance nodded.

"Mean Green Salad." Dolores appeared with their order. "And a yummy pizza." She smiled at Constance as she slid the pie in front of her. "You want Parmesan on that, hon?"

"Of course."

"Of course," Dolores agreed. She whipped out a handheld grater and went to town, leaving a fluffy pile of cheese on top of the saucy pie. "Enjoy, ladies."

"That's the same look one of the guys had on his face when he saw the shirt," Constance said as soon as Dolores disappeared. "Kind of amused, but without the horror. That stricken look of horror you've got going on there." Constance waved her fork in a circle near Sunny's face. "Hey, the unicorn was the only clean shirt that fit. I got really slender during my running days. Even in high school I was thicker. From all the cheerleading."

"You were definitely really slender when you were running all those miles," Sunny agreed. "But wait. A dude laughed at your shirt?" She dug into her bed of greens. "That doesn't sound very friendly."

"No, he didn't laugh." Constance forked in some pizza and chewed thoughtfully. "Not with his voice. He kind of laughed with his eyes. They're this cool brown color. With a hint of mossy Irish green." She looked out the window, like she was remembering. "Hazel? Like they're brown *and* green, but can't make up their mind." She turned back to Sunny. "He wasn't laughing at me. He was just kind of…smiling without smiling. And when I touched him, his energy was *rough*. Not rude, like you're thinking. Just rough. And…" Whatever else Constance was going to say ended in a shrug.

"Uh-huh." Sunny dabbed her lips with her napkin. She wanted to meet this guy. Pronto. "So, when you going back?"

"Going back?" Constance's gaze shot up from her plate. "Who said I was going back?"

Sunny stuffed more salad in her face to squelch the gurgling her stomach made at the aroma of Constance's hot, cheesy pizza. "You seem kind of excited about it." She chose her words carefully. "In fact, you look a little different." She wasn't lying, even though Sunny wasn't above that sort of thing. But Constance really did have a certain glow about her that she hadn't seen in a while. When Sunny had walked into the restaurant and spied her sister by the window, she'd attributed the bright skin and tiny smile to the new puppies. Constance always got a little high from a rescue, even though she pretended to be all business about it and acted like she helped the dogs purely for Sunny's benefit. Now, Sunny wasn't so sure that glow had anything at all to do with dogs.

"No." Constance waved her hands over her pizza. "No way. That workout was horrible."

"Okay." Sunny shrugged. Unable to stand it anymore, she reached over and stole a slice of Cici's pizza. Cici didn't even blink. "But you went," she pressed as she bit into the cheesy slice. "And you stayed. And you're kind of glowing." Sunny chewed and swallowed. "Holy shit, this is good."

"I am not glowing." Constance stabbed her fork into Sunny's salad and stuffed the greens into her mouth.

"Whatever you say."

They ate in silence for a while, both their own food and each other's.

When Sunny next spoke, she changed the subject. "I'm going to do the Christmas fundraiser again this year." She crunched on a crouton and waited until she'd swallowed completely before continuing. "You're coming, right? I'm going to run the whole thing, like I did before. I'll need you to massage my biggest donors. The more important they feel, the more they open their wallets."

Constance laid down her third slice, half-eaten. "Of course. Anything for the dogs."

Sunny dabbed her lips with her napkin and slid her empty bowl to the edge of the table. Daddy had died midway between Halloween and Thanksgiving last year. Six months ago, Josh had packed up his sorry ass and moved out. The year hadn't been easy on Constance, and Sunny hadn't been one hundred percent sure her sister would be on board for the holidays this year. "You don't have to do the party if you don't want. Just the massages. You'll do those, right?"

"I just said I would."

"I know. It's just that—" Sunny drew a deep breath "—I know you've said you don't feel like you bring the same energy to your work since Daddy died and since Josh…well." Sunny pressed her fingers over her mouth. "I was just checking."

Constance shrugged. "I'll do the massages." She shoved her remaining pizza away. "Those rich donors want the classic spa massage. They want to say, 'My shoulders hurt,' and have me rub their shoulders. They feel smart and in charge and you get money for the dogs. It's a no-brainer."

Dolores came by with the check, which Sunny grabbed. "Are you cooking for Thanksgiving?" Sunny's intention had been to steer the conversation toward something that made Constance happy, like cooking. But then, she hadn't cooked a Thanksgiving feast last year, with Daddy being gone.

Constance was staring out the window again, and Sunny got the distinct feeling she'd ruined whatever glow her sister had come in here with. "Yeah, I'll cook."

Sunny slipped a bill in the little folder. "I've got to get home to the brood."

Constance nodded, still not meeting Sunny's gaze.

Sunny reached out and covered her sister's hand with her own. Constance snapped her head around. "I think you should go back to the rope-climbing, tire-flipping gym tomorrow," Sunny said. "If you want my opinion."

Constance slid her hand away. "Did you hear what I said?" Her tone held the cold iron of Daddy's voice when anyone tried to tell him what to do. "I hated that place."

"Yeah." Sunny grabbed her purse and rose up. "I heard you. You hated that place."

seven

It sounded like bullets were raining down on the roof of the Humvee. Thousands and thousands of bullets. How were that many bullets even possible? He waited for the roar of the rockets, but they stayed just inside the ghost of his memory, taunting him.

Rhett woke in a cold sweat, well ahead of his alarm, to a black, sleeting sky. He held his head between his knees for a second, drawing air steadily in and out of his lungs, before he threw back the covers and stepped onto the cold floor. He peeked out the window. The side streets that led to his town house looked dicey, but the main roads had probably been sanded. Still, with schools closed and miniature hail hitting the windows, attendance at the gym would be minimal. He sent out a mass email, canceling classes for the day, and followed that up with notifications on social media.

Then he fixed himself a protein shake and limped his way to the front door. The colder it got, the worse his leg felt.

Going in was probably a stupid move; no amount of warming up was going to get his muscles functioning today. He opened the door and faced the dark sky. His breath turned to steam. At 5:30 a.m., the moon still hung like a yellow beacon. Ice pelted him gently in the face. Nobody else was stirring.

Go back to bed, his body screamed.

Fat chance, his mind responded.

Rhett unlocked his Jeep with his remote, sprinkled the stairs with salt, took his steps gingerly, slid once, reflected briefly on the stupidity of his journey and got in the car, anyway.

He put the Jeep in low gear and drove slow. The ten-minute drive took twenty, but he got there in one piece. He spent some time salting the perimeter of the building, but then settled in the office and turned on the computer.

Rhett kept telling himself he didn't have anything better to do, and that the roads weren't so bad. He pulled up yesterday's waivers and dug through them. Once he found hers, he admitted, for a brief second, this was one of the reasons he'd come into work today.

There were three forms, but only one was for a woman. Specifically, the redhead who had the balls to come in here wearing a unicorn T-shirt. It wasn't the standard—not like one of the "special unicorns" that were in fashion right now, the tight tank tops meant to suggest how unique its wearer was, despite the fact that a dozen other women were wearing the same damn unicorns.

No. My Pretty Pony had come in here wearing some kind of early nineties throwback that reminded Rhett of the dolls Mel favored when she was a little kid. Mama used to say, "Go on, Rhett. Play with your little sister. Brush the ponies' hair."

And he'd been forced to scrape miniature plastic brushes

through the rainbow-colored manes of the little horses that gave Mel so much delight.

Constance Morrigan.

That was her name. She was thirty-three years old, and she'd come in here wearing a fucking My Pretty Pony T-shirt.

Rhett laughed to himself. He pictured her again as the sleet pattered a relaxing tune on the tin roof. The ragged short hair—not classic red and not blond, but both; what did they call that? Strawberry?—looked like a little kid had taken scissors to it. Ironically, her hair had looked much like what Rhett had once done to one of Mel's ponies in revenge for losing his cap gun in Andy Simmons's backyard. Mama had grounded him for a week over that. Mel, forever a kind and forgiving soul, had begged Mama to shorten his sentence and declared she liked her "punk pony's" new do.

The luxurious hair on My Pretty Pony's unicorn shirt hinted at what Constance Morrigan's hair might look like if she weren't determined to have the ugliest haircut on the planet, which is what Rhett had sensed. She was trying to hide anything about her that might be attractive, including that oversize shirt that draped her soft, curvy hips. Everything about her had been soft and curvy, though Rhett had sensed a harder, firmer woman buried beneath it all. The ghost of an athlete was in her face, her concentration, her determination to finish that stupid workout Hobbs had programmed. Any other newbie would have run from it.

Rhett was certain he didn't know Constance Morrigan. Who could forget a name like that? But there was something familiar about her. Something about her eyes, which were the impossible blue color of an arctic glacier. Not cold, but vivid. Which could be good or bad. They were the kind of eyes that told it like it was, but also made it hard to hide anything.

A set of headlights washed through the gloom, over the

front of the building, temporarily blinding Rhett through the window he faced. Who the hell would be out in this weather? Besides himself.

The headlights disappeared around the corner. Maybe it was a salt truck, or somebody from the strip mall across the way. After a moment, Rhett heard somebody try the front door.

Seriously? Somebody had shown up for the 7:30 class? He shouldn't be surprised. His gym attracted a lot of diehards and addicts, even if their poison was fitness instead of a much less healthy drug. It was probably Tatiana, with her overworked body and bullish personality. No way in hell was Rhett giving her a one-on-one. She could do some open gym since she'd dragged her ass here in the sleet, but he'd have her out in an hour, tops.

By the time Rhett got to the front door, the figure was already moving away, taking steps gingerly along the sidewalk. He didn't recognize the person from behind, clad in a large blue jacket and stocking cap. Despite his better judgment, Rhett poked his head out.

The figure stopped and peeked over her shoulder. She turned and headed back his way, her boots crunching over the salt he'd put down. "Are you open?"

"No." Rhett didn't recognize her voice. "Didn't you get the email?"

She stopped when she reached the front door and peered up at him from beneath her beanie. "Oh, hi." Her voice changed. "Rhett, right?"

"Rhett Santos." He extended his hand.

Her big glove clasped his fingertips. "I don't get the emails. I'm not a member." Long lashes framed bright, clear blue eyes.

Well, damn. Rhett knew that if she pulled off that cap, she'd reveal strawberry blond hair, done in the worst haircut imaginable.

"How about this crazy weather, huh? When's the last time we had ice before December?"

Rhett watched her carefully. There was just something about her. An old-fashioned throwback who had grown up too quickly to give a crap about the little things. He wasn't sure how he knew that, but he did.

"Yeah," she said in the wake of his silence. "I don't do mindless chitchat, either. Forget I said anything."

Rhett laughed, despite himself. *We're not open today. The roads are too slick. Everything's canceled. Go home.* "C'mon in."

Constance stamped her feet and brushed ice balls from her coat before she hung it on the hook beside the door. She removed her cap and gloves, stuffed them in the pocket of her coat and ran her hands through her hair. Full of electricity, the pale red hair stood up on end, making it look like she'd stuck her finger in a socket.

"Am I the only one here?" She surveyed the empty gym, mostly in darkness. Rhett had only turned on the office lights.

He eyed her outfit for today. The unicorn shirt was gone, replaced by a Marine Corps Marathon tee that seemed old and too big and a pair of black joggers. "It's sleeting outside, My Pretty Pony. It's just you and me."

Her pale cheeks flushed. Normally, he might not notice but she had that porcelain skin only redheads could pull off, perfectly clear without a freckle in sight. "Right," she said. "I can go."

"You're already here." Rhett motioned toward the office. "Let's have a talk. Get some info, discuss your goals."

She hesitated. For an instant, fear ran through those crystal clear eyes. She cleared her throat. "Okay," she said. She took a seat inside the office without fuss. "I really don't need to take up your time. I thought there'd be a group. A large group." She twiddled her fingers together.

"I'm your group today." Rhett settled in his desk chair, went silent and waited for her attention.

She turned her chin up to face him. She was silent, her eyes searching his, like she had questions for him, rather than the other way around.

Rhett felt the look deep in his gut, which made him shift in his chair. He was hard to rattle; certainly didn't happen when a harmless, awkward woman came in to see about a gym membership. The longer she stared at him, her lips working in micromovements, like she was searching for words, the more uncomfortable he got. There went that feeling again.

Rhett cleared his throat abruptly. "So you were in here yesterday. How'd you like it?"

"It was torture." She didn't crack a smile.

"Yet you're back." Rhett kept his own smile suppressed.

She bit back anything she might have to say, because no words came out.

"Let's start with your history." Rhett decided to keep the ball rolling. "What kind of fitness background do you have?" He nodded at her shirt. "Runner?"

Her hand went to her chest, like she'd forgotten what she was wearing. "Once upon a time. I used to run the Marine Corps Marathon every year. Back before it was a lottery."

"Nice. What's your best time?"

"Three twenty-two."

It came out memorized, as if from pride. "Not bad." He let his eyebrows go up. Really decent time actually.

"Thanks. You, um—" she bit down on her lower lip "—you a runner?" She eyed his sore leg.

Rhett had thought she was paying close scrutiny to his limp, but he hadn't been sure until now. "I run on Sundays to clear my head." Running, for him, was more like meditation than exercise. Unless, of course, he was doing sprints. Those were a whole different story. "I've done the MCM once or twice. I think your time is better than mine. I'd have to look it up." His best time was exactly twenty minutes better than hers, but she didn't need to know that.

"That was a couple of years ago." A tiny smile crooked the corner of her mouth. "I was more into running then. I was… different then." She pressed her lips together and crossed her arms over her chest, covering the anchor, eagle and globe that made up the official insignia and emblem of the marine corps.

"You've still got the shirt." Rhett nodded toward the old tee. "You're proud of it. It's still a part of who you are."

She uncrossed her arms. "This was my dad's. None of mine fit. Well." She cocked her head. "I don't like how I look in them, anyway."

Only then did Rhett realize the shirt was from the Fifth Annual Marine Corps Marathon. Constance Morrigan, age thirty-three, wouldn't have even been alive.

She offered up that wry little smile. "The entry fee was two dollars."

Rhett laughed. "That's awesome. Your dad a marine?"

"Army. Vietnam vet." She waited a heartbeat, then added, "My parents had kids later in life."

Rhett felt a twinge, deep in his gut. "Thank him for his service."

"He's dead."

"Ah, okay." Rhett never said he was sorry when people were dead. Sometimes death was the way to go, especially if suffering was involved. Sometimes, the dead in question had been assholes in real life, and nobody was sorry they were gone. Why speak ignorantly about what you didn't know?

Constance got really quiet, sat there and blinked at him with lashes that were much darker than her hair.

"So you're here to get your groove back." Rhett refocused

his interview. Stay professional, find out her needs and do his best to meet those needs. "Used to be a runner. Maybe you've let things go, and now you want to get back into it. Maybe get a little stronger than you were before?"

She crossed her arms over her chest again. "I'm…um…"

"I'm listening."

Constance blew her breath out in a sharp exhale. "You know what? I'm not interested in running much anymore." She glanced toward the interior of the gym, still in darkness. "One of the ladies told me you're more into weight lifting than anything else. I've never actually touched weights. Not like you were doing yesterday. With the weights on your back? Maybe…" She paused and blew her bangs out of her face; they had lost some of their static and had started to dip into her lashes. "Maybe you can show me that."

Rhett thought for a moment. He'd done a lot of things yesterday. Right before class, though, he'd been doing back squats. Powerlifting. My Pretty Pony wanted to do power-lifting, which made her even more interesting than she seemed. He thought briefly on how he'd told Kitty to check in with Zoe, who was the Level 1 lifting coach, whether for power-lifting or weight lifting. Rhett didn't typically mess with the beginners.

"All right," Rhett heard himself say. "Let's see what you're made of."

Rhett Santos pointed to his phone, which he'd attached to the stereo equipment, and told her to pick some music she liked. He started to collect equipment. For just a mo-ment, Constance hesitated. What the hell was she doing? She'd woken this morning, after a pretty sleepless night, to roads covered in ice. Despite that, she hadn't been able to stop herself from driving here. She hadn't eaten breakfast or made coffee.

She just got in the car and drove to this insane gym, as if she weren't even in control of her own body. She hadn't really thought anyone would be here at this hour, in this weather, but the light that shone from one small window of the gym had somehow seemed like a lighthouse beacon in the middle of a stormy sea. Now here she was, alone, with a very large, strong man.

Rhett glanced up. "All good?"

Constance jolted, unfreezing herself. "Sure." She clicked on the Pandora icon, ignoring the voice in her head that told her she shouldn't have listened to Sunny. She couldn't blame Sunny. She'd have come here, no matter what, though she still had no idea why. She selected what Rhett had been listening to last—Reggaeton Radio. A song called *"Pobre Diabla"* woke the silent speakers with a Latin beat. She waited, the music livening her blood, as Rhett tossed a ginormous rubber band and a long plastic pipe into his pile.

"You can change the station," he offered.

"I don't want to."

He smiled a little bit. "I saw a bit of what you can do yesterday. You move pretty well. But let's just run through the basics." Rhett put his arms straight out in front of him, then settled into a squat, no bar on his back this time.

Constance's eyes were fixed on his quads. Those might be the strongest quads she'd ever seen in real life. He wasn't bearing anything but body weight and she could still see the delineation of vastus medialis. Too bad men's shorts were so long these days, affording her only a peek around the knee. She'd love to see those quads in all their glory, working together. Totally from a professional standpoint, of course. She'd been observing him for half an hour now, assessing him from an orthopedic standpoint, and had already figured out how she would go about helping him if he were her client. That sort of thing happened automatically in a variety of settings, but she wasn't going to deny that assessing Rhett's gait, posture and movement patterns was far more enjoyable than the average old lady with kyphosis.

"Hip crease below the knee. Knees stacked over the ankles and in line with the toes," Rhett was saying. He rose back up, towering over her. "Let's see it."

Constance squatted.

"Keep your weight in your heels."

She shifted.

"Good. Give me ten of those."

Rhett ran her through a warm-up of squats, something called Good Mornings with that giant rubber band, sit-ups, push-ups on her knees and lunges. By the time she was finished, her sweat had doubled, despite the meager heat running inside the gym.

"Are you sore from yesterday?"

Constance nodded. "Biceps." She squeezed her arms. "Hamstrings. Quads. Delts. Abs." She touched all the places on her body.

Rhett flashed a smile. So far, he had two different kinds. One was mostly in his eyes, with a tiny bit that escaped around the corners of his mouth. The other was a full smile that backed off at the very end, just enough to be genuine, but not enough to let you inside. "You know your muscles."

"Yeah. A little bit."

"Okay, Constance." He grabbed the long white plastic pipe and slipped it on his shoulders. "I want you to do that same squat, with this PVC on your back." He demonstrated. "Remember, keep your weight in your heels and your chest up."

Constance took the pipe and settled it on her shoulders.

"Nope." Rhett came behind her and moved it down a little. "I want the PVC right here, on the upper traps." He touched his own. "See how they make a shelf? Right there. Not up on your neck."

"Sure, yours make a shelf." Constance laughed, despite herself. "Mine are more of a slope."

Rhett adjusted her hands, his own large and warm over her cool fingers. "Right there." Then his hands went to her hips. "And right there."

His touch was light and professional, but it still sent something oddly electric through her core.

Rhett came alongside her to observe. She executed her squat, surprised at how much the addition of a featherweight pipe could challenge the movement. From an orthopedic standpoint, that shouldn't have surprised her, but it did.

"Hips down, back straight. Pretend you're pushing a car door closed, Constance." He shook his head. "This isn't going to work."

Constance rose up and brushed the sweat from her eyes. "Is it really that bad? It feels a little awkward, but—"

"Squat's fine." Rhett shrugged. "You'll be able to use weight before you leave today. I'm talking about your name. I can't keep calling you Constance."

Constance drew the PVC off her back and settled it between her feet, like a cane. "What?"

"Do you have a nickname?"

"No. Why?"

"You're lying." Rhett scratched the back of his head, ruffling his dark hair. "Somebody calls you something other than Constance. And I can't keep calling you My Pretty Pony. People will think we're into some weird S and M. We need a new nickname."

Constance pointed her chin in the air as heat rushed her cheeks. She didn't want to lie again so she blurted, "Don't you dare call me Connie."

He wrinkled his nose. "No worries there."

She didn't know whether to laugh or get pissed. She was kind of in between both. Maybe he lacked a filter. More likely, he just didn't mince words.

"Not Connie. You're more of a..." Rhett paused, looked her up and down and said, "Stanzi. That's who you are."

Stanzi. Nobody had ever called her that. She liked it. She liked it so much she felt that electrical sensation zip through her core again.

"Come on over to the rig, Stanzi." Rhett waved his hand as he strode to a racked barbell. "This is quite a bit heavier than your PVC. Let me see five."

Constance ducked beneath the bar and settled it on her meager upper traps, where it rested more on her C7 than her muscles. "What if I don't like Stanzi?"

Rhett fixed her hands. "Close grip," he said, then tapped her heels with the PVC. "Widen your feet a little. There. Good. Go."

She visualized bumping that car door closed and sent her hips back as she settled into the bottom of the squat. She rolled forward a little on her toes, but listened to Rhett's cue to keep her weight in her heels and chest up as she drove up out of the bottom.

"Not horrible," he said. As Constance made her way into her second, then third squat, he finally answered her question. "Doesn't matter if you don't like it. You don't get to choose your nickname."

"Is that right?" Though she couldn't argue with him. She'd been called Cici her whole life because that's all Sunny could pronounce when she was a little girl. Constance had never liked nor disliked the name Cici. It's just who she was. She swallowed down the ripple of excitement at the idea that this man was giving her an opportunity to be someone else altogether.

Constance finished her five squats, the last one making her sweat beneath the armpits, then settled the barbell in the rack. "That's a two-way street, though." She faced Rhett, all bundled up in a hoodie, arms crossed over his chest. "What if I give you a nickname and you don't like it?"

He gave that barely there smile. "Good luck shortening my name. You deserve an award if you succeed."

"I could just call you Santos."

"You and the entire United States Marine Corps."

"Well…" Constance swallowed down the unusual tightness that had filled her throat and willed her heart to slow. She faced the rig and clasped the barbell. She didn't understand this response. Lately, she had a hard time looking men in the eye without feeling some kind of aversion. That wasn't happening with Rhett, despite his brusque manner. Josh had never been brusque. Even on the day Constance interrupted his run with that other woman, he'd been all sweet and syrupy, talking like, *Oh, I had no idea you'd be coming. We haven't run in so long. You're just so tired all the time.* Constance shook off the memory and focused. "I never back down from a challenge. I'll find you a nickname."

"You do that, Stanzi." Rhett's voice came over her shoulder. "Now go grab two of those plates over there, the ones that have the number ten on them. Then come back here and put some weight on that bar."

By the time an hour was up, Rhett had run Stanzi through back squats and dead lifts. She was a good mover. A little bit of time and practice would take her far, especially if she was as persistent as she seemed. Deep into their training, she hadn't complained or wimped out; she'd just buckled down and tackled the work.

Now, he would get in his own workout, then go home, wrap the heating pad around his leg and hope tomorrow was warmer.

They reached the front door. Stanzi grabbed her giant winter coat, but paused, staring pointedly at his thigh. "Do you want me to look at that, before I go? It's the least I can do, for taking up your time today when you were supposed to be closed."

Rarely did Rhett find himself speechless.

"You've been limping all morning." She took a step closer. "You were limping yesterday, too, but it's worse today."

"Yeah." Rhett found his voice. "When it's cold it's... Um, what...what exactly would you do?"

A pretty smile hooked the corners of her mouth. It lit her face up in a way he hadn't seen before. Her body seemed to relax. "Sit down."

Rhett settled onto the closest bench, without argument. He wasn't sure what she was going to do, but the pain was so intense he didn't really care.

Stanzi kneeled down in front of him and pushed up his shorts, on the right side. "Oh." The word came under her breath when she spied the scars. "I see."

Rhett waited for her to ask what happened to his leg. Everybody did. For a rotten second, he found himself formulating a lie. "No big deal," he said.

"No? Okay. Wait here."

Rhett wasn't sure where she thought he would go, but she held up a finger as she rose, like she was telling a dog to stay. She put on that ridiculous coat and disappeared out the door. A few minutes later, Stanzi returned with a bottle of something in her hand. The coat came off again. "Lie down on the floor."

Again, Rhett was in too much pain to argue. He regretted not paying more attention to her occupation on her waiver. Physical therapist? Nurse? He settled himself on the floor and waited.

Stanzi kneeled next to his right side, squirted something into her palm from the bottle she'd fetched and rubbed her hands together. She slipped one of her legs under his knee. "Relax. Let me support your weight."

Rhett obeyed, closed his eyes and drew a deep breath into his stomach. Her hands, still warm from the workout, hovered above his knee. Even though he couldn't see her, he could feel her, just above his skin. When she finally touched him, he felt a little jolt inside, but contained it, keeping his body still. She sat there a few seconds, doing nothing while he breathed. He waited for questions. None came. Then her hands moved into long, gliding strokes from below the knee, all the way up his thigh.

"Keep breathing like you are," she said. "Achy pain is okay, but if you feel like you want to punch me, let me know."

Rhett laughed a little bit. "Do your worst, Stanzi." Despite his bravado, he felt himself bracing, in anticipation of the pain. He'd gone to a couple of massage therapists—he was guessing that was her occupation—for PT after he got back home and things always got excruciating. Afterward, he'd lie in bed feeling like he'd just beat the flu, weak and useless.

But as he lay there, and Stanzi worked his leg, he found himself relaxing. There was something different about her touch. She didn't just jam her elbow in his scars and try to make him cry. She didn't talk too much, either. Everybody else talked too damn much. He didn't want to open his eyes to see, because it felt too good and he didn't want to jinx it, but it felt like she was kneading his muscles more than squashing them. She could've had fifty hands for how deftly she worked his leg, all the way from below the knee, up into his groin.

"We could work this scar tissue more, at another time." Her voice was light and professional as her fingers grazed over the old wounds. "It would be a little more painful, though, and right now I just want to loosen up all the fascia and get the quads separated and warm. You'll feel a lot better, trust me."

He already did. His thigh was warmer and looser, like she'd chinked up and loosened his muscles from their old bonds. This reminded him of the time Papa had dug up a dying tree in a client's yard, and showed him the root-bound ball that was keeping the plant from getting the nutrients it needed. Papa had shaken out the dry dirt and worked the roots, combing his fingers through them like he stroked a lover's hair, until he'd been satisfied and had replanted the tree in a larger hole with fresh soil.

Twenty years later, Rhett drove past that tree, now large and robust, every time he went home to visit his parents.

"You doing all right?"

Rhett nodded, unwilling to speak, afraid his voice would come out lacking authority and control. So he just kept breathing and hoped whatever she was doing would never end.

All too soon, Stanzi straightened out his shorts and slipped her thigh from beneath his knee. "How do you feel?" she asked as he blinked his eyes open.

Rhett sat up, then rose slowly to his feet. He bent his knee a few times. "Not horrible," he said. *Amazing*, he thought. "Thanks. Now I can get through the day."

"You need a full assessment. Your old wounds could be causing an ascending disorder. I'm guessing you suffer a tight back and some neck pain most of the time, in addition to the pain you get in the leg."

Wow, how the hell would she know that? Rhett kept the surprise, and the laughter, out of his voice when he said, "Oh, trust me. I have an ascending disorder or two."

Stanzi offered a pretty, genuine smile. A matured version of the one he'd seen so far, like she'd grown more comfortable after massaging him. He noted that she didn't offer to give him the full assessment. He wasn't going to ask, either.

Stanzi drew on her coat, zipped it all the way up her neck and over her mouth. The hat and gloves followed.

Rhett suppressed a chuckle. "All you need's the mask and you're in MOPP 4."

"What?" The word came muffled from beneath the coat.

"Mission-oriented protective…never mind." Rhett chuckled to himself.

She giggled, anyway. "Thanks for the lesson. I'm going to be sore as hell tomorrow."

"That's okay. Long as you come back the day after."

All Rhett could see were those bright glacier eyes. Her mouth said nothing, but her eyes were conflicted. She was terrified, but excited. Overwhelmed, but had hooked into something she couldn't deny.

Stanzi left, saying nothing.

But she'd be back.

eight

"Everybody's good, ma'am. I'm turning in." Roger peeked into the living room, where Sunny sat by the fireplace, watching the pups and Chevy snooze while she nursed a glass of wine.

"Thanks, Rog." Sunny offered a tired smile. The day had been long, but rewarding. Despite the ice storm, she'd been able to place three of her dogs into successful adoptions today. "I'll see you in the morning. Oh, hey!" she called out before Roger disappeared. "What happened to the new girl? Yolanda? She wasn't here when I got back today."

Roger paused in the entryway. His shoulders rose and fell before he turned back. "Janice stopped by again." Roger waved in the general vicinity of the Matteri land. "When you were out. I didn't want to tell you, because you were so busy and look so tired. She threatened me and Yolanda. Made her hand into a gun—" Roger imitated "—and said we'd be sorry if we set foot on her land. Yolanda spooked. But I don't want her to get kicked out of the program. Yolanda is good people. She needs to be here or she's just going to be strung out her whole life."

Sunny's insides tightened, her fatigue filling up with the sizzle of adrenaline. "I'll talk to Kendra tomorrow. See what I can do. I'll make sure Yolanda doesn't lose her spot."

"Thank you, ma'am." Roger turned to go, but stopped again. He lowered his voice, even though nobody was around to hear them. "I know you wanted to go back for that beagle last time you raided her mill, but I don't think it's a good idea. That woman is on to you and she's crazy. Please don't go over there. At least for a while." He opened his hands in a stop gesture, which offered an impressive palm spread. Though only nineteen, Roger was a large man with a deep voice and a gentle demeanor that belied both his years and upbringing.

Sunny drained her wine and smiled. "You're sweet to worry about me, Rog. But I'll be okay. You go get some rest now."

"Yes, ma'am."

Sunny watched him through the window as he made his way out back and along the path to the cabin that was reserved just for him. It was the largest one, attached to the main kennel. Sunny would never forget the tears she saw in the young man's eyes when she offered him the place for his very own. "No rent," she'd said. "You live here and help me take care of my dogs for as long as you want to and the room and board is on me."

Despite the fact he shared his quarters with half a dozen dogs, all he'd said was, "I've never had a room of my own before."

Sunny's eyes had welled up fast. "Well, you do now."

As soon as Roger disappeared inside, she plunked her empty wineglass down, rose and snatched up her coat and boots. It was one thing for Janice Matteri to threaten her; it was another entirely to go pointing her nasty fingers at her crew.

Sunny trained her binoculars on the back of Janice Matteri's kennel. This is where Janice kept the dogs she cared the least about. Anything prized, which is what she'd shown to the police, was kept in or near the main house. Everything was dark, quiet and freezing. A shift to the left: the security camera was still disabled with black spray paint. Now was the time. Nobody would be expecting Sunny to raid the kennel just days after Janice had gone to the police. What kind of idiot would do that?

Me, that's who, thought Sunny.

She slipped the binoculars into her bag and approached the fence, feeling around until she had the first foothold. Sunny had long ago memorized the notches in the old wood fence that Janice was too cheap to replace. Divots just big enough to hook her feet and hands and pop herself over. Sunny landed with a thump, then slunk through the trees and stopped at the door of the kennel. The padlock Janice had put on the handle made her chuckle. Sunny withdrew bolt cutters from her bag. She paused before she put metal to metal, but all was silent. Despite the fact that common sense suggested a kennel full of dogs would bark at Sunny's noise or smell, she had learned early on that Janice's dogs were cowed into silence. They didn't like the sound of people approaching and never drew attention to themselves.

Her heart thudded in her chest as she braced to cut open the padlock. This time, she'd come armed with a leash and collar and a bag of raw meat to entice the poor beagle out of his corner. Even though some time had passed since she'd first tried to lure him away, now that she was here Sunny felt an urgency to get to him as quickly as possible. Her hands shook with anticipation.

"Hands up," a cold male voice came from behind her back. "Nice and slow."

★ ★ ★

Sunny's hands planted on the cold metal of her car as the detective spun her around. Her head was spinning, just as fast. What the hell had just happened?

You got busted trying to break into Janice Matteri's kennel and then marched out to your car, where you thought it was safely hidden on a back road nobody knows about, by a police detective, her brain shot back.

"Sunny Morrigan, I presume? I'm Detective Callahan. Would you like me to radio a female detective to come out here and frisk you?"

"Frisk me?" Sunny's heart hammered in her chest. "Listen, Detective, I'm not on any drugs and I'm not carrying a gun. I was only trying to check on—"

"Who said anything about drugs or a gun?" His voice got sharper.

Dammit. Where the hell had he been hiding? And why?

"I'll take that as a no." Detective Callahan kicked her legs apart with his foot and patted her up and down, cold and professional, until he was satisfied she wasn't packing. "Turn around. Stick out your arms and touch your nose, one finger at a time."

"Listen." Sunny pushed off the car and obeyed, her fingers going rapidly to her nose, back and forth. "I know what this looks like. But it's not what it looks like. If you'd just let me explain." Sunny actually had no idea what she would say if the detective suddenly agreed.

"Walk in a straight line, just there." He pointed. "One foot in front of the other."

"We both know I'm not drunk." A cold fist tightened around Sunny's stomach. "Janice Matteri's the one you should be arresting. She has dogs in that kennel who are suffering.

Shame on her, and shame on you. I'm the only humane one in this scenario."

Silence passed. A hand gripped her shoulder, stopping her midstride. Sunny turned and faced the steely gaze of the detective. He wasn't exceptionally tall, but he didn't need to be. His eyes looked like cold stars, the way they glittered in the dark, and his jaw could've been chiseled from marble. His light brown hair was cropped close on the sides, and the way he filled out his clothes, beneath his protective vest, left no doubt of his strength.

Sunny held up her hands, palms open.

Callahan's face softened, like he was seeing her for the first time. "You're under arrest," he said. "I'm going to put you in the back of my car and take you back to the station. Maybe a night in jail will make you think about how reckless you're being."

Sunny sensed the slight drop in his guard and moved in quickly. "You could do that. Or you could come back to my place to talk. I know what it looks like, but I swear I'm not the bad guy. She's been threatening me and my staff. Threatening to shoot us, no less."

Detective Callahan paused, stuffed his hands in his pockets and stared at her.

"Plus—" Sunny took a step closer "—I have whisky."

The detective gave a soft laugh. He looked her up and down. "Are you trying to bribe me?"

"Maybe."

Just enough silence passed to make Sunny nervous, but when the detective spoke, he surprised her. "Get in your car," he said. "I'll follow."

Without the vest, his shirt undone at the top two buttons and his sidearm safely holstered, Detective Callahan was a slightly less imposing figure as he leaned back on Sunny's couch. She poured him a glass of Scotch and passed it over.

"Are you going to get into trouble for not taking me in?"

The detective sipped his whisky and watched her awhile, maybe sizing her up or trying to decide what to say. "I'm not on duty. Nobody knows I'm out here but me." He rubbed the back of his neck. "But that won't stop me from taking you in and throwing you in jail for the night if I don't like what I hear."

"You're not on duty?" Sunny measured her words carefully. "Then why are you out here?"

"I spoke with your sister the other day." Detective Callahan's unflinching gaze was bright above the Scotch glass. "She suggested looking into the dog operations when no one was expecting it. I decided to come out here tonight, see the layout. Then I spotted your car. The way it was tucked off the road drew my suspicion immediately."

So, he was a good detective. Nobody else would've seen her car there, on that back road that only the Morrigans and Matteris knew existed. "I'm sure my sister meant you should check out Janice Matteri's operation. Not mine."

Callahan laughed a little. He rubbed the back of his neck. "I'm not seeing Ms. Matteri breaking into your kennels. Am I?"

Sunny silently agreed that she'd walked into that one. "If you talked to my sister, then you know that I rescue dogs. I also help kids who've been in trouble so they get a second chance. They're innocent. Janice Matteri, on the other hand, sells for profit. She overbreeds and keeps many of her dogs in inhumane conditions."

Callahan rolled his glass around in his fingertips, then ran it beneath his nose. "Is that who lives in your cabins, out back? Kids who work here?"

He had done more than a little sleuthing. "Only one resident works for me. Roger. He's an adult, but yes, he started here with the youth program. He was in foster care his whole childhood." Sunny dispensed with the fake pleasantness and loosed a little of her frustration by thunking a glass upright on the bar. "The other cabins are rented out by people who don't want to camp but also don't want to glamp. I'm a mix between the two. Helps pay the bills."

"I see."

"I'm surprised you came with me." Sunny poured herself two fingers and tossed it back. She braced herself for the burn, but the amber liquid went down much smoother than she'd expected. "Why not just throw me in jail?"

Detective Callahan ran the glass under his nose again and drew a breath. "Because I like your sister, Miss Morrigan."

"Call me Sunny."

"I like your sister, Sunny." He took a second sip and showed his appreciation by eyeing the glass with raised brows. "She shot straight with me. That's why I tend to believe your story about why I caught you breaking several laws tonight."

"Everybody likes Cici." Sunny rolled her eyes. Introverted Constance, who needed nobody. She just had a way with people. "She's like that grumpy aunt who doesn't like cats, but all the cats go to her, anyway." Sunny shrugged. "Except she likes cats. And she's not really grumpy. She's just kind of… intimidating, without being intimidating." Sunny expected confusion but the detective smiled.

"The opposite of you?"

Sunny poured herself another glass. "I get it." She spread her arms open. "I'm not large and intimidating." She threw back the second drink and was grateful for the warmth that spread quickly through her body. "Like you."

"Size isn't everything." Callahan shook his head and stood up. "A black widow can be just as dangerous as a great white shark." He approached her, his demeanor considerably more relaxed than outside Janice Matteri's, and took the bottle of Scotch from her hand. "Something tells me that you just might be a venomous little spider."

"Oh, yeah?" Sunny dropped her voice down. "What tells you that?"

"Everything from the way you invited me out here to the way you're guzzling this very, very, *very*—" Callahan eyed the label "—expensive Scotch, when you should be sipping it. Smelling it. Savoring the different aromas." He set the bottle on the oak bar and leaned his elbow there.

"I don't know anything about Scotch," Sunny said. "This was a gift."

Callahan nodded toward the bottle. "Macallan. Thirty-year-old single malt. Whoever gave you that likes you a lot."

"One of my frequent customers." Sunny opened her arms, as though to embrace the grounds. Mr. Healy. A wealthy property developer from New York City who came down twice a year, rented a cabin for two weeks, took all his meals alone and always greeted Sunny with a peck on each cheek. He'd never asked her out or gave her lascivious looks, but he always presented her with a "hostess" gift, and bowed when she accepted it.

The detective took another sip from his glass. It looked like he rolled the Scotch around on his tongue before he swallowed. "Starts off like oranges," he said. "Then turns to vanilla and toffee. Midway it goes woody. Finishes like silk. You should try it slowly. Here." He held out his glass.

Sunny took it and sipped.

Callahan's eyes didn't leave her mouth. "Where do you taste it?"

"Starts in the middle of my tongue. Then changes to the

edges." Sunny sucked in her bottom lip. "Then it sort of fizzes out, filling my mouth and warming my throat."

The detective took the glass back, without breaking their shared gaze. He drank, then nodded his agreement. "Mouth. Then throat." He put the glass to her lips and tilted it until she got another sip. "That's the way it should be."

The heat from the liquid spread from Sunny's throat, down across her chest. A couple of drops missed her lips entirely and trickled to her chin.

Callahan reached out and swiped the drops with his thumb. "Four grand a bottle," he said, sticking his thumb in his mouth. "You shouldn't waste any."

"Four grand?" Sunny said, even though she'd researched the gift and knew exactly what it cost. "That's insane."

"Like I said. The guy who gave you this likes you a lot."

"I never said it was a guy."

Callahan finished the Scotch and slid the glass to the oak counter. "I'd bet my salary."

Sunny tilted her head to the side and smiled. She had Detective Callahan right where she wanted him. Thing was, he probably knew that, which made it difficult to know how far she could push it. Then again, the beagle was still stuck at the Matteri mill, and Sunny was still in danger of being arrested. Her mission was singular and unavoidable. "You want something, don't you? There's some other reason you came out here."

The detective smiled and leaned in close. "I'm just here to enforce the law." His breath came warm against her cheek, smelling of oranges, chocolate, Scotch.

"Then the person you should really spring a surprise visit on is Janice Matteri. Not me." Sunny felt like she was swimming inside that expensive bottle of amber liquid. Dizzy. Warm. Sparkling. Desired.

"Maybe I'll do that." Callahan pulled back suddenly, and buttoned up his collar. "Maybe I'll forget about what happened tonight, too. With you and your bolt cutters, over on your neighbor's property. Which, by the way, are a lot harder to use than you think. You'll need really strong hands to get the job done. But once you do get the job done, it's officially breaking and entering. Savvy?"

Sunny swallowed hard. "Savvy."

"Good." He rubbed the back of his neck.

"You should have someone check that out," Sunny spoke carefully. It looked like he was going to leave, and she wasn't sure if that was good or bad. "My sister's got great hands."

"Tell me about it." Callahan collected his jacket and drew it on. "Your sister spent a total of two minutes, tops, working on my neck the other day. And even though it still bugs me a little, it feels better than it has in months."

Sunny licked the remainder of the Scotch from her lips. "She could help you as much as you need. I'd make sure of it." Constance's voice ran through Sunny's head: *Do you ever think before you leap? No, you don't. And then when you land in crap, you're always surprised you got dirty.*

Callahan's movement's slowed. He got a glint in his eye. "How would your sister feel, about you offering her up like that?"

Sunny shrugged. "She's used to it."

Callahan's glint deepened. Just like the way he'd spotted Sunny's car in the woods, he saw things most people didn't. He was on to her. Sunny was certain he was going to leave, when he stopped, turned back and leaned against the bar. "I have a friend." He lowered his voice. "A really good friend. The kind you have for life. A brother. You know?"

"Of course I know."

Callahan appeared to consider her words, puckering his

lips, then nodding. "My friend could use a pair of hands like that. He's struggling, even though he doesn't know how bad he's struggling."

Sunny shrugged. "Sure. I'll get you Cici's business card. Have him call and—"

Callahan was already shaking his head. "That won't work. I can't just hand him a card and tell him to call. He'd never do it. This would have to be done with…finesse."

Sunny bit down on her lip, which still tasted of chocolate and oranges. "I see. So what you're saying is, if I scratch your back—or your friend's back, more specifically—then you'll scratch mine. You'll look the other way on tonight, and I'll help you with your friend. Something like that?"

"Yeah." Callahan nodded, eyeing her up and down. "Something like that."

nine

Constance glared into her sister's innocent-looking eyes. How many times had she been through this? Sunny, plowing ahead with little thought to the endgame, leaping off buildings for shiny prizes. "I told you not to go back to Janice's yet. I told you to bide your time. Now that beagle is probably stuck in there forever. Does that make you feel better?" Constance gestured in the direction of the Matteri property, which started several miles down this path, deep into the Virginia woods.

Sunny's eyes welled up. "Don't say that." Her chin quivered. "I still think I can help him. You just have to help me first."

Fezzi gave a woof that sounded suspiciously like an apology. Constance stared down at him, but he only grinned, his tongue lolling to the side as he panted. The air was cold but Constance had walked him at a brisk pace from her place to Sunny's, down the worn dirt path she used to run on. The old boy could move at a pretty good clip with the hobble-hop-step he'd adapted to long ago on his three legs.

"I can't believe you're not in jail. You really should be in jail."

"I know," Sunny agreed. "But you have to help me."

"Now I know why you were so happy to see me this morning." Constance immediately regretted making her sister almost cry, which only happened if something terrible befell a dog. To Constance, Sunny was still just a five-year-old girl who'd lost her mother, platinum hair sticking to her wet cheeks and blue eyes an ocean of sadness. "Why can't this guy just set up an appointment?"

"He's the stubborn sort." Sunny swiped a knuckle under her nose, which was red from the cold air. "Doesn't need anybody's help for anything. You're good with guys like that. Remember, that's how you became a massage therapist. To help Daddy." Sunny shrugged. "So the idea is that you sort of cozy up to him and get him to let you work your magic without him knowing the detective had anything to do with it. I know you can do it. Just like with Daddy. You'd tell him you needed to use him for 'practice' and he had no idea what was going on." Sunny offered a smile—a little bow on the neat little package she'd just wrapped up.

A door creaked on the main cabin. Roger appeared a second later, food bowls in his arms, to start the morning rounds. They all waved at each other.

"But I lived with Dad. How the hell am I supposed to cozy up to some random guy?"

Sunny's smile deepened. "That's the best part. Turns out the detective—and his best buddy—go to your gym. You know, the gym you hate that you went back to, anyway?" She arched a perfectly shaped eyebrow.

"I shouldn't have told you I went back." Constance's cheeks went warm. "I barely know anyone. And I'm not going back again. I'm done there. I don't need a gym to get fit. I can do it myself. I will, I swear. Dang it, Sunny." She let out an exasperated sigh. "Why do you always make messes for me to clean up?"

"It'll be easy." Sunny clasped Constance's hands and squeezed. "I promise. Look." She dug a business card out of her purse. "You don't have to mingle with people and meet all the gym members. I know how you hate that." She pressed the card into Constance's palm. "The guy you're going to help is the owner. See? Easy. Have you met the owner yet? His name is some old movie star name. It's..." Sunny reached to take the card back.

"Rhett," Constance supplied, her heart suddenly thumping hard in her chest, like she and Fezzi had been on a run instead of a walk. For a second, she was back on the trail, lean and mean and full of the cool morning air. There wasn't anything quite like those morning runs she used to take, the cobwebs shook clean and the blood flowing smooth and her brain both alive and relaxed. She was an athletic, confident woman in her early thirties, running up and down these trails at least three times a week. The other three days, she'd run around the neighborhood or at the high school track, depending on her goals. She was a smart woman, who planned for everything. By training on trails, roads and the track, she was ready for any kind of race, both various distances and terrains. She planned for hydration on longer runs, knew to dress like it was fifteen degrees cooler than the actual air temperature, rotated her running shoes, carbo-loaded if necessary, scheduled taper weeks before a big event and never, ever wore new clothes or tried new foods on a race day.

Man, she had it all together.

Until Daddy got sick. Her running tapered off. She got

slow, sad and unmotivated. And Josh started running with somebody else.

"Yeah, that's it. Rhett." Sunny's voice was bright with surprise. "So you know him? You've met the owner? You've… Oh." She quieted. The color of her eyes deepened. "Ohhh."

"Stop." Constance regretted how quickly the word came. "Yes." Her voice was cool. "I've met him." *And*, she didn't add, *I've already massaged him. His leg, anyway.* Which hadn't been entirely altruistic. Her offer to massage Rhett had been as much for herself as a way to pay him back for his instruction in the gym. She wanted to know what he felt like. She *had* to know what he felt like.

And just as she'd imagined, based on the first time she'd touched him, Rhett's energy turned out to be strong, damaged and deeply rooted. It mimicked what the muscles in his thigh had done: in order to guard the destruction, deep inside, the muscles surrounding the wounds were a hard, protective gauntlet. The rigidity of the wall gave him pain, but it also served a purpose. Constance had to massage with caution. She could soften him a little, to ease his considerable discomfort, but to go too deep, too fast, would only do more damage than good. That wall hadn't been built in a day, and couldn't come tumbling down in one, either.

"This is the guy who smiled at your unicorn shirt, isn't it?" Sunny said.

Constance's gaze flew to Sunny's. She stopped herself from saying, *How did you know that?* "I'm not sure I can do this, Sunny. I understand now why the detective is hesitant. Rhett is…complicated." She closed her eyes and felt his energy again as she worked his leg. His was exactly the sort of energy she'd stopped working with since Daddy died and Josh left. His sort of massage was the polar opposite of the Classic Spa Massage.

"And?"

"And—" Constance didn't hide her exasperation "—remember when I worked at Walter Reed? With the wounded combat vets?" She waited, letting it sink in. When realization showed on Sunny's creased brow, she pressed on. "Yeah. Like that."

"Well." Sunny shrugged helplessly. "I get it, but...you helped those patients. You made things better. Most of the time. Right?"

Constance opened her eyes with a sigh. "I'd have to be very careful. He's not someone to mess with, and I wouldn't want to hurt him. He's a—" Constance glanced down at Fezzi and the words escaped her mouth before she could stop them "—dangerous breed."

Sunny's eyes were no longer teary. Instead, the yin to her yang had taken over and a sly glint had settled over the face she'd inherited straight from Mom. "So...is that a yes?"

Constance could barely believe the word that came out of her mouth. What the hell had come over her?

"Yes."

ten

Rhett took a few deep breaths and stretched his legs. He was not going to let stress ruin how good his quads still felt. Part of it was due to the weather, he knew. In typical Virginia style, Saturday's ice storm was nothing but a memory by Monday morning. Temperatures had risen twenty degrees and he needed nothing but a light jacket when he took off for the gym.

But there was no denying the magic Stanzi had worked on him. He had spent Sunday pain-free, even if he hated the quiet diligence of that day, the gym closed and the focus on paperwork, advertising and other things that required sitting still. Not Rhett's strong point. He hadn't even gone for his usual run because he'd wanted to milk the effects of Stanzi's massage for as long as possible.

By Monday morning, he was always antsy, and today was worse. Still, he pushed it all to the back of his mind as he arrived at the gym and drew in the scents of orange cleaner and cold steel. Connor had just finished mopping. He gave Rhett a salute as he dumped the bucket of dirty water out the back bay door.

As soon as Rhett got the morning classes rolling, his insides started to come unstuck, which was the closest he could come to describing what it felt like to live in the normal. The doldrums of everyday life were like flatlining; the intensity of gym life, with its loud music, clanging barbells, jacked heart rates and brisk pace was just enough to loosen the glue and keep his head above water. If he thought about it, he could compare what Stanzi's massage had done for his leg to what coaching and intense exercise did for his soul.

Rhett was just starting to think he'd been wrong about her, and about how much she'd enjoyed the powerlifting, when, right at ten, she walked through the front door, out of breath. "Just in time," he murmured to himself. He'd been thinking about slipping her in with an experienced bunch—a close-knit group of cops and firefighters and a few other professions that had shift work and a load of testosterone. Not the place he'd put any newbie. But the perfect place for Stanzi.

"Stanzi." Rhett watched her strip off her coat, a much lighter version of what she'd been wearing on Saturday. "I'm glad you're not late. That would piss me off."

She tilted up her chin to fix her gaze into his. "Late?" she said. "How'd you even know I was coming?"

Rhett shrugged. "I just knew."

Her eyes were fearless. "How's your leg?"

Rhett's hand went instinctively to his right thigh. "Not horrible. Thank you again."

"You're welcome."

Rhett almost smiled, but held it in. Instead, he checked out her outfit, just in case unicorns were back on the menu.

Today, she sported a pair of black leggings and a raggedy green T-shirt that read The Hick from French Lick.

That did make him smile. More of Dad's old wardrobe, maybe? "Go warm up, Larry Bird," Rhett ordered. "James, Doug, Duke and Benita will get you going." He nodded to the cop, firefighter, Secret Service agent, and mother of three small children, respectively, one tall and lanky, the other short and stocky, Duke both tall and stocky and Benita small but all muscle, and strong as an ox. "This is Stanzi. Warm her up."

She cast him one flash of helplessness before she sucked that weakness right back in, then turned up her chin and joined the others.

Rhett watched from a short distance, curious how his experiment would hold up. Within minutes, Stanzi was doing the stretches and drills with ease. Her no-bullshit personality fit in well with the seasoned group, and they were more than happy to have a woman with a determined spirit join their circle. Especially when they thought she was a basketball fan, and they turned out to be right. Rhett could hear her rattling off some Celtics stats with Duke as they lunged across the floor.

"What's this about?" Zoe came up beside him and flashed a curious grin. She watched Stanzi grimace through her air squats, obviously still sore from Saturday.

"She's new." Rhett felt stupid, stating the obvious. "I'm trying something out."

"What? You don't trust me with her?" Zoe elbowed him in the ribs. "You just put a newbie into your strongest group."

"I want to see who she is." The words slipped out before he could stop them. Stanzi was most certainly a newbie, especially today. They were going to focus on upper body and he'd bet his month's salary she wouldn't be able to bench-press much more than the barbell. But there was something seasoned about her, too. He sensed a fighter beneath all those baggy clothes. "So I threw her in a snake pit."

Zoe watched a little while. James had Stanzi doing overhead squats with the PVC, against the rig. Stanzi lowered herself methodically, the struggle to keep the PVC against the rig and keep her weight in her heels a challenge. "Cute," Zoe said. "Certainly has potential. I worked with her Friday. Not a quitter. I like that."

"Me, too."

Zoe elbowed him in the ribs. "What're you in such a good mood about?"

"I don't know what you mean."

"You've been supernice to everyone all morning. You didn't even make the latecomers do burpees."

"Eh." Rhett tried to think quickly of an excuse. "Guess I slept good."

It wasn't a lie.

"Uh-huh."

"I'm going to throw her in your eleven o'clock for some cardio," Rhett said. "My focus with her will be strength but I want her to get her conditioning back, too. Slowly."

Zoe clucked her tongue. "Whatever you say, boss."

For the next hour, the crew did weight-lifting work. Stanzi's workout was a little different. Rhett would keep her from the more complicated Olympic lifts for now.

"We're going to widen our grip for this." Rhett shifted her hands farther down the barbell. "This is a snatch grip. Eventually, when you snatch, this is where you'll finish, once the bar is overhead."

Stanzi nodded, without flinching, determined if confused.

"Dip and drive, just like I showed you," Rhett said. "The dip is just a break of the knees. The drive is powerful. You're using your hips to help get the bar overhead. When I say drive, I want you to fire those glutes. Then punch it overhead."

Stanzi struggled at first, to keep the flow from dip into drive smooth. At first she'd pause, the power of her hips lost, and would finish by muscling the bar overhead. She racked the barbell and watched the others, her eyes sharp like a hawk's. When she got back to the bar, her next set of reps was smoother. She repeated that through all twelve sets, every minute on the minute, sweat beading her brow, which was creased in concentration. By the end, the bar was almost flying overhead.

"You hear that clanking sound?" Rhett smiled at her. "That's the bar rattling in your hands. That's good. Means you're getting power into the lift."

Stanzi smiled and worked her arms in big circles. She was probably exhausted, but she said nothing.

"Duke." Rhett shook his head as the big guy failed the last rep of his last set. "This is medium percentage work. You shouldn't be failing. As big as you are, you aren't getting the power you need in the drive."

Duke racked his barbell. "I don't know what's going on, man." He rubbed his lower back. "I'm just sore today."

Stanzi, who'd been watching intently, stepped in. "I think—" her voice came out soft but authoritative "—that your glutes aren't firing correctly. I think your back is firing first. Do you want me to check?"

Duke blinked for a few seconds. His hair, which was always perfectly combed on arrival, like a black-and-white film star's, had a rumpled, sweaty look. "Um," he said. "Yeah. Sure."

"Lie down." Stanzi pointed at a spot on the floor long enough to accommodate Duke. "Facedown."

Duke stripped off his wrist wraps and, with raised eyebrows, obeyed.

Stanzi kneeled down next to him and waved Rhett closer. Rhett kneeled down on Duke's other side. The rest of the crew gathered in a curious circle. She pushed up Duke's sweaty T-shirt, exposing his lower back. "Can I touch your glutes?"

Duke laid his cheek against his crossed forearms. "You have to ask?"

"Yes."

"Then yes, ma'am. Touch my glutes."

Stanzi spread the fingers of her left hand, placing her thumb on Duke's right butt cheek and her pinky on the center of the back of his thigh. With her right hand, she placed her thumb and forefinger on Duke's lower back, one on either side of his spine. "Duke," she said, "when I say go, I want you to slowly raise your right leg toward the ceiling."

"Gotcha."

"Go."

Duke slowly raised his leg.

Stanzi watched carefully, then said, "One more time." Her eyes closed as Duke repeated the movement. Her eyes opened and locked into Rhett's. "Did you see that?"

"I think so."

"His back is firing before his glutes or hamstrings. That's not good." Stanzi ran a hand through her hair, making it stick up in places. "It can lead to a loss of power and low back pain. I want either the glutes or the hamstrings to fire first."

Rhett nodded. "Makes sense to me."

"Here." Stanzi came around to Rhett's side and took his hand. "You feel." She positioned his fingers on Duke's body, just as hers had been. Up close, that sweaty Larry Bird T-shirt smelled sweet; not like chemical perfumes, but something spicy and soothing at the same time, like a warm kitchen on a cold night.

"Hey, Rhett." James was smiling down at them. "You're supposed to ask Duke if you can touch his butt first."

Doug snorted a laugh. "Can Rhett touch your butt, Duke? And can we watch?"

"Shut up," Duke laughed into his arms. "Just let the little redhead fix me. I don't care who touches my butt."

"Duke—" Stanzi bit down on her lower lip, like she was trying to suppress a smile "—raise your left leg this time, slowly."

Rhett watched carefully. He was pretty sure he felt Duke's spinal erectors bump under his fingertips before his butt or hamstrings. He made Duke repeat the movement three times. "Yeah," he finally concluded. "Back's firing first on this side, too."

"Duke, I'm going to squash your glutes," Stanzi said. She pressed her hands over his generous butt cheek, like kneading bread dough. "I'm bringing the origin and insertion of the muscles close together."

"That's her fancy way of saying she's rubbing your butt, dude." Doug chuckled, his big arms crossed and his chest shaking as he laughed.

Stanzi broke a little smile and shook her head as she worked Duke's other side.

"I'm next," Benita piped in.

"Now I'm going to smack your ass," Stanzi said, "to be blunt."

"I'm all yours." Duke closed his eyes, like he was relaxed enough to sleep through the whole process.

Stanzi wasn't kidding. She slapped Duke's rear, one side after the other, for about twenty seconds each cheek. When she was done, and the laughter had died down, she ran her test again. "Rhett," she said, "check Duke's left side. Close your eyes this time and go by feel."

"I'll be damned," Rhett said, once he ran the test twice, both with and without eyes open. "His butt fired first this time."

Stanzi gave a proud little smile. "Yes, it did. All right, Duke. You can get up."

He rose to his feet and looked down at her. "Is my face as red as my ass?"

"It's a little pink in the cheeks," she said. "Seriously, though, I want you to work on activating your glutes every day. It can be as simple as squeezing your butt and holding for ten seconds, five times, a few times a day. Then do one cheek at a time. Glute bridges are good. You guys do those here?"

Rhett nodded. "Oh, yeah. We do those."

"Do them slowly," she told Duke. "Raise up slow and squeeze tight at the top."

"Thank you, ma'am." Duke's ruddy cheeks calmed down, going from reddish to pink as he offered a sheepish smile.

"Hey, you guys helped me all morning. Least I can do is return the favor." Stanzi turned to Rhett. "Now you can check any of your clients, if you're unsure what's firing first."

"Yeah, Rhett." Duke gave his shoulder a shove. "Where you been hiding her?" He turned to Stanzi. "He ought to pay you."

"You just got Duke's butt all ready to guard POTUS, free of charge," Benita added.

The group laughed.

Rhett gave her a thumbs-up. "Jump into Zoe's workout. It's just a short bodyweight metcon. We want to get your conditioning back up to speed." Rhett knew everybody had their flavor, but nothing irritated him more than lifters who had no engine and skinnies who had no strength. Balance was always the key.

"Guess I got a little weight to lose." Stanzi smoothed her

hands over her hips, stretching the Larry Bird shirt down to the top of her thighs, as though trying to hide her body.

Rhett resisted the urge to pull it up again. "Don't talk to me about the scale. That's just a number. You keep working hard here and your body will change, all for the better. We're looking for your body to be as strong as your spirit. Got me?"

Surprise widened her bright blue eyes. Her lips parted, but nothing came out.

Rhett lowered his voice and leaned down closer. "Just say yes."

The waver around her lips threatened a smile, but didn't prove up. Just when he thought she might obey, Stanzi bit down on her lower lip, turned and walked off toward the circle of people gathered around Zoe.

If she'd had enough hair, she would've tossed it.

By the time the workout was over, and Constance was covered in sweat from head to toe, Rhett had started another class. He was in a far corner of the gym, with about a dozen women, ranging in age and size. The only constant was the language—Rhett was teaching the class in Spanish. Constance didn't understand all of the words, but she got the gist, mostly through body language. He had them all in a circle, with light kettlebells between their feet. She watched for a little while, mostly hidden by the cubbies where people stashed their stuff while they worked out. Rhett's voice was strong without being brash, encouraging but forceful, and seemed to motivate the women without putting them off. A few of them hung on his every word, their body language obvious in how they felt about Coach Rhett. It was clear that he was a native speaker of both English and Spanish, his ease in either language like he'd spoken both since he was a babbling infant.

If she didn't have clients booked, Constance would've considered going back in for a third workout, just to listen to Rhett coach in Spanish.

She laughed at herself, and made to slip out unnoticed, but just as she turned away, Rhett looked over and caught her watching. He held up his hand in a wave. Constance waved back, then headed out into the cool air.

On the drive home, she looked into the bright blue sky and drew a breath deep into her belly. She called Sunny, even though she didn't normally talk on the phone while driving. "I just finished at the gym."

"Awesome! How'd it go?"

"Great. I learned a lot of new stuff. I was in this lifting group with some pretty intimidating people."

"I can't believe you're lifting weights." Sunny giggled. "But, at the same time, it totally makes sense. Did you see Rhett?"

"Yes. He coached the class."

"Good. Good. And were you able to talk?"

"You need to give me some time. This isn't going to happen overnight." Constance felt a zip of irritation. "I'm doing this carefully."

"Of course. I'm sorry."

"Listen. I didn't tell you this before, but I've kind of already worked on Rhett's leg. Before you even asked for my help. So, if you give me enough time, I'll try to help him. But you have to be patient."

"Are you serious?" Sunny's voice was somewhere in the range of giddy.

"When am I not serious?"

"Good point."

"And I'm doing this for him, just so you know. Not for you. I like him and I want to help him." Constance glanced at the clock. She had exactly an hour to get home, shower, eat lunch and prep the room downstairs for the human clients scheduled for the day. All easy-peasy spa massages. "Anyway. Change of subject. You're staying away from Janice's dogs, right?"

The pause at Sunny's end was a hair too long. "Yes. The detective and I have a deal. I'm not going over there, and I'm doing things lawfully. He'll help me if I help him."

Constance thought back to the day she'd worked Detective Callahan's neck. Like all men in power positions, he wasn't completely honest and he struggled with his own demons. But he seemed like a good guy, and probably had Rhett's best interests at heart. "Okay. Just give me some time. And don't do anything stupid."

"Who?" Sunny's voice went sweet as sugar. "Me?"

eleven

Sunny parked in a thin grove of trees a ways down from 13 White Fern Road. She'd made one pass, initially, then driven back around and settled her gaze on the house with a set of binoculars. Everything was old, dried up and rotting. Unlike the sparse neighbors, there wasn't a single holiday decoration in sight. There weren't a million cars in the driveway, as if all the family relatives had converged for Thanksgiving Day. The only life around the place was the black dog, out near the faded red barn. Even with the binoculars, she couldn't see much more than his head, due to the height of the grass around him.

Might as well get a little closer. She tossed her binoculars in the passenger seat and drove up to the house. She made no attempt to hide herself, even though that old car was parked out front. She'd just made her way in the direction of the dog when the front door of the house opened and a stout woman stepped out onto the rotting porch.

"Who're you?" she barked.

"Good afternoon, ma'am." Sunny cleared her throat. "I'm from the county. Just coming to assess the property."

The woman wrapped her brown knit sweater tight around her lumpy chest. She narrowed her eyes beneath her wiry gray hair, which looked to have been set with old-fashioned curlers. "You been here before? Driving a—" she pointed her nose at Sunny's truck "—dumpy old van?"

A dumpy old van?

Cici.

Sunny strode a little closer, wishing she had a clipboard or something else official looking. She hadn't decided on the county assessor angle until the moment it came out of her mouth. "That must've been my associate."

The old lady's face relaxed a little but the deep wrinkles in her cheeks were permanent. "I'll be watching," she said. "Don't you go near the dog, neither."

Sunny glanced in the direction of the barn. The dog had sat up, exposing skinny shoulders with brown patches. He looked more mutt and less rottweiler at a closer distance. He gave a sharp bark, followed by another.

"Actually—" Sunny patted herself "—I've forgotten the forms I need. I'll be back later in the week. Maybe you can make sure the dog's put inside?"

"The dog don't go inside."

"Ever?" Sunny drew the chilly air into her lungs. "It's cold."

"He got a coat." She drew a pack of cigarettes from the pocket of her brown polyester pants, knocked one out and lit it with a plastic red lighter.

"He seems like a nice dog."

The dog kept barking.

"He was my grandson's. He don't live here no more. Don't

know why I didn't take him to the pound. Still might. Shad-dap!" A stream of cigarette smoke escaped her thin, cracked lips.

"Oh, I could give him a ride." The words slipped out be-fore Sunny could stop herself. "I could take him to the shelter for you. Save you the trip."

The woman's eyes narrowed inside the curl of her cigarette smoke. "Like I said. Don't go near my dog."

"Okay." *Don't do or say anything suspicious*, thought Sunny. *Keep your head straight.* "Well. You have a nice day. I'll be back." Sunny turned slowly, like the old woman was a snake who might strike if she moved too quickly, and made her way back to her truck. The old bat watched her drive away, cigarette between her fingers and free arm smashed around her thick waist.

Oh, Sunny thought, *I'll be back.*

The traffic light was clearly broken. Sunny tapped her fin-gers on the steering wheel and sighed. This is what you get when you leave your kitchen to your sister and go scouting for abused dogs on Thanksgiving Day.

"Five minutes," Sunny muttered. "I've been sitting here for five minutes." There were two people behind her and three to her left. She kept waiting for the guy next to her to de-cide first that the light was never going to change and push through, but the blue sedan just kept sitting there.

The car behind her honked. Sunny looked in her rearview. The woman pointed at her watch, mouthed, *Go*, and pushed her hands forward, as though shoving Sunny through.

Sunny glanced at the clock, then looked in both directions going across traffic. No one was coming. Six minutes had gone by. She edged through the light and got about ten sec-onds down the street before a siren blared.

"Are you shitting me?" She looked in her rearview again

and saw that the blue sedan had a police light going. Of all the dumb luck. Sunny drew over to the side of the road, lowered her window, killed the engine and waited as the sedan pulled up behind her. She sat there, not even moving to get her license and registration. "Officer," she said as he approached. "That light clearly wasn't going to change. We sat there for six minutes…" Her voice trailed off as her eyes locked into his.

Detective Callahan.

"Happy Thanksgiving, Sunny," he said, devoid of smile. "Are you aware that you ran a red light?"

The emotions that rolled through her were varied enough to keep her in silence for well past a sufficient amount of time to answer the detective's question. Yet, he just stood there, waiting for her answer. She silently admitted that she'd been thinking about this man, the way he smelled and the cold authority of his eyes, ever since he'd shared her very, very, *very* expensive Scotch, but this wasn't the way she'd wanted to run into him.

"You ran it, too." Sunny bit down on her lower lip, but the words were already out.

"I'm allowed."

"Aren't you a robbery detective?" Somehow, Sunny had decided to answer his questions with one of her own, even though their past suggested this was not a smart move. "Who's not even on duty?" She eyed his jeans and sweatshirt.

He surprised her with a smile. Detective Callahan was even better looking in the daylight, where the gray sky highlighted the gentle wrinkles around his eyes. "I have a light." He pointed at the flashing siren. "Which means I can pull you over whenever I want."

"Don't you have anything better to do on Thanksgiving?" Despite her better judgment, Sunny pressed on. "At least go arrest some gang members. Not law-abiding citizens stuck at traffic lights that are broken."

"So I'm arresting you, am I? Should I have you step out of the vehicle now or radio for backup?"

Sunny sighed and wished she didn't enjoy the way his jaw ground down on his gum when he was annoyed. "I get it. You're still punishing me for trespassing on Janice Matteri's property. But I thought we had a deal. I'm working on my end, I promise. Can you just…do what you're going to do and let me go? I'm late as it is. My sister's going to be pissed."

Callahan sighed, his breath going to steam in the cold air. "Well, as long as you let me do what I'm going to do. Then I suppose I can let you go." He rubbed the back of his neck.

"What are you going to do?" Panic sneaked into Sunny's voice. She wished she could take back all her sarcastic questions. What the hell was wrong with her? Callahan had already demonstrated he was not someone to be toyed with. "Wait." She reached into the bag on the passenger seat and withdrew a bottle of champagne. "Here. Take this. To celebrate with your family." She pushed it through the window.

Callahan took it and examined the label. "Are you trying to bribe me again, Sunny?"

"No, of course not." Sunny started to sweat, right at the small of her back. "It's a gift."

He handed it back. "You know I like Scotch." The detective leaned in the window, close enough Sunny could smell his aftershave. "Especially the expensive kind."

"Well." Sunny took the champagne and rested it in her lap. "You know where the expensive Scotch is. Feel free to come by, anytime."

"Oh, yeah?"

"Sure. I'll keep it warm for you."

Callahan considered the ridiculous suggestion of warm Scotch with a sly smile. He rose up and regarded her. "All right, Sunny. You enjoy your day. And drive safe."

Sunny smiled over the heavy beating of her heart. "Thank you, Detective."

"Sean."

"Sean." She watched him go back to his car, get inside and take off, well over the speed limit. Only once he was out of sight did she start her engine, raise her window and chuckle under her breath.

The dining room table had been draped in white linen and decorated with leafy centerpieces of yellow and crimson. A roast turkey sat in the center, surrounded by myriad colorful dishes, like waiting footmen. Green beans, cranberries, oyster stuffing, mashed potatoes and parsnips, corn pudding and at least three different kinds of bread—buttery rolls, high-domed white loaves and some kind of rustic baguette, still crackling. On the serving board near the bay window rested an assortment of pies, each one colorful and flaky and sporting intricate latticework. Everything you could possibly want to eat was on or around Constance's Thanksgiving table.

Roger, closest to the stacks of plates, stared impatiently at the spread. He still wore his jeans and blue hoodie, but he'd shaved his face clean for the occasion.

"You know it's just four of us, right?" Sunny set the two bottles of champagne—her excuse for going to check out the rottweiler—on the counter.

Constance shrugged. "I don't know how to do less."

Sunny felt a twinge in her gut. "Daddy would've loved it."

"Roger loves it," Roger said, and didn't even crack a smile. "If that helps."

Sunny sputtered a laugh. "Dude. You are not disguising your eagerness very well."

"Oh, let the kid eat," Constance chided. She nodded at the plates. "Take as much as you want."

Just as Roger scrambled for a plate, Pete came in the back door, brushing off the cold. "That German shepherd you got is smart as a whip. Taught him a few basic commands in about an hour." His sparkling eyes settled on Sunny. "You're back."

"Champagne." Sunny waved toward the unopened bottles.

"Even though we have wine." Constance narrowed her eyes in suspicion.

"Some of us would like champagne with their turkey," Sunny protested. "And yes—" she changed the subject "—Buster is smart. He's got an application on him. I'll do a home visit tomorrow and he'll probably be all settled. Nice couple. No kids."

"Good deal. I'll open the wine." Pete dug the corkscrew out of the correct drawer, first time. He knew Sunny's house and grounds as well as she did.

Once they were all seated, Roger, as hungry as he was, asked to say a blessing. Constance dropped her phone and bowed her head to join in. She'd been cooking up a storm all morning, but now that the creative process was over, she looked deflated and worn out. Sunny almost asked her what was up; usually Cici was all about the food when a meal was on the table. She worked too hard to have people act distracted and ungrateful. But once the pleasant sound of forks clinking plates filled the air, she decided to let it go. This was their first holiday season celebrating without Daddy, and Constance's first in three years without Josh.

Sunny's gaze connected with the two empty chairs the men would usually occupy. She glanced at Constance and saw that her sister had been doing the exact same thing. Sunny offered a smile.

Constance just looked away.

"What's that dinging sound?" Mel's voice came from across the room, where Rhett had her on speakerphone. "Please tell me that's not the microwave."

"Okay." Rhett pulled out his platter of turkey cutlets and mashed potato buds. "It's not the microwave." He threw a handful of kale, which he kept in the fridge for smoothies, on the plate.

"You skip coming home for your father's beautiful Thanksgiving meal so you can microwave some trash?" Mama's voice soared over Mel's like a rocket launcher.

"You know how I love trash." Rhett had learned long ago not to argue with Mama. You just couldn't win. He drizzled some olive oil and vinegar on top of his kale. There. That should do it.

"Don't you get smart with me. You're not too old for me to go fetch the belt."

Rhett sat at the table and faced his Thanksgiving dinner. "That'd be one hell of a long belt, Mama." Not to mention, Rhett couldn't recall one single time in his life being hit by that belt. He was convinced that Mama used it as a tool to get her children to run like crazy. Not only would they get exercise, they'd get out of her hair and stay far away for hours. At least until the streetlights came on.

"Don't listen to her, *mijo*." Papa's soft tone managed to ride over the women. His calm voice and gentle personality had always provided an anchor of stability for Mama's storms. "If you want microwave food for Thanksgiving, that is your right. I'll freeze some of what I make for you."

Rhett had always wanted the softly accented English of his father, but no such luck. He could sound like Papa if he wanted to, but he had to fake it. Only when he spoke Spanish did they share that lyrical quality. Just listening to his father speak made his pulse slow. He was probably the only person Rhett could tell, "I woke this morning to the sound of Katyusha rockets, Papa," and have him not react with shock and concern and orders to get into therapy.

"Did you, *mijo*?" Papa would say, his voice a salve on the old wounds. *"Digame."*

But Rhett didn't tell him that. They were on speakerphone, and everyone was listening. "How are you feeling, Papa? How's the back?"

Papa made a dismissive noise. "It's good."

"It's tight," Mama chimed in. "More than usual. I told him he needs to retire, but you know how he is about his plants."

"I'm not going to retire, Meara," Papa said. "Not yet."

Mama started a new protest but Rhett cut her off. "He doesn't want to retire, Mama." They had to stick up for each other. It was the only way to survive Mama's determination to control everything. "And neither do I. Which is why I'm here for Thanksgiving. Christmas, too. I've spent my whole life in the marine corps and now I'm doing something else. I can't get away."

"Good for you, Rhett," Papa said. "You do what you have to do. We support you."

"But you're keeping the reservation," Mama said quickly. "At the cabin. I told you, your father and I stayed there one night last time we visited? Three years ago? It's fabulous. Just fabulous. You go and enjoy."

Rhett made a noncommittal noise that was neither agreement nor a lie. He was not keeping the Christmas reservation his mother had made for him at some random local cabin, which was her way of punishing him for not coming home. But Mama didn't need to know that. Let her think he was going.

"I already made a donation to the dog rescue," Mama said, as though she saw right through him. "You donate to the rescue and you get to attend the Christmas Eve banquet. There's food and music. You can mingle with other people."

Just the word *mingle* sent a crawling sensation up Rhett's

spine as he imagined having to spend Christmas Eve talking politics and religion with drunk strangers.

"Oh, and a massage! You get a free massage, too."

Rhett groaned. He couldn't think of anything worse than being alone, in a dark room, naked on a table, at the whim of a stranger. At least the massages in physical therapy had been clothed, in a chair, under a bright light, the only body part bared his wrecked thigh.

"You're going to love it."

Love it? First, a party. Then, a massage. He'd rather be back in Fallujah.

Mama made a suspicious *hmm* sound, but was quickly over-shadowed by the clanging and banging of Rhett's nieces. Brittany and Josephina were a wild pair. Rhett loved to rile them up when he visited, not only satisfying his need for physical activity by getting the girls running, jumping, screaming and being as obnoxious as possible, but also irritating his baby sister as much as he could in the process. They dominated the conversation after that, saving Rhett from any more argument over holidays and food. By the time he hung up, he faced his pathetic Thanksgiving dinner with a sigh.

He really wanted to go into the gym now. He'd wanted to since he woke, but had convinced himself to stay home and enjoy a rest day, despite the stir-crazy feeling and the stiffness in his thigh. "You can do this," he told himself. "You can sit here and enjoy a relaxing day, and some food, like a normal person."

He took a bite. Mama hadn't been far off when she'd called it trash. The kale was good, but he knew it would be bland. Rhett checked his email while he chewed a bit of dry turkey, his laptop open in front of him. There were a bunch of work emails he could check, but only one caught his eye. Stanzi had emailed him about an hour ago. Inside was a polite and professional email asking him to recommend a light body-weight workout she could do at home, since the gym was closed for the holiday.

Rhett laughed to himself. Stanzi was something else. Yes, there was a certain type that got hooked on his gym's brand of fitness: the constant variation, high energy, loud music and community atmosphere. But Stanzi took it to another level entirely. She'd come faithfully, to either the weight-lifting program or a cardio workout—once even to the Spanish class—all week long, with no breaking or slowing in sight. She'd show up in her oversize, outdated T-shirts, black leggings and zero bling (no makeup, nails or drama) and put in whatever hard work Rhett threw her way. He constantly pitched her curve-balls, just to see how she'd respond. During the Spanish class, he refused to clarify himself in English. "Why did you come to the Spanish class if you wanted to speak English?" he'd whispered. Stanzi had bit down on her lower lip, then simply rolled up her sleeves, pinned down the most experienced lady in the class and shadowed her for the rest of the workout.

Yesterday, they'd run out of barbells and he'd told Stanzi to give hers to one of the other women, who could lift more weight. Stanzi hadn't argued, and had looked around the gym for about twenty seconds before she solved her own problem and grabbed a set of dumbbells.

Rhett emailed back that he admired her dedication, but she should be resting today. He'd barely taken a bite of his coarse, bland kale salad when she replied, insisting she just needed something to Get her heart rate up.

Sounded familiar. Rhett emailed back. Can I text you instead? He had her phone number, but didn't want to overstep, even though he texted many of his clients.

Stanzi emailed back one word. Sure.

Why aren't you resting? he texted. It's Thanksgiving.

I know. Sorry to bother you. I'm not much into holidays. Feeling stir-crazy. Just want a distraction.

Me, either. Rhett smiled to himself. Why was he not surprised Stanzi wasn't much of a holiday person? Do you have a jump rope?

Yes.

Ten rounds of 20 jumps, 10 push-ups and 15 air squats.

Thanks! I'll hit that after the turkey digests.

Turkey? Thought you weren't much of a holiday person. Rhett shook his head at himself after he hit Send. He should have just said, "Great. Enjoy." Why was he getting personal?

I'm not. Socially, I mean. I'm still very much into the food. I've got a turkey, stuffing, potatoes and the works. Don't be mad. You told me not to worry about the scale.

Mad? It was like he couldn't stop himself. I'm jealous.

A longer amount of time passed before her next text, almost as if to register surprise. Why jealous? What are you eating today?

Rhett looked down at his shitty plate of food. Just some stuff from the microwave.

What? No. She added some shocked and sad emojis. You're welcome to share my feast.

Rhett took a deep breath and quelled the urge to satisfy both his hunger pangs for real, home-cooked food and that part of his personality that he kept stowed away as best as possible—the one that wanted to do things he knew he shouldn't do.

The one that craved excitement and things that made his heart pound out of his chest. But who was he kidding? Stanzi had those magic hands, and his thigh was starting to act up again.

So you're saying that if I meet you at the gym in an hour and run you through a quick workout, you'll bring me some of your home cooking?

Stanzi texted back, Deal.

A long time passed. Long enough, Stanzi probably thought Rhett had blown her off or fallen asleep. Finally, as if someone else were choosing his words for him, he texted back, See you in an hour.

Just as long passed on her end. When his phone dinged, her text made him laugh out loud: Just went and got changed. See you soon.

twelve

The gym was unlocked. Loud hip-hop music boomed from the speakers, which Constance could hear even before she stepped inside. She found Rhett, alone, on his back, lying in a pool of sweat next to the rig. "What'd you just do?" She stood over him, her hands full of the bags Sunny had helped her pack.

Rhett's long, dark lashes blinked until his brown-green eyes shone up at her. "Twenty minutes of twenty-five burpees and fifteen bodyweight back squats."

"Holy cow." Constance eyed the barbell in the rack. "How much weight is that for you?"

"Two forty."

"Holy cow," she repeated. "I guess we're not working out together?"

"Thought I'd get it done. No worries. I have good stuff planned for you."

More like, you couldn't stop yourself, Constance thought.

She was beginning to understand how Rhett Santos's brain worked. "I can't wait."

After Rhett had peeled himself off the floor, they made their way into the office. He leaned in close to the bags of food, drew a deep breath and let out a dreamy exhale. "Are you sure you want to work out? Can't we just eat?"

She caught a whiff of the soap, shampoo or deodorant that was coming off his sweaty shirt—something spicy and masculine. It surprised her to realize that he smelled better to her than the roast turkey and side dishes. He also got better looking every time she saw him. Rhett was striking to begin with, but as Constance got familiar with his movements and habits, his gestures and quirks and all the little things that helped create the contours of his face and lines of his body, the better he got.

"C'mon." Rhett waved her into the gym and pointed to the PVC he'd laid on the lifting platform. "This'll be fun. I'm going to show you how to snatch."

Constance's eyebrows rose.

"The most technical lift," Rhett went on. "The more places there are to mess up, the harder a movement is. We'll spend half an hour on it, just to wet your feet. And then we'll eat." She might've looked hesitant because Rhett added, "It's that, or we do a beep test."

"What's a beep test?"

"Running," Rhett said. "You have a set distance to sprint, and the beeps keep getting shorter, which means you have to keep running faster, as time goes on."

Constance stepped onto the platform and lifted the PVC. "Snatch, it is."

Rhett laughed. "You really don't want to run, do you?" He narrowed his eyes. "Come spring, there'll be a lot more running in the workouts. Just to give you a heads-up."

Constance shrugged. "Who says I'll be here in the spring? I still haven't joined."

Rhett stared down at her. "Free week's up. We'll get you a contract before you leave today."

"Maybe."

He grinned a little bit, then grabbed his own PVC pipe and said, "The object of the snatch is to get the bar from the ground to overhead in one fluid motion." He demonstrated once, slowly, then a little faster, then really fast, getting the PVC from down near his feet to over his head. "So let's break it down. Set up position. Feet are just under the hips. Wide grip on the bar."

Once her hands were right, Rhett instructed her to retract her shoulder blades and bend her knees, hips going straight down. "From here, we're going to roll that bar down to mid-shin. Keep the tension in your hamstrings. Keep your shoulders forward of the bar."

Constance got to midshin. Rhett came beside her and, touching her only with his fingertips, had her raise her hips a little. Just keeping correct form in a still position was hard work. She felt sweat trickle down her back, despite the chilliness of the gym.

Instruction after that was a blur of commands and tiny pieces—flat back, elbows out, chest up, engage the lats, squeeze, extend, shrug, pull under—all of which ended up getting Constance's bar from the ground to over her head. Never in her life would she have thought something so simple could be so complicated.

Rhett's eyebrows rose. "Not bad. Keep the bar closer, though. It should be able to lift your shirt."

Constance tried again, and was rewarded with, "Not horrible," which she had learned was Rhett's way of saying she was improving.

"You're pulling a little early, though, which is common." Rhett went through the movement again. "Delay the second pull. Then the arms look a little like a scarecrow."

Constance thought of Daddy's scarecrow, still out in front of the house, with its bent elbows, forearms hanging down and creepy grin. *I've got to become Daddy's scarecrow*, she thought, and rather than reflecting on the irony she imitated Rhett's movements, going slowly and getting quicker by her fifth try.

On her last setup, Rhett approached and grazed his fingertip, light as a feather, beneath her chin. "What've I told you? Eyes at the horizon. Don't look at the ground. You're not going that way."

A zip of electricity ran through Constance's body, starting at that gentle brush of his finger and going all the way deep, deep inside her core. She got an all-over little shiver that felt completely new. It was so powerful for a moment she forgot where she was.

"What's wrong?"

"Nothing."

"You sure?"

"Yeah." Constance drew a deep breath, lifted her gaze straight ahead, her muscles steeling with determination.

"Okay. Let's go again. Be patient. Don't rush that second pull."

Her first three tries, Constance was overthinking all the pieces. Were her shoulders over the bar? Were her hips too high? Was she looking up? Was she pulling early?

Then, a new song popped on. "Here Comes the Hotstepper," by Ini Kamoze. Constance recognized it from one of her running playlists. For some reason, her determination deepened.

When she finished the lift, the bar was overhead and her body deep in a squat, yet she had no idea how she got there.

Rhett clapped his big hands together and let out a whoop, which was the loudest noise of approval she'd ever heard him make. "You know what, Stanzi? You're actually pretty good at this. You sure you're just a runner?" Rhett winked at her.

"Well," she said, before she realized his question was rhetorical. "I was a cheerleader in high school."

A crease appeared between Rhett's eyebrows. "Really? Don't seem the type."

"My sister wanted to be a cheerleader. She wanted to do this summer cheerleader camp in sixth grade. The high school cheerleaders were camp leaders. I was a sophomore in high school. So my father made me become a cheerleader so that I could watch over my sister in the camp." Constance rolled her eyes. Not until she said it out loud did the extent of her forced mothering sink in.

"Wow." Rhett laughed. "And I thought I had it tough with my baby sister."

"You didn't have to become a cheerleader?" Constance smiled.

"Ha," he laughed. "I tried. They told me I was too big."

Constance giggled and passed over her PVC. "This might be why I'm good at snatch. I was always tossing the smaller girls up on somebody's shoulders."

"You know what?" Rhett grabbed the PVC and switched it out for a light barbell. "You might be on to something. Here. Snatch this."

"My mom died when I was nine." Stanzi took a bite of her turkey. They each had a plate of food at the desk in the office. When Rhett had grabbed one of the two drumsticks she'd brought, along with some sliced white meat, Stanzi had grabbed the other. "My sister was five. I pretty much raised her after that. My father tried, but he worked, and he was old-fashioned."

"I did a lot of caring for my sister, too. But nothing to that extreme. Both my parents are still alive."

"Do they live far away?"

Rhett took his time chewing and savoring the food. The turkey was moist and rich, the mashed potatoes fluffy, the stuffing both crisp and creamy and the green beans nothing like that awful casserole people served. These beans were bright green, with just the right amount of crunch and tossed in some kind of balsamic sesame-seed dressing and a shake of feta cheese. "Um." Rhett tried to remember the question. "I'm sorry. Did I tell you how good this food is? Like, really damn good."

Stanzi stifled a laugh with her napkin. "Like, twelve times. But you can tell me as much as you want. I love to cook, but have nobody to cook for these days. My sis is all I have and she's a busy lady."

Rhett took the time to savor another bite of each item on his plate. "You can cook for me whenever you want." He caught himself before he said more, hoping he hadn't overstepped. It was damn hard, though. To add to the growing list of things Rhett liked about her, she could cook as good as his father and wasn't afraid to eat it, either. Plus, she was a natural at the most difficult lift to execute properly. It wasn't every day you met someone good at snatch, especially right off the bat.

"My parents," he said, her question just now sinking in and providing a good topic change. He needed to be careful, keep things professional. "They live in North Carolina. The Outer Banks. So, no. Not too far away. Five-hour drive."

"Your parents live at the beach?" Stanzi arched one eyebrow. "And you stayed here for Thanksgiving?"

"You can't swim right now," he countered. "It's too windy and cold."

"You could walk on the beach," she countered back. "A long, windy walk in a hoodie after a rich Thanksgiving meal." Her voice sounded dreamy.

"That's exactly what my family does. Or we sit on the deck, which faces the ocean, and drink wine or whiskey and eat pie."

"You're not helping your case." Stanzi took a huge bite of her turkey leg, Viking-style. "Instead, you're sitting here with me, in an office you see every day."

"Eh." He eyed her messy red hair. "I could do worse."

Her cheeks turned pink. She cleared her throat. "Are you at least going down for Christmas? Or…do you celebrate Christmas?"

"Do I celebrate Christmas? I'm Irish and Mexican. I'm a Catholic hand grenade." Rhett polished off his drumstick and went to toss it in the trash. "But I'm not very religious. And I'm not going home for Christmas. I'm not much of a holiday person, either."

Stanzi grabbed the turkey bone from his hand before he could let it go. "I remember going to church with Mom. Daddy couldn't be bothered with it, once she died." She slipped the bone in a Ziploc bag, along with her own. "I'll make bone broth."

"Of course you will." Who the hell was this woman?

Stanzi bent over and lifted something out of the giant sack she'd brought. She shoved some papers aside on Rhett's desk with her elbow and set her treasure down.

A smooth, creamy pumpkin pie with a decorative crust, which included little crust cutouts on top, shaped like turkeys.

"Like I said, I was kind of the mom of the house," she explained when Rhett had stared at it a few seconds too long. "Not in a creepy way, just the whole motherly bit, which included making sure my sister didn't eat like shit. My father would've fed us TV dinners and hot dogs every night."

The pie looked like something from the cover of a baking magazine. The custard had not even a hairline crack and the golden-brown crust was perfectly roped around the perimeter.

"Where's the Cool Whip?"

It was meant to be sarcastic, but damned if she didn't reach into her sack and pull out a disposable container filled with what looked like homemade whipped cream. She offered it, her face as straight as his.

When Rhett finally smiled, Stanzi burst into giggles.

After they'd both eaten large slices of pie with mounds of whipped cream, Stanzi rose up and stretched. She cast a glance at his leg. "How's it feeling?"

"Good," Rhett said, which wasn't a lie and wasn't the truth. The work she'd done had felt amazing but was starting to wear off and, with the return of the cold, the pain was creeping back in.

"Do you—" Stanzi shrugged "—want me to check it out?"

Just the thought of her hands working the scar tissue made Rhett feel like melting to the ground. Which was why he had to say no. He couldn't rely on someone else to make him feel better. He couldn't rely on anyone else to understand anything about him. His burdens were his alone. "No, you've done enough." Rhett nodded to the containers of food. "Thank you again."

She might've frowned, but she recovered too quickly to know for sure. "Okay." Stanzi rose up and collected her coat from the peg on the wall. "I've taken up enough of your day." She offered a quiet smile. "Thanks for showing me how to snatch."

"Anytime, Stanzi. Thanks for the food." Rhett rose quickly and began to pack up the turkey and pie.

"No. Keep it. I've got plenty at home."

Rhett smiled. "I'm not going to argue with you. So if you're being nice, now's the time to change your mind."

"I'm not nice," she said, her tone matter-of-fact. "Well—" she slung her gym bag on her shoulder and tucked up the corner of her mouth "—not like that. The fake nice."

"I know."

"Happy Thanksgiving, Rhett." Her gaze flicked to his leg, then back up.

"Happy Thanksgiving, Stanzi."

He watched her go. Once she disappeared, Rhett realized she still hadn't officially joined the gym.

thirteen

"Holy crap," Pete whispered. "You're serious."

"Did you think I was kidding?"

"No." Pete shrugged. "Maybe."

"I need your strong hands," Sunny said. "Cut it."

Pete grunted and cursed. The chain dropped to the ground.

"You can still turn back," Sunny said as he rested the bolt cutters against the wall of the kennel. She grasped the door handle. "I wouldn't blame you." Despite her agreement with Callahan, Sunny just couldn't let another day go by knowing that beagle was stuck inside this grimy, freezing kennel. It was Thanksgiving, dammit, and she was going to set him free.

"I'm not letting you do this alone. Maybe we should both turn back." Pete looked around in the darkness, but everything was still.

"Janice is never here for Thanksgiving." Sunny noted the slur in her speech and regretted having that last glass of champagne. Constance had gone straight home after her trip to the gym, so Sunny and Pete had drunk a little more than their share. "It's the perfect time to get the beagle out. Besides, we've already cut the padlock."

Pete puffed out a heavy breath from his nostrils. "Okay. Let's do this."

The door creaked as Sunny pushed her way inside. She shone her flashlight around, just a pencil beam to mark her way, and a couple of critters stirred in their cages.

Most of them were empty, but Sunny could make out two figures in the metal structures. One appeared to be a Maltese, who should've been white and silky, but the matted layers of dirt made the animal's fur rough and brown. So, Janice had "restocked" since she'd been here last. The Maltese had not been here on the previous raid. It took Sunny a moment to even realize the creature's breed because she was so matted with grime. Worse was the smell. Deep inside this kennel, with a couple dozen cages stacked like egg crates, the ammonia burned her eyes and choked up her throat.

Sunny brought the back of her hand to her nose and blinked rapidly. The Maltese barked and snarled, but when Sunny opened the tiny, rusted cage and reached, it pressed itself into the rear corner. The dog whimpered. Sunny sank to her heels and drew a calming breath into her shaky lungs. "C'mere, girl," she said, her voice going soft and singsongy. She clicked off the flashlight and let her eyes adjust to the darkness.

The Maltese whimpered again, so Sunny hummed a little song under her breath.

"There's a beagle over here," Pete said. "A very small one. I think it's the one you're looking for." He reached into the cage and pulled out a squat little creature. The dog looked like a Popsicle, so stiff and hard at Pete's touch, but it was soon wrapped in the blanket he'd brought and held close to Pete's chest. "I'll take him out to the carrier, and be right back."

A wave of relief rolled over Sunny. Pete had found the little beagle, and had gotten him out much easier than her last attempt. She turned her attention back to the only other dog left in this shithole, the Maltese, and hummed some more. Soon, the little dog pattered closer. One step up, two steps back. The dog went like that for a minute or more before she finally bumped her muzzle against Sunny's knuckles. The dog's beard was sticky. She smelled like piss and shit and vomit and her whines were a deep, primal noise that blipped beneath everything else like a heartbeat. Sunny wondered, as the stench of urine seared her throat, if the dog could even see. The fumes from the waste and muck were enough to burn out her eyesight. "That's it," Sunny sang, enticing the dog into the blanket in her other hand. She scooped the Maltese against her chest. The dog bucked and whimpered, but Sunny held fast.

A man's voice burst out, splitting the room. "Who the hell are you? What are you doing here?"

Sunny's head whipped around. She peered at the shadowy figure in the darkness who stood by the open doorway. He marched toward her at a determined clip. Sunny backed herself into a corner, her arms tight on the Maltese. Just as the figure reached for her, something swept the man's feet, clipping his ankles. He hit the ground, on his back, in a big poof of dirt, but didn't even have time to wallow or catch his choked breath before Pete was on top of him. Pete slipped his arm under the man's neck, shoved his thigh up under the stranger's and pinned it across his other leg. With Pete's full weight over the man's torso, he reached up from beneath the man's neck and grasped his own bicep, squeezing his face into his shoulder.

A long, choking moment passed before the man started to squirm. Pete released his own arm, brought it over the man's chest, to the other side of his head, and planted his elbow on the floor, pinning his arm against his neck and the side of his

face. As if on autopilot, Pete's other arm came from beneath
the guy's neck and grabbed him by the wrist. He tugged on
that wrist, pulling the guy's body in one direction and pressing his neck in the opposite.

The man sputtered and choked curses as Pete kept his
weight braced.

Holy shit, Sunny thought.

The man grunted and tried to thrash, but he was trapped.
Finally, he stilled.

Pete released him and stood up. "He'll be out for a bit," he
said, his voice coming in short gasps. "We better get moving."

Sunny didn't have to be asked twice. She took the Maltese
outside and watched as Pete closed up the kennel behind him,
then collected the carrier that held the beagle, along with the
bolt cutters. He stopped next to Sunny, who felt frozen to
the ground.

"Well, c'mon," Pete hissed. "Let's get these poor dogs back
to your place."

Sunny and Pete shared the bathtub, each taking one end,
with the beagle and the Maltese. Sunny got the beagle, the
little dog she'd been after for weeks. As the grime and stench
washed away, and the little dog's shivering subsided, she regretted not getting him out the first time. He looked like he had
only one good eye, the other squeezed shut, and his tongue
stuck out between his teeth from dehydration.

"They need Dr. Winters," Sunny said. "Stat."

"Yeah," Pete agreed. "I can see their ribs."

He got the dogs dried and comfortable while Sunny texted
the vet. She arrived within the hour, asked no questions and
had them settled in her mobile van quickly. "I'll keep them
overnight. Maybe longer."

Once she was gone, Sunny turned to Pete. "Okay. Where'd you learn the cage match moves?"

Pete grinned, though his normally easy smile came a little strained. "Sunny, I've had those moves since my years in the army. I've just never had to use them around you. Thank God."

"Oh." Sunny noticed, maybe for the first time, that Pete had fine lines around the corners of his eyes when he smiled. They gave a layer of character to a face she'd always considered boyish. "Well, aren't you full of surprises." With a medium build and a quiet personality, Pete had never seemed like the MMA type.

"You don't know the half of it." Pete's grin was a little fuller now. "I'm not the geek you and Cici grew up with."

Sunny gave his shoulder a shove. "You'll always be a geek to me. Remember that huge calculator you'd whip out in math class? Got it for your birthday?"

"Hey, that calculator saved your sorry ass more than once. And that's when you weren't cheating off my paper during tests."

"True." Sunny didn't even try to argue. She squeezed that same shoulder. "Thank you. I can't believe you helped me rescue those dogs."

"Oh, really?"

Sunny smiled. "I know you rescue dogs, too, and people. But what I meant was, I haven't made you help me steal a dog since we were kids."

"You didn't make me do anything."

"I know. And don't worry, if the police come around, I'll take all the blame."

"Sunny, the police ought to be questioning her, not you." Pete's gentle Virginia accent thickened. "You ever call animal control?"

"All the time." Sunny kept the anger from her voice, because it wasn't aimed at Pete and she didn't want him to take it that way. "Janice keeps the dogs she sells in good condition and that's what animal control sees. The ones that don't sell eventually end up in dead man's land back there." She tilted her head toward the kennel they'd broken into. "She always seems to have it empty when animal control visits. Plus, there's only me to call her out. You're a bit too far away to notice and no one else is around for miles."

Pete nodded silently. "So you take matters into your own hands. Like you always have."

"What I need is a way to shut her down for good," Sunny said. "I'm working on something, though. I've got a plan."

Pete ran his hands through his hair and sighed. "What plan?" He flopped down on the couch.

"I got a deal with a detective." Sunny smiled and plopped next to him. "If I get Cici to help out a friend of his—this guy at the gym?—I have a feeling things will go my way out here."

"I see." Pete's face clouded. "Is that where she went after dinner?"

"Yes." Sunny leaned her head on his shoulder and closed her eyes. "But don't worry about Cici. This is exactly what she needs. And I think she already has a thing for this guy."

Pete grabbed a throw blanket from the back of the couch and draped it over Sunny's legs. "A thing? What kind of thing? Cici never has 'things.' Even with Josh, it seemed like she was going through the motions. He was a business deal. Fit her needs and her life. She's always been too busy taking care of everyone else to really know what she wants."

Sunny peeked up into Pete's face. Oh, man. How could someone have such a strong, unrequited crush for over twenty years? He wasn't wrong, though. Cici had spent her life taking care of both herself and Sunny, and then it was Daddy.

"Yeah, I think you're right," she admitted. "Josh was always kind of like the guy that happened to be there, right? Good enough. But not anything special."

"Definitely not anything special."

Sunny giggled, which turned into a big yawn. "I'm sorry," she said. "It's not the company."

"I know that. It's the hour, not me." Pete glanced at the grandfather clock across the room. It was after midnight. "I'm too riveting to make a lady yawn."

Sunny giggled again. "I feel bad you're still here. You should go home."

"Lay your head down, Sunny Skye." He patted his thigh. "I'll stay with you until you're out." Pete was the only person who ever used her middle name. "When that guy wakes up, he's going to have a headache. If he calls the police, I want to be here."

"I'd rather you weren't."

"I'm not leaving."

Only after Sunny had nestled her head in Pete's lap, and he'd straightened the blanket out so that it covered her entire body, did it dawn on her that he had intuited her fear. A fear Sunny hadn't even realized she felt—not until the huge relief hit when Pete insisted on staying. Never before had Janice caught her inside the kennel, taking the dogs. Tonight, a man had heard the commotion, and though it was dark, he might've seen her face. Sunny had no idea who the man was, or why he was there, but none of that mattered if he could identify her as the one who'd broken into the kennel.

A hand rested on her shoulder.

Sunny's eyes drooped. Pete smelled like pine needles and wet dog. Comforting smells, which soon had Sunny breathing deep and even.

"Go to sleep, Sunny Skye."

fourteen

"A week's gone by, and nothing's happened." Sunny hopped off her bike and stripped the seat of her gel cover. She had a small patch of sweat in the shape of a vee down her neck. "You know why? Because Janice clearly didn't want those dogs. Not only that, what's she going to say? 'Hi, Officer. The neighbor stole my dogs. They were abused dogs, dehydrated and living in their own filth, but she stole them.'"

"You're getting too cocky." Constance crossed her arms over the handlebars of her bike and laid her head there to catch her breath. She knew her seat, sans gel cover, was covered in sweat. But she'd finally taken Sunny's spin class, so could officially check it off her list. "Janice is pissed. Trust me. We just don't know what she's going to do yet."

"I don't care," Sunny said, her face twisting into a grimace. "You didn't see them, Cici. They were nearly dead. The Maltese is doing much better but the beagle is still with Dr. Winters. He's going to make it, but he'll probably never be adoptable." Sunny waved at a few of the women as they left the class. "Good work, ladies!"

The women dabbed their faces with the brightly colored towels. "Thanks, Sunny! Great class! As usual!"

Constance didn't dab. She mopped her face with the hem of her shirt. "I'm more concerned about Petey, to be honest. He could get taken in for assault."

"You should've seen him." Sunny did some kind of made-up karate moves. "Who knew?"

"Petey's taken martial arts for years." Constance shook her head. "Like, since we were kids. I swear, Sunny, you have tunnel vision most of the time." Constance dropped her T-shirt down. It was no use. The sweat was going to keep coming for a while.

Sunny's eyes narrowed. "Wait a minute." She reached out and lifted Constance's shirt.

"What're you doing?" Constance smacked her hand down. "People will see."

Sunny cocked her head to the side and smirked. "See what? Have you looked at yourself lately? You look awesome. Different. Can't quite put my finger on it, but it's working." She went for another peek.

Constance smacked her hand down again. "I don't know what you're talking about. I haven't had time to go preening myself in the mirror. Like some of us." Which was a total lie. Constance had actually done a double take in the mirror after stepping out of the shower last night. Nothing dramatic had happened to her body in such a short time, but something had stopped her. Something that, as Sunny had said, she couldn't quite put her finger on. Whatever it was, she knew it had something to do with Semper Fit. With the way she anticipated the next workout as soon as she finished the last. The way she dreamed about the barbell, the cold steel in her hands, the chalk on her legs, the squeeze of all her muscles as she snatched weight over her head. For the first time in a long time she felt...*strong*. In control. Able to face down whatever came her way. Maybe that feeling, prickling and glowing beneath her skin, was shining out, making her look different, even if she didn't really look different.

Sunny took a sip from her pink water bottle, grinning slyly at the same time. "That Semper Fit is sure working for you, huh?" She reached out and tucked some of Constance's hair behind her ear. "I notice your hair is growing, too. It's almost a bob now." She shrugged. "A really shitty bob that needs to be stacked and layered by a professional, but better than that hack job you had going for so long."

Constance ran her hands down the back of her hair. "Stacked and layered? Sounds like cake."

"And you like cake." Sunny winked. They moved toward the exit and now stood in the foyer in front of the floor-to-ceiling glass windows. "Have you done any running yet at the gym?"

Constance zipped up her coat, noting her sister's clever segue from gym talk to Josh talk. "Not yet."

"And what're you going to do when running's on the menu?"

Constance had thought about that more than once. In fact, she'd been surprised that Rhett hadn't programmed running after she'd rejected the beep test, as fond as he was of making her do things he thought she didn't want to do. "I'll tackle that road when I get there."

The cocky humor that often defined her baby sister melted away beneath the bright sunlight flooding the tall windows.

"What?" Constance hated when that happened. Hated when Sunny lost her shine.

Sunny stepped in a little closer. "It's just that...you loved running so much. It was such a big part of who you were, as long as I can remember. One of my first memories is of you making me run up and down that big, grassy hill out back of the house. The one with the enormous dandelion patch, always full of bees. I can still see it. The green grass. The yellow flowers. The zillions of bees that I was scared of, but you weren't. Your pale legs in those awful plaid shorts." Sunny paused to chuckle but there was little humor in her voice.

"What're you saying, Sunny?" Constance's voice went soft. Her throat tightened.

"I'm saying—" Sunny drew a deep breath and bulldozed ahead, like she always did "—that running's been a part of who you are since I've known you. Josh was only part of who you were for a few years. Don't let him take that away from you."

Constance was quiet awhile, blinking in the sunlight and ready to blame it for her watery eyes. But then she sniffed deeply and cleared her throat. "C'mon. Let's go. I got stuff to do."

Sunny parted her lips, like she might say more, but then offered a weak smile. "Okay." She pushed open the front door.

Constance was glad to hit the cool air and leave spin class behind her. Now that she'd tried it, she could honestly say she hated it, and would never, ever go again. She'd felt trapped, like her legs were spinning but her body wasn't really going anywhere. Nothing like the escape she once felt while running.

"I've got paperwork to do." Sunny stopped at the curb before they crossed to their vehicles. "You have clients?"

"Yep. Just a few. Let me know when the beagle comes home. I'll work on him."

"Thanks." She leaned in for a hug. "When you going back to the gym?"

"Tonight actually. At seven. I've never been in the evening."

"But you already worked out. Just now."

"I know. But I still haven't technically joined, and Rhett

told me I have to come in and do the paperwork. Might as well work out, too."

"All right." Sunny's brow narrowed. She looked like she was going to say more, but stopped herself. "Text me later."

"Yep. And, Sunny. Keep away from Janice for a while, now that you've got the beagle."

Sunny shrugged. "I can't make any promises."

Rhett ducked her right hook and blocked the kick from her left that followed. He'd missed his chance to sweep her feet because she'd seen it coming. If Angie had one thing going for her, it was speed. They were both drenched in sweat. Angie was the only woman Rhett had to entertain when he taught Semper Fit Combat. The rest of them did the moves solo or paired up and sparred without making contact. They got their heart rates up, learned some defense moves and nobody got hurt. Perfect. Until Angie came to town.

The rest of the gym circled around, cheering.

Rhett glanced at the clock. "One more minute and we're calling it."

Angie took advantage of his distraction and nailed him right in the gut with the flat of her foot. He'd braced for it at the last second, so he didn't lose his wind, but he stumbled, which sent a good roar through the gym, anyway. He laughed and gave her a high five. "Nice."

Thank God she only popped in once a year.

As the class dispersed, Rhett noticed a flash of strawberry hair in the crowd. The gym was packed tonight, which happened every Thursday evening when he ran Combat. Stanzi had been watching for at least a little while; he could tell by the look on her face. It was the same look she got whenever he taught her something new: interested, a little bit afraid and a lot determined.

"I don't think we've met." Hobbs stepped in front of her as Rhett took a few steps in Stanzi's direction. "I'm Steve Hobbs. One of the coaches."

"Constance," Rhett heard her say.

"You're new?"

"Not really. I never come at night."

"That makes sense, then," Hobbs said. "I'm mostly here at night. You taking the 7:00 p.m.?"

"Yes."

"That's my class. Go ahead and hop into the warm-up. We're running a little behind because of Rhett's Combat class. Pain in the ass. Happens every week."

"Yeah, I was going to ask…what is that exactly?"

Rhett popped up beside her. "I'll tell you about it after your class, if you want." He pointed at Hobbs. "This jerk bothering you?"

Stanzi laughed. "Not yet." The soft, half-moon dimple she had on her right cheek looked deeper than usual. It took Rhett a moment to realize it was just that she'd dropped some body fat, which seemed suddenly visible today versus a couple of days ago. Her hair was longer, too. In fact, this was the first time Rhett had seen it up in a tiny ponytail.

"She was just admiring my chest," Hobbs shot back with a grin. He made his pecs bounce.

Rhett shoved him away. "Go warm up," he told Stanzi. "We'll do your membership later. And talk about Combat."

"Okay." Stanzi's gaze went back and forth between the two of them before she shook her head with a laugh and moved off to do jumping jacks.

Hobbs turned to him with both eyebrows up in the air. Rhett had known him so long he knew what Hobbs's brows were saying, no words necessary. *Who the hell is that?*

"Not your type," Rhett said. He watched Stanzi do kettlebell swings like a pro. Hard to believe My Pretty Pony had come so far in such a short amount of time.

"Why not?"

"Too smart."

Hobbs blew out a sharp gust of air. "Guess she's more your type, then. Her whole body changed when you walked over. She was looking at me with that whole *Keep your distance, dude.* Guess I intimidated her with my good looks." He flexed his biceps, one after the other.

"Yeah, that's it."

Hobbs ignored him. "Then you come strutting over and she opened up like one of those videos where the flower blooms at hyperspeed."

Rhett shrugged, even though he really liked Hobbs's metaphor. Sometimes, Hobbs wasn't a complete idiot. "She's just familiar with me." He wondered if Stanzi had really bloomed like a flower. He'd been too busy studying her new look to notice. Coincidentally, Stanzi's T-shirt sported a bright red poinsettia, surrounded by presents—something like an Ugly Christmas Sweater pattern. It looked too big. Just as he thought it, Stanzi stopped her warm-up to knot the shirt in the back, making it smaller.

"Hey, sugar." Angie slid her arms around his waist and hugged him from behind. "You're not mad at me for kicking your ass, are you?"

"You wish. You got one hit." Rhett grabbed her wrist and pulled her off him. "Look at you. Any excuse to cop a feel."

"You're just too sexy to resist." She rolled her eyes.

"You two enjoy. I'm off to change the redhead's mind about my pecs." Hobbs flashed his big grin and gave the whistle he wore around his neck a trill, drawing everybody in for the seven o'clock.

Angie smiled and pushed back her long, dark hair. Her face

grew serious. "So, yes on Christmas? Since you aren't going home? Come out to Ohio and join me and the boys. They'd love to see Uncle Rhett."

Rhett wished he had lied when she asked about Christmas, but then, with as good a friend as she'd become to Mel, he couldn't risk her finding out that way. "I have to stick near the gym. Hobbs and Zoe are going out of town. My other two coaches are part-time. They can't cover all the classes."

Angie planted her hands on her waist and drew a deep breath through her Roman nose. "We can come here, then. Stay with you. I don't want you alone. Vic wouldn't have wanted it, either."

Times like this Rhett was left to think on the depth of character that Victor Devon had possessed; he hadn't exactly been a looker, but his widow was the stereotypical raven-haired beauty, complete with inky eyes and smooth, olive skin. She reminded him a lot of Mel, though Mel took after Papa and was a lot shorter. Angie had obviously married Devon for his dance moves and big smile—not to mention, he always had your back. Rhett had never worried about having Victor Devon in his foxhole.

"I've got reservations," Rhett blurted, the panic in him rising so high the words spilled out like they rode the edge of a big wave. "Mama got me this cabin. It's close enough I won't miss work and just a couple of days. There's dinner and a party. The works."

Angie's lips parted in surprise. "Really? And you agreed to that?"

Rhett lifted his hands in surrender. "You've met Mama. She doesn't take no for an answer."

Angie's face softened into a warm smile. "Your Southern accent only comes out when you talk about your mama." She reached up and squeezed his shoulder.

"That right?" Rhett flinched a little, but tried to hide it with a forced shrug. "I hadn't noticed."

Angie's smile fell. "I better get going. I've got a flight later. As always, it was good to see you. Thanks for letting me pop in here and kick your ass."

Rhett spread open his arms. "You know when you're here, I'm all yours. Arlington Cemetery in the morning and Combat at night. You get to cry on me and punch me all in one day."

"Yeah. C'mere." She slid into his arms and hugged him tight. After a long embrace, she tilted her chin up. "See you next year, then. But you know my door's always open."

Rhett glanced over her head and caught an image of Stanzi, executing three perfect snatches in a row. Hobbs, who was checking her weight before they started the workout, gave a sharp whistle. "Not bad, Red. You say you just started?"

Stanzi caught Rhett's eye. Her gaze traveled down to Angie, who still had her arms locked around Rhett's waist. Stanzi quickly turned back to Hobbs. "That's right."

Rhett looked down at Angie and gave her a peck on the forehead. "Have a safe flight. And say hi to those boys for me."

Sunny watched her sister go into Semper Fit around 6:55 p.m. The sky was dark, the gym was bright and the windows were tall, which gave her a good view of what went on inside, even from her car.

The place was packed, and the clientele had a wide range of ages, genders and body types. Sunny got a glimpse or two of Cici's coaches. One of them was so tall he literally stood out. Some of these people were in such good shape they belonged on the covers of fitness magazines, the tall guy most of all. Sunny wondered if he was Rhett Santos. If he was, that would make him one of Detective Callahan's closest friends. While Sunny had no doubt he was a good part of the reason

Cici was so into this place, it was obvious there was much more that kept her coming back.

Her sister slid in easily and fit like a crayon in a very colorful box. Sunny could feel the vibe all the way out to the parking lot, with the thumping music, sweaty bodies and satisfied smiles.

Once Cici had melted into the background, Sunny drove away. She wasn't sure what she was feeling. Cici seemed happy, which was good, but Sunny felt guilty about spying. Even the sight of her house and grounds—newly decorated for Christmas, with Pete's help—didn't put a smile on her face.

Especially when she saw a strange car in the driveway.

"Now, who could that be?" Sunny sidled up to the blue four-door, older make and model, and peered into the driver's seat. Her heart leaped into her throat.

"Evening, Sunny." Detective Sean Callahan greeted her as she stepped out.

"Evening, Detective." Sunny hugged her arms around her waist. "To what do I owe this pleasure?" The detective wore jeans and a button-down shirt beneath his casual jacket. Maybe that was a good sign. He'd have to be dressed up to arrest her, right?

"Oh, I'm a pleasure now, am I?"

"Depends on why you're here."

He shrugged. "For the Scotch, of course. You said I could come by anytime. Unless, of course, there's another reason I should be here?" His voice took on a hard edge, but Sunny couldn't tell if it was real or pretend.

Either way, she wasn't risking it. "Sure. C'mon inside."

After a quick tour of the house and grounds, Sunny took the detective into the living room that was just off the foyer. It had a stone fireplace that took up the entire east wall and windows that overlooked the frosty woods. She lit the paper beneath the layers of starter logs always waiting, then poured the detective a glass of the four-thousand-dollar Scotch and pressed it into his thick hands. It was best to keep him here, warm and liquored up, and nowhere near Roger's cabin, which housed the Maltese. Just in case he'd heard anything.

"Thanks." Sean stared into the fire as he took a sip. "This room is almost as amazing as this Scotch."

"I like it, too." Sunny went behind the bar and poured herself a glass of red wine. "Did you enjoy Thanksgiving?"

Sean rubbed the back of his neck. "Sure."

Sunny sipped at the cabernet. "You rub your neck when you're lying."

He fixed her with his appraising gaze, which seemed to always live just under the surface. "Now you sound like your sister."

Sunny could picture it. Cici noticed everybody's habits, posture, gait. It was difficult to be in public with her without her wanting to fix someone's rounded shoulders or pronated feet. "Just saw my sister. She's at the gym, making progress with your buddy."

Sean finally smiled. "It's a good thing your sister is stubborn. Or so she seemed when I met her. She'll need it, with Rhett."

"Oh, she's stubborn, all right." Sunny sat on the couch, right where she'd nestled into Pete's lap on Thanksgiving night. When she'd woken, the sun had been bright and Pete was gone, which had given her an empty feeling she hadn't expected.

Sean threw back his Scotch and helped himself to more from the bottle Sunny had left on the bar. "By the way—" he reached into his back pocket and withdrew a piece of paper "—I have something for you." He handed it to her as he sat next to her on the couch.

"What's this?" Sunny's stomach tightened back up.

"A restraining order," Sean said casually. "From Janice Matteri."

Her pulse thudded in her ears. The wine burned the back of her throat.

"This is a preliminary protective order," Sean went on, as though they were discussing the weather. "Basically, you have to stay away from her and her grounds for a period of time. There'll be a hearing to determine whether or not she'll be granted a permanent order." Sean sipped his Scotch. "I brought it over myself, so we could talk."

"I see." Sunny slugged her glass of wine. "And did Janice Matteri say why she was obtaining this order?" She dropped the paper on the couch, without looking at it.

Sean narrowed his eyes, which deepened the gray hue of his irises. "She claims you stole two of her dogs over the holiday. Her nephew was staying at the house. His story—" a small grin played around Sean's mouth "—is a lot more interesting." He sipped his drink again and swallowed with a satisfied sigh. "He claims he caught you in the act and you took him down with some fancy martial arts moves."

Sunny rose up and crossed slowly to the bar. She said nothing, gathering her thoughts as she poured the wine. Part of her was relieved that the man Pete had taken down hadn't even seen him, apparently, and thought Sunny responsible. The other part of her was calculating how much Sean knew and what to say next. "If this is true—" Sunny spun to face the detective "—then why aren't I under arrest?"

"Oh, they're not pressing charges." Sean set his glass down on the coffee table and folded his hands together, between his knees. "Janice Matteri just wants you to stay away, permanently."

She's afraid, Sunny thought. *She knows she could go to jail herself for abusing her dogs.* "That woman is a lunatic. Her nephew was probably strung out. That whole family is bad news. Like I told you before, you really ought to check into her operation. Not mine."

"Maybe."

Sunny leaned back against the bar and opened her arms. "Do I look like the type who could take down a fully grown male?"

Sean rose from the couch and approached her, his gaze steady on her own. "Depends on what you're using."

"You have some nerve." The wine had gone to Sunny's head. "Pretending you wanted to share my expensive Scotch when you really came out here to give me some silly protective order. You know who needs a protective order? Janice Matteri's dogs!"

Sean halted, just inside Sunny's personal space. "I wasn't pretending that I wanted your Scotch." His eyes glinted. "All of this could've gone a very different way. I came out here to make sure it went the gentlest way possible."

"Am I supposed to thank you?" As soon as the words left her lips, Sunny's eyes closed. Why could she never stop her mouth? If Cici were here she'd be shaking her head.

"Do you want to thank me?" Sean's voice came close to her ear. His breath danced over her cheek.

A little shiver zipped down Sunny's spine. Her eyes opened. Sean had closed the space between them. His hands went to the bar, on either side of her body.

"What happens if I say no?"

Sean shrugged. "Nothing. I leave."

"What happens if I say yes?" Her voice lowered, the words coming of their own volition.

Sean leaned in close and brushed his lips over her cheek, toward her mouth. He stopped there. "I don't know, Sunny. Do you want to find out?"

fifteen

Constance had just pulled on the door handle when a touch to her shoulder made her halt. Rhett loomed above, looking stern. "I thought you wanted to hear about Combat."

Constance pushed a few sweaty strands of hair from her face and decided she'd get out the scissors and cut it short again when she got home. Long hair was just a pain in the ass and served no purpose whatsoever. "It's late," she said. "I'm sure you're tired."

"I've got a few minutes." Rhett gave a wave to the stragglers from the last class as they headed out into the cold.

"Later, man." Hobbs held up a hand. "You locking up?" His gaze went from Rhett to her and back again.

"Yep."

"All right. Night, Red." Hobbs winked at her. "Great job on those snatches. You seen her snatch yet?"

"Of course." Rhett's voice had a tinge of possessiveness to it.

Constance forced a smile. "Thanks." She liked Steve. That

conceited persona he wore was about as real as a clown's painted smile. He was loud and boisterous but friendly, which kept him from being obnoxious. His energy was big, but thin. Constance sensed that there was a quiet, denser core that he kept tight and tucked away from scrutiny. She'd have to lay hands on him to find out.

Rhett locked the door behind Hobbs. His energy was big in a different way. Constance didn't even need to touch him tonight to know—he was wide-open. It emanated from his body, even though he stood about a foot from her. Constance wondered if the woman who'd hugged him earlier was the one to amp him up. Unlike Hobbs, Rhett's persona was typically cool and controlled, and his outward energy matched that, like a quiet, retreating tide that left a long, smooth pattern of wet sand in its wake. His core was where the storm lived. It was his source—a deeper, darker entity that drove him, crashing from the inside out, driving the power in circular ripples that calmed as it broke the surface.

Constance looked out into the dark parking lot. The strip mall across the street flickered with bright, festive lights. Everyone decorated for Christmas right after Thanksgiving these days, but she hadn't even put her electric candles in the windows. At least she'd taken down Daddy's scarecrow. "This was already my second workout today," she said. "And it's late. I should go."

Rhett's eyes narrowed. He silently appraised her. Constance swallowed the tightness in her throat, hoping he couldn't see what she herself didn't understand. What was her problem? Why had her mood changed ever since she saw that woman locked in his arms?

"We're not going to work out." Rhett took her elbow and gently pulled her away from the door. "I'm just going to show you a few basics. Then you'll know whether or not you want to try the class."

"Well—"

"C'mon. You can help me solve a problem at the same time."

Constance knew she really should just go home. Eat some leftovers and maybe dig out her miniature tree. She could hang her White House ornaments on it and light it up, which would make her feel cozy and cheerful while she binged on some Netflix before bed.

She felt her gym bag slip from her grip and hit the floor. "Okay. Sure."

They moved over to the area where the gymnastic mats still covered the floor from the Combat class. "Had a friend visit earlier," Rhett said, like he could read Constance's mind.

"I saw her." Constance pictured the pretty brunette with the toned body and long, silky hair. "She looked like she was really good at this." She nodded toward the mats.

"She is now. When she first tried, she fell flat on her ass." He laughed. "That was a few years ago. After her husband died. We served together. My last tour in Iraq."

Constance felt her insides open up in so many different ways it was impossible to decide what she was feeling. It was like getting a bite of something with multiple flavors and not knowing which way the dish would go. Salty? Sweet? Bitter?

"He's buried in Arlington Cemetery. She comes every year from Ohio to visit."

Bittersweet.

Constance regarded Rhett carefully, trying to absorb everything he said without words. "You go with her. You take care of her, as best as you can."

Rhett's eyes glimmered with surprise. It wasn't a look Constance was used to seeing on his face. "Yeah. I have to be here for her. I have to do anything I can. Which is why—" he shrugged "—I feel bad I lied to her. She wanted to be with me for Christmas and I just can't do it. I can't." He sighed, and rubbed a hand over his face.

Constance noticed how tired he was around the eyes. She stayed quiet, letting him open on his own.

He cleared his throat. "My mother rented me this cabin for Christmas Eve. Out at this dog rescue. Some kind of rustic getaway. I canceled the reservation. But when Angie suggested she come here and spend Christmas with me, I told her I was staying there. It just popped out of my mouth."

Constance stopped herself from laughing, because Rhett wouldn't understand. Had he really had one of Sunny's cabins booked for the holiday? Talk about a small world. "You don't want to spend Christmas with her?"

"No." Rhett drew a deep breath and sighed. "I can't be… I can't…" He stopped and drew another deep breath. "I think she wants more from me than I can give."

His deep, hidden energy rolled out and surrounded her, seeking somewhere to land. Constance let herself be open to it, rather than closing herself off to protect herself, which is what she mostly did these days. "It was a harmless lie," she said. "There's nothing wrong with lies sometimes. Life isn't as black and white as we'd like it to be."

"I know, but—" Rhett shrugged "—now I feel like I should call and try to get my reservation back. Just so I'm not lying. I'd feel better about it if I wasn't lying. Is that stupid or what?"

Constance stifled a laugh. It's not that she found anything about Rhett's story funny. Obviously this woman's husband had been close to Rhett. Rhett might've even watched him die. Her instinct told her not to question it. But his response to his lie reminded her so much of herself she couldn't help but feel amused. "Did you say a dog rescue? Was it Pittie Place, by chance?"

"Yeah." Rhett's eyes widened. "You know it?"

Constance hesitated. The direction they were taking was new, more intimate. Up until now their interactions had been mostly professional with only a little friendship. "My sister owns it."

A heartbeat of quiet passed. "Are you serious?"

"My sister, Sunny, runs Pittie Place. She built up a few of the cabins on the land as a source of income. Every year she does this Christmas fundraising dinner for her wealthiest donors."

Rhett shook his head. "Small world."

Constance smiled. Her body, once warm and sweaty, had grown cold. She suppressed a shiver. "I can talk to my sister if you want. Get your reservation back."

"Really?" The worry that creased around Rhett's eyes lifted. "That would make me feel better. I know it's dumb, but…"

"I'll take care of it." Constance knew, as she said it, that Sunny had already rented out that cabin. It had probably been snapped up within an hour of Rhett's cancellation and she probably had five more people on a wait list behind the current renters.

"I'd owe you one." The relief that washed through Rhett's weary eyes was palpable.

"Nah. We're square. After all, I still haven't joined the gym."

"Speaking of. We should do that. Or are you ready to get your Combat on?" Rhett held up his fists.

Constance smiled. As soon as she'd walked in tonight and seen Rhett sparring with Angie, she'd been drawn in like a hungry orphan to a banquet. She wanted—no, she *needed*—to know what they were doing, to learn how to move like that woman was moving. It scared and excited her all at once and she hadn't been able to think about much else since.

"It's late," she said. "I'm hungry. And you're tired."

"All right." Rhett looked both disappointed and relieved. "At least let me show you a good fighting stance before you go."

"Sure."

"Show me your fists." Rhett held up his own. "You're getting ready to fight. Show me."

Constance swallowed her sudden embarrassment and held up her fists.

"Okay," Rhett said. "Not horrible." He opened his hand. "Bend the middle set of knuckles first. Then the second set."

"Wait. The middle? What? This?"

"Middle first. Then the base."

"Oh, okay. DIP joint, PIP joint, metacarpals. Got it."

Rhett smiled. "The DIP and the PIP. I like it. Then thumb covers the first two fingers."

Constance followed his directions until he nodded in approval.

"Keep your wrist completely straight. When you strike, you'll use the first two knuckles. Pointer and middle finger. They're bigger, stronger and will cause more damage."

Constance wished she'd known that before she broke her hand on Frankie Rumbaugh's jaw, the day after he took Sunny to homecoming and tore her blouse trying to feel her up. "Do you really strike in class?"

"No. Well, not unless you're Angie." He rolled his eyes a little. "But I teach it like you'd use it on the street. We start by trying to avoid combat at all costs. But if you're forced to, we want you to be prepared."

"Makes sense."

"You want your dominant leg and punching arm behind.

You're going to put your hips and shoulders into the strike. Generates more power. Just like when you're lifting. Hands up. Hand not throwing the punch protects your face. Chin down. Elbows in." Rhett demonstrated, then came behind Constance and adjusted her posture. He put one hand on her right hip and turned it a little, then did the same to her shoulders. His warm hand closed over her left wrist. "And here," he said, fixing that side.

"Got it." Constance's voice came out a little thin, and her pulse rose. Maybe being so open to Rhett's energy hadn't been such a good idea.

"Your body delivers the strike." Rhett's torso just barely touched her shoulders as he guided her punching arm forward. "Use this hip. Deliver. Then pull straight back. Good."

Rhett came back around in front of her, leaving her body to feel cold and oddly weak. He peered down at her. "You okay?"

"Uh-huh."

"Now aim for anything vulnerable on my face. Eyes. Nose. Jaw. Throat."

Constance thought through all of the instructions, started, stopped, adjusted herself and started again. She stopped just short of Rhett's jaw, which sported about two days of dark growth.

"Not horrible," he said. "Just needs a little practice."

"You're so tall," Constance pointed out. "In a real situation, I don't see myself getting near your face."

"You will if you nail me in the groin first. But don't use your toes, like they do in the movies. Aim with your shin. Broader surface, much more likely to score a hit. Go ahead and try, but please—" he held up a hand and smiled "—stop just shy of your target."

Constance chuckled as she got into her fighting stance. She turned, using her body, and pantomimed the move, stopping her shin just inside Rhett's thighs. He bent double, as if she'd really scored a hit. "Now aim for my jaw," he instructed.

She swung, again turning into the move and aiming with her first two knuckles. Constance tapped Rhett's jaw and he acted like he was going to fall sideways. He caught himself on his knees and smiled up at her. "Simple stuff, right?" He took her wrist and brushed her knuckles over his jaw. "Here," he said, "or here." He tapped her hand to the side of his face near his eye, then his throat. "Anywhere below the forehead, which is likely just to hurt your hand."

Constance's increased pulse warmed her back up, but she still felt shivery. Like the flu, but also absolutely nothing like the flu.

"Hey." Rhett snapped his fingers. "Where'd you go?"

Constance blinked rapidly. Rhett was in front of her, still on his knees. His eyes sparkled in the dim light, his brow creased with concern. His scents, heightened up close, filled her. His laundry soap mixed with his shampoo—a hint of lavender and something woodsy. A few heartbeats passed, which thrummed in Constance's ears and burned around the back of her neck. She didn't even realize she'd uncurled her fist, which he still held, until Rhett's thumb grazed her palm.

"This is bad fighting form." His voice dropped an octave as he waggled her hand.

Constance stood only a few inches away, her hand loosely inside of his, her fingertips against his throat. She studied his eyes, sparkling in the dim light. His pupils were large, the heartbeat in his neck strong.

The tension in his body changed, loosening in some places and tightening in others. "Well?" There was no longer humor in his voice. "What now, Stanzi?"

Constance couldn't move. Rhett Santos didn't start where his body began; the beginnings of him were well outside his physical presence, that deep, dark energy throbbing all around her, an unseen shadow that held her captive.

His thumb stroked the center of her palm again.

Constance slid the fingers of her open hand behind his neck. The hair at his nape, which curled a little bit, was cool and silky. The feel of it sent a shiver through her body that raised goose bumps over her skin.

Rhett's free hand went behind the small of her back and rested there.

She leaned in close, pausing near his cheek.

Rhett's entire body stilled.

Constance gave him a gentle kiss on the mouth. She lingered long enough to feel where the tenderness ceded to the rough stubble on his upper lip. The only part of Rhett that moved was his hand. His warm fingers, rough with calluses at the base of his fingers, slid down to her forearm.

Oh, hell. Constance drew back slowly.

Rhett's eyelids fluttered open. "And," he said, his voice low, "she goes for the kill."

They studied each other in silence for a moment, the complete quiet of the gym so unusual it heightened the significance of what Constance had just done. Rhett released her and rose to his feet. Constance drew a deep breath to steady herself. She wasn't sure what to say or even how to feel. She still couldn't move.

Rhett ran a hand through his hair, his expression unreadable. "C'mon," he said. He nodded toward the doorway. "I think we'd better not do any more tonight."

"Right," Constance agreed, the word mostly a whisper. She thought about apologizing, but she wasn't sorry.

They said nothing as they stepped out into the cold and Rhett locked up the gym. He walked her to her car and opened the door for her. Constance climbed in and waited.

Rhett's hand was still on the top of the door so she couldn't slam it shut.

"Drive safe," he said.

"Yeah."

He let go and she pulled the door shut.

Just before she went to pull away, he knocked on her window. She lowered it. "I have this feeling," he said, "that you're going to be really good at combat."

The tightness in her throat eased up. She smiled and laughed under her breath.

Rhett smiled back and waited until she'd backed out before he headed off toward his Jeep. He had the tiniest limp to his step.

Constance took a shower, then faced herself in the steamy mirror, scissors in hand. She slid them back into the drawer, leaving her hair untouched, then ran her fingertips over her lips. Eyes closed, the scent of Rhett's skin hit her, even though she'd showered.

She put on her pajamas, snapped off the light, slid under the covers and thought about that kiss. In hindsight, she couldn't believe her nerve. It was as though she'd had no control over her body whatsoever. Or, maybe more rightly, for the first time in a long time, she'd had complete control over her body.

Constance didn't know if Rhett had expected, wanted or enjoyed that kiss at all. But it made no difference. She'd given it to him, and she wasn't taking it back.

Rhett lay awake in bed, reliving those last moments with Stanzi for as long as his sleepy mind would allow. He wanted to tell himself that he'd seen it coming, because Rhett didn't like being caught off guard. He also wanted to tell himself that she'd taken him completely by surprise, because then he'd be excused from letting the kiss happen.

Neither one was true.

There were many places along the way Rhett could have prevented that kiss. He should've let her walk out the door, right after class. Her demeanor was stiff, if not cold, and she wanted to go. Yet, he persisted she stay. During their Combat session, he should've stood up as soon as she'd made her last strike. Rather than take her hand and draw her in closer, he should've said, "This is the part where you keep hitting soft targets, or you turn and run like hell." That's what he would've said to a class, or to any other woman training with him.

Instead of running like hell, she'd let him draw her closer.

Now he was left to lie alone in his bed, thinking about the strawberry scent of her hair, the feel of her soft lips against his own and her breath on his cheek.

Shit happens, and Rhett was no teenager. But gentle seduction hadn't been on the menu for a long time. Even in his on-again, off-again with Katrina—an ex who was sort of an ex and sort of not?—their sex had become more like mutual masturbation than a connection of any kind between the two of them.

Despite the fact that Stanzi's lips had done little more than brush gently over his, Rhett couldn't remember the last time he'd been kissed like that.

Had he ever been kissed like that?

Stanzi's kiss, in and of itself, was a delicious thing. It was delicate, sweet and promising. Genuine, like her personality. But what was even more dangerous was *why* she'd kissed him.

Rhett didn't actually know why.

But he'd *felt* why.

The power behind that kiss had paralyzed him like dart venom. In that moment, Stanzi could have done anything—

kiss him more passionately, slip her hand into his pants or even slit his throat—and he would've let her. That's how good it felt.

And that wasn't a place he was comfortable with.

His phone buzzed. Normally, once he was in bed, he didn't touch his cell. He grappled for it on the nightstand and ended up knocking it to the floor. He cursed as he felt around for it, then clicked it open to reveal a text message.

It was from Angie. Letting him know they'd made it to the airport—her, the boys and Devon's mom—and would be catching the red-eye home. Rhett blew out a sigh of disappointment. He didn't realize just how much he'd been hoping the text was from Stanzi until it wasn't. He typed back, told Angie to be safe and, as always, to let him know if she needed anything.

He clicked off the volume and slid the phone back to the nightstand. If the phone buzzed again, he didn't want to hear it. He wanted to close his eyes, drift into hopefully dreamless sleep and make it to the morning.

As soon as his heavy lids shut, the kiss popped into his head. Rather than push it away, he embraced it. There were worse ways to fall asleep. Whether what came of that moment would be good or not, he couldn't say. But that moment itself had been amazing.

Fuck it. Nothing else had to come of it, but he wasn't going to insult the power of that kiss with wussy feelings like regret. Tonight, a beautiful woman had given him a beautiful thing.

No matter what happened, he was keeping it.

sixteen

"You slept with Detective Callahan?" Constance's eyes were so big they looked like the prized bright blue marbles she and Sunny used to carry around in the bags Mom had made before she died. Because their parents were older, a lot of their toys were old-fashioned. None of their friends understood the fun of shooting marbles, or carrying them around in homemade drawstring bags made by your dead mother. Sunny used to pretend she remembered Mom stitching them on her sewing machine, because Constance remembered it, and Sunny hated that Constance had way more memories of Mom than she did.

"You kissed your coach," Sunny shot back.

"That's way, way—" Constance made big circles with her arms "—different. What you're doing is pushing the envelope on bribery, Little Miss Restraining Order. What I did was just a classic caught-up-in-the-moment mistake. And, unlike you, mine won't happen again."

"And why not?" Sunny was happy to deflect the conversation back to Cici.

"It's complicated." Constance hovered her hands over the rescued beagle's shoulders, who sat up tall and rigid on his dog bed. He flinched, squeezing his one good eye shut. Constance massaged the air above him, not touching his body, moving slow and rhythmic, until he relaxed. "Humphrey's a mess," she cooed. "Even after a week with Dr. Winters."

"You've named him already?"

Her hands finally lit, just barely, on his black-and-tan fur. "It came to me immediately." Cici sat there, without moving, her hands on his shoulders. Her face broke into a delicate smile when he didn't move away.

Chevy, jealous of the attention, sat at Constance's feet and offered a sympathetic whine. "Hey, girl." Constance gave her a nod, but didn't move her hands from Humphrey. "Where are your babies?"

"I still keep them in the back room." Sunny was glad for a topic change. "Chevy roams around as she likes. She's starting to wean them." Often, if they suckled too long, the mama would stand up and walk away, irritated. It was funny to watch the pups cling to her nipples. They'd run after her, tripping over their own paws as they tried to hang on.

After a long wait, Constance ran her hands down the beagle's back, skimming his fur with her palms. A moment later, he sank to the dog bed. "That's it."

Sunny plopped down in the armchair across from her. "And what's so complicated, then?"

Constance sighed and flashed Sunny a look. "Well, let's just start with the easiest reason. You and the detective want me to help him. If I end up being Rhett's massage therapist, I can't go around kissing him. It's unethical."

Sunny rolled her eyes. "You haven't massaged him yet. Not

really. So you kissed him first. Does that count? And it was barely a kiss, from what you told me. It's not like you kissed him during a massage. That's way different."

"Doesn't matter." Constance continued her therapy with the beagle. Humphrey's breathing, always shallow with fear, had deepened. His ribs, still prominent through his coat, spread, rose and fell at a steady pace.

"You think too much." Sunny watched her sister work her magic and, as usual, was slightly jealous of her power. "But I'm not going to get into an argument."

"That reminds me, I need a favor."

Sunny's brows rose.

"Are all your cabins rented out for the Christmas Eve event?"

"Of course."

"You had a cancellation recently." Constance had reached Humphrey's back feet. She ran just her fingertips over the left one. He didn't move. He might've even been asleep. "Rhett's mother had rented one out for him, and he canceled it. I need you to give it back."

"Seriously?" Sunny thought back, and remembered that just after Thanksgiving a man had called and canceled a reservation that had been booked by his mother, even though the cost was nonrefundable. "He had a deep voice," she mused.

"What does that have to do with anything?" Constance lifted Humphrey's foot and began massaging the pads underneath. The dog took a deep breath and huffed it out in a satisfied sigh.

"It doesn't," Sunny said, marveling that the dog was letting her sister touch his feet. "But I can't give him the cabin. It's booked."

"But the massage comes with it," Constance pointed out. "This is the perfect way for me to help you and Callahan. Or do you not need my help anymore, now that you're sleeping with him?"

Sunny snapped her gaze up into her sister's glaring eyes. "So you're assuming I'm using him."

"Aren't you?"

Sunny shrugged. "I'm playing his game. That's all men do. Play games. He's the one using me. Or he thinks he is."

Constance shook her head. "This is why I have to be very careful helping Rhett. This kind of work—" she glanced at Humphrey "—is serious and can't be messed up with complications. At my end, this is no game."

"Okay, okay." Sunny didn't see as much of a problem with her own situation. She had no idea what was going on with her and Callahan and she really didn't want to categorize it, one way or the other. They were consenting adults. They had a great time. What was wrong with that? "Rhett can use your room," Sunny said. "You'll just have to go home to sleep Christmas Eve. Unless you want to be on the couch. Everything else is rented out."

Constance finished up Humphrey's other paw, then rose carefully to her feet. Humphrey didn't move a muscle. They were all jelly and he was nothing but a happy puddle. "Perfect. Thank you. In the meantime, I'll try to work Rhett's leg again. Before I spring a whole-body massage on him on Christmas Eve."

"Good plan. And yes, I still need your help. Sean and I had a deal that didn't involve sex and I'm assuming that's still a go."

Constance shook her head. Her face had gotten slimmer over the weeks at Semper Fit and she seemed sterner now when she gave Sunny that classic, disapproving look. "Be careful, baby sister. You're playing with fire."

Stanzi stood outside the office, holding up a small jar. Despite the fact she'd pretty much avoided him for a week,

Rhett smiled. She wore a pair of black leggings, a T-shirt only one size too big rather than three and had her hair up in that little ponytail. Her bangs had grown past her eyes and were pulled back with a small barrette. Up close, Rhett could see that the barrette was metal, with a small, plastic cat on it, like a little girl might wear.

He laughed to himself. *Who dresses you?*

"Your limp has gotten worse all week." She nodded toward his leg.

Rhett raised his eyebrows at her. "Hi. How are you?"

"Oh, I mean. Hey." Stanzi smiled, then bit down on her lower lip. "I've been a little busy this week. But I made it for Combat class tonight."

"You've been to the gym," Rhett said, crossing his arms over his chest. "Just not to my class."

Stanzi rolled the jar she'd brought around and around in her palms. She looked up toward the ceiling, then parted her lips to speak.

"What you got there?" Rhett let her off the hook and nodded to the jar. Watching her squirm was fun, but no need to push it. He didn't want her mad at him before Combat.

"I want to try this on your leg. It's great for pain relief. Before I try it on clients, I want you to be my guinea pig."

Rhett took the jar, which had a graphic of a leafy plant on the label. He read the ingredients. "Cannabidiol extract?" He smiled. "You trying to get me high, Stanzi?"

She rolled her eyes. "Of course not. It's nonpsychoactive. There's no THC in this. The compounds in here disrupt pain signaling in the body. It works really well. Sit down." She motioned to his desk chair. "It's perfectly legal."

Rhett narrowed his eyes, leery of tricks. But logically, that made no sense. She was asking for his help. He'd be a jerk not to accept some free work in exchange for being a guinea pig, right? "Go ahead." He sank into his office chair. "I don't care what you use on this damn leg." He motioned to the door and she pushed it closed.

Stanzi unscrewed the cap and dipped her pinky into the cream. "I should have an applicator, but this is my own personal jar. I don't use it on other clients."

"Will you quit going out of your way to be professional and just help my stupid leg?" He waited for that suppressed smile to play around her lips before he leaned back and closed his eyes, allowing the full power of her magical cream and magical hands and whatever magical thing she had going on to work its will. It didn't matter whether she had cannabidiol or Love Potion No. 9 in that jar, if Stanzi was going to rub it on him, he was going to feel good. He still remembered the last massage she'd given him. Dreamed about it sometimes.

"You've got a lot of scar tissue here." Her hands were right over the leg wound. She rested there a moment, then told him to take a deep breath. On the exhale, she sank in with her fingertips. Slowly, she worked around the scar, moving in short strokes forward and back, and side to side. "Feels okay?"

Rhett opened his eyes and saw she watched his hands and face for signs of pain, rather than watching his leg. Just like when she tested Duke's firing sequence, she took sight out of the equation. "Hurts, but in a good way."

"That's what we want." She worked her fingers awhile longer, and the pain slowly eased. "When you're hurt," she explained, "your body rushes to fix the damage. It doesn't care how the new fibers get laid down to patch the wound. It throws them down any which way, which is why scar tissue is so lumpy. It's kind of like, if you're putting out a fire, you don't care if you get water all over the walls. You'll throw buckets around if it puts out the flames, and you don't care what kind of mess it makes."

Stanzi grasped his calf and leaned back, putting him into traction. "We'll stretch the quad when you stand up. Keep in mind, you may actually feel worse after this, at least at first. But a change is good. Eventually, you should feel a bit better."

Rhett met her gaze, stifling the urge to reach out and fix the hair that had fallen out of her cat barrette. "There was an explosion." He spoke without really deciding to. The sound of his own voice surprised him as much as it showed on her face. "Rockets were launched at our firebase. We raced for the bunker when the sirens went off. I had to make sure all my men made it inside. Just three of us were left outside when they hit. One missed us, the other hit close by. My leg took a hit before I dragged myself into the bunker. I thought Devon and Masters made it in, but I was wrong. They took hits, too, but not in their legs."

He waited for her to say what everyone else said. What was it Katrina had said, over and over again? *You can't blame yourself that you didn't die, too. That's a classic mistake.*

Rhett had always wanted to say, *You're a classic mistake*, but had never been able to bring himself to be that mean to someone he was sleeping with.

Stanzi was quiet awhile as she released his calf and ran her hands back up and over his quads, this time using only the flat of her palms in long, smooth strokes. This part of the massage didn't hurt-so-good. It just felt good. "Was one of them Angie's husband?"

"Devon." Rhett watched her hands work. She had long, slender fingers and clean nails filed down smooth, past the tips. Perfect for her job. Perfect to wrap around a barbell. He stopped short of thinking about a few other things they'd be perfect for. "He had good dance moves and a big, stupid grin."

"Was Masters a good dancer, too?"

"No." Rhett wondered when the last time was anyone had

asked about Scott Masters. He'd been single and didn't have much to say about his parents. His death seemed to have gone mostly unnoticed back home. "He was terrible. But he made everyone laugh being terrible."

As usual, Stanzi said nothing with words, but her hands spoke volumes. Her pressure eased up considerably. Her touch was so light Rhett felt goose bumps rise on his skin. This was the sort of touch that could get him going in a direction she probably didn't intend. She stopped, as though realizing the change, squeezed around his knee and stood up quickly. "Let's get you on your feet and stretch that quad."

"You're the boss." Rhett rose, leaned against the wall and grasped his ankle, bending at the knee and stretching his thigh. After a minute he let it go and bounced around on his toes, like a boxer. "Not horrible." His lips twitched into a smile. *Fucking great.* "Thank you."

"Anytime."

"And not just for this." Rhett touched his leg. "Thanks for asking about Masters. Nobody ever does."

Stanzi stood by the door, her hand on the knob. "You can tell me about him anytime."

Silence passed. "You done avoiding me?" he finally said.

"I'm not avoiding you."

Rhett stepped closer and stared down at her. "Yes, you are."

She met his gaze, but her hair fell in her eyes. She adjusted her little cat barrette, gave her bangs a blow and faced him again. "Okay. But I'm not avoiding you now. I'm here, right?"

Rhett took another step closer and planted a hand on the wall behind her. He narrowed his eyes and waited, but she didn't elaborate.

Her breathing grew shallow inside the cage he'd made around her body.

Rhett laughed. "Okay." He pushed off the wall. "Go get

ready for Combat. Make sure your bangs are up." He brushed a thumb over the fringe of her hair. "You can't punch what you can't see."

She pressed her lips together and nodded. "Yep."

"Today, we're going over what to do when you're grabbed from behind. I need a crash dummy." Rhett looked around the circle of women.

Several raised their hands, but Constance remained quiet and still.

"Stanzi." He leveled his gaze on her. "You're up." He pointed at the spot next to him.

No thanks rose quickly to her lips, but for some odd reason the words didn't come out. Curious looks went in her direction as she walked slowly toward Rhett.

Rhett turned to the class and said, "Everyone, this is Stanzi. If you haven't met her yet, introduce yourselves."

A chorus of greetings rippled through the group.

"As always, by staying in tonight's class, you are giving each other permission to perform these movements on you. If you don't wish to be touched in the manner I demonstrate, please move on to Zoe's kettlebell class." Rhett pointed to the far corner where the buff blonde and her group were gathered in a circle, kettlebells in various sizes at their feet. "And, as always, perform these movements without actually harming each other. It's important we are realistic but not emergency room realistic."

Everyone laughed.

"All right. Stanzi has her back to me." Rhett touched her shoulders until she turned, facing away from him. "She's already done a check of her surroundings and every other precautionary thing she could do, but despite her efforts, I grab her from behind."

Rhett's arms went around her waist, pinning her own arms to her sides. "What should she do?"

The air smelled spicy, like Rhett's soap. As soon as the scent hit her, her lungs opened a little. His chest was hard and warm against her back.

"She could throw her head back, into yours," someone suggested.

"She could—" Rhett's voice came from near her shoulder "—but I've stooped down, to give myself leverage, and my head's lower than hers right now. Even if it wasn't, she's in danger of hurting herself just as much as she hurts me by using her head as a weapon."

"She could kick back."

"Kick me, Stanzi." Rhett's voice came close to her ear.

Constance struggled to, but didn't have balance.

"She could try kicking me." Rhett's voice came loud and authoritative, commanding attention. "And she might get a hit. Or she might lose her footing, and make her situation worse. What I want her to do is drop her base. Stanzi, I want you to bend your knees and squat, just like we do with a barbell. And fast. Just as fast as you get under that bar when you clean or snatch."

Constance dropped, fast and straight. To her surprise, she found herself nearly free of Rhett's arms. They were still around her, but up near her head, and he no longer had a solid hold.

She'd actually gotten herself free.

"Now that she's out, she can hit me in my vulnerable spots," Rhett said. "She can turn and nail me in the groin, keep kicking soft targets or run like hell. Watch, we're going to do it again."

Rhett demonstrated one more time, and this time, as soon as he had her, she dropped. "Now's a good time for her to hit."

Rhett took her by the forearm. "She can hit, downward, on my groin as hard as she can." He pantomimed the move. "Or turn and kick me there. Or aim upward for my throat." Rhett ran her through all the moves, gently turning and guiding her body to attack his. "You get the idea. Now, I want you to pair up and practice this on your own. I'll move around the room and take a look." He put his hands on Constance's shoulders as everyone broke off into chattering teams.

Constance went to walk away but Rhett held her back. "You stay with me."

"I did it." Constance beamed up at him, unashamed of her joy. She wondered why this made her feel so gloriously free. It was like she'd been a bird in a cage all her life but hadn't even known it until the bars were gone. "I really broke myself free."

"Sure," Rhett laughed. "I'm not going to teach you crap moves. I want you to always break free, Stanzi. Do you want to run through this again?"

Constance didn't have to think about that at all. "Absolutely. And I want you to teach me all the other stuff, too."

"All right. One rule." He held up a finger, his face growing serious. He leaned in close to her ear. "No kissing." When he drew back, the seriousness cracked, like a false wall, and he gave her a deep, genuine smile.

Whatever tension might've been left in her body erupted into a laugh. "Right," she said, looking around at the crowded room of women, all grabbing each other from behind and pretending to kick each other in the family jewels. "No kissing in Combat."

"No kissing in Combat," he agreed.

"That reminds me," Constance said. "I got your reservation back. At my sister's. For Christmas Eve."

"Ah." Rhett's expression was mixed. "Great. Thank you."

"Don't worry. You'll have fun."

"I don't know about fun, but...thanks."

"You're welcome."

"C'mon, Stanzi," Rhett said after her giggles had wound down. "Let's give you a few more chances to escape."

Then he opened his arms and waited.

seventeen

Sunny woke to the smell of aftershave. When she blinked her eyes open, he was nothing but a shadow in the dark, straddling her body. Sunny could feel the ties on her pajama top coming undone. As her sight adjusted, she saw the final tie in between Sean's teeth.

She'd almost forgotten it was Saturday night. Sean, sneaking in after his shift and waking her in a variety of ways, had become an unspoken tradition throughout December. He never woke her the same way twice, but he also never disappointed.

When they were done, they collapsed into darkness and didn't regard each other until they'd satisfied themselves just as greedily with sleep as they had with sex.

The next morning, as she watched Sean dress in silence, she said, "Your buddy is coming here tonight. He'll be getting a massage from my sister before the Christmas Eve dinner."

"Good," Sean said, buttoning his shirt. "I think she's had some kind of effect on him already. He's less grumpy and limpy all around. This should really help fix him up."

"She's really good with her hands," Sunny said. "If he's in pain, she can help."

Sean glanced up from his task but didn't slow. "There's a lot about him she doesn't know."

Sunny sat up in bed, keeping the sheet tight around her chest.

"Don't worry," Sean said, watching her. "He's a good guy. There's just a lot she doesn't know. It's not just physical pain. He's done one too many tours in the fucking sandbox."

Sunny loosened her grip and the sheet fell below her breasts. "Cici has a lot of experience with that. She was at Walter Reed every week for years. Massaging the wounded who came home. All volunteer."

Her naked body caught his eye. "I didn't know that."

"It's the whole reason she became a therapist," Sunny pressed. "My father was closed-off, half-deaf and walked with a cane because of Vietnam. He never let anyone help him, but Cici was able to do it without him knowing. Worked it in, a little at a time, until her foot, leg and shoulder massages became routine."

Sean came over to the bed and sat down on the edge of the mattress. "You've certainly lived up to your end of the bargain."

"And what about yours? You get Janice Matteri's restraining order off my back yet?"

Sean grasped her ankles and pulled her toward him. He leaned over her, renewed hunger in his eyes. "I can't do anything about that. But I am biding my time to send animal control over there when she's not expecting it."

"Really?" Sunny's arousal grew as she pulled him closer. "Then I guess I won't have any reason to steal her dogs."

He silenced her with a rough kiss. Sunny had learned that she could say just about anything to Sean and he wouldn't blink. In fact, the bolder she sounded, the more aroused he seemed to get.

"Not that I was ever stealing her dogs." Sunny undid the

shirt that Sean had just buttoned. "Or other abused and ne-glected pets that I see. I'm totally a law-abiding citizen, De-tective Callahan."

Sean stripped off the bedsheet. He pulled her into his lap. Sunny ran her hands up his stubbly face and sucked his lower lip in between her own. "There's this place out on White Fern Road." In fact, now that she spoke the address out loud, Sunny felt guilty she hadn't made it back out there. "Can you send animal control over there, too?"

"What, you have a list for me now?" Sean's fingertips ran up her spine. "You start throwing more stuff into the pot, I might have to do the same."

Sunny was just about to let things go where they may, even though this would be the first time they had sex that wasn't under the cover of darkness, when she caught a glimpse through the window of Pete's truck, rolling up the drive. "Oh!" She jumped up and grabbed her robe, slipping it around her shoulders while she struggled to get her arms in.

"What's the matter?" Sean's brow creased.

"Pete's here."

"Who's Pete?" Sean looked around the room, like Pete might be hiding somewhere.

"A friend." She got her robe tied and fluffed out her hair. "He's going to finish some decorating for me. For tonight's party. Stuff I can't reach. He helped with all the rest. He helps with everything. Meet you downstairs."

"Um." Sean stood up and started buttoning his shirt again. "Okay."

Pete slammed his truck door, which didn't shut properly because it was dented. It required Pete opening and closing it twice more before it latched. "Morning, Sunshine!" he called as Sunny stepped out.

"Morning!" Pete was the only person Sunny would allow to make that joke. She collected the newspaper from the stoop and straightened her robe. "You're earlier than I thought."

"Some of the new dogs are early risers," Pete agreed. "Decided to get a head start. You can go back to bed, Sleeping Beauty." He nodded toward the house as Sunny approached. Then his gaze shifted to over her shoulder.

Sean had just closed the door behind him. He blinked in the sunshine as he ambled over, straightening the sleeves on his jacket. He stopped next to Sunny and kissed her on the cheek. "Maybe I'll see you later." He turned his gaze to Pete. "Hi."

"Hi." Pete's big grin fell.

Sunny's face went hot. "Pete, this is Sean. Sean, Pete." She did some clumsy gesturing.

They nodded at each other.

"Pete's a knight in shining armor." Sunny gripped his shoulder and squeezed. "Always helping me out when I need something. Been like that since we were kids." Her voice had an odd, high pitch to it. "Right, Pete?"

"Yep."

Sean's gaze went from Sunny's hand on Pete's shoulder to Pete's face and back again. "Sure," he said. He turned to Sunny. "Enjoy your day. Hope you get all your decorations up."

"Great." Why did her voice sound so funny? And why did she say *great*? That didn't even make sense.

After Sean left, Pete turned to her. "Sean a new friend?" He gestured toward the sedan as it disappeared down the road. "I don't remember seeing him before. Though he does seem familiar."

"Yes. New." She didn't feel like getting a second lecture on promiscuity, so she kept her answer short. Luckily, Pete was not the sort to pry.

"All right, then." Pete eyed the giant Douglas fir that

reached all the way up to Sunny's bedroom turret. "So what's our deal? I help you put balls on this sucker and you let me start training the pups in January, right?"

"That's the deal." Sunny nodded toward the ladder that lay on the ground next to the tree. "I'll bring your balls out soon as I'm dressed."

"Speaking of balls." Pete eyed her up and down. "You must be freezing yours off right now." His breath turned to steam as he laughed.

Sunny pulled on the hem of her silky robe but did not succeed in making it cover any more of her bare skin. "Why, yes, I am," she agreed. "Which is why I'm going inside."

By the time Sunny had showered, fixed the coffee and taken a thermos out to Pete, he was already on the ladder, wrapping garland around the fir. "I found it in the foyer," he called from his perch ten feet in the air. "Found your balls, too!" He pointed to the bag of giant ornaments on the ground. Sunny had spied the big balls on clearance after Christmas last year and had bought as many pink ones as she could find.

She gave Pete the thumbs-up. "I brought you some coffee." She peered up at Pete and shielded her eyes from the sun. Despite the cold, he'd peeled off his jacket and had it tied around his waist. His flannel shirt was rolled to his elbows, giving him a rugged look of concentration as he wound the gold garland on the branches.

Pete climbed down the ladder and accepted the thermos. "I know where I've seen him." He pointed toward the end of the driveway, where Sean had disappeared. "I've seen that guy at the police station. When I've gone out to visit Kyle." After a pause Pete clarified, "Kyle, from the K-9 Unit. Your visitor is a cop."

Sunny wasn't sure why she felt a twinge in her stomach. "Maybe."

"He is." Pete nodded. "Everything okay?"

Sunny took the thermos from Pete's hands and opened it. She took a sip, but it burned her tongue. "He's the friend I told you about. Don't worry. Like I said, nobody saw you at the kennel the night we rescued the dogs. They think I beat up the nephew. Not you."

Pete took the thermos back and narrowed his eyes. "I don't care about that. I just want to make sure you're okay." The morning sun played over Pete's face, changing his eyes from light brown to gold and back again. He sipped the coffee, and didn't seem to mind the heat.

"I'm fine." Sunny reached out and squeezed his shoulder again. Only after she did it did she wonder how often she did that. "You know you don't need to worry about me. I got it all under control."

Pete took another drink. Then another. Then he handed her the thermos and winked. "All right, Sunny Skye. Leave your big balls out here and get inside, where it's warm. I'm sure you've got plenty to do before tonight's party."

"Thanks, Pete." Sunny kissed him on the cheek. She didn't pull away as quickly as she expected. He smelled different somehow. His skin felt different, too, under her lips.

"Go." Pete drew away and stepped onto the ladder. "You got all those rich people coming to party. Get to work, girl."

"Right." Sunny smiled. She went inside, but for a few minutes more she watched Pete as he worked the garland around the tree, slowly but surely making her Douglas fir bright and happy.

The grounds were decked out in full, tasteful Christmas glory. A single live pine wreath, complete with red berries and bows and electric candles, adorned each window of the house. The twelve-foot-tall Douglas fir on the north lawn had been decorated with white lights and large balls in ecru and pale pink. The grand foyer had another large Christmas tree, this one with fat, colored bulbs, bubbling lights, Victorian Santas and old-fashioned ornaments that hinted at years gone by. Garland wound the railings and the air had a subtle hint of pine.

Sunny wore a fashionable dress in a red-and-black checkered pattern that clung to her slender body. "You remember, now that you made me give him your room, you have nowhere to stay." She pushed her golden hair behind her ear and fixed Constance with a stern look.

"I don't care." Constance, wearing her navy blue scrubs, looked far less classy than her sister. What else was new? "If I choose to sleep here tonight, I can sleep in the massage room. Or on your floor."

"Uh-uh." Sunny shook her head. "You're not sleeping in my room. I know what you're like since Daddy died and Josh left. You don't sleep. You toss and turn, call out, wake in night sweats. Unless I get you drunk. Hmm." She pinched her chin with her thumb and forefinger. "That's an idea."

"I can just go home. After work." Constance reached down to pet Fezzi's ears. He sat like a perfect gentleman just outside the kitchen. He could smell the big Christmas Eve feast being prepared but didn't beg for it like a normal dog. He waited outside the kitchen for anyone to walk by and notice what a gentleman he was. Those who were charmed by his no-begging begging would go back in and fetch him some scraps as a reward. His missing leg only helped his case. "Oh!" the rich women would coo. "Look at the good boy. And he's only got one leg, poor thing. Oh, James, grab me some of that meat from the appetizers for the cute boy."

It was a brilliant plan. He wouldn't even need his dog food tonight.

"You will not go home." Sunny's eyes narrowed. "You already told Rhett that you'll be at the dinner, right? You can't let him down."

"I did. He seemed happy about that. He'll have someone to talk to that won't insist on mindless pleasantries and witty banter."

Sunny rolled her eyes. "You two are a match made in heaven."

Constance waved her comment away, even though it gave her a quick flash of unexpected jitters. "I've got a full day. And so do you." She grabbed the stack of intake forms for the massages lined up.

"True. I need to make sure everything's going well in the kitchen." Sunny clacked away on her high heels, off to inspect the meal being prepped by two close friends who were chefs. Much of the food had also been donated. Sunny knew somebody everywhere, which was one of the reasons she'd been so successful. If there was one thing Sunny had always known how to do it was schmooze, to get what she wanted, when she wanted it.

Constance took the forms to the massage room and sat down at the desk in the corner to leaf through them. She needed to make sure no one had absolute contraindications that would end a massage before it got started. Most seemed like no-brainers, but Constance had seen clients show up with everything from the flu to poison ivy, expecting the massage to go on as usual.

Everything seemed pretty straightforward, with her day booked from morning to just before dinner, with a one-hour lunch break built in.

When she got to her last form, the five o'clock, Constance saw Rhett's name. So, he hadn't canceled it. He also hadn't mentioned it, which meant Sunny was probably right: he'd filled this form out weeks back and forgotten about it.

She scanned the form. Rhett Santos was thirty-four years old, took no medications and had no allergies. He listed no conditions, but under "soft tissue/joint dysfunction" he'd checked the box for right leg. Under miscellaneous, there were boxes he could've checked for stress or insomnia, but neither was ticked. Nowhere did he indicate he had PTSD or TBI.

Constance knew the next thing she should do was text Rhett and let him know she was his massage therapist for this afternoon. But then he'd probably cancel it. She'd had good success with his leg twice, feeling the release and the relief she'd been able to provide much more than he'd let on with his words. But she also knew he wouldn't be eager to do full body, especially if it was a surprise.

Text, or no text?

Quit being so professional and just help my stupid leg.

Constance shrugged. "I can do that."

Rhett coached a morning class on Christmas Eve, which was packed to the gills and had equipment all over the place, followed by two personal training sessions. The first was with Kitty, who'd refused Zoe as her trainer and agreed to pay the outlandish fee Rhett charged for a one-on-one that was more of a deterrent than a way to make big money. She wanted to work on clean and jerks, which went about the way Rhett predicted. Despite the cold air, she wore booty shorts and a sports bra the entire time. Rhett suggested a T-shirt when she started shivering, and trimming her long nails when she couldn't execute a proper hook grip, but Kitty did neither.

She also couldn't clean and jerk. But Rhett did his best, staying patient and keeping her weight to the PVC pipe for half the session and the training bar for the other half. She dropped a few hints about getting drinks later, which Rhett skillfully dodged.

His second one-on-one was with Tatiana, who was the complete opposite of Kitty. Tatiana was strong and a decent lifter, but she had limited range of motion and didn't like to take criticism, so her progress suffered from both. Her voice was an octave deeper than the last time he'd done a private session with her. *Steroids won't replace daily stretching, enough recovery time and taking the feedback of the people you pay to help you*, Rhett wanted to say. He took the time to filter his thoughts and said, "No amount of overtraining will replace the benefits of increasing your range of motion through the daily exercises I've given you, proper rest so your muscles can heal and actually listening to and taking the feedback that you pay me for."

Tatiana's jaw dropped, like she'd expected a little more Christmas cheer. But all she said was, "Yes, Coach. I'm gonna rest for the next few days. I promise."

Once everyone cleared out, the chaos was over and everything was quiet. Rhett knew he should do himself a favor by catching some z's before he went to this stupid Christmas party, but he knew as soon as he got to that filmy membrane that separated sleep from consciousness, he'd start to think about things. His pulse would rise and he'd sweat. He'd toss and turn and get so frustrated he'd find the nearest thing to throw against the wall. He'd broken more than one cell phone that way.

Instead, he went home and packed an overnight bag. Which meant he threw some clean underwear and his toothbrush in a duffel. He glanced at his watch and saw that he could check in anytime. Rather than mill aimlessly about the house, he fired up the Jeep and headed out to Pittie Place. The only reason he was going to see this through was because Stanzi would be there. He wondered what she would wear, and when he pictured her in a Larry Bird T-shirt and a cat barrette he broke into laughter.

The place was dressed to the nines in Christmas stuff, but it was classy Christmas stuff. None of those inflatable creatures or flashing lights. Pittie Place, even though it was a dog rescue, sparkled in the twilight like it was festooned in crystal. The parking lot was packed, but Rhett managed to find a spot for his Jeep that was farthest from the house.

The foyer was warm and smelled like mulled cider. A willowy blonde sat at a makeshift desk near the staircase. "Hi." She greeted him with a wide smile. "Are you here for the charity dinner? The guests are already out back, touring the rescue."

"Yes. Name's Rhett Santos."

A long pause followed. "Mr. Santos." She looked him up and down, and didn't even try to disguise it. "Welcome." She had bright blue eyes that were just a shade darker than Stanzi's. "I'm Sunny Morrigan. I'm happy you decided to join us for the holiday."

"Thanks." Rhett took his time studying Stanzi's sister. She was taller, thinner, had no trace of the strawberry in her blond hair and had a brand of confidence that was different from Stanzi's. While Stanzi's was quiet and resolute, Sunny's was bold and bright, like her name.

"You'll be staying upstairs." Sunny held out a brass key. Not a key card, but an actual key. She pointed to the winding staircase, the banister roped in red lights and red garland. "Top of the stairs, to the right."

"Thanks." Rhett took the key. "No cabin?"

She tucked her lips into an apologetic smile. "I'm afraid that after you canceled, the cabin was snapped up. The room upstairs was all I had available."

"No problem." Rhett noticed that none of the guests, many of whom milled in and out of the foyer and the sitting room with the large fireplace, went upstairs. In fact, the front of the staircase was cordoned off with a padded rope, like you'd find in a fancy theater. "I think I like that better."

"Excellent." Her apologetic smile turned a little wry. "The massage room is just around the corner here." She pointed past the staircase. "Your appointment is at five. Drinks and hors d'oeuvres will be served in the great room—" she nodded toward the roaring fireplace "—at six, and dinner is in the dining room at seven."

The massage. Rhett had forgotten all about that. He'd filled out the intake form weeks ago, before he'd canceled. His hand ran absentmindedly over his thigh, which felt stiff and icy. "About the massage—"

"Oh, you can't cancel now," Sunny interrupted, her voice kind but stern, like you'd talk to a toddler. "I could have filled your slot with five other people. Don't worry. My therapist is the best in the county."

Rhett bit back his words. Something about this woman kept him from being as harsh and forward as he could with the likes of Tatiana, and just about everyone else. "Five o'clock," he said.

"And don't forget, for this evening, ugly sweaters are encouraged, but not required."

Ugly sweaters? Sunny wore a striking dress that highlighted her long legs. Rhett had packed jeans and a button-down, and not much more. He'd literally sweat through a sweater in a matter of minutes. "Thank you." Rhett grabbed his duffel bag. He was pretty sure Sunny smirked at it as he made his way to the staircase. She gestured for him to unclip the barrier that closed off the stairs. Rhett undid the metal clasp, then closed it behind him. Sunny gave him the thumbs-up, then turned and headed into the great room.

The metal key slid into the large lock on the heavy wooden door and made a clicking sound when he turned it to the right. He pressed the door open to a room that smelled faintly of roses and vanilla. There was a four-poster queen bed in the center of the room, surrounded by curved windows. Rhett realized he was inside the tower that was farthest to the back of the house. The windows overlooked the garden, most of which had been turned over, but there was also a large greenhouse. It was a great view, even in winter; the ice on the trees gave everything a frosty glitter. In the spring, he imagined it sang with fresh blooms and insects and all sorts of life.

He peeked in the bathroom and saw a tub with claw feet and a deep, old-fashioned sink. He dropped his toothbrush there and went back to the main room, where he flopped on the bed. He closed his eyes and tried to breathe deep into his belly, slowly, for counts of ten. But sleep would not come. The silence made him feel almost itchy. He popped in his earbuds and started a fitness podcast, trying to focus on the main points and secretly hoping that he'd doze off.

No such luck. Before Rhett knew it, it was ten minutes to five. He sighed and made his way downstairs. The foyer was packed with people, coming and going in and out of the great room. Some were well dressed and others wore a wide range of ugly sweaters, everything from Santas in sequins to sweaters that actually flashed with lights.

Rhett hopped over the barrier at the bottom of the stairs and slipped around the corner to where Sunny said the massage room was. The wooden door had a glass insert that read Healing Touch Massage. It was ajar, so Rhett poked his head in. The room was lit with an assortment of electric candles. There was a table in the center, freshly made, and soft spa music was playing. It smelled of lavender and eucalyptus.

Rhett stepped inside and looked around, but nobody else was there. He sat down on a rolling stool and sighed. This wasn't going to go well. He pictured himself lying there, wanting to toss and turn but unable to because a stranger would be rubbing lotion on his body and questioning him about his scars. The more he thought about it, the more anxious he got.

He rolled around the room, to keep his legs busy, and checked out all the stuff. There was a towel warmer, the power light on, a small sound system, stacks of clean linens and a rolling laundry basket with discarded ones. In a cabinet, behind glass, was an assortment of small jars with rubber stoppers, oils, creams and lotions.

After he'd seen all there was to see, Rhett stood up and headed for the door. Just as he pulled it open, she came walking in, stopping just shy of slamming into his chest.

Rhett almost laughed. Of course. Why hadn't he put two and two together?

Stanzi stared up at him, her hair pulled back in a pretty but professional barrette in a solid gold color. She wore blue scrubs and looked better to Rhett than any of those women in their tight dresses or flashing sweaters.

"Hi." She held out her hand, a guilty crook to her mouth. "I'm Constance. I'll be your massage therapist today."

eighteen

Rhett perched on the edge of the massage table and Constance settled herself on her rolling stool, which had been moved. She pictured Rhett, rolling around the room, unable to sit still even when he was sitting. She looked down at her clipboard, which held his intake form. "So no medications or allergies?"

"Nope."

"Not pregnant?"

He smiled. "I'm pretty sure."

Constance could tell her joke had defused some tension. Now to pose her next question, in just the right way. "Anything you didn't mark that I should know about?"

"Sure." He pressed his hands on the edge of the table and leaned forward a little. "How about 'If your name happens to be Constance, give me a text and let me know you'll be my massage therapist today.'"

Constance looked up and saw he was doing the smile that

was contained mostly in his eyes. That meant he found humor in this, but didn't want her know it. "I should have texted," she agreed. "But, had I texted, would you have canceled?"

"Probably."

"So I made the right choice."

"I could still leave. My leg feels fine. I don't really need to waste your time."

"Your leg doesn't feel fine. And there are other issues I could address. You wouldn't be wasting my time."

"Oh, yeah?" Rhett's voice had a challenging edge. "Like what?"

Constance rose and stepped closer to him. She studied his face, his posture and his energy. "You're exhausted." She noted the fatigue around his eyes. "My guess is you have trouble sleeping most of the time. One of the reasons you love your job is that it takes you here—" she held up a hand, over her head "—so that when you come back down to here—" her hand sank to eye level "—it feels normal. Even though you should be here." Her hand went near her heart.

"Hmm." Rhett made a noncommittal noise. "And how did you get all that? Are you reading my aura?"

"I don't see auras." Constance brushed off his comment as a rare show of self-defense. "But energy is real, and I've had a lot of experience with it. Yours is big, like most introverts. But it's even bigger than most introverts. Bigger than most people I've met."

His eyes widened just the tiniest bit, like she'd said something that interested him and he hadn't reacted quickly enough to hide it. "Big? I thought introverts were supposed to be anti-social wallflowers, collapsing in on ourselves."

Constance noted the sarcasm. "Quite the opposite. It's my experience that introverts have big, wide-reaching energy. We absorb more, and if we're not careful, we take in more than we want. Some of us have too much energy, which makes us overly sensitive to our surroundings. Extroverts, on the other hand, have to absorb energy from others in order to function at their best. Which is why they love groups and can't be alone and all that noise. Most of us are a mix of the two. You—" Constance held up her hands near Rhett's chest "—start well outside your body. This keeps you strong without needing a lot of fuel from the outside world. That's good. But it also leaves you vulnerable to taking in things you might not want to, and to reacting stronger, and harder, than those who have duller senses. It's helped you survive. That's its purpose. And I'm guessing it's served you well. But when you don't need to be in survival mode, it can be exhausting."

Rhett grew quiet, twiddling his thumbs as he stared down at his hands.

"Right now, everything about you is a bit…" Constance drew a deep breath and let it out in a sigh, gesturing with her arms in a dropping motion. "Like that. You need to recharge."

Rhett looked up at her with narrowed eyes, all sarcasm in his face gone. "And you can help me do that?" He swallowed hard, his Adam's apple bobbing.

Constance stopped herself from saying yes. She couldn't make a definitive promise, so her words had to be chosen carefully. "Your sympathetic nervous system is in overdrive. My job is to get you into parasympathetic. That's easier to do with some than others. But I'd love to try."

A soft smile played around his lips. He spread his hands open. "You're great with the leg. But this is different. Some things just can't be fixed, Stanzi."

Constance leaned next to him, against the massage table. "I had this guy I used to see every week, at Walter Reed. The first week I met him, all he would let me do is hold his head in my hands while he lay faceup on the table. We stayed like that for the full half hour. Just a blanket over his body, music in the air and my hands supporting his head. He barely relaxed." Constance watched Rhett's eyes change. Usually, he had some form of guard up. Now, she could see him opening. "Week two, same thing. But by the end of the session he'd relaxed enough I could feel his weight grow heavier. Week three, he fell asleep about twenty minutes in. Week four, he let me move around to other places, just putting my hands on his shoulders, his arms. No massaging, just placing my hands on him. It went like this for months. By the time he went home, I was able to do light massage over his clothes and he called me by name. He even gave me a hug goodbye."

Rhett sucked in his lower lip. He looked around the room. After a while in silence, he turned back to her and shrugged. "Okay. I'm all yours."

Constance started with a warm towel to his back. This would begin the massage on a relaxing note. She checked in with Rhett once, who gave one-word answers to her questions about being comfortable and the temperature of the table, and then went quiet. She let the music fill the room. For the first few minutes, she didn't even touch him. Just as she'd massaged Humphrey, Constance worked only the energy that lived several inches above Rhett's body before she finally rested her hands on his back. His muscles twitched as she neared, but once she finally laid her palms on his bare skin, he didn't resist.

Over time, she slowly deepened her pressure. This was the first time she'd seen Rhett with his shirt off, so was the first time she saw the tattoo he had on his heavily muscled upper back, between the shoulder blades. He had a cross there, the horizontal portion done in Celtic knot-work and the vertical portion in colorful Mexican tiles. The center read USMC.

Constance hadn't seen one like it, and she'd seen a lot of tattoos. The unique blend of cultures and affinities suggested Rhett had had a hand in creating it himself.

The lower portion of his back had several scars on the left side, the most lateral one a circular shape. Constance slipped her hands around the front. As she suspected, there was a similar scar there, just outside the obliques. She didn't touch him there right away, just swiped over the wound a few times before finally giving a light massage to the affected tissue.

Constance worked Rhett's back longer than most clients. She found tension in all the muscles along his spine, which was no surprise, based on all the heavy gear he'd have worn for years. Despite that, she kept her touch medium. This session wasn't the time to go deep, risk him bracing or focusing on breathing to keep his mind off the pain.

He did that every day.

This session, Constance aimed to focus on flow, energy transfer and rhythm. She let her own mind go, feeding into the movements and allowing her body and his to guide her strokes and pressure. She covered his back and moved on to his left leg, adjusting the drape for modesty. When it came to lifting the legs to undrape, there were two types that always tried to help: women and military men. Constance usually told people up front that they didn't need to help support any part of their bodies during the massage but that had slipped her mind this time.

Rhett's leg was dead weight. She draped and adjusted him carefully, then watched him breathe for about fifteen seconds. Just a quarter of the way into the session and Rhett was out. Constance could tell by the stillness and weight of his body and pattern of his breathing that he was fast asleep. Many people did fall asleep during massage, which was normal. Most did not go quite that quickly.

She smoothed some oil in long strokes onto his leg and up into his hamstrings, which were large and strong, before moving into the hip muscles, finding tightness in the glute med but not so much in the lateral rotators. Just like with his back, Constance worked with medium pressure and focused on flow and energy, noting that her breathing was in time with his own.

Once in a while, Rhett twitched in his sleep, but that was the closest he came to waking, even when Constance covered his left leg and moved on to his right. When she was done, she slipped out the bolster under his ankles, straightened the sheets and blanket and came up near his shoulder. His back rose and fell with deep, slow breaths.

Worst part of the massage, every time, was waking a client to roll over. But you only got so much time on the table and nobody wanted to waste it. Constance leaned in close to his ear and whispered, "Rhett."

Nothing.

"All right, then." Constance put one fist on his shoulder, the other on his hip, and rhythmically rocked his body while he snoozed. Rocking was a legitimate finishing stroke in Swedish massage. At the end of the day, she had to be a body detective and give each client what he needed most. Her mind went back to the countless massages she'd done at Walter Reed, on the many, many service members who'd come home injured. Every case was different, everyone an individual. Her gut told her that this was what Rhett needed most.

After a while, Constance eased up the rocking and found her stool. She settled down and closed her eyes. When his body was ready, he would stir.

Sometime later, her own mind caught between a medita-tive state and the first wisps of sleep, Constance heard rustling. She opened her eyes and saw Rhett, up on his forearms, peering around the room.

"Rise and shine, sleepyhead."

Rhett grasped the sheets and rolled over on his back. He blinked up at her. "How long have I been out?"

Constance looked at the clock on the wall, behind the table, where clients couldn't see it during the massage. She was surprised it was 6:15. "You fell asleep about fifteen minutes into the massage. So you've been out about an hour."

He folded his hands beneath his head, propping himself up a little farther, and sighed. He offered a wry smile. "Aren't you supposed to do the other side?"

She rose and stood over him. "Typically. But it felt like a crime to wake you." With his arms bare, Constance got a look at the tattoo on the inside of his left bicep, which she'd only had a glimpse of from beneath the sleeve of his T-shirts. Now that it was completely uncovered she could see the all-black ink tribal-style wild horse. The mustang was in motion, left foreleg raised, his mane and tail whipping out to the side like flames.

Rhett followed her gaze, his eyes sleepy. "Outer Banks wild horse. Back in the day. They're mostly gone now. One day when I was a kid, I was playing in my backyard. Two of them appeared out of nowhere and started playing, winding their necks around each other. Gave real meaning to the phrase 'horsing around.' I just sat and watched them until they took off running. As more and more vacationers came down over the years, they started getting hit by cars in big numbers. They've moved the remaining ones to sanctuary."

"That's a great memory. Sad about the horses, though."

"It is." Rhett's voice was gravelly with sleep. "Eventually everything wild gets taken out by the modern world."

Constance offered a sad smile.

"No comment?" he said. "You don't like tattoos?"

"I do." She shrugged. "I like yours, anyway. But I can't comment on them. That could be considered sexual harassment."

Rhett stared at her a moment before the corners of his mouth turned up and his body started shaking with silent laughter. "Okay," he said. "Well, I won't tell."

"Hey, don't laugh," Constance said, even though she smiled. "We have to work our asses off to be taken seriously in this profession. Not only is there the stereotype of the illicit 'massage parlor,' we've got physical therapists and chiropractors who often don't take us seriously, either. Even though, depending on how much continuing education and experience we get, we can be quite knowledgeable. And often have more freedom than other professions to try different things, because insurance companies and Big Pharma don't have us in their pockets."

"Eh, you don't have to convince me. I've seen—and felt—you in action."

Constance smiled. "Mission accomplished today," she said. "I got you into parasympathetic, big-time. Do you want me to do anything else? Your hour's up, but it's my fault I let you sleep. Cocktails are well under way out there." She nodded toward the door. "But I'll do your front if you want."

"Oh, no." Rhett rolled his eyes in mock disappointment. "We're missing cocktails."

Constance laughed. "At least let me do your neck." She plopped down on her stool and rolled around behind him. She lowered the face cradle, squirted some warming liquid into her hands, rubbed them together and slid them under Rhett's shoulders. "With the tension you had in your lower back, and the issue with your leg, I know you're going to have neck issues. We all do."

"I'm sure I've got issues."

Constance let the weight of his body sink into her fingers

as she drew her hands upward. "Don't help." Now that he was fully awake, he was trying to raise his head for her. "Just lie there. That's all you need to do."

Rhett chuckled, but kept whatever amused him to himself.

Constance warmed up his neck with palm strokes, then slowly worked deeper. He had more tension than she'd expected, even though she'd expected plenty. Rhett's breathing changed, like he was focusing on keeping still and letting her work. She moved down to his upper traps, which were bulky and tight. He gave an audible, contented sigh. Constance worked them until they were like putty, then smoothed her hands back up his neck and beneath his head, where she held him in traction. She slipped her fingers into his hair and rubbed his scalp in slow, deep circles.

"Don't go back to sleep," she said with a giggle. "We've already missed cocktails."

"I'm not sleepy anymore," Rhett said. "But that feels amazing. You can do it as long as you want. I don't need cocktails."

"What?" Constance joked. "It doesn't feel 'not horrible'?"

Rhett laughed a deep, genuine laugh.

By the time Constance finished, the clock read 6:36. "Take your time getting up. I'm going to go change for dinner. Sunny will kill me if I show up in scrubs."

Rhett sat up and stretched, turning his head from left to right.

"How do you feel?"

He winked at her. "Not horrible."

nineteen

Rhett had to admit, he was impressed by the Christmas Eve banquet. The dining room had its own tree, decorated in the annual Christmas ornaments sold by the White House Historical Association, and poinsettias on every table. A professional harp player sat in the corner, playing angelic Christmas music. The dinner fare included standing rib roast, Yorkshire puddings, salad, potatoes and dark chocolate cakes shaped like old-fashioned Christmas puddings. People were lined up out the door to fill their plates.

Rhett took a drink of his beer, which he'd gotten from the bar, and searched the crowded room for Stanzi. He hoped to catch a glimpse of her strawberry hair, pulled back with cat barrettes, and her curvy body, growing stronger every time he saw her, dressed in either scrubs or a unicorn T-shirt. But all he saw were other people, many of whom looked like they came from money. Even their ugly sweaters managed to look designer.

Instead of getting annoyed, or breaking a sweat, Rhett took

the crowd in stride. He had to admit, he hadn't felt this way in a long time. It was hard to pinpoint what was different, but the closest he could come was to say that he felt level. Not too high, not too low. Hungry, relaxed and alert, without being edgy. His body was in less pain than it had been in years, an overall tightness to everything that he hadn't even realized he'd been carrying around, now diminished.

He almost felt content. Just to be; even if all he was doing was standing there in a roomful of strangers, during a time of year that had lost most of its meaning for him. It was kind of weird, feeling this way, but Rhett wasn't going to complain. With the line long and Stanzi nowhere in sight, he headed for the foyer to get some air. He had his head down, admiring the shine to the old wooden floor. When he looked up again, his strides halted.

She stood by herself, just inside the entrance, scanning the crowd.

Whoa. Rhett wasn't sure if he thought it or spoke aloud, until a guy next to him said, "No kidding." He stared at Stanzi, who wore a knee-length blue dress with fluttery little sleeves that showed off her arms. A modest pair of heels made her calves pop and the scoop neck revealed creamy, smooth skin. Her hair had been styled with a few big waves and it looked, as Rhett drew near, like her full lips were dotted with something tinted and shiny.

"Hi," she said, sounding out of breath. She scanned him up and down and smiled at his jeans and button-down shirt. "I've never seen you in anything but T-shirts and shorts."

"Yeah." Rhett tried to find his voice. The awkward girl in the My Pretty Pony shirt was nowhere to be seen. Dressed up like this, in clothes that actually fit, Rhett felt she was giving him a peek at her personality outside of the gym. The pretty blue Christmas dress was like the shiny wrapping on a present that you knew held something amazing inside.

"What's wrong with you?" Stanzi narrowed her eyes and waved a hand in front of his face.

Rhett shook his head and laughed. She sounded genuinely concerned. "Nothing. I'm just hungry. Starving actually." He realized he was still staring at her, so he quickly cleared his throat. "For the…the food. C'mon. Your sister went all out." He nodded toward the buffet.

Stanzi followed him toward the food line, which had dwindled.

Rhett guided her in front of him, and they took their time loading their plates, taking a little of everything. The place was packed with people chowing down, but they managed to find a table near the window that seated only two. "Your sister knows what she's doing," Rhett said, an unusual nervousness in his gut that he kept covered by talking about the food. But his statement was the truth: the meat was rare, the puddings crisp and flavorful, the salad not overdressed, the potatoes creamy.

"Sunny doesn't cook." Stanzi laughed. "Unless you ask her to mix dog food." She ate a bite of meat and potatoes. "Great businesswoman, though. I'll give her that. And, of course, amazing with the dogs."

"The two of you are alike. But different."

Stanzi's chewing slowed, as if she were considering that. "Yeah. Sunny's a lot like my mom was. Bright and perky and comes right at you. I'm more like my dad."

"Which is how?"

"Well." Stanzi's fork stopped, poised in front of her lips. "My father lost most of his hearing in Vietnam. He came home legally deaf. According to Mom, he could've used hearing aids but he learned sign language instead. Nobody else was really willing to learn, so Daddy didn't talk much, because when he did, everyone had to practically shout. Mom said I learned sign language from Daddy and was proficient at it before I was proficient at speaking—because I adored my father and would do anything for his attention. It wasn't until I was an adult that I realized that Daddy used his hearing loss to tune out the world. He liked it that way. He didn't miss anything, but he didn't have to hear all the noise, either. But—" she got a sly smile on her face "—he had to talk to me more than anyone, because I knew sign language."

"So what you're saying is—" Rhett thought it through "—you learned early on how to communicate without words. To absorb everything going on around you, without much noise."

Stanzi smiled. "To be honest, I don't know what I was trying to say…until you just said it. I guess I learned early on that we can learn most of what we need to know from other people in silence. More than eighty percent of communication is nonverbal. I mean, the reason I learned to cook was the only surefire way I had to my father's heart was with food. He never raved over anything I made, mind you, but I knew he loved and appreciated it. He'd never take a damn thing from me, but he couldn't refuse my food. Dinner, lunch, dessert—he'd eat it all. I couldn't make him praise me, go easy on me or even talk to me, but I could make him eat, dammit."

Rhett polished off the crumbs on his plate. "This is good food, but yours is even better." At the sly look on her face, he insisted, "I mean it. I'm not blowing smoke up your ass."

"Like you've ever done that." Stanzi rolled her eyes.

"Speaking of. You didn't show up for the workout this morning."

"I know. I've been here all day. I've done nine massages, though, so I think that counts."

"Eight and a half." Rhett arched an eyebrow at her.

Stanzi laughed and threw her napkin at him. "I'll get the rest of you later, I promise."

"Nine seems like a lot for one day." Rhett looked around at the crowd. "How do you fit them all in? All the donors get a massage, right?"

"Oh, hell, no." Stanzi shook her head. "Just the people who book a cabin. That's eight." She tilted her head toward him. "You make nine. The rest of these people donated to the rescue just to come to the party."

"That's a lot of donations."

"I know. I told you, Sunny's got a knack for this stuff. C'mon, let's get more food." She rose with her empty plate, and Rhett was happy to follow. They even helped themselves to the puddings this time, which turned out to be rich, decadent chocolate that needed the shot of whipped cream on the side.

"I think I'm officially full." Stanzi scraped her fork around the chocolate crumbs left on the plate. "But give me about an hour and we'll see."

Rhett finished the beer he'd been nursing and looked around. The room had emptied out considerably. The harpist was packing up her things and louder, peppier music was just revving up from somewhere else in the house. "What now?"

"The party's downstairs." Stanzi pointed at the floor. "Sunny renovated the lower level into this huge party area, with a bar and a place for a band or DJ."

Just the thought would normally send Rhett to his room for the night, but this time he rose, stretched and said, "Let's check it out."

They pushed their way through the crowded foyer and downstairs to the party area. Like the rest of the house, the room had a lot of wood, though the walls had been done in stone. It almost looked like something out of the late 1800s, except for the DJ, in the far corner, spinning out everything from Christmas tunes to classic rock. The air smelled of pine and sugarplums, which probably came from the fresh greenery and the big bowls of punch at the bar.

They made their way over and sampled cups of the brew, which turned out to be stronger than Rhett expected. Stanzi took about half of hers, fast, and held the tiny cup in both hands. He guessed she didn't quite enjoy crowds and noise much, either.

"By request," the DJ's smooth voice came over the speakers, "Anne Murray."

A slow country song started to play—"Could I Have This Dance"—causing Rhett and Stanzi to exchange confused glances. The abrupt change in tempo had everyone scrambling to either pair up or get off the dance floor and have a drink.

Rhett eyed Stanzi, still rolling her cup around. He extended his hand.

She looked at it, blinked, then looked up at his face and blinked again.

"What? You don't know how to waltz?"

"Wait. What?" She set her cup on the bar and fiddled with her hair. "Waltz?"

"Sure." Rhett nodded toward the handful of couples who were starting to push around the floor. "This song is a waltz. Somebody's favorite." He nodded toward a couple with gray hair who were moving so well together they had to have danced a million times in each other's arms. "Maybe them."

"I, um… No. I don't. I don't dance. Do you?"

"A little."

Stanzi twisted her lips into a wry smile. "Okay. Show me."

Rhett took her hand and guided her to an outside corner, where they wouldn't run into the people gliding around the floor. He settled her left hand on his shoulder and took her right hand in his left. "Come in a little closer. We can't be that far apart to dance."

A soft ridge of pink colored her cheeks as she stepped in, close enough Rhett caught a whiff of a bright, rosy scent, not unlike his room upstairs. "We'll just do a simple country-western waltz, since this is a country-western song. You're going to step back with your right foot first, just as my left goes forward. Then your left will step parallel to your right. Then your right will close with your left. It's a little box step. Light and airy, up on the balls of your feet. Just think one-two-three, one-two-three, with the downbeat on one."

Stanzi held tightly to his shoulder as he guided her out to the floor. She counted silently, her lips moving, as Rhett spoke the tempo. "Back, side, together…back, side, together." At first, she stumbled and her steps were a little clunky, but after one lap around the dance floor she started to let go, her body taking over.

She looked up at him for the first time, her eyes bright and questioning, looking for approval. "Not horrible," Rhett said, noting that she trembled slightly. He resisted the urge to draw her in, to feel that soft tremor against his own body. Not only did he not want to mess her up, he wasn't confident how his own body would react if he held her that close. "Now try to add a rise at each count and a fall between counts. Like this." Rhett added the rhythm of the hips and feet that gave the waltz its elegant lift.

Stanzi went back to counting beneath her breath, her sweet, flowery scent enhanced by a light sheen of sweat that warmed her body wherever Rhett touched it. He slid the hand that was on her shoulder down to her lower back, drawing her a little closer, despite the warning in his head.

"How'd you learn this?" Her voice was soft and tentative. "Your mom?"

"Yeah, Mama taught me this stuff early. You're not the only one who had to take care of their baby sister."

Stanzi smiled, her lips no longer counting, her body gliding more smoothly, the hand he held in his damp with sweat and squeezing tight.

Just as the song wound down, they neared the edge of the bar. Rhett slowed his steps, but wasn't quick to let go. The hand on her lower back tightened a little, his urge to draw her against him, inhale all those scents and press her warm, damp body against his almost too much to resist.

"So, when I asked if you knew how to dance and you said 'a little,' you were being sarcastic."

"You're in trouble if they play salsa."

She smiled, but didn't pull away.

"May I cut in?"

The words took a beat to register. The tone, however, was quick to stab him directly to the core. The hair on the back of his neck rose. *It couldn't be.*

Stanzi released him, her blue eyes big and questioning as she turned in the direction of the voice. Rhett reluctantly let her go and turned to the sound of the bold, shrill notes.

"Rhett? It is you! What are you doing here?"

There she stood, towering over Stanzi in her four-inch heels, her brunette hair waving down her back and her eyes on fire with both determination and jealousy.

Katrina.

twenty

From across the room, Sunny watched as a tall brunette grabbed Rhett by the front of his shirt, drew him in and planted a long, hard kiss on his mouth. After a second, Rhett took her by the wrists and pushed her back.

"Who the hell is that?" Sunny whispered, close to Pete's ear. "I don't recall her being at the tour of the grounds earlier."

Pete shrugged. It looked like he smiled a little bit.

"I'm going to get closer." Sunny pushed her way through the crowd, until she was close enough to listen in, but still hidden.

The woman was about six feet tall with her heels on—still shorter than Rhett but well taller than Constance. She seemed to enjoy the height difference as she looked down her nose. Her black dress, which was most definitely not an ugly sweater, clung to well-muscled curves.

"What are you doing here, Katrina?" Rhett's brow wrinkled, his eyes still blinking, like he was seeing things.

"More like, what're you doing here?" Katrina dropped the arm that held a fancy gold clutch, but the other hand remained planted on her slender hip. "My mother donates regularly to this dog rescue—" Katrina waved her clutch around the room "—but she couldn't make the party this year. I came instead." She turned to Constance and pointed the gold purse in her direction. "Who's this?"

Just then, the music started back up. Hip-hop replaced Anne Murray, so Sunny couldn't hear the answer, but she saw Rhett's mouth moving as he gestured in Constance's direction.

Katrina looked blank for a second. Then she held out her hand. Constance clasped her fingertips.

Pete was suddenly at Sunny's side. He tugged on her elbow. "You're eavesdropping."

"This woman doesn't care about my rescue." Sunny narrowed her eyes in Katrina's direction. "She's using her mother's ticket. I don't like her."

"What I meant was—" Pete eyed all the happy, tipsy, rich people and pulled Sunny in her sister's direction "—if you're going to eavesdrop, do it right." He smoothed out his ugly sweater, which had a group of drunken reindeer on the front, threaded her through the people dancing and halted next to Constance. "How's it going, guys?"

Rhett's eyes were hard. Constance wasn't quite the stereotypical deer in the headlights; she was more like a deer trying to *recover* from the headlights. Katrina eyed Pete's sweater with distaste.

"Hey, Pete." Looking relieved, Constance leaned in for a hug. "Haven't seen you tonight."

Pete squeezed her shoulder as they embraced. When they broke apart, he extended his hand toward Rhett. "Name's Pete."

"Hey." Rhett clasped his hand. "Rhett Santos. Nice to meet you."

"Pete runs Canine Warriors," Sunny piped in. "He trains rescue pups to be service dogs for veterans. Were you able to see his demo this afternoon, out back?" She nodded toward the vicinity of the grounds and kennels.

"I missed that." The corners of Rhett's mouth turned down. "Sounds really interesting, though." He looked torn between wanting to be polite to Pete and wanting to get away from the tall brunette who appraised everyone with cool detachment.

"I'll take you out there tomorrow." Constance offered a small smile. "If you want."

"I need a drink," Katrina said, her voice abrupt. "Let's get a drink." She nodded toward the bar.

Constance scanned the room, like she was looking for escape.

"I don't want a drink," Rhett said.

Katrina's eyebrows, perfectly plucked and shaped, knitted together. "Are you back on the meds?" Her voice sounded hopeful.

The muscles at the front of Rhett's neck tightened as his jaw clenched. "No. I'm *not* back on the meds."

"I'm not going to lecture you. But you know you should be on the meds." She gave Constance a pitying smile. "He's a mess when he's not on his meds." She patted his chest.

"You don't know what you're talking about."

"Let's not fight. Let's get a drink." Katrina took his arm and turned away from the group, trying to guide him toward the punch bowl. "A good bourbon buzz always beats lying awake, listening to the spiders talk, right?"

Rhett's face paled.

Pete worked his jaw in silence.

Constance made a little gasp that Sunny was sure no one

else heard. A second later she was off, her legs taking her as fast as she could go in the high heels she wasn't used to, wobbling through the center of the dance floor and up the stairs to the main level.

"Excuse me." Sunny went after her. Much more used to high heels, she quickly took the stairs and caught up to her sister. "Slow down." Sunny took her by the arm.

"Where's Fezzi?" Constance scanned the room, but Fezzi wasn't snoozing anywhere obvious, his belly full on the many treats given him tonight. "I'm going home."

"He's here somewhere." Sunny grasped Constance on either side of her shoulders. "Calm down. This isn't like you."

"I know. I just need to find Fezzi and go home. I'm exhausted from the day." Constance drew away and whistled for Fezzi.

"Don't worry, he's got to be here."

"Unless someone let him out." Constance's voice sounded high and thin.

"In which case, he'd just sit there on the porch until we let him back in. He's done this before."

Constance stared back at her awhile. "That woman was horrible," she finally said. "I can't believe I took off and left Rhett alone with her."

"Do you want to go back down? It's time for the silent auction, anyway."

Constance's fingers played around her lips. "No. I can't meddle in whatever relationship they have. Or had. Or... whatever. It'd be best if I just went home."

"I'm sure you're exhausted. You massaged all day. Speaking of. How'd it go with Rhett today?"

"Good." That's all Constance would say. She was very protective of anyone she worked on. "Though that woman is down there, undoing everything I did today."

"Pete's still with him." Sunny wasn't sure how to act. She'd never seen Cici this rattled before; she'd taken down more than her share of bullies over the years. "I better get back down there. Pete will be mad I left him."

"Go." Constance nodded toward the stairs. "I'll see you tomorrow."

Once Sunny was gone, Constance went into the living room and ordered a vodka tonic from the bartender, who was busy wiping the bar and tending to a couple of loners, nursing whiskey. She threw it back, had another, then went to the only place she knew she could be completely alone: the massage room.

Constance locked herself inside, laid down on the table, which still had Rhett's sheets on it, and closed her eyes. Behind her throbbing temples she pictured Katrina, gorgeous and slim and reeking of power. She had the sort of energy that had to be fed constantly, like a roaring, greedy furnace.

Her biting words about medication came back into Constance's head, along with the pained look on Rhett's face. Constance couldn't believe she'd fled, leaving him there. Then again, they obviously had a history together. Constance hadn't any choice but to leave. She had no place there, between them, a third wheel while they argued.

The vodka started to work its magic. Constance drew in deep breaths, felt herself drifting. The room still smelled like Rhett, his spicy scents mixed in with the lavender and eucalyptus. It was soothing enough she allowed her mind to drift back to the waltz they'd shared. Rhett was smooth on his feet, touched her with just the right amount of pressure, had been just daring enough to slip his hand to the small of her back without being so forward as to slide it any farther down, and he'd held her up during every stumble.

These probably weren't the things Constance should be thinking about. Nevertheless, that's where her mind went, and stayed, until she felt sleep swallowing her up, little by little.

When Constance woke, forty minutes had gone by. She sat up, still buzzing from the vodka. The foyer was quiet, and Fezzi was not behind the desk. He wasn't in the kitchen, where all the food had been packed up. He wasn't waiting by the back door, which is what he'd done many times in the past when he'd slipped out with guests, gone exploring, then wanted back inside.

Constance sighed. Aw, damn. That left only one place he'd be.

Rhett tried to use his big gold key to get into his room, but the door wasn't locked. In fact, it was ajar. At first he found that odd, but figured the door didn't catch when he'd left earlier. There was nothing inside worth stealing, and if someone was hiding inside, waiting to mug him, great—he wouldn't mind some combat practice. He fumbled his way into the darkness, intending to gather his meager belongings and go. He should've trusted his instincts. This whole idea with the party had been bad from the start. No good ever came from Mama's meddling.

Rhett pushed the door closed behind him and didn't even flip on the light. Moonlight from the garden shone through the windows of the tower, affording him enough to see by. He took a few steps toward the bathroom, but only made it to the edge of the bed, where he sank to the floor. He'd felt so good after his massage. Now, his pulse was up and the urge to throw things against the wall was at an all-time high.

"Woof."

Rhett lifted his head. Either those two shots of whiskey he'd had before coming up here were way stronger than he thought, or there was a dog somewhere in this bedroom. The sound was low, like a greeting, rather than a growl or a warning.

A second later, something licked his ear. Rhett turned his head and a tongue lapped at his cheek. He blinked in the darkness until the shape of a thick, stocky dog came into focus. Possibly a white-headed pit bull. There was a pit bull on his bed. Medium-size, white head, multicolored body.

A soft knock came at his door.

It couldn't be Katrina. She'd stormed out half an hour ago, and even if she'd come back, it seemed unlikely that Sunny would give out his room number to anyone. She was professional and, as Stanzi had said, a good businesswoman. Besides, Katrina wouldn't knock like that. That knock sounded like, "Hey, you in there? Can I bother you a sec?" Katrina's knock would've sounded like she was going to beat the door down.

"It's open," Rhett called. He didn't feel like getting up. Since he faced the door, nobody could surprise him, and if it was housekeeping they could just put the extra towels in the bathroom.

The moonbeam that shot through the room lit her silhouette as the door swung open. She sparkled in the light—red-blond hair, mussed like she'd been sleeping, and tight blue dress. The dog gave a happy whine and its tail thumped hard on the mattress.

"There you are, Fezzi." Stanzi's voice sounded warm and relieved.

It was the kind of tone you wanted for yourself, but Rhett knew it was for the dog. "His name's Fezzi?" He nodded at the mutt, who rolled over on his back and stretched. Rhett noticed the dog was missing one of his front legs.

"Yeah. Fezziwig. Like the guy in *A Christmas Carol*? Who does the silly dancing? Fezzi hops around like that, because of his three legs."

Rhett chuckled, despite himself.

"Sorry he's on your bed. This is my room whenever I stay here. Fezzi knows how to open the doorknob with his one paw."

Maybe it was the alcohol, but Rhett laughed. "No shit." The dog thumped his tail, harder this time. Rhett reached up and petted his head.

"Yeah, Pete trained him, a long time ago, to do stuff for my dad. The doorknob thing wasn't one of them, but Fezzi just kind of picked up on stuff on his own. He opened doors for Daddy when he struggled with his cane."

"No shit," Rhett said again.

"It didn't even occur to me, when I gave you my room, that Fezzi might come in here. I'll get him out of your way."

Rhett leaned his head back on the mattress and appraised the woman in the moonlight. "You gave me your room, huh?"

Stanzi shrugged. "Cabins were full. I told you I'd take care of it."

That's the Stanzi he knew. Always adapting. Always finding a way. He wished he was still downstairs, dancing with her. If he'd had enough time, he'd have requested a salsa himself. "Don't stand in the hallway."

Stanzi hesitated only a second before she pushed the door shut and closed the distance between them. Her heels were missing, her feet bare, so her steps were silent as a mouse. She sank down next to him on the floor.

True to form, Stanzi didn't ask any of the typical questions: *Why are you sitting on the floor in the dark? What happened to Katrina?* Instead, she was quiet awhile, perhaps absorbing the moonlight.

"My dad heard the spiders, too," she eventually said softly. "He told me about it once, but only when he'd been drinking a lot of whiskey, which was unusual for him. And he'd only talk about it in sign language."

Her words rippled inside him. At first, it felt like she'd poked the sensitive underbelly of the beast. That feeling changed to surprise. Then came the aftereffect—which Rhett didn't have a name for—the recognition that Stanzi had not only remembered what Katrina said, but understood it.

"He said that sometimes, at night, even though he was partially deaf, it was like he could hear the dust in the beams. Or the spiders, talking in their corners."

They were quiet again. "Well," Rhett finally said, "that's just fucking crazy."

Stanzi, who had her arms wrapped around her shins and her chin on her knees, sputtered a laugh. She rolled over on to her back, clutching her middle, as she collapsed into giggles on the floor. Fezzi gave a soft woof of concern.

Rhett nudged her with his foot. "You're scaring the dog."

She kept laughing, until tears ran down her cheeks. Stanzi swiped at them with her knuckles, her chest rising and falling in gasps. Rhett hadn't found his comment all that funny, but he thoroughly enjoyed watching her dissolve in front of him. The sleeves of her dress dipped down and the hem pushed up, which made it hard to divert his eyes. The room was dark, so hell with it. Rhett enjoyed the color of her creamy skin in the moonlight and the way the dress draped her legs.

Help her up, he told himself, but he just kept watching her, imagining the dress was gone. He held out a hand, she grasped it, and Rhett pulled her to sitting. He pulled a little too hard, and she fell against him, her hands planting on his chest. Her laughter died down but she still had a smile on her face. Rhett caught her wrists.

Stanzi's smile slowly melted.

He loosened his grip, but didn't release her.

For a moment, he thought she was going to kiss him again. Then she drew away and sank down next to him. He was both disappointed and relieved.

"Was that your girlfriend?"

Stanzi's question marked the first official time that Rhett considered Katrina a buzzkill. "She's a girl," he said. "And she's a… Well, I'm not really sure she's a friend."

"She wasn't very friendly," Stanzi agreed.

"I'm not feeling very friendly about her right now."

"Though you usually do."

He shrugged. "She fills a slot. Sometimes. The girlfriend slot. She travels a lot so we're together when she's in town and we're not when she's not. And we don't talk about when she's not."

"Sounds lonely."

"It can be. But I'm okay with that."

"You're all stressed out now. After all my hard work."

"Half your hard work."

Stanzi giggled and gave him a shove. "Do you want me to do your front? You can just lie down on the bed."

Rhett rolled the evening through his head. Stanzi, in that blue dress. The good food. The dancing. He wondered if a massage to his front was the best idea.

"I'll just work the leg," she said, as though she'd read his mind. "Then keep you relaxed."

There was no way in hell he was going to say no. "We only have the one room. If you don't massage me, I'll have to wrestle you for it. And that could be dangerous."

She laughed and shoved him again. "C'mon." Stanzi stood up and extended a hand. Once he was on his feet, she disappeared into the bathroom. Rhett stripped off his clothing and got under the bedsheet. The dog picked up one of his socks and sat politely by the side of the bed, sock in mouth.

"What?" Rhett adjusted the covers. "Why are you bringing me my sock?"

Fezzi whined.

Stanzi poked her head into the room. "Now that, he was
trained to do. He brought Daddy his socks every morning.
Along with other articles of clothing."

"That's amazing."

"That's Pete," she said. "Fezzi. Drop it."

The dog dropped the sock.

"Come." Stanzi pointed at the floor in front of her, and the
dog obeyed. "Down." He lay down and settled his chin on
his paw. Stanzi crossed the room, opened the drawer to the
nightstand and withdrew a bottle.

"You have massage lotion everywhere, don't you?"

"Pretty much."

Rhett closed his eyes. The sounds of partygoers mingling
in the cold out back, mixed with music from the basement,
hit his ears. He hadn't noticed those sounds before. The bed
squeaked and dipped as Stanzi climbed up next to him. She
carefully undraped his bad leg and started in on it, her hands
cool, soft and professional.

Just like earlier, Rhett felt himself relax as soon as she
touched him. His breathing deepened and his mind started
to spin into another place, one deeper and softer than his day-
to-day world.

Her hands moved in long, slow strokes, deep enough to get
into his muscles but not deep enough to cause pain. There
was something about him that moved with her; not a tangible
part of his body but something connected, nonetheless, like
she pulled on his shadow. When she'd massaged him earlier,
he'd lain there, tense, certain that it would be just like lying
in bed at night, with him unable to relax, unable to not hear
every little thing, and the panic in his chest compounding

with every second that he realized he didn't want to go to sleep, because he didn't want to dream, yet he didn't want to stay awake, because he didn't want to think.

Which left him nowhere to be at all.

But this wasn't like that. Just like earlier, Rhett started to drift, soft and slow, until there were no more party sounds coming from downstairs, no chatter from partygoers out back, dancing in the moonlight or stealing cigarettes in the cold.

There wasn't sound. There wasn't silence.

There was just this.

It felt really, really good.

And not one spider was whispering.

twenty-one

Rhett was surprised to find that the dog rescue, full of dogs, didn't smell like dogs. Sunny's sanctuary smelled like pet food, old wood and dog shampoo. It was well made, clean and tidy.

"This is actually Roger's place," Stanzi explained. "He cares for all the dogs who don't have foster families while we try to place them." She nodded toward the closed doors, which must have been Roger's bath and bedrooms.

Many of the dogs were out running the fenced-in grounds, but many remained inside. Most of them were pit bulls, and they all had their own personality, but seemed to share a sort of calmness Rhett wouldn't expect of this setting.

Stanzi nodded toward a small white dog, balled on a pet bed in the corner. "Maltese," she said. "Her name's Willy."

Rhett stepped closer. Willy pressed herself tighter into the corner. Ah. A sweet little thing. Her hair all silky white and her eyes doe-y behind her bangs. "What's wrong with her?"

Next to her bed was a small, stone statue of a man. On close inspection Rhett could see animals carved all around his robes.

Saint Francis.

Stanzi shrugged. "Hard to say. By the time Sunny gets them, they're all kinds of ruined. Willy came from the puppy mill next door. Though—" she lowered her voice "—don't tell anyone that."

Despite the sadness of looking at a dog like Willy, and guessing at her past, Rhett didn't worry for any of these dogs. They were like a collection of geeks at a *Star Trek* convention—a bit misunderstood and left of center, probably picked on all their lives, but all the more interesting and colorful. Sunny wouldn't give up on a single one of them. Rhett knew that, without having to be told.

"You help your sister with the rescue?" Rhett watched Fezzi hop around on his three legs, seeming to divide his time between overseeing the other dogs and following Stanzi wherever she went.

"I massage them," Stanzi said, cocking her head to the side and smiling.

"Of course you do." He still couldn't believe how great he felt this morning. When he'd rolled over in bed, Stanzi had been gone, but he'd been able to get dressed without bracing his leg and felt almost pain-free. The best part was how his head felt, which was clear. Like he'd actually slept eight hours. He literally couldn't remember the last time that had happened.

"I name them, too."

"Really?" He gestured to the Maltese. "Willy?"

Stanzi giggled. "You may not think it fits, but it does. Just get to know her, and you'll see. She's a Wilomena. Willy, for short."

Rhett shook his head. "Now, Wilomena I can see. You come up with a nickname for me yet?"

Stanzi twisted her lips. "I'm still working on it."

"And this guy." Rhett petted Fezzi's ears. "You said he was trained for your dad?"

Stanzi gave Fezzi a fond cock of her head. "Yeah. Like I told you, Daddy was legally deaf. Fezz was his ears and also his butler. He'd bring Dad his socks and other clothing items in the morning. Daddy was a different person when Fezzi came around. Calmer. More patient."

A metal crate in the corner of the room caught Rhett's eye. "Who's that?" He pointed to the furry form that nestled silently inside the cage.

Stanzi followed his gesture. "Oh, him." Her voice dropped a notch in timbre. "That's Humphrey. The beagle."

Humphrey. *The* beagle. Well, true. Rhett hadn't seen another beagle here. He squatted down to get a better look, but only caught a flash of a droopy head. "Why's he in a crate?"

"His choice. You see it's not closed. He prefers being in there. Makes him feel protected, maybe. He's been stuck in one all his life, so… Old habits are hard to break."

Rhett peeked inside. Humphrey was all the way in the back, his head sagging.

"He can't see very well," Stanzi said. "His eyes got burned from all the ammonia in the urine that built up in the cage he was stuck in." She nodded toward Willy, who'd fallen asleep in a white ball of fur on her dog bed. "Same people had Willy. Cruel, nasty woman." Stanzi peered inside the crate at Humphrey, who hadn't shifted an inch. "People come here and want to adopt. But some of these dogs are just too ruined, you know? No chance left. Humphrey, he stays in here most of the time because the other dogs smell his fear and mess with him and then he fights back. It gets ugly, and Humphrey is too small."

Rhett leaned against the wall and slid down until his butt hit the floor. A few of the dogs came over to sniff him. He petted them and let them smell all around, until they moved off to do their own thing. "Hey, Humphrey." He hoped the pathetic creature would look his way.

"I have to pull him out of there to massage him," Stanzi said. "After I get him out, I go slow and then he's okay. But then he rushes right back in the cage."

"I'm just going to sit here," Rhett said, even though he had no idea why. He wanted Humphrey to come out. That's all he knew.

Stanzi smiled softly. "I'm going to go check on Sunny. She's in a mad storm of cleaning up after her party. I'll be back."

Rhett waited until she was gone, then leaned his head back against the wall, closed his eyes and cleared his mind. He was hoping to feel a little like he had last night, during Stanzi's massage. That sense of letting go, of release, of connection. He stayed that way awhile, focused on his breathing.

Then came a soft, scratching noise. When his eyelids fluttered open, Rhett used every muscle in his body to keep himself from reacting. Humphrey sat only inches away, staring at him from rheumy brown eyes. With his head drooped like that, his ears hung forward, he looked so much like the vulture persona Snoopy did in the old comics Rhett had to stifle a laugh. He suppressed the urge to reach out and pet Humphrey on the head. Any movement he made might send the dog back into his crate, faster than he could blink.

"Hey, old man. You come out to say hi?"

"Am I seeing what I think I'm seeing?"

At the sound of Stanzi's voice, Humphrey fled. With a wild

scamper, he was back in the crate, nothing left to prove he'd been there but the sweet smell of his freshly shampooed fur.

"Shh!" Sunny, who'd come inside with her, gave Stanzi a nudge.

"Sorry." Stanzi covered her mouth. Rhett stayed where he was at, on the ground, observing Humphrey inside his cage.

"Did I just see what I think I saw?" Sunny squatted down and peered into Humphrey's cage. She turned to Rhett with narrowed eyes. "You didn't pull him out against his will, did you?"

"I'm insulted."

"Sorry."

"All right."

Stanzi laughed, but tried to stifle it. "I don't even have words."

Rhett cast a glance inside Humphrey's cage. The little dog had tucked himself away as far in the back as he could go. "I thought he didn't like people."

"He doesn't." Sunny watched him in silence. She planted her hands on her hips.

Rhett rose to his feet and dusted off his jeans. "I should get home."

"What did you think of the tour?" Sunny opened her arms to the rescue.

"I think—" Rhett looked around at this hodgepodge of dorky mutts, the special food, the carefully built and maintained structure "—that you and your sister are something else." He glanced over at Humphrey. "What will you do with him? If nobody adopts him?"

Sunny shrugged. "We'll keep trying."

"Before you go." Stanzi had a glimmer of hope in her eyes. "Let's be real quiet. Just sit in silence and give Humphrey another chance."

Sunny gave a slow nod. "All right. But I'm stepping out. I think three's a crowd, in this instance. Humphrey will never come out with this many heartbeats in the room."

After she left, Rhett shrugged. "I don't think he'll come out again." But even as he said it, he sank back to the floor and closed his eyes. Stanzi followed suit. At first, his mind chattered away with noise, the events of last night and all the things he wanted to do today, but then he thought about the massage, and his mind gave up on thinking altogether. His thoughts drained away like water down the pipes. He imagined his troubles choked up before they let go, like that bubbly, sucking sound when the suds reach the hole in the sink. After that, it was a blank sort of bliss and random splotches of color and light. His body relaxed like a rag doll, and the peace inside gave him a buoyed feeling of being suspended in water or air or somewhere else he could become weightless.

After a while, Rhett sensed a presence, close by. There was a change in the air. Someone else's breath. His eyes opened, and though the blissful feeling vanished, he couldn't help but laugh under his breath.

"Aw, hell, no," Rhett muttered, even as he smiled.

The little beagle was about a foot away from Rhett's thigh and staring like a vulture as his ears drooped forward.

"Stay very still," Stanzi said. "He likes that. Quiet people. Still people."

Humphrey seemed to watch him, with those brown-tinted eyes. His black, tan and white coat looked a little dull, even though he'd clearly had a bath. His paws seemed bigger than usual, but that was because his body was too skinny.

Rhett's gaze lingered on the dog's feet. Humphrey's nails were all pale, like a yellowed ivory. Except for the fourth nail on the right paw. That one was a reddish-brown color, like an extension of the few tan spots he had on his white feet. Like a shard of his clinging hope, or a tidbit of his youth, before life had been so cruel to him.

"Look at that," Rhett said. "He has one dark nail on his paw." Humphrey's nose bumped Rhett's fingertips. The little beagle inched closer. His paws nearly touched Rhett's thigh.

"He bumped you," Stanzi whispered. "I can't believe it."

Rhett raised his hand a few inches off the ground and extended it in the beagle's direction. Humphrey stretched his neck out and bumped Rhett a second time.

"Wow," Stanzi gasped. "He really likes you."

"He's not so bright, then."

"He's actually very smart."

As if to settle things, Humphrey took a couple of steps closer to Rhett, then lay down on his stomach, on the ground next to Rhett's thigh, and rested his head between his paws. There, he closed his eyes.

"Well, look at that."

Rhett stretched his hand a little closer, but stopped just short of touching him. "What now?"

Stanzi elbowed him in the ribs. "Want a dog?"

Rhett's smile fell. "Nah, I couldn't." Unexpectedly, his pulse rose. Aw, dammit. Not now.

"You're the only person he likes, so far."

"He likes you."

"He tolerates me. There's a difference."

Rhett's breathing changed, became shallower. The feeling about him changed, too, thickening and darkening, like heavy clouds. He hated this feeling. It had been a while since this had happened, long enough Rhett had thought maybe he'd beat the panic attacks. Why now? Not now. Any time but now. "I can't." He stood up slowly, but despite Rhett's effort to be quiet and careful, Humphrey woke and bolted back into his cage.

"Why don't you come inside and have some coffee? Think about it. Maybe visit him again before you go."

"I can't." Rhett looked down at her, and his head clouded as he struggled to breathe. "I'll just mess him up."

"He's already messed up."

"I'd mess him up more." Rhett cleared his throat sharply and drew air steadily into his lungs. "Thanks for entertaining me all night. And for showing me all this." He scanned the rescue. "This is amazing. But I've got to get going."

"Go where? It's Christmas Day."

Rhett shrugged. "Best day to get managerial stuff done. No gym to run and nobody to bother me." He cringed after the words left his mouth. That's not how he meant it, but he didn't have enough time left to explain or apologize.

Stanzi watched him, her eyes changing, like she knew a little about what was going on. "All right," she said softly. "See you at the gym?"

"Yep."

Then he left, not even looking back to wave. The zero pain he felt in his bad leg allowed him to get to his Jeep as quickly as possible. He dropped the keys twice before getting them in the ignition, but finally he got the engine going and peeled out and down the driveway as fast as he could go.

twenty-two

"Humphrey's not trainable as a service dog," Pete explained, "but he also doesn't have to be. If Rhett had the effect on him that you described, then they already have a synergy I don't need to mess with."

"Slow down," Sunny panted. She leaned forward, hands on her knees, and drew cold air into her already gassed lungs. "God, I hate running." She stood up, hands pressed to the small of her back, and arched into her palms. "How can you talk so much?"

"Quit being a baby. You can ride that bike all day long, but you can't run a few miles?"

"I repeat. I hate running. I don't have the legs for it." Sunny extended one leg and pointed her toes.

Pete blew off her comment with a smirk. He swiped some sweat from his forehead with the back of his sleeve. He had about two weeks' worth of a beard now, which Sunny hadn't realized he was growing until this moment. "So this guy must be okay, if Humphrey likes him."

"He seems like the real deal." Sunny bent down to tie her shoe. The trails were wet and muddy from melted snow. She drew a deep breath to calm her lungs. The air smelled like a fireplace. "Though Cici said he acted weird about Humphrey. Well, she didn't use the word *weird*. She said he 'retreated.' Didn't want to even consider taking him home. Cici thinks he was having a panic attack, but he would never admit it."

Pete watched her tie her shoe, then nodded toward the trail, to indicate he'd be starting up again. "It might not have been the dog. Or not just the dog."

"What do you mean?" Sunny was relieved when Pete started at a fast trot, not a run.

"That woman at the party—" Pete glanced over his shoulder "—was way out of line. The way she talked to him. About the medication and the spiders. If she were a man, I'd want to punch her in the face." He jumped over a felled tree with a quick little hop.

"I'll punch her in the face for you." Sunny climbed over the log, then pushed after Pete, who was picking up the pace. She'd never noticed how muscular his calves were until she ran behind him and watched him navigate the rocky trails with ease.

"Whatever Rhett is going through," Pete continued, "he feels all alone. To have that girlfriend or ex-girlfriend or whatever she is act like she's got it all figured out is insulting and condescending. Then along comes Humphrey, who for whatever reason, makes a connection. So the only person that's connecting with him is a messed-up dog who's lived in a cage all his life. That might've spooked him a bit."

Sunny realized she'd never really talked to Pete much about his experiences in Afghanistan. He never brought it up, and she was afraid to overstep by asking questions. But there was a reason he trained service dogs for service members, at no charge. Nobody took on that kind of work unless they were passionate about it. Nobody took on that kind of work unless they truly wanted to help.

"I think Cici has made a connection, too." Sunny's words came labored. "I've never seen Cici react like she did last night. Rhett's gotten to her somehow."

Pete went silent. After a second, he said, "Well, that would spook him even more." After that, Pete picked up the pace considerably. Sunny realized she'd pushed Pete's buttons, or more like his one big button: Constance. She briefly wondered why she'd done that, but her body was in too much pain to ponder too deeply. Her lungs were ready to burst by the time the rescue came into view. Roger was out running the dogs, and just looking at the mutts' tireless energy made her jealous.

Sunny sagged against a tree. Pete turned around and began stretching his legs. He smirked at her.

Sunny was just getting ready to call him a jerk when a van, driving past the house along the road out front, caught her eye. "Pete." She barely whispered his name. "I think it's happening."

Pete followed her gaze, but the van was gone. "What?"

Sunny's insides warmed instantly, which hadn't happened in three miles on the trail. "Animal control," she said. "An animal control van just drove by."

twenty-three

"Show me how to climb the rope." Constance grasped the hemp and looked up at the high ceiling, where the rope was attached. There was a piece of black electrical tape wrapped at the fifteen-foot mark, which seemed really high from her place on the floor.

"On your list of goals?" Rhett slid a bench over.

"Rope climbs were in the very first workout I did here. I remember being in awe of how fast you zipped up and down. Now that it's January, it's time to work on a resolution."

Rhett smiled and patted the bench. "Have a seat."

That smile felt like a warm ray of sunshine. Since Christmas, all of Rhett's responses to her texts had been tight and short. Not rude, but distant. Constance had been coming to class like a regular member, with no special instruction from Rhett and little exchanged between them but a few nods and waves. The gym had been crowded since the first of the month and snagging alone time with him had been impossible. Today, Constance came in early on purpose, saw Rhett in the office as she went by, but left him alone. She tried a rope climb by herself, failed miserably and found herself on her back, staring up at Rhett.

"It seems impossible."

"It's not." Rhett sat down on the bench. "Two ways to wrap your feet. You can snake the rope—" Rhett wrapped his leg with the rope several times, like he was doing needle-work "—or you can do the J-hook." He made a little shelf with both of his feet, one on top of the rope and one beneath.

"Ah, okay." Only now did Constance realize that the rope climb, like so many lifts with the barbell, was more about the lower body than the upper. "But you didn't even use your feet, that time I watched you."

"I know—" Rhett arched an eyebrow at her "—but it takes a lot of upper body strength to do a legless rope climb."

"Show me. I forget what it looks like," she lied.

Rhett stood up, grabbed the rope and, using only his upper body, pulled himself all the way up to where the electrical tape was wrapped. Then he rappelled himself back down, the same way. Constance silently admired his smooth athletic ability. He made that look so easy. She couldn't help but picture him without the shirt on.

"Let's try the J-hook. Just sitting on the bench, I want you to make a shelf out of the rope, with your feet." He demon-strated a second time, then passed her the rope. Once Con-stance got it right, he said, "Good. Now, in order to minimize how much upper body you use, I want you to focus on lean-ing your body back and getting those feet as high as possible on the rope for your second hook." He stood up and showed her what he meant, climbing his feet up near his hands. With his height, he was able to climb the rope to the black tape in only a pull and a half.

Constance started from a seated position on the bench, then worked her way to standing. At first it was awkward to hook her feet, then when she finally did she'd run out of upper body strength while she hung there, trying to hook her feet a second time. Rhett told her she "wasn't horrible" and made her rest before trying again, and again.

By the time she'd put in a solid twenty minutes of work, Constance could get two mini pulls that moved her a third of the way up the rope.

"Make sure you come down the same way," Rhett said, arms folded over his chest, something of a proud smile on his face. "Don't slide down and give yourself rope burn to the hands or legs. Control your descent."

Constance tried, but that was easier said than done. Her arms fatigued quickly and she slid down the rope. She sank to the bench and peered down at the rope burns on her inner thighs. This was the first day she'd felt comfortable enough about her legs to wear shorts to the gym, and now she had rope burns.

Rhett knelt down in front of her. "Let's see." He pushed her knees apart and grazed his thumbs over the reddened, scraped skin. "All right. Not too bad. We'll clean it, and next time you'll control your descent better."

Chills popped over Constance's skin.

Rhett looked up into her eyes, his hands going still on top of her thighs. "I've been wanting to talk to you about the night of the party. About Katrina. And Humphrey." Rhett tilted his head from side to side, as though shaking his thoughts around to sort them out.

That warm ray of sunshine expanded inside Constance's stomach.

"That's not how you taught me rope climbs, Santos. I'm jealous."

Constance and Rhett both jerked their heads in the direction of the amused male voice that came from the vicinity of the entrance. It was obvious neither one of them had heard him come in.

"Callahan!" Rhett smiled and rose to his feet. "You haven't been in much. Just when you promised you were going to start taking your fitness more seriously."

Constance's breath caught in her throat. Detective Callahan stood a few feet away, wearing gym clothes and toting a giant gym bag. He grasped Rhett's outstretched hand and pulled him in for a man-hug, that one-armed-shoulder-bump dance that the American male favored.

"I'm back for sure now," Callahan said. "I've done some soul-searching over the holidays and I made a decision that's got me back on track."

"I hope so." Rhett popped him in the gut. "You're not getting my special rope climb instruction package without a serious commitment."

Callahan laughed as he took the hit, giving a sharp exhale. He rubbed his midsection, which was mostly flat, and looked over at Constance. After a second, his eyes narrowed. "Miss Morrigan." He dragged out her name with recognition. "What are the odds? I was just going to tell Santos here how this one little lady, a masseuse, got me back on track. You told me to quit saying yes to something I wanted to say no to, remember?" He walked over and stuck his hand out. "Well, I finally told my ex that getting back together was not going to happen. Told her on Christmas Day. My neck hasn't hurt since."

"You broke it off on Christmas Day?"

"Best present I could give myself."

"I'm glad to hear it worked, Detective." Constance rose from the bench and accepted his handshake.

"Call me Sean," he said. "And yeah, it did. Thanks again."

"Anytime."

"Wait." Rhett pointed at Constance. "You two know each other?"

"There are better ways to meet, but yes," Sean said. "And it looks like her magic is working just as well on you as it did on me." His gaze went from Constance to Rhett and back again. "I knew it."

The room went quiet. Rhett's eyebrows knitted.

"Sunny has had some trouble with the law," Constance said quickly. "Between her and the neighbor, who has a puppy mill. But I think that's been ironed out. Right, Detective?"

"Got a court order. Animal control did a preliminary last week and should be back over there any day." Callahan smiled. "Now, as long as your sister behaves, all should be good."

Rhett's knitted brows slowly relaxed. He rubbed his chin as he looked at Sean, then slowly over to Constance.

"I'm going to warm up. You two carry on." Sean walked off toward the rig, leaving Constance alone with Rhett, who was watching her with a curious glint in his eye.

"You guys get arrested for something?"

"It was nothing." Constance waved a hand. But even as various excuses rolled through her mind, she knew that lying wasn't an option. "What I said about Sunny and the neighbor is true. My sister has this little habit of taking the law into her own hands when animals are abused. That's where Willy and Humphrey came from."

"Dog bandits." Rhett laughed under his breath.

Constance decided the rest of it needed to come out. If the detective was back at the gym, there was always the chance he'd say something he shouldn't—like he had just now. Constance didn't want anything popping out on Rhett when he wasn't expecting it. He'd had too much of that in his life already. "I just want you to know that, a little while back, Sunny asked me for a favor. A favor from Sean, who would in turn do her the favor of getting the law in gear over the neighbor's puppy mill."

Rhett was silent, his face showing no emotion.

"Sean asked if I'd help you with your leg." She nodded toward Rhett's right thigh, which hadn't been giving him any visible trouble today. "But it's not like I planned it." Constance scrambled to speak as she watched the light in Rhett's eyes change. "Coincidentally, I had already met you. I had already worked on your leg, too. They just wanted me to keep helping you." Constance shrugged. "Which I wanted to do, anyway."

Rhett's head drooped, and for a second, he looked a little like Humphrey. When he next raised his gaze, his hazel eyes were heavier on the green than the brown. "I was part of a bargain?"

"It wasn't like that." Constance nodded toward Sean. "They may have thought so. Though nobody meant anything bad by it. Everybody just wanted to help everybody else. But no, it wasn't like that."

"I see."

"Rhett." Everything drained away: the joy she'd felt at making it a third of the way up the rope, the arousal she'd felt when Rhett's large, warm hands had run up her thighs and the anticipation of what he was going to say about Katrina and Humphrey. He'd come to trust her.

And now he didn't.

The world became colorless and flat. "This is kind of like a huge coincidence," Constance said. "We'd already met. I could have made up anything. Why would I tell you the truth if the truth was that I thought you were part of a bargain? It wasn't like that for me. It never has been."

People were starting to fill the gym. They walked by and greeted Rhett, then Constance, then headed over to warm up. Chatter filled the air, and it seemed out of place inside the heaviness that hung between them. "I don't need anybody's help," Rhett said. "And I don't like the idea of people I'm close to talking behind my back about how to fix me."

The blood drained from her face. "It wasn't like that." Constance knew her words wouldn't carry the weight she needed to convey, but she also knew that words weren't going to fix this.

"I have to start setting up for class." Rhett's eyes were no longer fiery, but they held none of the joy from earlier. "You should go warm up."

As he walked away, Constance bit back the burning that simmered behind her eyes. She gathered her things and slipped out while no one was looking.

twenty-four

Sunny trained her binoculars on the Matteri property. The air inside the car was so cold her breath was turning to steam. A couple of weeks had come and gone since the animal control van's visit, and it was hard to tell if Janice's operation had changed much. Other than there was a certain stillness over her house and back kennel. Were all the dogs gone? Even though there was only one road in and out of this neck of the woods that housed Sunny's, Janice's and Pete's holdings, it was a vast stretch of land, encompassing dozens of acres and many miles. Sunny could easily have missed a second pass of animal control while she was out, asleep or merely not looking at the road.

She sighed. What the hell was she doing out here? She had a pile of adoptions and fosters today, including Pete's collection of Chevy's pups to take back to Canine Warriors for training, and she had to be at her best. A late night with Callahan hadn't helped, either. Just a little too much wine and not enough sleep made a baby hangover press around the edges of her temples. She'd just tossed her binoculars to the passenger seat and started the engine when she saw it: the animal control van creeping around from the back curve of Janice's house. Excitement pumped up Sunny's heart as she watched it edge out onto the road. The van was too dark, and Sunny was too far away, to see if the van held dogs, but she'd been peeping at Janice's house for fifteen minutes, watching for comings and goings, which meant the van had been back there for at least as long.

A smile plastered her face as she took the short drive home. She went inside and collected Chevy, who'd taken to following her everywhere, and brought her back out to do her business. Chevy had just finished squatting in the grass when an old station wagon screeched to a halt.

Chevy gave a sharp bark. Sunny grabbed the newspaper off the front stoop, even though it wouldn't make much of a weapon.

"You!" Janice's tall, skinny form made it out of the car and to the driveway in a flash. She fisted her hands on her hips, her lips pursed and sporting premature wrinkles at the corners. "You got my place shut down! You got my dogs taken away!"

Sunny drew a steadying breath, her grip on the newspaper tightening. The last time Janice had come over, she'd shaped her bony finger into a gun and pointed it at Sunny's head. This time, Janice was a thousand times as angry and might actually be packing.

"I did nothing of the sort. You got your own dogs taken away by abusing and neglecting them." Sunny snapped her fingers at her side, and Chevy came around and sat there. Sunny stepped in front of the dog, just in case Janice pulled out a real weapon.

Janice's eyes, drawn over in heavy black eyeliner and clumpy mascara, narrowed. "You did this," she repeated. "And this time you've gone too far. Too. Far."

Sunny pressed the newspaper to her chest. "Get off my property."

Janice pushed back her stringy hair. "You just wait." Her voice was quiet. Almost a whisper. "You just wait." She threw her shoulders back and marched to the driver's seat of her ancient car. The engine roared to life, but Janice poked her head out the window and repeated her directive one more time. "You just wait." Then she pointed at Chevy, peeking around Sunny's knees. "And you, too."

Sunny remained frozen to the end of her driveway long after Janice was gone, despite how her body shivered in the cold. Chevy shifted around, dancing, her nails tapping on the concrete. "All right," Sunny murmured. "Let's go inside, girl."

Constance made sure the cast-iron pan was smoking hot before she seared off the chunks of beef. In just a few minutes, she'd have a beautiful crust on the meat, the juices and the flavor sealed in and ready for the long, slow stew in the oven. She chopped the veg while the meat cooked. Onions, celery, carrots and potatoes. Simple, down-home ingredients.

"Is that Daddy's magic stew I smell?" Sunny's voice called out from the foyer.

Constance waited until Sunny was in the kitchen and could see for herself.

"Whose ass are you trying to kiss?" Sunny popped around the corner. "Daddy's dead. Is this a celebration for Janice losing her dogs today?"

Constance said nothing, even though Sunny's text this morning regarding the dogs had made her week. Using tongs, she flipped each meat chunk over so they were evenly caramelized on every side.

"Ohhh," Sunny said. "Right."

"Go get undressed and get on the table," Constance ordered. She didn't want to discuss her "magic stew," which Sunny had named back in the day when she discovered that Constance always made this meal when she knew Daddy was going to be pissed about something. Daddy wasn't a picky eater. He ate everything Constance made. But the stew never failed.

"You don't have to tell me twice." Sunny disappeared downstairs, to the massage room.

Constance finished the meat, then washed her hands and went downstairs to find her sister, already undressed, under the sheets and half-asleep. "You're hungover, aren't you?" She could always tell when Sunny had had a late night. She still had that perpetual spring in her step, but she got these dark rings under her eyes that were easy to spot on her pale skin.

"Maybe a little. It's mostly worn off."

"You know I can make it worse."

"You won't. You've massaged me hungover many times."

"Comforting."

Sunny went quiet after that, until the end of the massage. During the neck routine, her voice came softly from the table. "I'm sorry I got you in this mess with Rhett. Though, I can't lie, I'm only a little sorry. If you hadn't agreed to the deal, animal control might've never been able to completely shut down Janice's operation." Sunny went silent, and when Constance didn't respond, her voice went meek. "All right, I'm completely sorry."

"That's probably smart. Especially while I have your neck in my hands." Constance applied pressure down either side of Sunny's cervical spine.

"You have to talk to him about it, eventually."

Constance moved her way slowly back up to Sunny's mastoid processes and held there. "Your neck's a mess. It's all that texting and typing and spinning."

"Just fix me. I'm not giving up any of those things."

"I can't fix you. Only you can fix you. I can only try to help."

"And what are you doing to fix you?" Sunny tilted her head back to look up at Constance. "What have you done to fix things with Rhett? Which, by the way, you didn't have to say anything about our deal. You could have made up anything."

"Lie still." Constance flicked Sunny's forehead. "Quit staring at me."

"Ouch." Sunny settled back on the table. "Do you flick all your clients?"

"Just you. And I did have to tell him." Constance cradled Sunny's head in one hand and grasped her right SCM with her thumb and forefinger of the other. Sunny hated this part of the massage, because the muscles were right near the windpipe. Constance decided to spend extra time here. "You wouldn't understand, but I can't lie to Rhett. About anything."

Sunny stiffened as Constance worked the anterior neck muscles. All was silent until the massage was over.

"So are you going to talk to him?" Sunny sat up, holding the sheet over her chest. "Obviously you're making him Daddy's magic stew. So, you're going to talk to him, right?"

"Maybe." Constance swallowed a tremor in her voice. "I haven't been to any of his classes this week. I can't give up the gym at this point. It's doing too much for me. I think I'd die without it. But I've been going to classes where I know Rhett won't be coaching."

Sunny tossed back the sheet, stood up and strode to the opposite side of the room, where her clothes were. "You can't keep that up forever."

Constance had long ago stopped telling her sister that she

was supposed to wait until the room was empty to get dressed. She'd been massaging Sunny for over ten years and Sunny was probably the least modest woman who existed. "I'm going to Rhett's class tonight, okay?"

Sunny dropped her tank top over her head and slid into her Lululemon leggings. "Good." By the time she was fully clothed and ready to go coach spin class, she looked like she'd never been touched. Every hair was in place and her makeup was perfect. "Talk to him. You owe him that much."

"And you—" Constance followed her out the door and upstairs "—watch your ass. If you've really shut down Janice's puppy mill, then you've taken this war to the next level. I don't trust that woman."

"Animal control shut down Janice's puppy mill. The courts. Not me."

"She's going to blame you."

Sunny shrugged, but despite her cavalier attitude, Constance saw a glimmer of worry in her sister's eyes. She was hiding something. "Anything you want to tell me?"

Sunny sighed. Her head hung down, like a scolded child. She looked back up and faced Constance. "Janice came by today. Right after animal control left. She's livid. Threatened to get me back."

"Are you serious?"

"I swear to God, Cici, it was like something out of *The Wizard of Oz*." The skin on Sunny's arms popped with goose bumps. "I'm going to get you, my pretty!" She raised her voice to a cackle and pointed her finger at Constance's chest. "And your little dog, too!"

Constance's jaw dropped. "This is not funny, Sunny."

Sunny swallowed hard. "I know. It was really kind of freaky, how quiet Janice was. She kept saying, 'You just wait.' I don't even know what to do with that."

Constance got a tight feeling in her gut, like she'd eaten something bad. "Sunny. I think you should tell Callahan."

"No." Sunny waved her hands. "Our relationship isn't like that. I'm not about to whine to him that Janice Matteri pointed a finger in my face. You know I don't like looking helpless in front of the men I'm sleeping with. In front of any men."

Constance had about a million things she wanted to say about stubbornness, pride and bravado, but she knew her words would be wasted on her headstrong little sister, who was already sliding on her coat and heading for the door. "At least tell me you'll be careful. Lock everything at night. Tell Roger to watch his back."

Sunny nodded. "Already on it."

Once she was gone, Constance pulled out Callahan's business card and considered calling him. Just how pissed would Sunny be, and just how much would Constance care? After some thought, she put the card away. Maybe she'd see the detective at the gym and find a way to bring up Janice and her threats.

Constance pushed the mess from her mind and fixed herself lunch from last night's leftovers. Nothing was going to taste as good as the beef stew in the oven, but that was going to take hours. Her plan was to take some to the gym tonight and leave it in the fridge, with Rhett's name written on the top of the disposable container. Maybe that would be a good segue into having a conversation.

She hoped Rhett would accept it.

That evening, she dressed carefully for the workout, which was a first. Typically Constance would throw on one of the few pairs of leggings she owned and top that off with whatever T-shirt wasn't dirty. She'd scrape her hair back into a ponytail that was getting longer and longer each week, and secure her bangs with whatever clip was handy. Tonight, she actually fished out one of her old tech tees from her running days and was surprised enough at what she saw in the mirror that she sucked in her breath.

"Is that me?" she whispered.

The woman who stared back at her was someone she had never known before. Whatever ideal, whatever goal she'd had in her mind had been shattered by what she now saw. Had she wanted to be "thin" again? Had she wanted to be "in shape"? Had she wanted to be someone that didn't spend the larger part of her days nursing an elderly, sickly father? Or had she just wanted to be the woman that Josh had fallen in love with?

Constance wasn't any of those women, even if any of them had been an achievable or worthy goal. Whoever those women were, they no longer existed. The woman in the mirror now was someone else entirely. There was a glow to her skin that seemed fresh and bright; an angular shape to her cheekbones that hadn't even graced her teen years; a tightness to the tech top in places she'd never expected, nor paid attention to, like her biceps and shoulders. The woman who stared back at her wasn't a woman she had thought she could be, or even wanted to be, until she saw her. The woman who stared back at her wasn't "thin" or "ideal" or "the new you."

The woman who stared back at her was just strong. A woman who had been doing something for herself, pursuing her own goals.

Constance smoothed the shirt, then brushed her hair back into a ponytail, careful to catch all the strays. She used a pretty gold clip to secure her bangs and finished the whole thing off by dotting her lips with tinted gloss.

When she was done, Constance resisted the urge to wipe off the gloss and muss her hair. She didn't want to appear eager, and she was pushing that line. She drew a deep breath, headed downstairs, grabbed the container of stew and raced out to her car before she could change her mind. By the time she got to the gym, she was sweating and her heart was beating fast. She checked herself once more in the rearview mirror, tucked the stew into her gym bag and headed for the entrance.

Just as she'd grasped the handle of the door, it pushed open, making Constance jump back. Rhett strode out, his own bag on his shoulder. He stopped short of running into her, apologized, then said, "Oh," when he saw who he'd almost plowed down. "Hey." His eyes roved over her, from leggings to snug tech tee to the gloss on her lips. He smiled, just the littlest bit. "How are you?"

"Good." Constance hated how forced her voice sounded. "I mean, okay. How about you? Aren't you coaching the 7:00 p.m.?" She felt a wave of uncertainty. It certainly looked like he was leaving.

"Hobbs has that shift tonight." Rhett pointed toward the gym, but his eyes were still on Constance. "I'm cutting out a little early."

"What's this?" A familiar voice rang out from behind Rhett. A second later, Katrina popped into view. "Oh." Her dark eyes looked Constance up and down, examining her with a much different expression than the one Rhett had. "Aren't you the—" Katrina snapped her manicured fingers "—the girl. From the resort."

Constance felt hot all over, the sweat from her nervous drive here drying up like a blister in the sun. "Constance. My name is Constance."

"Right." Katrina pushed her hair behind her ear and straightened her shoulders. Beneath her open coat she wore a tight pair of shorts and tank top, which accentuated the perfect contours of her hips, quads and boobs. "I knew it was an old-fashioned name. I just couldn't remember which one. For some reason, I had Matilda in my head." She barked out a laugh. "That's nowhere near Constance, is it?"

"No." Constance glanced at Rhett, who looked like he'd eaten something bitter. "It isn't."

"Going in to work out?" Katrina nodded at the door. "It's brutal, so I hope you wore your big-girl panties. Rhett's a great coach, though. Got me through it." She ran a hand over his shoulder.

It looked like Rhett flinched, but Constance could've been seeing things. "I hate that expression," she said.

"What expression?" Katrina narrowed her brown eyes, which would be a lovely chocolate color if they'd held any kindness. As they were, they looked more like crude oil.

"Big-girl panties. It's just dumb." The weight of Constance's gym bag felt like it was biting into her shoulder. "Little girls don't wear panties, they wear underwear. And besides, girls have been forced to act mature and grown-up before their time for ages, so it's not like putting on our 'big-girl panties—'" Constance made air quotes "—is anything new or special. You know?"

Katrina blinked at her in silence, her lips twisted like she'd sucked a lemon.

Rhett smiled with his eyes.

"I better get inside. Nice seeing you." Constance pushed past them. As soon as the door swung shut behind her, a wave of restrained nausea rolled through her body. She paused at the trash can and closed her eyes.

"You all right, Red?"

Constance looked up and saw Hobbs giving her a concerned appraisal. She forced a smile. "Yep."

Then she took the stew out of her bag and tossed it in the garbage.

Katrina glanced up from between his legs. "Are you ever going to come?"

Rhett realized he'd gone limp, despite the time Katrina

had spent trying to blow him for the last ten minutes. "Sorry. Guess I'm tired."

"Fine." Katrina rolled her eyes in exasperation. She stood up and fastened her bra, closing up the perfectly round mounds of flesh and saline. "Five hundred ccs," she liked to say proudly as she cupped them.

He rose and pulled up his shorts, then drew his shirt over his head. He couldn't remember why he'd agreed to have her back here. Now that he thought about it, he hadn't agreed. It's just what they'd always done whenever she was in town.

"Rhett." She grabbed his arm. "What's going on with you?"

Rhett drew his arm away. "I don't know what you're talking about."

Katrina followed him into the kitchen and watched him take a beer from the fridge. "Are you seeing that girl?" Katrina narrowed her eyes. "The one at the gym? The one who was at the Christmas party?"

"No." Rhett pictured Stanzi tonight, standing in front of the gym. She'd looked so good he'd found it hard not to stare. He'd found it even harder not to draw her in for a hug, even if that was a bad idea. She looked like she needed a hug. Rhett sure as hell needed one. Even Katrina hadn't hugged him— she'd gone right for his pants. "You should go. I'm not going to be much company tonight."

Katrina was frozen for a moment, her face blank, then cold, then melting into something Rhett couldn't pinpoint. She lifted his hoodie from the back of a chair and pulled it over her head. "Okay, Rhett. I'll go. You know what I'm thinking, though." She fluffed out her hair. "You wouldn't be having this problem if you were on the medication. You're limping like an old man and you're acting squirrelly. I'll get this back to you after I wash it." She touched the hoodie. "I don't feel like wearing my big coat in the car."

"You don't need to wash it," Rhett said, ignoring her other comments. "And no rush. I have others. Spring is coming."

Katrina smiled. "See you soon."

Once she was gone, Rhett went out to his Jeep and tried to decide where he was going. He needed to go. Somewhere. So he just started driving. At the first traffic light, he considered turning left and heading back to the gym. The late class was over and most people would be gone, but Stanzi tended to linger, one of the few athletes he had that paid close attention to her mobility and flexibility and often spent a good fifteen minutes postworkout stretching and foam rolling.

Without another thought, he hooked that left. The gym was still lit up. Rhett didn't see Stanzi's car but she often parked on the other side of the building if she was going to come out after dark because the brightest streetlamp sat there and Rhett let her go out the side door.

"Hey. What're you doing back here?" Hobbs was finishing up work in the office.

Rhett's stomach sank when he saw that no one else was there. He was surprised at how disappointed he felt. "I thought I left my hoodie here." Rhett pretended to look around the gym for it.

"Haven't seen it." Hobbs didn't get up to help. "Check the bin."

Rhett dug around the bin full of clothing that was home to every article the clients forgot. Most were claimed within a week. Some stuff, like a pink water bottle and a black jacket with holes in the sleeves, had been there for a year. He used the opportunity of his fake search to pluck those items out and pitch them in the trash. Just as he dropped the jacket, he saw what looked like a throwaway container with his name on it. He reached in and dug it out. Yep, that was his name. He knew it was from Stanzi. Nobody else at the gym had ever fed him. He couldn't tell what kind of food was inside, but he knew it would've been good.

He shook it, testing the integrity of the lid. Seemed pretty well attached. God knows he'd eaten grosser things…

But no. Damn.

He tossed it back in the trash. "Thanks for covering class."

"No problem." Hobbs shut down the computer, stood up and stretched. "Was a small class tonight. About six guys and Red. She held her own, as usual." Hobbs got a devilish grin on his face. "You think I should ask her out?"

"No."

"That came out too fast." Hobbs's grin deepened. "What do you care? You're back with Katrina, I'm assuming?"

"Katrina and I have no commitment."

"Yeah, sure." Hobbs ran his hand through his wavy blond hair. His sandy, rumpled good looks and blasé attitude made him seem like a California transplant, ready to surf at any moment, though he was a corn-fed Nebraska boy, born and bred.

"We're not a couple."

"Why'd you guys leave together?" Hobbs pulled on his sweatshirt and grabbed his backpack. "Quickie in the parking lot?" He held up a hand. "I'm not judging. If you called me in to cover your class because you were banging Katrina in the parking lot, I totally understand."

"Nope." Rhett snapped off the office lights and followed Hobbs to the front door.

Hobbs stopped at the door and offered a grimace. "That makes me feel less happy about covering for you."

"Trust me, I'm not happy about it, either."

"So that's a yes on asking out Red?" Hobbs's smile was both teasing and serious. "She's really shaping up. I mean, she was always hot, in an intellectual librarian who's really a wildcat between the sheets sort of way. But now that wildcat is starting to shed its winter coat, eh?"

"Quit talking about her like that." Rhett shoved him out the door. "She's not your type."

"How do you know?" Hobbs locked up the gym and turned to Rhett with a set of raised eyebrows.

"I just know."

Hobbs shrugged. "You going to ask her out, or not?"

"I'm not."

"Then she's free game."

Rhett flashed him a warning look. "She's a client, Hobbs. I expect you to treat her professionally."

Hobbs laughed, but his eyes narrowed. If Rhett wasn't seeing things, he actually looked offended. "When have I ever not been professional?" Hobbs said. "I'll let it slide. For now."

"See you tomorrow."

"Yep."

Once he was home, Rhett took a long shower to stave off the chill that had built from going out without a hoodie or a coat. He scraped together a decent dinner from stuff he found in his fridge, wishing he had whatever Stanzi had brought for him, and then obviously thrown away.

So Rhett hadn't been imagining things. Stanzi had come tonight thinking she would see him. Take his class, then offer him the food that ended up in the trash, thanks to Katrina. He couldn't say he blamed her. Well, it was probably for the best. Let Katrina be the reason Stanzi kept her distance. That would make things easier for him.

Rhett made it through his bland dinner, then grabbed the beer he'd opened earlier and never drank. He thought about it, grabbed two more and headed to bed.

Too many empty carbs, but he had a feeling that the spiders were going to be talking up a storm tonight.

twenty-five

Sunny could hear the spa music playing from outside Roger's quarters. Sounded like Enya. Sure enough, Cici was inside, with Humphrey out of his cage, lying on a dog bed. She ran her hands over and around him, not actually touching his fur or skin, but about an inch above. The beagle twitched when Sunny entered, but he didn't flee. This was his norm. He'd let Cici get him out of the cage for about an hour, but then he'd be back inside.

Constance shot her a glare.

Roger chuckled under his breath as he fed the rest of the dogs, all of them politely eating from their bowls, lined up in a row.

When Humphrey started to squirm, Sunny went back outside and began to work the grounds. She collected toys, cleaned up dog poo and eyed the bins of food kept under tight seal outside the structure. She clucked her tongue. One barrel had been shifted outside the protection of the awning and the lid was askew. That meant everything could get wet, or worse, infested with bugs or mice.

Roger came out with the dogs a moment later. They went running at top speed.

"Hey, Rog," Sunny called out. She waved him over. "I'm not sure why you moved this, but it wasn't covered by the awning anymore. Worse, the lid wasn't fastened. It'll be full of vermin within a couple days if you don't keep it covered."

"I didn't move that, ma'am." Roger shrugged. "I thought you did. Was going to mention it soon as I came out. Does that mean you weren't bumping around out here last night?"

Chills popped over Sunny's skin. Despite how brave she'd acted in front of Cici, she'd been walking on eggshells since Janice's visit, waiting for the mean old hag's next wave of attack. She'd been hypervigilant when her dogs were outside, and she cringed any time a strange vehicle drove by. When weeks went by and nothing happened, when mid-January turned into February and February to March, and no tornado sent by the Wicked Witch befell Sunny or her rescue, she'd decided Janice really might be all bark and no bite. Now, she wasn't so sure.

"Roger," she said, her voice low, "did you feed the dogs from this bin?"

Roger shook his head. "I gave them the chicken formula today." He nodded at the bin next to it, closed up tight and in the right place.

Sunny felt so much relief flood her veins she trembled. "Okay." She pressed her hands to her cheeks, which were hot. "We're going to dump this food. Get rid of it."

Roger's eyebrows rose. "Ma'am?"

"I wasn't out here bumping around last night, Roger." She gazed off into the woods, which were silent, other than the drip of winter melting into spring. "Which means someone else was. Someone like Janice. Or her nephew."

"Dang." Roger's eyes bugged out. "Yes, ma'am. I'll get rid of it. That's a lot of food, though."

"I know. But I can't risk it." Sunny thought about texting Sean, telling him everything, just like Constance had wanted, but she decided not to overreact. Maybe all Roger heard was raccoons or deer. A large animal could've moved that bin. Sunny had never seen a bear out this way, but it wasn't unheard of for one to lose his direction and end up skimming trash cans or other places food was easy to find. She wasn't going to tell Constance, either. She'd just get that disapproving look on her face and say, "I told you so."

Sunny watched her rescues, a handful of whom had been here a long time and would never be placed, as they variously ran, hobbled and hopped around the grounds, content to live out their days at Pittie Place. There were a couple new pitties from the kill shelter, too. The shelter always called Sunny the night before a dog's final day, to see if she could take them before they were put down. Sunny never said no. These new pits were not aggressive, nor afraid of the other dogs. They'd been able to slip right in with the pack. They hadn't been fought or abused, but they also hadn't been trained or well cared for. The shelter had said the brindle one was from a family who decided they just didn't want a dog anymore. He'd been a Christmas present and after the newness wore off and he started getting bigger, their daughter lost interest. He had a circle of brown around one eye, which looked like a patch, so Cici had named him Sinbad. The other, a female, was a blue pittie who presented with a silver coat. She was well into adulthood and had been dropped off at the shelter by a man moving overseas who couldn't take her. Cici had named her Calypso because she came in at the same time as Sinbad, plus the blue tint to her fur. The first time Sunny had let her run out back with the pack it became obvious Calypso had spent most of her life in a crate. The pure joy with which she bounded, jumped, sniffed at the grass and rolled in the sunshine made it seem like she'd never before experienced wide-open spaces.

Either pittie would make a good companion for someone ready to devote some care and attention. Neither was a "dangerous breed." In fact, there was only one dangerous breed around here. Sunny's gaze went off in the direction of Janice's property, even though she couldn't see any of it from here. She turned back to her pack, playing under the bright blue sky.

If anything happened to them…

Sunny stopped herself from thinking it. Her heart squeezed so hard she gasped aloud.

Roger paused as he went by with the food bin. "You okay, ma'am?"

Sunny offered a weak smile. "Of course. I'm fine."

Sean Callahan.

Oh, that's right. Detective Callahan had booked a massage last week. He'd be coming directly after the morning workout. His intake form pointed out the neck pain he'd suffered in the past, as well as frequent back and shoulder pain, which was no surprise considering the vest and equipment he carried as a detective and also his history in the USMC.

Constance prepared the room, then sat, closed her eyes and did her box breathing until she felt calm and centered. By the time Detective Callahan entered the basement walkout, she was ready.

"Detective Callahan. C'mon in."

"Sean," he corrected.

"Don't know why I find that so hard."

"Callahan is fine."

"So tell me, Sean—" Constance tested out his name and found that it wasn't so weird, at least not in her domain "—what are your goals for your session today?"

He shrugged his shoulders around and groaned. "Just take care of all of this, and I'll be a happy guy."

Constance smiled. "I can do that. Get undressed to your comfort level. We'll start faceup so I can release your pecs before we check your back, and we'll go from there."

More often than not, Constance started her massages face-down, simply because it sent a relaxing, silent message that it was time to turn everything off and put all their cares, worries and pains in her hands, at least for the next hour. Other than checking in with her client about table temperature and pressure level, Constance kept quiet unless the client spoke first. Most clients were happy to be quiet and melt into the experience, even if they were receiving deep tissue work, but once in a while she got a chatty one.

Women tended to talk more than men during massage, and tough guys like Callahan were more silent than most, as a rule. They didn't like small talk and tried to hide their pain, even if Constance could clearly see them bracing or controlling their breathing.

Constance's hands hovered over Sean Callahan before she touched him. As before, he was warm, fizzy and edgy, but something had changed significantly. Perhaps his finally saying no to his ex had done the trick. Whatever it was had not changed who he was, but had softened him, making him more malleable—possibly more vulnerable.

"By the way, thanks for helping Santos," Sean said, almost immediately upon Constance's first pass over his left pectoral.

Constance hesitated. She hadn't expected Sean to be a chatty one. "I was happy to."

"I think he needs you again. Just when he was starting to

seem more centered, he's looking more ragged every week." Sean breathed a deep sigh as his tight pectorals released, one after the other, with Constance's pressure.

"I haven't seen him much," Constance said. "I think he's busy with work and...Katrina?" Her tone went bitter over the name, which always reminded her of the devastating Category 5 hurricane from 2005.

"Oh." Sean made a groaning sound. "Her."

"You don't like her?" Constance felt guilty at her wave of amusement. She settled on her stool and slipped her hands around Sean's side, to work out his boxer's muscles.

"I don't like her for Rhett," Sean said, then went quiet. Just as she rolled her stool over to his other side, his voice came softly through the dark. "Closest I can figure, he dates her exactly because she's a stuck-up, self-centered bitch. Which means she can't get close to him. She's safe."

Constance applied a little oil to her hands and rubbed them together. She considered Rhett's energy, which was large and open and susceptible, and Katrina's, which had a greedy, selfish pull. If Rhett let her inside, she'd drain him. The thing was, Katrina did not seem the type to want to get too deep. She'd happily feed on the crumbs that came easiest. Like a bottom-feeder.

"I've known Rhett a long time," Sean said, his voice low and careful. "Since Seven November in 2004—when we started ground operations in Fallujah."

Constance's hands slowed their work. She got a mixed feeling that was equal parts sinking and rising. "I didn't realize Rhett was in the service that long."

"Right out of college. He's done at least four tours. Maybe five. I got out after Fallujah." Sean was quiet awhile longer. Constance was just about to tell him to flip over when he added, "That was bloody. Really bloody. And ugly. We're talking IEDs. Booby traps. Spider holes. That's where Santos got shot. You seen it?"

Spider holes.

"Yeah, I've seen it." Constance remembered the scars on Rhett's left side, particularly the round one that resembled a bullet wound.

"His last tour was no picnic, either," Sean said. "There's a guy I work with who was in Makhmur with Santos. That's where he hurt his leg."

"He mentioned that. He got hit in the leg but a couple of his men got hit worse and didn't make it."

"Ah," Sean said, the word more of a grunt than an agreement. "Way I heard it, Santos got hit in the leg because he went back out to drag one of his men into cover."

"He didn't tell me that."

"He wouldn't."

Constance let some silence pass. It wasn't lost on her that Sean's willingness to talk about one of his closest buddies—a brother no less—was significant. Detective Callahan trusted her.

"Roll over, Sean. And once your face is in the cradle, I want you to be quiet and relax. This is your time to let go. Can you do that for me?" Constance considered herself a strong person, but she was no magician. She needed Sean to be quiet now and accept her help.

He sighed and settled into the face cradle with a satisfied grunt. "Yes, ma'am."

Sean kept his word and didn't speak after that. The music filled the room and gave Constance a mood to anchor to as she concentrated on Sean's wrecked back and hips. He had a lot of ink, a few scars and one hip well higher than the other. Constance commented on none. She worked the muscles, fixed the hip and stretched and smoothed everything out as his words sunk into the back of her mind. Here she'd been judging Rhett for choosing to be with a woman like Katrina when, really, she was no one to judge. Katrina, when you put the pieces of the puzzle together, made a whole hell of a lot of sense.

By the time she was done, Sean was asleep. She found her stool and moved up toward his head. Constance sank her fingers in his hair and gave him a scalp massage for about ten minutes, which didn't rouse him in the slightest. She rested her hands on his shoulders and did her box breathing until she felt him stir. Only then did she rise and remove the bolster from beneath Sean's ankles.

He groaned and lifted his head. "Did I nod off?"

"Just a little." Constance rarely told clients if they fell asleep. Even though her job was to get them into "rest and digest," most were embarrassed over the prospect of sleeping while being massaged. To Constance, it was the seal of approval that she'd done her job. "I'll step out while you dress. Take your time."

Sean came out a few minutes later, squinting against the sunlight. "That was great," he said, stretching his arms. He bent over and almost touched his toes. "I haven't gotten that close to my feet in years." He stood up with a grin. "You know who needs a lot more of this?" He pointed to the massage room. "Rhett."

Constance offered a rueful smile. "I know. But he found out about your deal with my sister and he's not happy with me right now."

Sean pulled out his wallet and handed over some cash. "Go easy on him, Red." For some reason, Hobbs's nickname had taken off at the gym. It was simpler, and Hobbs was more vocal than Rhett. Constance didn't really mind. She liked both nicknames, for different reasons, and if she was honest with herself, she liked it even more that only Rhett called her Stanzi.

"I'll try," she said. "But he makes it hard."

Sean laughed. "Ain't that the truth. But please don't give up on him. His strategy is to push people away so that they never get the chance. You just have to keep coming at him. You know. Like a pit bull."

Constance bit back a smile.

"I'll see you at the gym."

"Yep," Constance agreed. "Not today, though. You'll be resting and letting those muscles heal and get the full benefit of my massage for the rest of the day, right?"

"Yes, ma'am." He stuffed his wallet in his jeans pocket. "I worked out this morning. It's a good one. Enjoy it if you go tonight. There's running."

"Running," Constance said. "Running used to be my jam. But I haven't run in a long time."

"Well, then." Sean got a big grin on his face. "Today's the day."

Constance wasn't so sure about that.

Stanzi flailed the rope around her feet and hung there, swinging. Hobbs put his hands on her hips to steady her and she dropped to the ground. She pushed her lip out and muttered something, then made a few gestures with her hands.

"You gotta grab it with your feet," Hobbs was saying. "You don't have the upper body strength yet to get up there any other way."

Stanzi glared at the rope. "I know what I'm supposed to do, I'm just not doing it."

So, Stanzi was continuing her quest to climb to the top of the rope. With Hobbs. Rhett felt an odd twisting in his gut, even though it made sense. She'd obviously just done Hobbs's class and had stayed after to work a skill. Rhett knew he should feel proud of her for not giving up—instead of whatever it was he was feeling. He shoved it aside and headed for the office, but at the last second, Stanzi caught his eye. To his surprise, she waved.

Rhett walked over and stopped near the rope. He crossed his arms over his chest. "Getting in some skill work after class?"

"Before class," she corrected. "I'm doing the three o'clock."

"My class?" Rhett didn't try to contain his surprise. She'd avoided him for weeks, and he'd done the same.

"Yep." She pushed her chin up and crossed her arms over her chest.

Rhett bit back a smile. He tilted his head toward the top of the rope. "So get up there."

Stanzi's bravado faltered. Her arms loosened and her lips parted. "We've been trying." She glanced at Hobbs.

"Get your feet hooked," Hobbs said. "I'm going to go eat. I'm starving." He shot Rhett a look that said, *Fine, then. She's all yours.*

Stanzi turned back to Rhett, looking helpless.

"Well, go on." Rhett nodded at the rope again. "You come in here to climb a rope, or what?" He looked down at her chest. "Did you wear that shirt just to talk shit?" As the weather had warmed, and her fitness had improved, Stanzi's joggers had slimmed first to leggings, then to running shorts, and now to a pair of tight but tasteful bike shorts. Her shirts were still loose, but today the sleeves were gone, and she wore a loose-fitting tank top that read Don't Give Up! Don't Ever Give Up! with Jimmy Valvano's signature in the center.

Stanzi's hand covered her chest, as if remembering what she wore.

"Well? What's it going to be? If you're wearing a Jimmy V shirt, you better get your ass on that rope."

She glared at him, but grabbed the rope, drew in a deep breath and let it out with a gush.

"Wait." Rhett pulled the rope away from her. "Try jumping into it."

"What?"

"Jump into it." Rhett stepped back, jumped into the rope, caught it, hooked his feet and stood. He was more than halfway to the tape. He dropped down and released the rope. When he stepped back, he was careful not to limp so she wouldn't see it.

She eyed his leg suspiciously, but then turned back to the rope, drew another deep breath and jumped.

"Hook your feet! Now!"

Stanzi's sneakers searched around the rope. Rhett stood nearby. The longer she took to grab it, the more tired her arms would get. She growled in frustration, ready to drop. Rhett steadied her hips, taking the bulk of the weight off her arms. "Grab it. Get as high as you can, as close to your hands as you can. Lean back."

This time, Stanzi hooked her feet into a successful J-hook. Her back was against his chest, using him for support. Her sweat smelled sweet. Flowery, but not overwhelming. The rosy smell made him think of Christmas Eve, and how she'd looked in that blue dress.

"Now stand up," Rhett ordered. "Stand up on the rope." He moved away, not just to leave her to her own devices, but to avoid the unusual arousal that was rolling through him.

Stanzi rose up, straightening her legs with a grunt.

"Good," Rhett said. "That's one step. Now take another."

Stanzi hung there, flailing.

"Don't let go," Rhett said. "Lean back, move your feet and

hook again, as high up as you can manage. Don't think about it, just do it."

She slid her feet up the rope, trying to hook it. She struggled and made a desperate, angry noise, but eventually got her feet secured.

"Stand up!"

Stanzi obeyed, and her body was now just shy of where she needed to be to touch that tape with an outstretched arm.

"You're almost there." Rhett stood beneath her, in case she panicked and let go. He wasn't afraid she'd fall, but she might shred her hands bailing down the rope. "One more hook, stand up and touch the tape! Let's go!"

Stanzi's feet flailed again. She growled in frustration as her face flushed with her struggle. Her hands slipped a little, but she held on, stopping her slide.

"Don't you dare give up," Rhett ordered. He planted his hands on his hips and stared up at her. "Who's it going to be, Stanzi? You, or the rope? Only one of you is going to win this war."

She let out a roar of frustration, her biceps bulging as she clung to the rope like it dangled over an alligator pit.

"You let go of that rope and I'm going to make you change that shirt before you work out." Rhett circled around, ready to minimize her damage if she dropped, but he stood a foot away.

Her cheeks got so pink it looked like she was wearing rouge, but Stanzi finally hooked her feet. She stood up, reached and her fingertips tapped a good six inches above the tape line.

"That's it!" Rhett barked. "You did it! C'mon, now, don't celebrate yet. Scale down slow. Don't let go and don't slide. Ease on back down."

Stanzi rappelled as slowly as she could, but slid a little bit. Near the bottom, she jumped off and bent in half, hands on her knees, breath heavy and hard. She had a rope burn on her left shin and inside her right thigh, but when she raised her head, she beamed from ear to ear. She sighed and sank into a sumo squat.

Rhett stopped in front of her and held out a hand. "Nice work, Stanzi."

She peeked up at him and accepted his high five with a sweaty smack. "I didn't do it all myself," she said. "You helped steady me for that first hook."

Rhett shrugged. "All I did was help you make the first step. Now your body knows what it should feel like and you can do it easier, when you're not tired."

She nodded, her breath winding down as she gingerly poked at the burn on her shin.

"Clean that off before the workout. So you don't get cellulitis. The ropes are nasty."

Stanzi looked up, like she might say something, but her gaze went past him, toward the front door.

Rhett turned. There, just inside the entrance, waving one hand and holding up his hoodie in the other...

Katrina.

twenty-six

She wore a pair of red booty shorts that cupped her firm bottom and a tight white tank top that thrust her breasts up and together. Her long brown hair was brushed back into a perfect ponytail and she wore enough makeup to make Constance wonder if it would melt during the workout. She wrapped the hoodie around Rhett's waist and attempted to tie it in the back, forcing her chest against his. He brushed her off and tossed the hoodie on top of his duffel bag, which sat in the corner.

Stanzi walked past them, toward the office. The first aid kit was in the top drawer of the desk; she'd seen several people get it out to use on torn hands from too many pull-ups.

"Oh, hi." Katrina waggled her fingers at Constance as she walked past. Her nails were painted red today. "Matilda, right?"

Constance didn't even look her way. "That's right," she called over her shoulder. "You can call me Tillie."

"That's not her name," she heard Rhett say.

Constance smiled at Hobbs, who was chewing the last of

his sandwich and was giving her a thumbs-up. "Saw the end of the rope climb," he said. "Heard Santos shouting and peeked out. Good work, Red."

"Thank you." She ripped open an antiseptic wipe and dabbed her thigh and shin. The sting felt good.

Hobbs glanced out the door, in the direction of Rhett and Katrina, and shook his head. "You should celebrate." He leaned back in his chair and laced his fingers behind his head. His biceps and pecs bulged. He swiveled around. "What's your favorite food?"

"Potatoes."

Hobbs squinted. "What?"

"Potatoes," Constance repeated. "Mashed. Baked. Fried. In a soup. I don't care what. I love potatoes."

"No." Hobbs shook his head. "Your favorite food is Italian or Thai or—"

"No. It's potatoes."

Hobbs stood up and sighed. "Vodka. Your favorite food is vodka."

Constance nodded. "I see where this is going. Okay. An old-fashioned. My favorite food is an old-fashioned."

"What's in that?"

"Sugar is muddled with bitters and…" Constance suppressed a laugh at the look on Hobbs's face. "Whiskey," she said. "It's whiskey."

"See?" Hobbs smiled his big, perfect smile. Constance's mood lifted a little. Hobbs's cheerful grin could perk up anybody. "That wasn't so hard. Would you, Red—" he grabbed his bag from the floor and slung it over his shoulder "—like to join me later for an old-fashioned?"

"Oh." So Constance had not, in fact, seen where this was going. It'd been so long since she'd flirted she'd missed Hobbs's obvious impending segue into asking her out, and merely thought they were talking about food. Slick. She stammered at first. The word around the gym was that Hobbs liked women. As in, all the women. The more he could charm, the better. Not the type Constance went for. She caught sight of Rhett and Katrina, standing near the whiteboard. Katrina kept stepping into his personal space. Rhett would retreat, and she'd follow.

"Is anyone else coming?" Constance turned back to Hobbs.

"Like who?" Hobbs's smile had an amused tinge. He peeked out of the office. "Like Rhett?"

"I didn't mean that," Constance said quickly. "I wasn't sure if it was a group thing or…" She tried to shrug it off but the awkwardness hung like a cloud.

"It's okay, Red." Hobbs stood up and clapped a hand on her shoulder. "I know when I've been beat." He glanced at Rhett again. "Lucky son of a bitch," he muttered.

After he left, Stanzi stood there, her face flushed and her stomach doing flip-flops. She considered heading home for a nap. The workout today was going to be intense: seven rounds for time, with each round consisting of ten power cleans, ten push-ups and ten calories on the rower. Plus the dreaded running Callahan had mentioned—eight hundred meters at the start. All she had to look forward to was getting crushed by Katrina, who would look gorgeous the entire time she was doing it.

Rhett caught her eye and waved her over to the growing circle. The clock read 3:00 p.m.

Constance remembered she was wearing Daddy's old Jimmy V shirt, drew a deep breath and joined the group.

"Couple of changes," Rhett was saying by the time she got there. He uncapped a dry erase marker, erased "10 power cleans" with a swipe of his finger and wrote "5 snatches," leaving the weight at 115 for men and 95 for women. People groaned. Katrina's face crumpled into a glare.

Constance perked up a little. Snatches almost made running seem bearable.

At the bottom of the workout, Rhett wrote, "Buy out: 1 rope climb."

His gaze connected briefly with Constance.

"Rope climbs?" somebody said. "The workout you put online last night didn't have rope climbs. I didn't wear my long socks."

"And I'm wearing shorts," somebody else whined. "I like leggings for rope climbs."

Rhett raised his voice above the din. "Complainers," he said, "you know where your car is." He pointed at the parking lot. The room went quiet. "Part of general preparedness is being able to adapt to and overcome what you're not prepared for. I don't care if you don't have pants, socks, body armor or a gas mask with you today—you can still execute a rope climb."

The room tittered.

"And I don't care if you hate snatching." His gaze went briefly to Katrina. "If any part of this workout is not doable, you are free to scale it, or go to Fitness Universe, just a five-minute drive away. They're open twenty-four hours, have a juice bar and don't care if you do rope climbs or eat doughnuts while you're in the gym. Any questions?"

The laughter intensified, then died off, though Katrina's face remained stony.

"Good." Rhett clapped his hands together. "Let's warm up."

Constance tried not to think about the run while she went through her air squats and push-ups. If she asked Rhett to row instead, she might as well go home. The snatches and rope climb caught her eye while passing the whiteboard during warm-ups. If she made it through the run, she got to do snatches at a weight and rep scheme that was challenging or impossible for most of the women here but was easy for her, as well as see if she could do another rope climb, especially while exhausted. This workout both terrified and thrilled her.

Constance wondered if Rhett had known that all along.

Once he'd gone through the snatch warm-up and demonstrated the standards and scaling options for all the movements, everyone began loading up their barbells. Constance warmed up slowly, but once the weight was on her bar, she felt confident she could do five in a row, seven times. Katrina had the prescribed weight on her bar, too. Constance overheard Rhett suggesting she scale back ten pounds, but Katrina insisted she would be fine.

Constance had heard arguments like this before, and Rhett always won. Mostly, they consisted of the athlete telling Rhett that he would be fine, followed by Rhett telling the athlete to demonstrate a few reps for him to observe. Once that was done, Rhett would say, "Like I said, strip ten pounds." Today, when Katrina argued, Rhett shrugged at her and said, "Suit yourself."

Katrina rolled her bar so that she was directly in front of Constance. "You okay with that weight, Tillie?" She raised her eyebrows at Constance's barbell.

"Yep." Constance sounded braver than she felt.

"Aren't you kind of new to this?" Katrina looked Constance up and down.

Constance resisted the urge to cover all the places on her body that weren't as perfect as Katrina's. "Almost five months. Snatch just comes naturally to me."

"Uh-huh." Katrina turned away.

Once Rhett told everyone to gather outside the bay door for the two laps around the building, Katrina spent a few minutes putting on her wrist wraps. Even though Constance knew Rhett was growing impatient, she used Katrina's intentional slowness to gather her own courage as she headed outside. The chatter and nervous energy of the group became like white noise as Constance stepped into the soft spring wind.

The sky was bright and the air smelled clean, like daffodils and March wind. New growth. This was a day not unlike the one last year, when she'd gone to the park to surprise Josh on his run, and Constance had been the one to be surprised instead. She remembered thinking how dainty and cute his new companion was, all decked out in a pink tank top the color of roses and tiny shorts that showcased skinny legs, complete with thigh gap. At the time, Constance had wanted to look like her. Slender. Toned. Obviously in charge of her weight, her body. Now, the memory of Josh's new running partner was different. The picture Constance had in her mind's eye was more breakable. The woman seemed less in charge and more like a damsel in distress, which was something Constance had never wanted to be.

She barely heard Rhett count down to one and yell go. The last thing Constance remembered was Katrina, her lips in a sneer as she shoved her way in front, leaning forward like she was on a starting block. What happened next was one of those things Constance didn't understand until she ran it through her mind later. She took off, not quite at a sprint but maybe two notches under, knocking Katrina out of her way with a well-placed shoulder check. Like a hound that's found a scent, Constance's feet just kept pumping as she tore around the building. She heard nothing. She saw nothing but her target: two laps around the gym and then back inside.

By the time she was at her barbell, Constance was shocked to see that Rhett was the only other person in the building. That meant she'd beaten everyone else inside. He stood there, arms crossed, a smile on one corner of his mouth before he shouted over the music, "What're you standing there for? Pick that shit up!"

With Eminem's "Till I Collapse" booming from the speakers, Constance snapped to, set herself up in a proper starting position and pulled her first snatch. She dropped beneath the bar with ease.

"Keep up the good form," Rhett said, stepping closer. "You're going to get tired, but don't sacrifice good form for speed, even though you're going for speed, too."

Clear as mud, but Constance knew what he meant. She'd spent enough time in barbell class, as well as the high-intensity conditioning classes, that she knew both sides of this coin. She pulled another snatch, this one feeling just as good.

By her third snatch, the rest of the class started to filter back into the gym. By the time Katrina made it inside, Constance was halfway through her push-ups. She felt a surge of energy, a natural high that propelled her through the bicep burning push-ups and on to the rower to knock out her calories. She'd gained just enough time, through her speedy run and ability to execute the snatches quicker and smoother than Katrina, that Constance actually had a chance to beat her. Katrina's push-ups were ten quick bounces and her row would be slightly quicker, too, with her longer body and better technique. But Constance had the lead and the snatches were going to be the great equalizer.

Constance drew a deep breath and focused on her own work. She ignored the clock and put Katrina out of her sight. All that mattered was that she did this workout as quickly and as well as she could. She didn't even think about the fact that she'd done her first eight-hundred-meter run outside in over a year; she could celebrate that later.

Once her five rounds were complete, Constance's legs and arms were on fire. She faced the rope, stood there staring at it while she caught her breath and sweat dripped into her eyes. The electrical tape looked really high, almost impossible to reach.

"Jump into it!" Rhett shouted. "Hook those feet! I don't care if you're tired! Embrace the suck! Go!"

Constance summoned any energy left and leaped onto the rope. Her feet flailed around while she tried to grab it and she dropped back down.

"C'mon, Red!" Duke was a few feet away, all finished and clapping his hands together. "Get your ass on that rope!"

Constance leaped a second time, this time bringing her feet up as quickly as she could. She got the J-hook so fast she hung there a moment, stunned.

"Go on!" Duke circled around her. "Don't burn out! Go!"

Holding the rope tight, Constance leaned back, brought her legs up and hooked her feet again. She remembered Rhett's command—*stand up*—and fully extended her body. She looked up at the tape and found herself only one tiny step away from being able to tap it.

"Don't let go now!" somebody yelled.

Out of the corner of her eye, Constance saw Katrina fail her snatch. She'd pulled too early and couldn't get under it. In fact, Katrina had failed a lot of her snatches and that had kept her behind. *Focus*, Constance told herself. *That woman is not your problem.*

Dredging up every last ounce of blood and sweat Constance had left in her, her arms screaming, she bent her knees, secured her feet—this time not much higher than where they'd been before—and stood up on the rope. She reached, and her fingertips just barely tapped the tape. Her heart surged, and in her excitement, she slid more than she rappelled her way back to the floor. At the bottom, she landed on her feet, but quickly sank to her butt, then flat on her back. Eyes closed, heart pounding, Constance remembered back to her first day. She'd lain on the floor then, too, after doing her rope climb. But back then, she'd done the scaled version, and was the last to finish.

Her eyes opened as soon as the pain started to recede, just in time to watch Katrina jump on the rope, climb it in about fifteen seconds, and drop to the ground.

Katrina, covered in a sheen of sweat, looked lithe and supple and made the rope climb look easy. Constance lay there, unable to move, and grateful for the people that weren't done yet so that she had more time to recoup before she had to clean up her equipment.

By the time Rhett turned down the music and told everyone they'd done "not horrible," Constance could stand. Everyone was giving high fives. Katrina, face stony, accepted the high fives that came her way but offered none of her own. She was intent on cleaning up her barbell as quickly as possible.

"Nice work," Constance offered. "Your rope climb was beautiful. I hope I get mine that quick someday." She held up her hand.

"Thanks." Katrina gave her palm a swipe that barely counted as a touch. Then she grabbed her water bottle and walked away.

"Red!" Duke stormed up to her, like he was angry, but then stopped, wrapped his arms beneath her backside and lifted her up. "Heard it was your first rope climb! Good job!" He bounced her against his sweaty chest, then set her back on her feet.

"Second rope climb," Rhett's voice corrected as he strode out from behind her. "And nobody wants to touch your sweaty body, Duke."

Duke smoothed back his hair. "Don't be jealous, Santos. I'll pick you up, too. Soon as you do something awesome. Which is never."

Rhett gave the smile he did only with his eyes. He shoved Duke in the chest, then turned to Constance. "How was the run?"

"I honestly don't remember it." Constance wanted to laugh and cry, all at the same time. Only now, with her adrenaline dying down, did everything that had happened this afternoon sink in.

"I'll take that as a good thing. I knew you could do it."

"Makes one of us." Constance laughed at herself, but let it die off when she saw that Rhett wasn't joining in her humor.

"You knew you could do it, too. That's how you got it done. Same as that rope climb." Rhett's jaw tightened. He had about two days' worth of dark growth on his face and his hair was getting a little long in the back, so was starting to curl up around his neck and ears. His gray T-shirt was just tight enough across the chest and shoulders to show how big his muscles were, even fully clothed. His sleeve was shoved up just the tiniest bit, and Constance could see the hooves of the stallion tattoo.

"I think you pissed off your girlfriend." Constance nodded in the direction of the open bay, where Katrina exited with a great show.

Rhett followed her gaze, then shrugged. "She's not my girlfriend."

"I don't think she was happy about you changing up the workout," Constance pushed, even though she probably should've let it drop.

Rhett eyed her in silence for a moment before he said, "I don't think she'll be back."

"Oh, that's a shame."

"Is it?"

Constance remembered everything Callahan had told her today. Rhett's energy was changing by the second, like a storm coming suddenly to sea. "First time I've run in a long time," she said, not wanting to talk any more about Katrina. "I still don't think I want to make it regular, but I'm glad I ran today."

"Warm weather is here." He nodded toward the open bay,

where Katrina had made her huffing exit. "We run a lot after winter's over. Sometimes into the woods and back."

Constance eyed the leafy green trees across the street. This was the first time she'd noticed that Greenview Park butted up to the gym. Greenview Park was where she used to run with Josh. Greenview Park was where he gave up on her. "Trail running used to be my thing. Once upon a time. Not sure how my mile would fare these days."

Rhett stared down at her, silent, his eyes unreadable. A few people walked past and said goodbye or slapped him on the shoulder. He responded to all, but then turned back to Constance and looked down at her again.

"I'll run with you." His eyes softened. "I'll run with you different places outside. On Sundays, when we're closed. Get your legs back. If you want."

Constance bit down on her lower lip. That was not at all what she had expected him to say. She'd expected him to shrug and tell her to man up. She had tremors and butterflies and no way to tell which was which or what they meant. "Okay. But you have to let me help you, too."

He narrowed his eyes. "I don't need any help."

"Yeah, you said that," Constance pressed. She wasn't going to let him put up his facade this time. "We'll swap. You run with me, I'll massage you." She nodded at his leg. "That limp is bad again, and it's not even cold. And you look tired, even though you hide it. You're not sleeping well at night. And even though we've never talked about Humphrey, I think you were having a panic attack. These are all things I can help with."

A long silence passed. Duke went by and yelled goodbye to them both. Neither one of them broke their shared gaze, even when they both muttered, "Bye, Duke."

Finally, Rhett stuck out his hand. "Okay. Deal."

twenty-seven

Sean sat in front of the window, bathed in full sunshine. He'd pulled the chair from Sunny's vanity and plunked it right there, with a view to the gardens. His skin looked tanned and his hair tinged with blond in the bright light.

"What're you doing over there?" Sunny sat up in bed and stretched.

"Watching." His chin rested in his hand, so the word came muffled.

"Watching what?" In all their weeks of weekend mornings, she'd never found him anywhere but in her bed, getting dressed or gone.

"Your rescue." Sean continued to stare out the window. Eventually, he stood, flipped the chair around and settled it back at the dresser with Sunny's makeup and mirrors. "You've got some loyal people helping you. Impressive."

"Thanks." Sunny glanced at the clock and jumped from the covers. "Oh, jeez. I'm going to be late."

"For?"

"Meeting with Pete about the pups." Sunny yanked on a pair of leggings. She hurriedly pulled on a T-shirt, then realized she'd forgotten her bra and stripped it off.

"You hang out with Pete a lot." Sean watched her scramble around. "I think he's sweet on you."

Sunny's fingers slowed on the clasp of her bra. "I've known Pete since I was a kid. And it's Cici he's sweet on. Besides, he knows we're sleeping together." Top on again, she glanced in the mirror, saw she'd put on a black bra beneath a white T-shirt and stripped the top over her head again. She balled it up and tossed it in the corner. "Sorry. I'm not a morning person by nature." Sunny dug a black shirt from her drawer and pulled it over her head.

"No need to apologize." Sean leaned against the wall, like he was settling in for a show. "I'll watch you undress as much as you want."

Sunny gave his reflection a smile as she fluffed her hair with her fingers. No time to make it look good.

"Is that what we're doing?" he asked.

Sunny dabbed gloss on her lips and rubbed them together. "What?"

"Sleeping together. Is that what we're doing?"

Sunny tossed the gloss on the table and turned to face Sean. "Well—" she shrugged "—aren't we?"

"Yeah." Sean pushed off the wall. "Sure."

Sunny rubbed her lips together again, slowly. "Are you...? What are you...?" She put her hands on her hips as the question faded out. This was a new scenario for her. Now that she thought about it, she wasn't sure she'd ever had a man ask her where they were at in their relationship. She'd certainly never asked it herself. Besides, she knew Sean was technically still married, even though he was separated.

"I was thinking." Sean's expression was his typical cool, calm and collected. "We should have dinner, maybe."

"Dinner?" Sunny shifted her weight from foot to foot. Shoes. She needed shoes. "Um…sure." She disappeared into her closet and returned with a pair of red Italian sandals.

"Sure?" Sean narrowed his brow, gave a little shrug.

"Sure." Sunny slipped on the sandals and grabbed her purse. "We can have dinner."

"When?"

"Soon." Sunny glanced at the clock. "I need to get going. Just text me and we'll figure it out."

Sean shrugged again. "Okay."

Sunny walked over, planted her hands on his chest, leaned in and gave him a peck on the lips. "Gotta run. You know the way out."

Sean caught her arm as she turned to go, drew her back in and gave her a long, slow kiss that made Sunny want to get undressed and get back into bed. The way Sean's hands slipped beneath her shirt told her he felt the same way. "No, no, no," she whispered, pushing him gently away. "Oh! White Fern Road." In all the mess with Janice Matteri, Sunny had completely forgotten about the poor dog that lived out by the barn. "Have you had a chance to peek over there?"

He held on to her another second, then released her. "White Fern Road. Yeah, I peeked over there. Didn't see a dog at all."

Sunny's chest tightened. "Maybe he was around the other side, where you couldn't see him."

"Maybe. I'll drive by again."

"Thank you." She kissed him once more. "Okay. Now I really am late." When Sunny made it to the door, she glanced over her shoulder and saw that Sean was once again staring out at the grounds.

★ ★ ★

Pete was letting Chevy's pups have the run of his living room, which used to be his parents' living room. He'd taken over the house when his folks moved to Florida a decade ago. This was the same living room where Sunny, Cici and Pete used to play—Twister on the hundred-year-old floor or *Space Invaders* on the boxy television. The irony was not lost on Sunny that Pete's mom had hated dogs, and would never let him have one, and now canines ruled this roost.

"That one." Pete pointed to Ziggy, a wiggling ball of energy. Her brindle coat was heavy on the black and her ears were larger than a typical pit bull's. "She's being trained for mobility service. And that one—" Pete pointed to Munchkin, the smallest, who had a large caramel spot around his left eye "—is being trained for psychiatric service. And that one—" Pete pointed at Zelda "—the one rolling around on her back like a buffalo wallowing in the dirt?" She was mostly white, with random splotches of tan and black that looked like continents on a map. "I still haven't figured that one out."

"Different personalities for different jobs," Sunny agreed.

"I'm tempted to rename them." Pete gave a sly grin. "Cici, Pete and Sunny."

"Oh, no, you didn't." Sunny giggled. "I'm the one wallowing in the dirt?"

"You know it."

Sunny gave him a shove. "I hate you."

Pete tilted back the brim of his baseball cap and grinned. "I'm happy to see that smile. You've been really tense lately."

"I didn't know you'd noticed." Sunny reached out and ran her fingers down the sides of his chin. His beard was softer than she'd expected. "How long you going to grow this?" Personally, she liked it right where it was. It gave him a sexy, rugged look, but any longer and Pete would start to look like a guy from a Civil War photo.

"Don't change the subject," Pete said. "But since you asked, I was thinking a little longer. What do you think? You like it?"

"I do like it." Sunny was surprised. Typically, she preferred clean-shaven. "But any longer and you'll be trendy." Pete grimaced. Sunny pointed a finger. "I knew that would get you."

"Yeah?" Pete's humor died a little. "And what's getting you? You haven't been yourself lately. That guy you're dating treating you right? The cop?"

"Sure." Sunny sank to the original hardwood floor of Pete's living room. Sunny often thought about all the feet that had walked on this wood, what kind of shoes they wore and where those shoes had roamed. Zelda, the little crazy one who Pete couldn't figure out, streaked into Sunny's lap, her head hitting Sunny's abs as she flopped onto her back. "We're not really dating, anyway. I'm not sure what we are, other than the product of a bargain. Sean lived up to his end in spades. Took out Janice Matteri's puppy mill in one fell swoop. I've been picking away at her for years, and along comes Sean, with his badge, and she's down for the count." Sunny shook her head. "Who knew?" She left out the part about Janice's threat. Even though weeks had gone by and nothing had materialized but a moved feed bin, Sunny still felt Janice's icy words in her veins.

"You're the one that took her down," Pete corrected. He rolled his eyes as Sunny indulged Zelda's "crazy" by rubbing her tummy. "Your cop wouldn't have had any interest in Janice Matteri without you in the pot."

"In the pot?" Sunny gripped Zelda's ears gently in both hands and stroked them, enjoying the silky feel in her palms. She was pretty sure that the stray who mated with Chevy was a lab, based on the puppies' ears and coloring. "You make me sound like a bargaining chip."

"No offense to you, Sunny, but your cop isn't helping you out of the goodness of his heart or for the love of the dogs. You're not just part of a bargain to him. He's helping you because he's sweet on you."

Sunny kissed Zelda on the head and rose up to face Pete. "That's funny. Sean said the exact same thing about you."

"What thing?" Pete's eyes narrowed.

"He said you were 'sweet on me.'" Sunny laughed as she made air quotes. "He brought up how much time we spend together and suggested you like me. Isn't that the most hilarious thing you've ever heard?" Sunny giggled and waited for Pete to bend in half, his body racked with laughter.

"Oh." Pete's face relaxed, all lines erased as he considered her words. He watched the puppies race around with each other. "I guess he's a pretty good detective, then."

"I know, right? I told him how dumb he sounded. I told him how you've always had a thing for Cici and… Wait." Sunny's mouth closed. She did a mental rewind. "Did you just say he was or wasn't a good detective? I don't think I heard you right. Or maybe you didn't hear me right?"

Pete crossed his arms over his chest. "I said he was. And I heard you right."

"Oh." Sunny thought back on her words, just to make sure she'd said them the way she meant to say them. "But that means that…"

"Guess we know who isn't a good detective." Pete's seriousness ceded to a half smile. That was his uncertain smile. One side of his mouth would tuck up at the corner and his eyes would get big. He'd been doing it since that day, ages ago, when he'd come upon Sunny and Cici in the woods, halfway between their homes, and said, "I'm Pete. You guys wanna play hide-and-seek?"

"So you're sweet on me how? Like a sister?" Suddenly, she was sweating.

"That's not what 'sweet on' means. Nobody's 'sweet on' their sister."

"But you have a thing for Cici." Sunny rubbed her sweaty palms down the front of her pants. "You always have. You even said so recently, back when we first found the pups." Sunny pointed at him, like she'd caught him in a lie. "I said you had a thing for Cici and you said, 'A little bit.'"

"Yeah." Pete shrugged. "A little bit. But with you, it's a lot."

Silence passed. Their gazes locked and didn't waver. Sunny had looked into Pete's eyes so many times, but not once had she noticed *this*. Had it always been there? This tension? This *ache*?

"You're messing with me." Sunny's voice seemed thin and high.

"My crush on Cici was always the kind I could show. My crush on you is the kind I don't want anybody to see."

Sunny became aware of her shifting feet only after Pete glanced down at her sandals. The world felt unreal and unstable all of a sudden.

"Look, Sunny, I've been around you guys a long time. Like, all my life. I've watched you grow and turn into women. I've watched you go from little backwoods thugs who could build a tree house better than any boy to taller backwoods thugs who steal dogs from abusive owners. I've seen Cici get her heart broken and I've seen you break about a million others. I've seen how your father raised you tough as nails and what good and bad came from that, and I've seen you both break in half when he got cancer and died. I've seen it all. I know you in and out." Pete paused and drew a deep breath. "Friendship like that doesn't come around every day. Women like you two don't come around every day. I've never wanted to muck it up by pushing for more." Pete stripped off his baseball cap and swiped his forehead, like he might be sweating, too. "But dammit, Sunny. With you, I want more."

"You know—" Sunny's voice came out sounding less joking than she'd intended "—if you kissed me, you'd probably feel like you were kissing your sister."

"Well." Pete tossed his cap on the couch. "There's only one way to find out."

Sunny swallowed the giant lump that'd formed in her throat. What was wrong with her? Why wasn't she laughing this off? Why wasn't he?

"Unless you feel like you'd be cheating on the cop. You just said it wasn't serious, that you're not dating. But if it is…"

"It's not." It wasn't for her. Was it for Sean? After this morning, she wasn't so sure. Still, they had no promises, no exclusivity. What harm would come from kissing Pete, then dissolving into laughter when they realized how silly they'd been?

Pete smiled at whatever expression arrested her features. "C'mon, Sunny Skye." He took her hands and drew her in, against his chest. "It won't be so bad." He pushed the hair back from her face, his fingers calloused and knuckles bruised from all the outdoor work.

Sunny was suddenly aware of all of her body parts, like she was a million pieces of a jigsaw puzzle. She didn't know where to put her hands, so she just rested them on his biceps, which were firm. Images of Pete last summer, in a T-shirt, sleeves rolled up and sweat on his brow as he built a new structure for his dogs, flashed through her mind.

"I don't understand what's happening," Sunny whispered as he drew her closer and his breath passed over her lips. She'd never fantasized about Pete in the past, not even as a teenager. He'd always just been Pete. Good ole Pete. Or, as Cici said, Pesky Petey.

He didn't feel like that now. He didn't feel like a comfortable shoe or a pesky neighborhood boy. He felt warm and arousing, the nearness of him getting in Sunny's blood and under her skin. Maybe he'd been doing that for decades, and only now was Sunny realizing just how much of him she'd absorbed.

His fingertips were on either side of her face, gentle, like the way she'd stroked his beard. "Last chance," he whispered.

Any reply Sunny had was swallowed up in the sensations that enveloped her body once Pete's lips touched hers. Her words melted and her body dissolved against the soft tease of his mouth and tongue. His kiss wasn't greedy or forced, but drew her in, an invitation to peek inside, to know him differently. She felt different layers of him come alive beneath her touch. Some were familiar, but heightened, such as the tender and selfless man who spent his time working tirelessly for others. And some were strangers, the owner of deep desires kept under careful control for a long, long time.

Sunny's knees buckled, and she held fast to his arms. Pete slid one around her waist to steady her, then kissed her once more, soft and deliberate. He drew back slowly. "Well, I don't have a sister," he said, his breath ragged. "But I don't think kissing her would feel like that."

Sunny touched her fingertips to her cheeks, then her lips. Her heart thundered in her ears. Only one thing was going to happen if she didn't leave, right this second. "I have to go."

She expected Pete to get angry or ask her a million questions, but he only gave that half smile. "Was it that bad?" he said. "Or was it that good?"

"I have to go," Sunny repeated, the words coming too quickly. She grabbed her purse, didn't even pause to pet the puppies and bolted toward the front door.

Behind her, coming through the raging pulse in her ears, she heard Pete say, "Okay, Sunny Skye. You know where I am."

twenty-eight

By the time Constance arrived at the gym, she was both relieved and dismayed to see Rhett's Jeep parked in his favorite far left corner of the lot. It'd taken her forever to get dressed and get herself here, and she was twenty minutes late.

Constance approached the Jeep and found Rhett sitting in the driver's seat, eyes closed, window down, a classic rock station playing on the radio. He wore a blue T-shirt with the Semper Fit logo and had a clean-shaven face. She reached in to shake his shoulder and he caught her wrist just before she touched him. He squinted at her through the sunshine, sighed and let her go. "You're late."

"Sorry."

Rhett got out of the Jeep and stretched. He put his hands on his hips. "You good to run?"

Constance spread her arms open. "I'm here." That was the closest she'd come to agreeing. "How about you?"

"I've been here."

"You look tired."

He stopped short of saying something, probably *I'm always tired*. Truth was, he'd learned to function quite well on too little sleep. Constance knew what that looked like, and Rhett was a master.

"You're a little overdressed," he said. "It's already sixty-nine degrees. You know as well as I do that means it's going to feel like eighty once we get moving."

Constance looked down at her joggers and oversize T-shirt. She touched her hair when she saw Rhett eyeing her sloppy bun. She hadn't wanted a ponytail and loose wasn't an option, so she'd done her best to twirl it up into a knot. It kind of looked like a frayed pincushion. "I'll be okay."

Rhett looked skeptical but didn't press the issue. "I figured we'd run the sidewalks up and down the main road there." He pointed to the road behind the gym. "I've run it many times. You can go seven miles out before you run out of sidewalk. That's fourteen if we go out and back. Obviously we won't run that far today."

Constance smiled. She hadn't talked in runner's speak in ages.

As they walked through the parking lot and alongside the building, Rhett sketched out his plan. "Since we're running along a main road, there's a lot of traffic. But it's a good way to get your legs back without too many hills."

"Hey," she said as they climbed down to the sidewalk. "I was thinking about your nickname. Does anyone ever make *Gone with the Wind* jokes?"

Rhett actually did a double take. He'd turned to scope out the traffic but looked back to her quickly. He was smiling with his eyes. "Are you stalling, Stanzi?"

"No," she lied. She grabbed her ankle, pretending to stretch her quads as she bent her knee. "I've just been meaning to ask you. I never did find a way to shorten your name and it got me thinking. If anyone ever makes jokes."

"I've had a few people over the years call me Butler," Rhett admitted. "But the joke's on them, because that's my middle name. My mother's maiden name is Butler."

"Your name is Rhett Butler Santos?"

"Yeah. You got a problem with that, Morrigan?" He poked her in the chest. The smile in his eyes had melted down to the corners of his mouth. Clean-shaven? Five-o'clock shadow? Beard? Didn't matter. He was striking, any which way. It was like getting different flavors of your favorite dessert.

Constance felt stupid just staring at him. But not stupid enough to run yet. "I don't think I ever apologized." Now was as good a time as any, and it was long overdue.

Rhett didn't insult her intelligence by asking for what. He did look out at the traffic again, like he was either searching for or hiding an expression. When he faced her, he just shrugged. "I understand why you kept it to yourself."

"I'm not sure I'm sorry I kept it to myself," Constance clarified, "because I'm not sure I could have done anything different. But I am sorry I hurt you. I know what it's like to lose trust. And I never meant that to happen. You were never part of a bargain."

"Well—" Rhett tilted his head from side to side, like he was shaking her words around "—I appreciate that."

Constance nodded. "So." She squeezed her hands together, then stuck one out. "We're good?"

Rhett glanced at her attempt at a handshake, then ignored it and took off at a warm-up clip. "Yeah," he called over his shoulder, "we're good. C'mon. Move your ass!"

"Hey!" Constance started running after him. "I wasn't ready yet!"

Rhett turned around, so that he was running backward. He smiled, wide and unmistakable. "Frankly, my dear, I don't give a damn."

★ ★ ★

They didn't need to run a great distance today, or any day, really, to get ready for the running they did in the gym workouts. He didn't think he'd ever programmed anything more than a 5k. All Rhett wanted to accomplish was getting Stanzi on her feet again. Any short distance would do, but despite her year off, her body was going to quickly remember all those miles she used to put in. It already showed when she did the high-intensity workouts at the gym. She might not be able to lift as much weight or do as many of the skills as the more experienced, but her engine was strong. Rhett was never worried about Stanzi being a quitter. He figured a relaxed 5k was all she needed today.

Rhett kept her on the inside of the sidewalk, away from the traffic. She had a quick pace, which didn't surprise him. Her form was good and she knew how to breathe, how to negotiate traffic so she didn't lose her stride nor get plowed over by a semi.

But she'd made a classic rookie mistake that no seasoned runner would: she'd overdressed. By mile two, which Rhett had let slip by without remembering to turn around at the half mark on his GPS watch, Stanzi was panting like a husky in the desert.

She didn't complain, though. She just kept going, her cheeks on fire and sweat flying from her face to the pavement. Then she started tugging on her collar, mopping her face with the hem of her shirt, gasping a little bit. She must've finally had enough because she stripped her shirt over her head and stuffed it in the waistband of the back of her pants. Beneath, Stanzi wore a red sports bra that was supportive but still couldn't completely contain her generous chest. There was no longer much excess around her middle; she'd built muscle and dropped resting body fat at the same time.

A loud, double-tap honk rang out from a utility truck that flew by. A man in the passenger seat leaned out the window and whistled. Stanzi's pace slowed. She petered off into a walk and veered into a shady area, next to a kids' playground. She chose an empty picnic table beneath a large maple tree, sank to the bench, clasped her hands between her knees and rested her elbows on her thighs. She leaned forward, the sweat dripping from her forehead, and cursed softly to herself.

"Why'd you wear these winter pants?" Rhett sat down next to her, wishing he'd brought water. Another thing seasoned runners didn't do was carry water during a 5k.

Stanzi gasped a short laugh. "I don't know. Actually, I do. I think it's as simple as not wanting to wear running shorts. Every time I think about running, including the eight hundred meter the other day at the box, I think about the day I went to surprise my fiancé on the running trail and found him running with someone else."

Ah. Now they were getting somewhere.

"Josh and I met on that running trail. In Greenview Park actually. During a Turkey Trot. We were using each other as a pacer all throughout the race. At the end, when I beat him by ten seconds, he asked me out." She smiled at the memory. "We were together for three years, but…" She twirled her forefinger. "After my dad got sick, I had little time or energy for running. I got slower and slower and more and more out of shape. Josh withdrew. Told me I was making excuses. But running was such a large part of our relationship." She shook her head. "Too large, I realize now. After Dad died, I realized I needed to dig myself out of the hole I'd let myself sink into. I went to the park to surprise Josh. He was such a creature of habit, I knew exactly what trail he'd be on. I knew I'd find him there. What I didn't know was that she would be there with him." Stanzi's voice got softer, almost dreamy.

"It was her legs. Her bare legs in those running shorts. Slender to a fault. Easy to move for distance. She looked like I looked, once upon a time. Josh was pretty much dating me again…or the person I had been when he met me. The person I no longer was."

Rhett leaned back, elbows on the picnic table. He knew this was a moment when speaking less and listening more was the right thing to do. He stared out at the playground, a few yards away, and enjoyed the breeze cooling the sweat on his face. The equipment was covered in screaming children. Young moms, a few dads and a handful of grandparents followed them around, from slide to monkey bars to swings. The trash receptacles were overflowing with junk food wrappers, fast-food containers, apple cores and banana peels. Birds and squirrels pecked at the spillage on the ground. The chatter going on around them was one hundred percent parental: "Decker, stop poking your brother!"

"Hey, my kid was playing with that!"

"Good job, Buddy! You climb that all by yourself?"

"I didn't stop because of the pants," Stanzi admitted. "It may sound weird, but it was the honk. And the whistle." She shook her head. "I know it sounds dumb. But after I gained weight and Josh ditched me for a newer, slimmer running partner, all I wanted was to be that woman again. The sexy, skinny chick that got Josh's attention. But then, when I was honked and whistled at just now, I was ashamed of myself that I had ever wanted to be a certain way for Josh. It's bad enough we have to dwell on our appearances every single day, for every little thing we do. We have to ask ourselves, every time we go out for a run, should I wear this? Are my shorts too short? Is my bra pushing up my breasts too much? If I run this way, rather than that way—" she gestured with her hands "—will I get more or less catcalls? And, when I do, should I be nice and smile and wave? Or should I flip the middle finger? If I do that, what are the odds someone comes after me? What are the odds they'll come after me if I smile? Am I a bitch if I ignore them? A slut if I whistle back? Why do I even care? Why am I measuring myself, my beauty and my worth by how skinny I am or how many catcalls I get? And it's not as though catcalls are even compliments! Just a comment on women existing. And what if I just don't feel like dealing with all that shit? What if I just want to run in peace?" Her voice rose in pitch by the time she sputtered her last question.

Rhett kicked up some dirt with his shoe. He'd always found Stanzi brave, beautiful and sexy, both when she started at Semper Fit and now, her resting body fat having little to do with the equation or his attraction.

"I know I just went off on a tangent," Stanzi admitted with a rueful smile. "But I guess what I'm trying to say is, I dressed like this today because I didn't want to have to care how I looked while I ran with you. Josh clearly wanted to run with—to be with—a woman who looked a certain way. I wanted to run with you while looking as frumpy as possible. And then the honk reminded me of everything that I don't want defining me anymore."

Rhett tried to keep silent, to stay neutral, so that Stanzi would keep letting it all out, getting rid of it, making sense of it. But he felt himself smile, just the littlest bit.

Stanzi smiled back. "You've never had to plan your outfit before a run, have you?" Her question wasn't accusatory, just curious. She didn't wait for him to answer. "You've probably never even thought about what you wear to work out. And I bet you can count any catcalls you've gotten on one hand, which has nothing to do with how attractive you are. It's just different for you. Different rules. Same world."

Rhett stared out at all the kids, running, screaming, jumping, their lungs bursting in the sunshine, their voices exploding against the blue sky. He rested his hand on Stanzi's back, right above her bra strap, on the sweaty skin between her shoulder blades.

She didn't flinch.

They sat like that for a while. In the silence that passed, one kid fell off the top of the slide, but hopped right back to his feet, despite his mother's horror; another kid got yelled at for spitting on another boy, and a football landed at Stanzi's feet. She picked it up and winged it back to the teenagers who were tossing it around while they watched what must've been younger brothers playing on the seesaw. Damn. Good arm.

Stanzi's skin had grown cool under Rhett's hand. "We can walk back, if you want," he said. "You ran more than two miles already."

Stanzi offered a weak smile. "Progress is progress, right?" She stood up and stretched. "And I will celebrate progress by running some more."

Rhett followed suit. "You going to wear your giant shirt?" He nodded at the tee stuffed in the back of her pants.

She shook her head. "Nah."

"All right." Rhett stripped his off, too.

Stanzi giggled as they headed out of the park, back onto the sidewalk. "Hey, baby—" she mimicked a dude's voice "—you running my way?"

Rhett rewarded her attempt at humor with a laugh. "My eyes are up here." He gestured with his first two fingers.

After he got a few steps ahead, he heard her mutter, "Can't go wrong either way." He was pretty sure he wasn't supposed to hear that, so he kept his second laugh to himself.

By the time they made it back to the gym, Stanzi was drenched in sweat again. Rhett nodded toward the bakery across the street, which had been strategically situated between his gym and the one on the opposite corner that offered spin classes, resistance machines and every type of electronic exercise gadget on the market. "Let's get some fuel."

Cinnamon, vanilla, coffee, chocolate and butter wafted out of the warm interior of the shop as Rhett held the door open. Stanzi stood there, a little smile on her lips.

"What's wrong?"

"Nothing." Her smile deepened. "It's just—" she swiped back the hair from her face that had gotten loose from her messy bun "—the last time I stood in front of this shop, I was miserable. I'd skipped the spin class on the corner and I felt depressed and defeated. I saw your gym across the street and I just stood here, staring, while some guy held the door for me."

"Déjà vu, eh?"

"Yeah. Except this time I feel way different. Not perfect, but different." Her blue eyes were brighter than the sky, her skin kissed by the sun and wind, and her body lit by a sort of glow that made Rhett want to throw her over his shoulder, carry her back to his house and toss her on his bed. If she asked, all of that would be done in a classy, romantic sort of way, but in his mind things were way more primal than that.

"Get inside already." Rhett nudged her foot with his. "And maybe put on your shirt. You'll get cold in the air-conditioning."

"Oh!" She yanked it from her sweats and opened it up, slipping it over her head with a little bit of a struggle as she searched for the sleeves. She popped her head through, her hair full of flyaways, and marched forward. She ran smack into the chest of a blond guy, average height, well dressed, who was coming out the door. A blonde woman by his side scooted to the left, so she wouldn't get run over. Between the hair, the clothes and the bland smiles, they looked like Malibu Barbie and her surfer date.

"Sorry," Stanzi said. Then her smile crumpled.

"Connie!" The man's eyes widened. "Is that you?"

Josh stepped back, to allow her inside. Constance entered the bakery, the sweet and spicy smells settling in her stomach like heavy dough. "Hi," she said, because she couldn't think of anything else. The sight of Josh, along with the woman from the park, made her skin go cold all over. Constance was glad she'd put her shirt on. Oh, my God. Had she put her shirt on before Josh saw her? Her hands ran over her midsection, an old habit she hadn't performed in months.

"Hi, I'm Rhett." He stuck out his hand. They were all lined up by the pastry case, the glass shiny and showcasing its wares. The top row had a rustic cherry pie, a classic carrot cake with orange carrot icing decorations, blueberry muffins with giant domes and whoopie pies with oozing marshmallow filling. Constance suddenly wanted them all.

"Oh, I'm sorry." Constance knew her face had paled. "Rhett, Josh. Josh, Rhett."

Josh accepted Rhett's handshake.

Even though Constance had never considered Josh a small man, he didn't look as large as he used to, next to Rhett.

Josh's hand tightened on his bakery bag, making a crumpling sound. "Nice to meet you." His gaze settled on Rhett's bare, ripped torso, a concentrated look on his face. Constance remembered that look. That was the look Josh got when a drunk at a bar tried to pick a fight with him, or when his boss asked Constance to dance at an office party. Didn't like it, but wasn't going to do anything about it, either.

The obliques, Constance thought. That must be what Josh couldn't look away from. Everything on Rhett's torso was gorgeous. The big pecs, the anterior delts, the upper traps, the abs. But the obliques were something special. Ropy, and the way they disappeared into his shorts, almost like little arrows pointing the way to heaven…

"Connie." Josh's voice sounded like he'd said her name a few times. "This is Jenna." He motioned toward the woman next to him; she wore a silk tank top, a long skirt and an uncomfortable smile.

"Hi, Jenna." Constance extended her hand. Jenna brushed her fingertips. "We've met, remember? You're the woman Josh was jogging with, that day in the park. Right?"

Jenna blanched.

Rhett laughed out loud. He pulled his shirt over his head. Several women, seated throughout the small bakery, looked disappointed.

"You look great," Josh said, ignoring her comment. His gaze toured her body as much as it had Rhett's, but with a different expression. "What've you been doing?"

"Little bit of everything." Constance shifted her weight from foot to foot. There was a dispenser on the counter to take a number, and as more people entered the shop and the line got longer, she resisted the urge to grab one. She knew she was supposed to be polite and give Josh compliments and ask him questions, too, but words wouldn't come. After the story she'd just told Rhett, seeing Josh and his girlfriend in real life was a strange sort of gift that she didn't quite know what to do with. *Here's the guy who's kept you from doing something you loved. Here's the woman you were jealous of. What do you think of all that now?*

"Well, you look great." Josh's eyes traveled over her again. "How's your sister?"

"Excuse me." Rhett pushed between Josh and Jenna, causing her to jump back, clutching at her collarbone. He snagged a number from the dispenser and held it up. "We're hungry."

"Sunny's fine," Constance told Josh.

"Great. That's great."

Jenna pursed her lips together and shot Josh a dark look. An arm slipped around Constance's waist. The light pressure wasn't possessive, just an invitation. Constance contained her surprise and sank against Rhett's chest. He was warm and damp and smelled like fabric softener.

"Well." Rhett stared down at Josh. "It was nice meeting you."

Josh's gaze went toward the embrace, then back up to Rhett's face. "Nice meeting you, too." He turned to Constance, and his expression warmed. "Good seeing you again, Connie. Whatever you're doing, keep it up. You really do look great."

"I feel great. That's what matters."

"Oh." Josh's forehead wrinkled. "Good. Good."

"Bye."

"Bye, then."

Once they were gone, Rhett withdrew his arm and led her to a tall, round table in the corner by the window. It seated only two, with old-fashioned high stools. "Arm wrestle for the stool facing out?"

Constance stroked her chin. "Take it. I don't have the same need to have my back to the wall that you do, and I wouldn't stand a chance at arm wrestling you. But I will fight you for who gets the coffee." She nodded toward the coffee station: a row of cups, carafes and stirring sticks. You could pour while you waited, then pay when your number was called.

They did Rock, Paper, Scissors and Rhett won.

Constance got the coffee—black for Rhett and a splash of milk for herself—then climbed on her stool and stared out at the Sunday crowd. Some were churchgoers, headed out to shop or eat after service. Others were dressed in fitness clothes and aimed for the gym on the corner. A few wore sweatpants and even pajamas, headed into the grocery store at the other end of the strip mall.

"Sorry about that." Rhett set their paper ticket on the table. It read 135.

"You're not sorry. You're enjoying your win." Constance's pounding pulse was slowly coming down. Seeing Josh felt so much different than it had last time she was having trouble sorting through it. Last time, his classically handsome, slightly arrogant face had filled her with longing, and the sight of Jenna had made her feel sick. She'd gone home, eaten an entire bag of tater tots, then climbed into bed and binge-watched *Psych* for the rest of the day.

This time, seeing Josh almost made her feel foolish. That's who she gave up running for? That's who she'd wanted to be?

"No, I mean I'm sorry about pretending we were together," Rhett said. "When I put my arm around your waist. I couldn't help it."

Constance's body grew warm thinking about it. "Nothing to be sorry about."

"I wasn't trying to be possessive. I just wanted him to stop looking at you like that. And to shut up." Rhett pulled the ticket toward him and started to roll it up into a cylinder.

Constance laughed. "It's not like he had anything to look at." She held up the hem of her oversize T-shirt and stuck her legs out straight to display her sweaty, long pants.

"He saw you with your shirt off."

She wrapped her arms around her chest. "Are you sure?"

Rhett nodded. "Positive."

Constance waved a hand. "I don't care." Part of her was actually glad. *I don't know you anymore.* Take that, Joshua Stoneford. You really *don't* know me anymore.

Rhett smiled. "That was kind of freaky, huh?" He tilted

his head toward the door Josh had exited. "That we bumped into them."

"I was just thinking that." After suffering her first public run and growing cold while talking to Josh, the coffee filled her insides like a warm hug. "But I'm so glad it happened. I can't even imagine being with him now. He clearly only wanted to be with one version of me. When that side of me struggled, the fit runner who had it all together, Josh bailed. Went out and found himself a new Connie."

"One thirty-five!"

Rhett unrolled his ticket and stood up. "Know what you want?"

Constance eyed the pastry case. To her surprise, none of the sugary fare sounded appetizing anymore. The aromas coming from the savory section were like heaven, though. "The bacon, egg and spinach bites." She nodded to the flourless muffins that came in a set of three.

Rhett smiled. "You read my mind."

They got the same thing, though Rhett got two orders for himself. Constance refreshed their coffees while he got the muffins, and once they'd dug into their food he said, "So what made the fit runner Constance struggle? You said your dad was sick?"

"He had a long, hard battle with cancer." She glanced up, but Rhett didn't flinch. "Josh didn't exactly understand how I coped with that. In fact, he hated how I coped with that."

Rhett stuffed an entire muffin in his mouth and still managed to chew without any spilling out. "Which is how?"

Constance nibbled at her second muffin. The eggs were creamy and the bacon salty and crisp. The spinach offered just enough vegetal tang to bring it all together. "I kind of shut down. While Dad was sick, I was consumed with taking care of him. Sunny helped as best she could but she's so busy with the rescue—plus, she's the younger daughter so doesn't have as many duties. People might say that's bullshit, but it's not. As the eldest, his care was more on me than her, just as it was all our lives. When Daddy died, I didn't cry." Constance sipped at her coffee. "Josh really hated that I didn't cry. Told me I was holding it all in. I said, 'What do you expect? I was raised by a Vietnam veteran. I was never allowed to cry.' Except I did cry. Every time I overate, or ate like crap—" she nodded at the pastry case "—I was crying. Whenever I missed a run because I was just too worn out or sad or getting too slow on the trail, I was crying. Josh told me I was just being lazy. Told me running would make me feel better if I just got off my ass and went. When he started running with that woman, Jenna, he said it was because who I was turning into wasn't what he signed up for. He didn't know me anymore."

All of Rhett's body movements froze. A second later, he swallowed what he'd been chewing. He chased it with a long drink of coffee. "So that's how you found out he was cheating on you? You found him running with her?"

"Oh, I don't know if he was cheating on me or not." Constance shrugged. "He said he wasn't, but it didn't make any difference. Still doesn't. When I found him running with her, I could literally see what it was that he loved most about me. And it wasn't enough."

Rhett nodded thoughtfully.

"I broke it off," Constance admitted. "Everyone, including Sunny, thinks Josh dumped me. I just said we broke up and everyone figured he dumped me for that woman." She shrugged. "I never corrected them."

"Why not?"

She shrugged. "Doesn't matter. I don't honestly think we ever loved each other. In hindsight. I guess in one way that woman saved me from a bad marriage."

"You'd have figured it out."

"Maybe." Constance had thought about this before. "I'm a different person now. Weaker in some ways, stronger in others. But I see people more clearly now. I was pretty good at it before, but I'm even better now. Feeling what others are feeling. Guessing what they're going to do before they do it. I see more details. Which can be debilitating, but also saves me from a lot of hurt." Constance finished her food and slid her empty coffee cup to the edge of the table. "What about you? How did you deal with…things?"

Rhett, who'd been staring out the window, shook himself. "Eh, I don't know," he said. "I was combative with my therapist. I hated taking the meds. I didn't cry." He let a beat pass before he smiled.

Constance laughed as she crumpled up her napkin. "Are you making fun of me?"

"Not one bit."

The bakery had grown even more crowded since their arrival. Every available inch of space was now occupied by people sitting at the tables or the counter, standing in the line that wound out the front door or milling around, searching for a spot to settle. "C'mon." Constance stood up. "Let's go to my house. I owe you a massage."

Stanzi had him lie faceup this time, and she worked his bad leg first. She started at the hip and worked her way down, massaging, stretching and rubbing cooling oil into his muscles that helped kill the pain and stiffness. Once she moved to the less painful side, Rhett felt himself starting to doze. He was aware of her in the back of his mind, when she moved up to his chest and arms, working his pecs and delts and the muscles around his ribs. Just when he thought he might slip away, she had him roll over, facedown, and started in on his back.

Her hands were pleasantly cool on his skin, but warmed with her increasing pressure. Stanzi's whole body flowed into her movements—her hands, her arms, her breath. The way she moved was kind of musical, with patterns, rhythm, repeats, a chorus. Nothing like the work he'd gotten as part of his PT. Nothing like anything, really.

As much as Rhett wanted to pay attention to every little second of her therapy, as soon as he was on his face and her hands lit on him, he started to drift. She rubbed and rocked at the same time, which gave him the impression of being swaddled in a giant quilt.

The last thing he remembered was wishing Stanzi could come over at night, before bed, and rock him to sleep. If he had her there, hands on his back, rocking and caressing him, he just might not hear the spiders in the corners, or the dust in the beams. He could sink away and not blink again until morning.

When he did blink again, the room was still dim, lit only by the yellow glow of Stanzi's electric candles. Enya floated out of the speakers. Stanzi sat on her rolling stool, a couple feet away, her back against the wall, her eyes closed. Her shoulders rose and fell slowly.

Rhett sat up. As soon as the linens fell away, he felt cold. His skin was damp. So were the sheets. He swiped his forehead, which was clammy and cool.

"Oh, you're up." Stanzi stretched her arms and arched her back. "You've been out awhile."

Rhett looked around the room for a clock, but there was none, and he'd stripped off everything, including his watch. He remembered the few massages he'd had at PT; the therapist had a ticking timer that she'd slap as soon as Rhett entered the room. After fifty minutes it would ding like someone's order was up.

"You were having night sweats." Stanzi wheeled over next to the table. "Shaking a lot. I just let you ride it out. Kept a hand on you."

Rhett gathered the sheet around his waist and slid to the edge of the table. He sat there, thinking about her words. He didn't know what to say, so he stayed quiet. He wondered if there was anything she wasn't telling him. Had he talked in his sleep? And what did she mean by shaking? Was it a little? Or a lot? Rhett wasn't sure how to feel. Physically, he felt like when you've been sick, finally fall asleep, sweat it out and wake up knowing you've broken through and you're going to make it.

Mentally, he felt like he'd just fought his way out of a battle and successfully made it to the other side.

"It's your body's way of healing," she said. "Getting it all out, through sweat and vibration."

"Is that normal?"

Stanzi took a while to answer. "It's normal for you, at this point in your life."

Rhett laughed softly. "So no."

"It's not typical," Stanzi clarified, "of the average Joe getting an average massage. But yes, the process you are going through right now is, in my experience and scope of practice, very normal."

"I like how you say exactly what you mean. No more, no less."

Stanzi stood up and put a hand on his shoulder. "You okay?"

"I feel weird," he said. "It's not bad. It's actually good. But it's weird."

"Lie back down and I'll do your neck. C'mon."

Rhett allowed her to guide him on his back. She rolled her stool toward his head and slid her hands beneath his shoulders. Rhett breathed deeply into his stomach, held it, then breathed out just as slowly.

"Good." Stanzi's pressure was light and comforting. She drew her fingers up his neck, to the back of his head, and held there, cradling him. She scooped the back of his neck, one hand after the other, and told him it was called Mother Cat.

She talked a little while she worked, a few words in a low tone, just making sure he was okay while her hands and fingertips rolled around like magic on his upper traps, neck and head. She even worked some muscles in the front of his neck that he didn't think anyone had ever touched. If he was honest with himself, he probably wouldn't have let them, as they were too close to his throat. When her fingers sank into his scalp, he sighed aloud. That, she could do forever.

Eventually, her fingers slowed. After they stopped, she rested there before she gently drew away. "How are you feeling now?" Her voice came close to his ear.

He reached up and squeezed her wrist.

"Good," she said. "I'll step out. Get up slowly. Take your time."

Rhett took her at her word. Once she was gone, he took his time getting off the warm table, stretching, and searching for his clothes. He felt wrung out, but also lit up. It was an odd competition between his physical body and his mental state. He stepped out into the lower level of her house, which they'd entered through the back gate and the walkout door of her basement. She had a waiting area with a couch and chairs, a coffee table with magazines fanned out and a desk with a computer.

Stanzi was nowhere to be seen, so Rhett took the stairs to the next level. The door at the top of the steps led to the kitchen. The room was medium-size, brightly lit by lots of windows, with a small island in the center of the tiled floor. Stanzi's back was to him, in front of her stove.

"Oh!" She gave a little start as she turned around. "I put

the kettle on." She gestured to the stove. "In case you wanted tea. If you stay hydrated, your muscles will stay in the gel state. Soft and open to healing."

Rhett could smell the spring air on the wind that came through the open window over Stanzi's sink. The clock on her microwave read 3:12 p.m. Yep. He'd been out awhile.

"Sit." Stanzi gestured to a stool tucked beneath her island.

Rhett obeyed. His head was fuzzy and his body weak. He was still puzzling through what had happened during his massage, and he didn't know what to think or say. He looked around the room, saw Fezzi, asleep in a dog bed by the kitchen table. He remembered that the only reason Stanzi had come to his room at the resort on Christmas Eve was because she couldn't find her dog. Rhett made a mental note to buy Fezzi a giant box of biscuits.

The kettle whistled. Stanzi poured bubbling water into two mugs and set one in front of him. It smelled flowery.

"Thanks."

"You'll like it. The bergamot will open up your senses."

The tea was too hot to drink, so Rhett stirred it with the spoon Stanzi had left in the cup. He sniffed it, enjoying the steam on his face.

"You feeling better?"

Sweat sprung up on the back of Rhett's neck, even though the kitchen was cool. "My leg feels great," he said. "No pain. And I feel like I slept for a week. Wrung out and hung to dry. I haven't felt this way in ages."

Stanzi settled in the stool next to him and peered into his face. "But what else?" Her eyes narrowed. "There's something bothering you."

Silence passed.

"You know, it's okay. Today, when we ran, I kind of fell apart. Then my ex showed up. You saw all that. You've seen me fall apart more than once, at this point. So, it's fine if you let go during your massage." Stanzi's hand went to his forearm and rested there. "That's all it was. A release. Your body is so used to being in the sympathetic nervous system—the fight or flight—it just needs a little help coming down. Letting go."

Rhett used his spoon to sample the tea. It was strong and wasn't as sweet as it smelled. "Remember today when you asked me if I ever have to plan my outfit before I run? Or worry about what route I take?"

Stanzi nodded. She slowly stirred her spoon around in her cup.

"You were making a point about things men can take for granted." Rhett took another sip of the tea from his spoon. He liked it even better the second time. "And you're right. As a civilian, I've never even thought about what I wear when I leave the house, other than in relation to the weather. I don't worry about getting honked or whistled at or treated like shit if I reject a woman's advance. If I'm objectified, I'm free to enjoy it or ignore it. I have that choice. That privilege. But..." Rhett watched her go to the fridge and withdraw a couple of containers of fruit. Looked like strawberries and raspberries. "There are things women can take for granted, too. Like... letting go."

Stanzi looked up from her task, her fingers poised over the raspberries as she took them from container to decorative bowl.

"It's okay for you to be weak," Rhett said. "Maybe you, personally, don't want to be, but you can be, if you need to. You can open up and let go. In fact, it's not only allowed, it's expected. What was it you said today about your ex? He hated it that you didn't cry? You're not only allowed to cry, you're supposed to cry."

She didn't answer, merely took out a handful of strawberries and sliced off the tops with a small knife, then added them to the bowl with the raspberries.

"Guess what happens if I cry? Or—" he gestured toward the basement, where they'd had their massage "—sweat or shake or hear spiders talking? Fall asleep while a beautiful woman is giving me a massage? I'm a special fucking snowflake, that's what."

Stanzi watched him carefully. "You really mean that?"

"It's the truth." Rhett took a big gulp of the tea, which had cooled to the perfect temperature. "My job is to be tough. Strong. Protect others. Never let go. Not just because I'm a veteran, or a coach, but because I'm a man. Not even a man, just male. It's expected of us as soon as we take our first steps. And I'm not whining about it. It's just the way it is."

"No, I meant—" Stanzi ate a raspberry and slid the bowl in his direction "—you think I'm beautiful?"

After a second, Rhett laughed. Then he threw a raspberry at her.

She ducked the fruit and smiled. The raspberry made a miraculous landing in the kitchen sink. "Everything you say is true. But you can let go here. You can be whatever you need to be with me. People think a massage therapist's only job is to relax and stretch your muscles, but truth is, we're in contact long before I rest my hands on your skin. My job is to connect with you, wherever you're at, and help make a change for the better. That may be a deep tissue massage or just a light touch in a safe environment."

"It still feels weird. It's like wearing clothes that don't fit or talking to that weird relative in your family who does everything against the rules—everyone's kind of afraid of him but he also makes perfect fucking sense."

She smiled. "Clear as mud."

"Okay, how's this." Rhett polished off his tea. "Remember

today, when you got so hot you said hell with it and stripped your shirt off? You didn't want to. You knew what was coming. And like clockwork, those assholes in the truck honked and whistled at you. Exactly what you thought would happen. But you took your shirt off, anyway. Because you were just…so…damn…hot." Rhett made a blade with his hand and sliced the counter to mark his words. "That's how I felt, when I knew how my body would respond to your massage. I knew I was going to be a special fucking snowflake. But I just didn't care anymore."

"You can be any kind of snowflake you want, on my table."

Rhett smiled.

"Did you say they put you on medication? After your last tour?"

"I took them a little while. They weren't for me. Not the pills. Not the cortisone shots."

Stanzi nodded. "Cortisone eventually just breaks you down."

"Katrina liked me on meds," Rhett said. "They dulled everything. And the cortisone shots. I got one, and never got another. Yeah, my leg felt better, and I walked straight for a couple weeks, but it was just a bandage. Eventually, the bandages have to come off, or the stuff underneath won't ever heal."

"This is true." Stanzi came around to the other side of the counter and sat next to him again. "You can only use quick fixes so many times before what's really going on underneath collapses. I should know."

Rhett rubbed his face and knew he already sported a tinge of five-o'clock shadow. He could smell the eucalyptus from the massage lotion on his skin. "I don't think Katrina cared what was going on underneath," he said. "As long as everything seemed perfect on the outside. She liked the medals and the stories and the false gratitude. The kind of shit everyone wants to reduce to a ribbon of an unspecified color."

Constance sipped her tea in silence.

"I don't know if this will make any sense to you." Rhett fiddled with the handle of his mug. "But I just…" He paused. "I just couldn't be…" He trailed off and sighed. "Dammit."

Constance bumped his shin with her toes. "Couldn't be what?"

"You know." He drummed his fingers on the counter. "A hero. That's what." He watched her in silence, then rubbed his hands over his five-o'clock shadow. "I don't want to be a hero all the damn time."

The corners of her mouth turned down. She covered his drumming fingers with her own. When they quieted, she said, "You don't have to be a hero with me."

Rhett pressed his lips together. He drew a breath and sighed, then rose to his feet. "You know what we both need?"

Constance slid off her chair and tilted her chin up at him. "What?"

"A change of scenery."

"Well." She shrugged. "My kitchen's not the biggest or best. But it's pretty cozy, if you ask me."

"No." Rhett laughed. "I mean, we need a big change. We need somewhere totally different to run together. Somewhere wild and open and nowhere near all our old haunts. Somewhere to get lost."

"Oh, yeah?" The little dimple on her cheek deepened. "What'd you have in mind?"

twenty-nine

"Sunny, wake up."

The words worked their way through her slumbering brain. Sunny didn't want to move. Her world was warm and safe, like she could stay this way forever. In this world, she was in Pete's arms, tight against his chest. He'd just finished kissing her, making the world spin and her heart implode. She blinked in the dim, orangey light of her salt lamp.

"Sunny. Wake up. Call off your dog."

Sean stared back at her. Right next to him, on all fours—threes?—and pointing his muzzle in Sean's direction was Fezzi.

Oh, right. "Fezz," Sunny said. "Down."

Fezzi settled on his stomach and thumped his tail on the mattress. This was the first time Cici had gone out of town since Dad died, and Sunny had taken pity on Fezzi and let him sleep on the bed with her. She sat up and gathered the sheets close to her chest. It took a moment of blinking her eyes and rousing her brain to realize that it was Friday night.

The week had flown by. This was a busy time of the year for the rescue, and Sunny had barely had time to breathe. She'd meant to text Sean and tell him not to come this evening, that she was just too tired and needed to turn in early. Which was true. Even if it wasn't the whole truth.

"You called me Pete," Sean said. "I kissed you in your sleep and you called me Pete."

And *that* was the whole truth. Sunny rubbed her face in her hands, then looked up at Sean with a sigh. She might be dreaming now, but the kiss she'd shared with Pete was real. And so was the way she'd felt during that kiss, after that kiss and every moment since that kiss. She hadn't told anyone. Not Sean. Not Pete. Maybe most notably, not Cici. Telling Cici would make it real, and then Sunny would have to accept that something unacceptable had happened the moment Pete had drawn her in and pressed his lips to hers: Sunny had cracked. He'd edged his way in somehow, behind that just-for-kicks barrier she'd built around her heart.

Long ago, after watching her steely father spend his days a hardened widower, Sunny had decided that a serious relationship was not for her. No way was she going to spend her days trying to get a man's attention in all manner possible, only to be rewarded with the hardened crumbs of whatever he might choose to toss out. She kept her relationships with men fun and convenient. They could be as gruff as they wanted, long as they went home afterward.

Sunny had a heart, but it belonged to her dogs. Men could have her body, but the heart was off-limits.

Then Pete had gone and kissed her. Pete, whose heart also belonged to his dogs. Pete's kiss had changed something. Awoken something? Sunny wasn't sure. She had no idea what Pete had done. But she didn't like it, so she'd avoided Pete all week and kept all this nonsense to herself. It would pass if she gave it enough time. Like everything fleeting, it would blow over.

Sean's expression was changing.

He rose up from the edge of the bed. "I should probably go." He headed for the door.

Sunny threw back the covers and went after him. "Sean." She stilled him with a hand on his arm. "I'm sorry."

Sean turned around to face her. "Nothing to be sorry about. We weren't exactly dating. Just keeping it casual. Sex. Court orders. Animal control. No big deal." He tried a laugh.

"I know, but…" Sunny paused, shrugged. "I'm still sorry. What you said to me about Pete. About him being sweet on me. It got me to thinking. And it turns out you were right. I honestly had no idea until…" She stopped. How much honesty was too much? Even if she and Sean hadn't been serious, they'd still spent a lot of nights together. She didn't want to hurt him.

"Hey." Sean raised his hands. "Relax. You don't need to explain anything to me."

"I do," Sunny insisted. "Even though we were kind of just messing around, I—" she shrugged "—I like you, Sean. It just turns out that I…well, I don't know what I…" Sunny closed her mouth.

Sean offered a tired, sad smile. "I like you, too, Sunny. Even if you are a dog thief." He paused a heartbeat to let her giggle softly. "And I'm not going to lie. I wanted this to be something more. But I could tell, you know? About you and Pete."

There's nothing between Pete and me, she wanted to say. The words wouldn't come. Sunny wrapped her arms around Sean and gave him a tight, solid hug. Sean returned it, then pulled back and grinned. "Keep your nose clean, Sunny. Don't think what we had will keep me from locking up your thieving ass."

Sunny laughed. "Yes, sir, Detective Callahan."

"I'll let myself out."

Once he was gone, Sunny sank back to her mattress and pulled the covers to her chin. She grabbed her phone off the nightstand and considered texting Pete. She even typed out a brief, goofy message with no serious emotion attached before Fezzi crawled up next to her and nudged the cell out of her hand. "You're right," she agreed, kissing him on the head. Sunny deleted her text and stuffed her phone under her pillow. Fezzi curled up against her and let out a great sigh.

"I hear you, boy." Sunny stroked his fur. "I hear you."

thirty

"You're a friend?" Rhett's mother had a barely there Southern accent, like good perfume. She was around six feet tall, had smooth skin that belied her age, dark hair streaked with gray and green eyes that reminded Constance of the moss that grew on ancient stones lying in the crooks of fertile hills. It was the same green Rhett had in his eyes.

"Yes, ma'am."

"Call me Meara."

"Meara."

"Hmm." She tapped her chin with a forefinger. "My son is a master of brevity. So, when he walks in and says, 'Hey. This is my friend, Constance,' I just assume that Rhett is being Rhett. But you can tell me the truth." She whipped her kitchen towel over her shoulder and smiled. "Your secret's safe with me."

"We're friends," Constance repeated, which wasn't a lie. That didn't change the fact that Constance felt like she was being stared down by a hungry tiger. A strikingly attractive hungry tiger, but a tiger nonetheless.

"You're uncomfortable there." Meara tapped her chin again as she observed Constance. "Let's move to the back deck." She didn't wait for an answer, but collected both cups of tea, walked by Constance's perch at the dining table and tilted her head to follow.

Constance rose a little too quickly and slammed her knee into the neighboring chair. "Ow." She clutched at it, but Meara hadn't slowed down. She was already using her foot to push open the screen door that separated the dining area from the deck. "Let me help you." Constance scrambled for the door, but it was too late.

Meara had already settled both cups on a wooden table that was connected to two chairs, one on each side. She reached behind Constance and slid the screen shut.

The Outer Banks breeze was cool and welcoming. "Wow." Constance could see the ocean, rolling beneath the orange ball of the setting sun. It looked like a clementine floating in a golden pool of dying sunlight. The sound of the surf washed over her as the salt air bathed her skin. To her left, a long set of stairs led to the sand below. All the houses out here were elevated well above sea level. On the drive in, Constance had seen more than one beach house whose stairs had been washed away by last year's hurricane winds and roaring waves.

Meara joined her against the deck rail and stared out at the ocean. "It never gets old."

"It's so beautiful." Constance went quiet after that, unable to speak as she watched the dusk happen before her eyes. In the wake of their quiet, punctuated only by the sound of the lapping surf, she could hear soft male chatter coming from the deck below, which sat outside Rhett's bedroom. He'd shown it to her after they arrived, had said, "Put your stuff in here. It's got a bigger bed. I'll sleep in Mel's room," and left her to the cozy space that sported a queen-size bed, simple wooden dresser and bookshelves and an adjoining bath. Constance couldn't make out any of their words, but eventually realized the reason for that was because they were speaking Spanish.

Rhett and his father. Every once in a while, they'd break into laughter, then would pick back up again in the language they both seemed most comfortable sharing. Listening to Rhett speak Spanish was like listening to another person altogether, but with the same deep baritone. His words rolled together, musical and light. Goose bumps rose over her skin. Constance blamed it on the North Carolina wind.

"Those two." Meara held up her first two fingers, crossed. "It's funny because Rhett is way more like me than he is his father. Tall. Persistent. Some would say bullish. We don't back down and we like to have things our way. Domingo, he's more soft-spoken. Conciliatory. Got the biggest heart of any person I've ever met in my life." Meara's face glowed in the darkening sunset.

Constance understood. Domingo, who had given her the biggest hug she'd ever received in her life from a father figure, had a heartbreaking smile and a personality that accepted you immediately. He seemed like the kind of person who liked you by default, and saw the best in everyone. Standing at around five feet seven, he was still taller than Constance but well shorter than his wife or son. "My sister, Mel, got the small person genes," Rhett had said with a grin, and Domingo had laughed harder than anyone.

"Rhett and I are too much alike, maybe," Meara continued, "to be as close as that. He and his father have always been inseparable. Did everything together, though I was the sportier of the two. I would push Rhett hard at soccer practice or cross-country training and Domingo would say, 'Ah, it's just a game, *mijo*.'" Meara waved a hand. "Just a game. When is anything just a game?" She gave Constance a knowing smile.

Constance figured that between Rhett's insistence on pushing people out of their comfort zones and his proud acceptance of any performance that was given with full effort, he'd gotten the best of both of his parents. "I was a cheerleader," Constance said, then wondered why she'd led with that. "Not just at games but we'd travel and compete. I was actually pretty good."

Meara glanced down. "You got the quads for it."

Constance followed her gaze and ran a palm over her bare thigh. "Thanks. I think."

"Yeah, it was a compliment. Who wants skinny legs?"

Constance didn't say, *Me, most of my life.* She actually liked her legs now.

Meara reached out and tucked a windblown strand of hair behind Constance's ear. "Constance Morrigan," she said. "An Irish girl, then."

"Dad's side. My mother's people were Russian."

"That explains the eyes. Pretty." Meara turned back to the ocean. She opened her arms. "Our house has been here ages. Long before all these beach rentals that have a thousand rooms. I understand why people do it, but I like my little space."

"Your home is lovely."

"Thanks. Rhett told me you're a massage therapist."

"Yes. I've been helping him with his leg."

Meara chuckled. "Oh, no." She waved a hand at Constance's startled expression. "I'm not laughing at your profession. I'm a physical therapist myself. I was just thinking that you're about as chatty as my son. You two must have a lot of wild conversations." She snorted with soft sarcasm. "Do you both wait for the other to start talking?"

Constance giggled. "Sometimes," she said. "I guess I'm kind of quiet. My father raised me, after my mother died, and he was legally deaf. He lost his hearing in Vietnam. He could still talk, because he wasn't born deaf. But he rarely did. He liked silence."

"You're the type that doesn't need to fill the silence," Meara suggested. "People think you're aloof or disinterested, but that isn't true. Am I right?"

Constance thought it through before she replied. "I guess I just don't see silence as empty. Therefore, it doesn't need to be filled."

"Huh," Meara said. "That's really interesting." The rise in Meara's pitch told Constance that she meant what she said, wasn't being sarcastic or patronizing.

"A physical therapist, huh? That's great." Constance felt a surge of pride at starting a new thread of conversation. "I have a lot of background in orthopedic massage."

Meara made a fist and they bumped them.

The sun was nearly set, but a jogger went by, down by the edge of the retreating tide. He was shirtless and shoeless, wearing only a pair of swim trunks. Meara pointed. "Rhett brought you on a five-hour drive down here to do that, huh?"

Constance nodded. "We're going to have a beach run in the morning. Then head back to Virginia, later in the day."

"You two have been running a lot, then? A new program at the gym or something?" Meara crossed her arms over her chest and rubbed her hands over her skin. With the sun almost down, the temperature had dropped and the wind felt colder. "Rhett's done a lot of running, obviously, but he's been more into lifting these years past."

"He taught me how to lift, too. That's what we did first. We added running to the mix only recently."

"Training for a race?"

"Sort of. I used to run all the time. Then I…quit. He's kind of been helping me—" Constance chose her words carefully "—with some running issues."

At first, she'd thought this a bad idea. A really bad idea. Sunny, on the other hand, had loved it, and couldn't show up fast enough to collect Fezzi to babysit. Sunny's eagerness had only made the idea to take a short trip to the Outer Banks seem even worse. If Sunny was on board, it was probably going to be a disaster.

But ever since she'd gotten here, Constance had felt a sort of calm wash over her body that she couldn't deny. It was like the breeze got inside her, along with the salt and the dry air, and had soaked up some of the heaviness that'd been bogging her down for so long. "He thought the beach was a good idea," Constance added. "Nothing like running on the beach."

"He's right." Meara nodded. "I'm not a runner, but even a good walk on the beach can cure a lot of ills." She glanced at Constance, a little grin on her face. "Ever been to Virginia Beach?"

"Sure." Constance refrained from telling Meara that Rhett had said Virginia Beach was too crowded. Too busy. Too commercial, to achieve what he wanted to achieve. The Outer Banks, he'd said, was special.

"But not this time, huh?" Meara said. "Not for this run?"

Constance laughed softly to herself. She'd been right about Meara being a tiger. One who knew how to move with stealth. "You know, Meara," she said, "being more of a listener than a talker all my life makes me really good at the subtle art of innuendo."

A few seconds passed before Meara broke into loud, hearty, natural laughter. Her laugh matched her personality. Big. Bold. Nothing held back. "So you're on to me," she said. "I'm usually pretty good at making people talk without them even knowing I'm doing it."

Just before they lost the last curve of the setting sun, Constance said, "Where did Rhett see the horses? The wild horses playing?" She touched her own arm, where Rhett had the tattoo, eager to see the spot where, as a boy, he'd watched the last of a dying breed frolic in their happy freedom.

Meara turned to her slowly. She planted a fist on her hip and smiled. "Shut your mouth. He told you about that?"

"Sure." Constance touched her arm again. "When I saw the tattoo."

Meara gave a deep, motherly sort of laugh. "He always tells people he got that tattoo because he's a wild stallion. He says it sarcastically, but—" Meara waved a hand "—he never tells anyone the wild mustang story. That's too...too—" she waved her hand again "—sacred, in his eyes."

Something funny happened inside Constance's gut. Not a squeezing, but a tingling, like the sparkles over the ocean were inside her instead, sparking and popping. Constance quickly turned back toward the beach, to avoid Meara's knowing gaze.

"I'll let him show you the spot," she said. "That'll be important to him."

The chatter below grew louder, then turned into raucous laughter. Constance had never heard Rhett laugh that loud. She wished she could see his face, the way being with his father might make the skin around his eyes crinkle up and bare all of his teeth into what had to be a huge smile.

"Sounds like they're going to head inside and start a late dinner." Meara tucked one corner of her mouth into a guilty smile. "I think. My Spanish is not as good as it should be after being married to Domingo for almost forty years. I don't cook, by the way. But Domingo is excellent in the kitchen. You're in luck. He froze a batch of the tamales Rhett missed at Christmas, even though it's Rhett's own fault he missed his father's Christmas tamales. It's quite the effort. Masa and corn husks everywhere." She waved a hand.

"Rhett's crazy to miss Christmas here."

"Because he gets his dad's tamales?"

"Because he gets a dad." It popped out of her mouth before Constance could stop herself. "And a mom," she added. She suddenly wondered what her mother would have looked like if she'd lived to be Meara's age. Would she have the same fine lines around her eyes? Streaks of white in her hair, instead of gray? That confident way of speaking, filled with the sort of wisdom and easy love that comes with age?

"Oh, bless." Meara put her hands on Constance's shoulders and drew her in for a hug. "That boy missed Christmas *and* Thanksgiving. And yet, here he is now. Interesting, don't you think?"

She wore a pair of tiny swim trunks and a sports bra bikini top that she said were "surf to turf." They were both different shades of blue, the best color to highlight her hair and eyes, though Rhett didn't think she'd planned that. Her body looked smooth and strong.

"I couldn't find you in the house," Stanzi said. "So I came down here."

"I've been up awhile." Rhett dug into the wet sand with his toes. "Came down here to warm up."

He had, in fact, been down here well before sunrise, using the light on his watch to observe the sand crabs scurrying between the hidden holes that led to their vast labyrinth underground. He'd always been fascinated at how quickly and silently they moved, and at how well they camouflaged themselves. Crabs, he'd decided, were ninjas.

Once sunrise peeked over the ocean, a few fishermen had shown up, planted themselves in lawn chairs on the sand and cast their lines. One man had brought a black Lab. He raced up and down the beach, fetching a bright yellow tennis ball, even if it went into the surf.

"Did you sleep okay?"

"Decent enough."

Better than at home, not nearly as good as after one of her massages. But Rhett wasn't tired. He was eager for today, as he'd planned everything. Hobbs was covering the gym for the weekend. Mama knew as much as she needed to know about why he'd spontaneously come home, for no apparent reason. The weather was clear and cool but warm enough to make for a perfect morning run. The sound of the ocean, paired with the feel of sand between her toes and the wind drying the sweat on her skin, salt water in her hair and the scent of the beach in her nose, was the perfect formula to pair a new memory with the act of running. He hoped it worked.

Rhett hadn't planned for the bikini, though. How was he supposed to run while she was wearing that?

"This is perfect." Stanzi scraped her hair into a messy bun that looked like it'd been mauled by a cat. She sniffed deeply, then jumped up and down on her toes a few times. "Let's get moving. A little chilly."

"After you." Rhett motioned ahead, toward the long stretch of beach that went on for miles. He started his watch. "We can go as far as you want," he said, keeping her in his sights as she stayed a few feet ahead, "but we'll have to decide when to turn around. There's no way to go in a loop out here."

"Got it." Stanzi's cheerful voice matched the airy strides of her light gait.

The little shorts rode up her firm backside as she ran, which helped shake out the remainder of his cobwebs and gave Rhett incentive to keep moving, but also stay a few steps behind. The tide was out, leaving a wavy length of wet sand once the foamy water was dragged back out to sea. The sun was half-way up on the horizon, peeking its round, red dome like a mole from its tunnel, filling the sky with streaks of yellow that hovered behind the last dim drape of night. There were a couple of other runners and early birds on the beach, but mostly they had the place to themselves.

They ran in silence for several miles, nothing but the screech of gulls and lapping of the waves to punctuate their heartbeats. As light overtook the sky, vacationers crawled out of their rental houses, toting chairs and buckets, picking along the shore to collect shells left in the wake of the tide.

Stanzi made a circular motion with her hand as she turned around, indicating the halfway spot to head back to the house. Rhett wondered what she'd used as her marker: the bright pink house or a blue umbrella, sitting lonely and unguarded up near the slope of dunes?

Her pace dwindled a little on the return trip, their second three miles going slower than the first three. Rhett didn't mind, though. He could see the old runner inside her, coming alive after hibernation, hungry and dying to leave the cave.

"The uneven terrain was a challenge," she said as they slowed to a stop near the edge of the ocean. The private staircase that led to the back deck of his childhood home was visible in the distance. "So was the barefoot run." She pointed at her feet. "But I loved it."

"Yeah?" The water that lapped up around Rhett's ankles was cold, but not overly so. The breakers were yards out, leaving enough ocean to dip into before things got rough. "Think we should finish it off with a swim?"

His question left Rhett with an image of Katrina, the one and only time he'd suggested they go to Virginia Beach for the weekend. Her face had wrinkled up, matching the "Hell, no" that came out of her mouth. "Why would I want to swim in the Atlantic? It's so dirty. Take me to Hawaii if you want me to swim."

Stanzi bounced up and down on her toes and tapped her

fingertips together, marking the first time Rhett had seen her behave like a little girl. He wondered, based on the stories of her past, how often she'd actually gotten to be a little girl when she was growing up. Her smile was so big he could see that half-moon dimple on her cheek. "Should we inch our way in or just go for it?" She sidestepped a little ways into the lapping waves.

"Well." Rhett scratched the back of his head. He'd never seen somebody so excited to dive into the ocean. "I'd say, maybe just…" He reached out, planted his hand between her shoulder blades and gave her just enough of a shove to make her lose her balance.

Stanzi went down, shrieking. She hit the water with a giant splash, then jumped up, clutching her arms around herself. "You jerk!" She dove for him, drenched from head to toe, her smile still big and eyes bright.

She didn't slam into Rhett's chest so much as he caught her, and went down willingly. The cold water hit him like icy needles, but he quickly acclimated as he bounced to the surface. Stanzi was next to him, shoving the surface of the water to drive it into his face, over and over.

Finally, he could catch his breath. Stanzi grinned and dove beneath the surface. When she popped back up, she was a few yards out. "C'mon, Rhett!" She stuck her feet up, floating on her back.

They swam until it felt warmer to be in the water than out, until their fingers were wrinkled up and their bodies were full of salt. When they were finally done, the sun was bright and the beach was getting fuller. Rhett collected his T-shirt from the sand and tossed it to Stanzi. She caught it and slipped it over her head. It fell down to midthigh, covering everything Rhett had enjoyed looking at for the past few hours, but the warm smile on her face more than made up for the loss.

Until this moment, he hadn't been sure about fulfilling all of his reasons for coming down here. She'd had a great run, in a place as removed from home as was possible. That was enough, wasn't it?

"I want to show you something." As they neared the house, Rhett took Stanzi's elbow and guided her to the side yard, which butted up to the sand dunes. Their house was the last in the row before the dunes rose up like a giant, tan wall, dotted with the dense, squat shrubbery native to the area. If you climbed those dunes, the sand and shrubs went on as far as the eye could see.

Stanzi followed, until they were alone and out of view from any of the beachgoers or other houses. She looked around, taking in everything. Her face lit up. "Is this the spot?"

Rhett couldn't hide his surprise. "You know what I'm showing you?"

"The horses." Stanzi's voice went to a reverent whisper. "This is where you saw the horses." She clasped his forearms. "Isn't it?"

"Yeah." He laughed and nodded toward the dunes. "They came down over the hill. Stopped, right here." He pointed a few yards away. "I was kicking a soccer ball around over there. I stopped, put my foot on the ball. I was scared if I moved even one muscle, they'd spook."

"What did they look like?" The ocean had polished her skin with its salt and made her face glow.

"They were white with brown spots." Rhett briefly closed his eyes, to recapture the memory. "Slender and agile, like teenagers. They grunted and snorted while they played. Long, silky manes that blew in the wind. Obviously they had no shoes or saddles or reins or blinders—none of that stuff we're used to seeing on horses. They were completely free."

When Rhett opened his eyes, Stanzi opened hers, too. "I was picturing it," she said.

"I can't believe you remembered that story."

"Why not?"

"I only told you one time. And it was months ago."

She shrugged, her cheeks going a little pink. "Nobody forgets a story like that."

They held each other's gazes for a moment before Rhett glanced up at the dunes, at the place the wild horses had both come from and disappeared to. This was the spot he always came to when he needed to be alone. When he needed to think, or make a hard decision. When he felt lost. This was the first place he came to, after every deployment. He didn't even go to his own house. He came straight here, did not pass go or collect two hundred dollars. Came straight out here with a six-pack of Fat Tire and just basked in the freedom and isolation. Something about staring up at the dunes and picturing those horses made everything a little bit easier. The wild horses were his reset button. His reason to keep going.

Stanzi turned her body to face him. "You okay?"

Rhett rubbed his hands together. He was starting to feel cold. "Yeah. You?"

Stanzi shrugged and took a step closer, as though she sensed his chills and wanted to share her body heat. "Yeah."

"How was the run for you?"

Stanzi's mouth turned down at the corners. "It was—" a little dent over her eyebrow that she got when she was confused deepened "—like I'd never run before." Her skin sprung with gooseflesh and she gave a little shiver.

Rhett smiled. The air smelled just like it had the day he saw the wild horses playing—like salt and sand and crabs hiding in their tunnels. "Good. Let's get you inside before your lips turn blue."

★ ★ ★

They went inside to an empty house. Meara had left a note that she and Domingo had gone shopping. The air-conditioning felt like ice and the house was silent as stone. Constance closed herself in her bedroom and turned on the shower. She slipped Rhett's shirt off and held it to her nose. He'd sweated all over it during their run. His sweat smelled like lavender and sea salt. She held it there a long time.

Then she took a long, hot shower, which felt amazing after being in the cold ocean. She'd forgotten her body wash, but there was bar soap in the tray affixed to the wall. As soon as she sudsed it up and smelled the lavender, Constance knew the soap had been here since Rhett's last visit home.

Once she'd gotten the chill from her bones and all the sand and salt from her hair, she turned off the water and wrapped herself in a big blue towel that had been folded neatly and set on the closed toilet lid. Meara had probably put it there before she went out, as it hadn't been there this morning.

Constance made her way back to the bedroom, where there was a full-length mirror on the closet door. The vertical blinds over the sliding glass door that led to the deck were open, letting in a wash of natural light. The room had sand-colored walls with a seashell border done in a stamping design, which led Constance to believe Meara had redone Rhett's childhood room into a guest room. Nothing screamed teen angst like dark walls or old band posters. Instead, the decor was Modern Beach Daydream.

Constance opened her towel and looked at herself—really looked at herself—for the first time in weeks. Yes, she'd noticed changes in her face and body over the passing months but never, even in her running days, had she given herself such a hard appraisal while completely bare.

She closed the towel up and walked to the bedroom door.

"Rhett?" she called, wondering if he would answer. Silence passed, which told her his parents hadn't yet come home. She was just about to close the door again when soft footsteps came down the hall. Rhett's dark head appeared around the corner. His pace quickened when he saw her peeking out. Constance opened the door for him.

He eyed the towel.

Constance waited.

He came inside and pushed the door closed behind him. "Are you all right?"

"Yes."

He stood there in silence, wearing a fresh pair of shorts and a T-shirt. His hair was wet, a glossy black color like raven's feathers, and he smelled like the same soap Constance had used. "Are you sure?" He eyed the towel again.

"Yes." Constance was highly aware of the single piece of fabric that separated her naked body from Rhett's searching gaze. "I just wanted to ask you something."

"Sure."

"Why'd you invite me down here?"

Rhett hesitated, but finally spoke. "I told you. Wanted to get you running in a new environment. Reintroduce it, so it wasn't attached to negative stuff in the past."

"So you were being a good coach," Constance offered. "And a good friend."

At first, Rhett's face was tight, like he was waiting for the hidden trap. Then it relaxed. "Okay," he said, then shrugged. "I wanted you to see the spot." His voice was low. "The place where I saw the horses." He gestured toward the outdoors.

"Why'd you want me to see it?"

Rhett gave a soft laugh. "Because." He scratched the back of his head. "Because," he repeated. "Because it's my spot." He shrugged helplessly. "I don't know how to say it. Sorry if that's dumb. If dragging you down here just to see some sand and shrubs was…"

Constance let the towel fall to the floor.

Rhett eyed her naked body up and down. His Adam's apple bobbed. Constance could tell he tried not to stare, but failed. Eventually, his gaze settled with her own. The intensity she felt, when he chose to look into her eyes, was so strong the back of her neck started to sweat.

Constance didn't move to lift her towel and cover up, or even to find a set of clothes to put on. For the first time in a long time—maybe ever—she was completely comfortable being totally bare. He'd liked her in the My Pretty Pony shirt, and all of Dad's old tees. He'd liked her in the bulky sweats she wore on their very first run together. He'd liked her in anything. Which meant he didn't care what she wore. What size she was. How far she ran. He just liked *her*.

Rhett's jaw tightened. He swallowed hard.

"Well, at least tell me what you think." Constance didn't know why he stood there, in silence, looking angry and frustrated and helpless all at the same time. She closed the distance between them and took his hands in hers. "Am I not horrible?"

His warm fingers traced up her palms, which sent gooseflesh over her skin.

Constance felt like they were back in the gym, alone in the quiet. He'd just taught her some combat moves and they were staring at each other, unsure how to handle the heat and energy that grew between them. It got hard to breathe. "Why are you mad?"

"I'm not mad."

"What are you, then?"

Silence.

"Remember when you kissed me during Combat?"

"Of course." She almost smiled, but kept it to herself.

"Do you think about it?"

"Yes." Her pulse was loud in her ears. "Do you?"

He ran a finger under her chin, tilting her head up. "Every single night." He leaned in slowly, but stopped, just shy of her lips. "Do you feel that?"

"Yes." Constance's voice was a whisper.

"It's hard to breathe."

She waited, her blood growing warmer with each passing second. He was teasing her on purpose, but still, she waited. She'd kissed him last time. She wanted him to kiss her this time.

Her eyes closed. After an eternity, his lips touched hers. Contact was like a glowing poker, straight from the fire, right to her core. That moment of intensity when you can't tell if you're frozen or burned, but it doesn't matter because the effect is the same: it's almost too much.

Almost.

Rhett's kiss deepened slowly. He took only a little at a time, like he absorbed her in pieces. Constance's fingertips and palms rolled over Rhett's body, beneath his shirt, touching all the places she'd already touched before, but in a new way. His lips found her neck, the curve of her shoulder, her collarbone, his touch light and coaxing, exploratory, inquisitive.

"You really want me to tell you what I think?"

"Yes." Constance opened herself. Whatever he said, whatever he did, good or bad, she would take it.

He sank down, to his knees, and drew her against him. Constance's hands went into his hair, thick and damp. His scents filled her nose and his warm, wet lips trailed over her abdomen. She tilted her head back and gasped softly. "You're beautiful," he whispered. Her legs shook, making it hard to stand. "I've always thought you were beautiful. From the second you stared up at me, from the floor of my gym, drenched in sweat, I was lost." His hands lit on her wrists and pulled her down against him, into his lap.

He kissed her again, firmer this time, his lips urgent but sweet, his energy roaring over her like a wave at high tide or winds out of control. Constance was caught up in the storm, her only choice to ride it out. She stripped his clothing, one piece at a time, parting from him only long enough to rid them of the irritating material that kept her from being completely bare against him. He felt hard and smooth, tasted like warm skin, lavender and beach air.

A perfectly good bed remained untouched, the sheets still made from this morning, as Rhett flipped her beneath him on the floor, cradling her neck in his arm.

Constance whispered his name and begged him to make her forget hers. She traced the lines of his muscles, drank the sweat of his skin, touched as many places on his body as she could with hers, drinking, swallowing, becoming. He pressed inside her, just as slowly as he'd kissed her, as though gaining permission for every inch. She lost herself in the rising and falling of thousands of tiny explosions inside her body, outside her body, inside his, in a place where they both existed and ceased to exist at the same time. Her mind and body shattered, over and over.

Rhett drew back and looked down at her, his grip on her waist like he clung to something keeping his head above water. His body went hard and tight and slow. He gasped aloud, pressing deep inside her, before he arched and groaned, then slowed, his breath coming shallow as he collapsed against her chest.

They lay there awhile, Constance's arms around his back, his chest slick on hers, neither willing or able to move, bound in the heat and the energy that pulled and clung. Her lips pressed against his throat, the thrum of his blood strong in his neck as his heart pounded in his chest. Her hands continued to explore his body, instinctual, habitual, the touch changing from greedy, back to inquisitive, discovering how he felt after he'd emptied into her, sharing his hurt, grief, anger and ecstasy. Everything was fizzy and hot and wild.

When the world had settled, Rhett rose and extended his hand. She smiled as she imagined him, the first time they met at the gym. He'd stuck out his hand and helped her to her feet then, too.

Rhett smiled back, as though he'd read her mind.

He scooped his arms under her legs and tossed her on the bed, then climbed in next to her. She nestled into the crook of his arm, her head against the wild horse tattoo, and listened to the sounds of his body: his heart, his lungs, the whispers of his skin.

Within a couple of minutes, Rhett's chest rose and fell in a slow, deep pattern. He hadn't slept well last night. She'd learned to read him and she knew.

She closed her eyes.

Constance floated in a world where she truly had forgotten her name. She didn't know who she was then, whether Constance or Stanzi or Cici or Red—or just a woman who continued to escape death by being reborn.

It didn't matter.

Just this.

thirty-one

Sunny woke to a text from Cici, saying she was going to stay at the Outer Banks another day. Was that okay? How was Fezzi? Did he miss her?

Forget about Fez, Sunny texted back. Tell me instead what "staying another day" means. Does it mean things are going well? Then she tossed in a grin and the eggplant emojis.

Not telling, Cici said, and that was the last she heard from her for the rest of the day. Normally, Sunny would've pushed and pressed until she finally got Cici to talk. She knew just how to do it, had learned when they were young where that line was, that she could come at Cici "like a pit bull" just far enough to get her to spill if she was careful not to go just one push too far, in which case Cici would clamp her jaw and after that… Alcatraz.

But not today. Today, Sunny spent most of her time with two families, one who wanted to adopt Sinbad and the other who wanted Willy. The family who wanted Willy was a retired couple in their sixties. The wife was a mother of four grown children; she took care of the grandkids and quilted in her spare time. She wanted to rescue an older dog who needed a home. Someone quiet who might like lying next to her while she worked at the sewing machine. Her name was Martha and she was absolutely perfect for Willy. Her husband, George, was a mild-mannered ex-accountant who just wanted whatever made Martha happy. The vibe was good. Willy went right to them after they'd spent a quiet hour in the spring sunshine, and Sunny was happy to schedule a home visit for the following weekend. Martha was eager to show them her sewing room. She petted Willy gently on the head—she always held it sort of cocked to the side—and cooed, "You want to quilt with me, don't you, sweet thing? Don't you?" Willy beamed beneath her fluffy white bangs.

Sunny wasn't as sure about the people who wanted Sinbad. Two men, brothers, in their late twenties, who wanted a dog to hang out in their autobody shop. Sunny had images of chain link around Sinbad's neck, left to wallow outside, maybe trained to be mean. The brothers insisted he would be inside the shop, like their sidekick. They'd seen a similar dog on a popular television show and thought it'd be cool to rescue a dog for their own.

It was borderline. They could be telling the truth, and Sinbad would be entirely suitable for such a situation. It could also be a line of bullshit. This is where Cici came in handy. Often, Sunny had her over during visits. She'd sit off to the side, billed as a dog therapist, and people paid little attention to her once they got in with the dogs. Sunny would glance over midway through visits and either exchange a grin of agreement with Cici—*these people are perfect*—or perhaps uncertainty—*let's get to know them better.* Every once in a while, Cici would purse her lips and shake her head. It was a micromovement, barely perceptible, but also absolutely, certainly *no*.

This was a situation that required Cici's intuition. But Cici wasn't here. Cici was getting laid in the Outer Banks by a hot fitness coach with the body of Adonis, while Sunny was stuck here with two possibly shady men, no night of fun from Sean and a lack of Pete, a decidedly gaping hole in her week that Sunny had only dug herself.

"Let's schedule a visit to your shop for next weekend."

"We were hoping to take him home today." The larger of the two brothers was over six feet tall, head shaved bald, muscular beneath a thick layer of body fat.

"My policy is a visit here, and a visit there." Sunny spoke in a large voice, calm and steady, and kept eye contact. She'd learned long ago how to speak to convey authority.

Whatever the bald brother lacked on his head, the other brother had on his chin. Beard Brother shrugged at Bald Brother. "What's another week?"

"I'm ready today. There's no reason I can't take him today," Bald Brother said, but he spoke to his brother, not Sunny. Typical male entitlement. But not necessarily a sign of bad people.

"I have my policies for a reason," Sunny said. "My reasons are for the dogs' benefit. I don't break them. If you're interested in Sinbad, following my policies should be important to you." Sinbad, meanwhile, thumped his tail as he sat between them. Technically still a puppy, everything made him happy. He was excited to be at the rescue with the other dogs. He was excited at the brothers' visit. He was excited just to be alive.

Bald Brother blinked in silence, meeting her gaze. "All right," he said finally. He pulled out a business card and handed it over. "This is the shop. This is where we spend most of our time. We live above it. Sinbad would almost never be alone." He shrugged. "We'd treat him right."

Sunny took the card, more confused than ever. She had learned long ago never to judge by stereotypes. The elderly couple looking at Willy weren't necessarily any safer than the motorhead brothers.

"Everything okay, ma'am?" Roger poked his head in. He always checked in when Sunny was alone with male customers.

"Yes, thank you, Roger."

By the time the men left, the sun was going down. Sunny took a shower, poured some wine and considered texting Pete. He would've been busy with his own dogs all day, but she could get his opinion on the brothers. Maybe ask him to go with her to the shop next weekend. Of course, if she texted, he might bring up the kiss. Or had enough time gone by that Pete would realize the kiss had been mistake and wouldn't mention it again? After all, he'd made a point of saying he didn't want to risk their friendship. After a second glass of wine, Sunny realized she wasn't texting Pete because she didn't *want* him to say the kiss had been a mistake.

Oh, boy.

Sunny decided this day was done. She went to bed, but tossed and turned, her brain on overdrive. She was sure this was one of those nights she'd be awake until the wee hours. And maybe she was. At some point, though, she drifted.

Until the smell of burning toast woke her. Toast? Or was that a fireplace?

Fezzi was barking madly. Sunny sat up in bed and rubbed her head. Dawn was just breaking. Fezzi stared at her, his three feet dancing over the hardwood floor as he woofed and tossed his head.

A rush of hot wind blew in from her open bedroom window, and she smelled it again.

Smoke. Burning wood.

The realization came slowly to her, like fog that thins over empty streets.

"Oh, my God!" Sunny grabbed the closest garment, her silken robe. Just before she dashed toward the doorway, she snatched up her cell phone and texted Pete two words: Something's wrong.

She stumbled outside, Fezzi on her heels, barking and running beside her, keeping stride despite the fact he could've easily streaked ahead, even with one leg missing. Black smoke billowed in the air, orange flames licking against the outside of Roger's quarters. "Roger!" Sunny shrieked.

Her legs got going so fast she stumbled on some underbrush and nearly fell on her face. A strong arm hooked her waist, saving her. She looked up, into Roger's frightened eyes.

"I woke to Fezzi, barking at me. I guess he opened the door somehow, with his paw? He saved my life. I woke to smoke and fire. I called 911 and ran inside your house for this." Roger had a fire extinguisher braced against his hip. "C'mon."

They took off after Fezzi, who hadn't slowed his pace. A siren blared in the near distance. A few seconds later, emergency lights flashed near the end of the road. The firefighters were nearly there.

Roger rushed in and aimed his extinguisher at the flames on the west side of the compound. Dogs swarmed around, leaving off barking in vicious howls at the fire so they could jump against Sunny's legs and lick her hands and arms. "Did they all make it out?" she shouted, though she doubted Roger could hear her. "The dogs?"

Chevy ran behind them, nipping at their heels and herding them away from the smoke. Sunny counted them, saying their names as she went, touching each one, her heart pounding in her chest as her gaze wove frantically among the pack.

Smokey Bear. Sneakers. Butter Bits.

Some of them barked excitedly at the firefighters, who were just now stretching a long hose through the yard and toward the blazing cabin, while others cowered in the bushes. Chevy relentlessly tried to collect them all, leaving Sunny to think she might have some sheepdog or heeler in her.

Tubby. Ranger. Willy.

Water shot out the hose, drenching the building as firefighters ordered Roger back, away from the fire.

Sinbad and Calypso shot out of the bushes, where they'd obviously been hiding. Who was left? Was anyone left?

"Humphrey," Sunny said, her skin going cold. "Where's Humphrey?" She turned to Roger, who was again by her side. He had a helpless expression, his face matching the faded blue hoodie he always wore. "He's the only one who wouldn't run," Sunny whispered. "He hid inside that cage. Do you think…?" Sunny pictured the little beagle, huddled in the cage, rearing from everybody's touch. Even loud noises didn't send him running. He just balled up harder.

Sunny bolted toward the enclosure. The flames were nearly doused, and about two-thirds of the structure was still intact, but the other third had been wrecked completely, the roof caved in, charred beams sticking up like giant burned matches.

It smelled like wet ashes and singed wood. All the food bins were half-burned and soaking wet. Saint Francis was a giant lump of coal. Humphrey's empty cage peeked out from the rubble, the metal blackened.

Just then, a firefighter emerged from the building, holding a blanket that enveloped a small form. "No," Sunny whispered. Her hand went to her mouth as her throat sealed up with smoke and grit.

"Stay back, ma'am." Another firefighter held his arm out and pushed against her chest, guiding her away from the compound. "Too much smoke."

Sunny ignored them, her gaze on the blanket. One corner slid away. Tufts of fur poked up from the mass, which was covered in soot. "Found a pet," the firefighter said as he drew near. "I'm sorry, ma'am. This one didn't make it. Probably died from smoke inhalation."

"No," Sunny repeated, her voice caught up in a choking sob. "Humphrey."

"Let me have him." A voice boomed over Sunny's shoulder. Pete shoved in front of Sunny and took the bundle from the firefighter. His ball cap was missing, his hair mussed from sleep. He wore a pair of long pajama pants covered in images of the starship *Enterprise* and a white T-shirt. "Text Dr. Winters. Now. And your sister."

"Cici's out of town."

"Text Dr. Winters."

"I'm doing it."

Pete kneeled on the ground and opened the blanket, adjusting Humphrey so he was on his side. He laid a hand on Humphrey's chest for about two seconds, then leaned his cheek in close to his muzzle. He took Humphrey's leg and pressed his elbow back toward his chest, then pressed his fingers there, touching Humphrey's wrist and finally the rear pad on Humphrey's foot.

"Does he have a pulse?" Sunny's voice was barely audible, even to her own ears.

Pete ignored her, opened Humphrey's mouth and swiped out what looked like vomit. He pulled Humphrey's tongue forward, then covered Humphrey's mouth and nose with his own and blew gently. Sunny watched Humphrey's chest rise. Pete drew back and let the air escape, then drew Humphrey's elbow back again, positioned his hands and gave him chest compressions. Pete repeated the breath and chest compressions while Sunny stared in silence, her own breath held as Pete continued to share his with the little beagle.

Sunny covered her face with her hands and tried to steady her feet. It wouldn't work. It was too late. Humphrey, who had been abused his entire life, had died in a fire. A sweet little animal who wouldn't hurt anyone had been rewarded by living a life of torture and suffocation. Sunny slid her hands into her hair and squeezed. The pain at her scalp kept her from sinking to her knees. Janice Matteri wasn't all bark, after all. She'd sworn to get even, and she had. In the worst imaginable way.

Sunny would've preferred a gun to her own head. Anything but this.

Pete assessed Humphrey, then continued with his chest compressions and blows of air.

Sunny couldn't hide anywhere. She desperately wanted to hide, to escape the devastation she felt. She let the sobs come until something heavy went around her shoulders. One of the firefighters had draped her with a blanket. He didn't look more than a teenager.

Sunny swiped away her tears and looked around at the mess, the chaos of the dogs and the ruin of their home. Roger watched in silence with bloodshot eyes.

"Ma'am." The elder of the two firefighters turned to her. "You live here?"

"Yes," Sunny said. It felt like her body floated above the wreckage. Her ears buzzed. She leaned over and coughed a few times, to clear her lungs of the smoke and ash. "This is Roger," she choked, between her tears. "We both live here."

"Anyone else? What about all these other buildings you have on the property?" The firefighter pointed out some of the cabins, farther off in the distance but still visible through the trees. Thankfully, the fire had not reached them.

"I rent those out," Sunny said. "But they're empty right now."

"Any idea how this happened?" The firefighter had a gray mustache and closely cropped hair of the same color. His eyes were sympathetic, but cautious.

"It was Janice Matteri," Sunny said. "One of my neighbors. I shut down her puppy mill and she vowed to get even. She said she was going to hurt my dogs. And I think someone was fiddling with my food bins some weeks back." There were also those brothers today, Sunny remembered. The ones who wanted Sinbad and didn't get to take him home. They hadn't seemed angry when they left, but...

"Good thing you reacted quickly," the firefighter said, and glanced toward the mess. "Or this could have been much worse. When the police arrive I'm going to suggest an arson investigation. There's a heavy smell of alcohol near the site. Especially around there—" he pointed "—where the burned and unburned sections meet. Do you store any kind of alcohol back here?"

"No, sir," Sunny said, shaking her head. "It's where Roger lives. With many of the dogs. It...it was..." Sunny paused as her eyes welled with fresh tears. "It was a rescue. A place where those who don't have anywhere can go. I had the dogs, along with their food, combs, toys, leashes, a few crates. A wooden table. That kind of stuff. No accelerants. I swear."

"All right." The firefighter watched the dogs mill around, many of whom were dirty and shaking. "I know you want to take care of your animals," he said. "I'm going to talk to the police." He pointed toward the main house, where a man in plain clothes was heading their way. "Stay close."

Sunny nodded, her feet suddenly freezing. She glanced down and saw that Roger was barefoot, too. Her dog enclosure was in ruins, her feed contaminated. She hoped Dr. Winters got here ASAP. As the last puffs of gray wisped into the sky above the compound, which sat in eerie silence, Sunny's mind reeled, her body alternating between hot and cold, cold and hot.

Pete once again assessed Humphrey.

Sunny's hand covered her mouth as fresh tears rose, hot and fast. She kept picturing the little beagle, gray and still, his life choked out of him because he was too scared to run. And when the firefighters arrived with their hoses, he'd have been even more terrified because that bitch Janice had abused her dogs by spraying them with water from a hose. He'd have cowered more from the water than the fire. Humphrey had never stood a chance.

And it was all her fault. She could've apologized to Janice, or at least asked for a truce. Instead, Janice Matteri had driven right up to her driveway, threatened her and her dogs, and Sunny had done nothing. She hadn't told Sean or Pete. She hadn't told anyone but Cici, because Sunny had never really thought something this awful would happen to her. Even though she'd seen the extent of Janice's cruelty firsthand, she'd had too much of an ego to think that woman would go this far.

"Pete," Sunny said, her voice raspy with smoke and tears.

Pete glanced up from the little beagle.

"Stop," she said. "Just stop." Then she collapsed into tears.

thirty-two

Rhett could see the yellow beacon from a distance, moving slowly in his direction. He assessed the height and size of the shadow, as well as the pace and gait of the person by the pattern of how the lantern's light bounced.

Stanzi.

He clicked off the light on his watch and left the crabs in peace, then sank to the damp sand and waited for her to reach his side.

He smelled her before he got a glimpse of her face. Her sweet scents made his heart thud and his loins tingle. She settled next to him and stared out at the ocean by what little light the lantern afforded. The moon helped; it hung in a bright, eggshell-colored orb in the dark sky.

"What're you doing out here, at this hour?"

Rhett checked his watch: 4:00 a.m. "What're *you* doing out here at this hour?"

"Looking for you."

"Did I wake you?"

"No. I got up for a drink of water and you were gone. I checked the back door and it was unlocked." Stanzi dug her bare feet into the sand. "You've been doing this your whole life, haven't you?"

"Pretty much. The first time Mama caught me, I was ten years old. She freaked out when she saw I was gone, but Papa kept her calm. He told her he knew I was fine because the tactical flashlight I'd begged for at Christmas wasn't on my dresser where I always kept it. They found me out here. Mama threatened to ground me for a week until Papa cussed her out in Spanish. They got in a huge fight and didn't speak for days. I felt bad. Not for sneaking out, but for causing a fight."

"You should feel bad. Giving your mama a heart attack like that."

"The crabs," Rhett said, pointing at one that scurried past the lantern. "They act different at night. You can't get to know their secrets during the day."

Stanzi flicked sand at him. "That's so you."

He laughed. "I was planning special ops and recon from my bedroom to the shoreline from about age seven," Rhett mused. "I even got Mel to do it a couple times, but she wouldn't go very far. She'd get freaked out, worried we'd get caught." Rhett could still picture Mel, standing on the shoreline in the dark, clutching her My Pretty Pony doll with the chopped-up rainbow mane, her lips turned down and eyes wide in fear.

"Smart girl."

"Pain in the ass, you mean."

"I bet she thinks the same about you."

Rhett wasn't going to argue. He found Stanzi's hand and clasped it. What he felt for her was a dangerous thing. Like liquid nitrogen living in his gut, he had to be careful how he stepped, or everything could explode. He watched a tiny crab skitter out of his hole and dart in front of the lantern light. "You like it here, then?"

"It's beautiful."

Rhett watched the moonlight ripple in a wavy line over the water, which sucked in and out in a soothing roll. It was hard not to think about the morning he'd spent with her. He'd been thinking about her, anyway, all day long, whether she was in his presence or wasn't. Neither one of them had wanted to stick to their plan to drive home, so they'd spent the rest of the day hanging out with his parents, cooking dinner, having some wine, laughing, walking to the shops across the street for ice cream. All day Rhett could smell her on his skin and taste her on his lips. He could feel her body, all around him, holding him close and tight. Heat would rise over his skin at random moments, like in the middle of dinner, and he'd look up and find his mother regarding him with an odd expression.

Rhett leaned back on his elbows, in the sand. "Should I apologize for…anything?"

Her soft laugh rippled over the sounds of the water. "You know the only thing I regret?"

"What?"

"Not getting a snap of your face when I dropped the towel."

He pictured what he might've looked like, based on how he'd felt in that moment, and he laughed, loud and open. "My chin was on the floor."

"A little bit."

Rhett knew, in that moment, that she'd come into his gym to find him. Even if she hadn't known it. Conceited as it might be, she was his for a reason. There were plenty of girls out there, like Katrina, who would stay fit and strong and help keep him in tip-top shape. Plenty of girls who would keep him on his toes. But Stanzi was different. She wasn't a unicorn. She wasn't perfect. She wasn't pretending to be, or even trying to be, perfect. She was a dorky My Pretty Pony who wore cat barrettes. She massaged dogs, for Christ's fucking sake. She was a mess. A good mess. His mess.

Rhett clicked his watch and the light popped over the sand, casting its green glow. The little creatures froze, some with claws in midair. Stanzi giggled, because she wasn't just the kind of girl who would indulge his need to drive himself to the edge, or bring him back from the brink with her magical hands.

Stanzi was the kind of girl who would sneak out of the house and watch the crabs with him.

Rhett slipped his arm around her waist and drew her in, against him. One thing led to another, their shared urgency a need Rhett had never experienced. Their lovemaking was like a storm that came on sudden—thick, intense, with bright flashes of light that left them spent and happily confused. They lay back in the sand and she snuggled into the crook of his arm. There was nothing but the sound of the ocean, lapping the shore and crashing in on itself.

The next thing Rhett heard was the sound of a classic telephone ring. For a moment, he was a kid again, inside his house while the rotary on the wall pealed out.

He blinked his eyes open to the sunshine. It looked about 7:00 a.m. Stanzi was just sitting up, her cell phone in her hand, which was the source of the ringing. "H'lo?" she said, her voice sleepy. A long silence followed. Moments later, she turned to Rhett with an ashen face. "Rhett," she said. "Something terrible happened to Sunny."

thirty-three

Sunny jolted awake, certain that she smelled smoke in the air. She blinked in the darkness, her heart pounding in her chest.

The room was dark. The clock read 2:15 a.m. Chevy was at the foot of the bed, fast asleep. Sunny drew air into her lungs and smelled only the ghost of tonight's roast chicken and potatoes, which she'd barely picked at.

She slipped out of bed and peeked out the window. No fire. She couldn't see the blackened remnants of the dogs' house and Roger's rooms, but she knew it was there, in the darkness, smelling of ash and cinders. She'd moved all her dogs into the smaller cabins, along with Roger, until the structure was no longer a potential crime scene and she could rebuild. When Sean had heard what happened, he'd sent a car to patrol at random times throughout the night, along with a promise to look into the investigation.

Sunny padded over to the guest room, Constance's room,

and stood outside the closed door. Pete had stayed with her all day, then offered to sleep here until Constance made it out of North Carolina. Sunny had insisted Constance not rush home—the damage was done. Cici had promised to be back by the following morning.

She knocked softly. So softly, she wasn't even sure Pete would hear it.

Pete opened the door within seconds, his hair ruffled, chest bare and eyes squinting with sleep. He wore only a pair of boxer briefs. Sunny wasn't sure she'd ever seen Pete in anything that bared his legs, at least not since they were kids. They were more muscular than she'd expected.

"What's the matter?" Pete looked over her head and peered around her shoulder, searching for villains. Only after he saw that Sunny was alone did his gaze halt on her flimsy sleep tee. It was white and came to the tops of her thighs. Sunny knew it was see-through, but hadn't given that any thought before she came here. Knocking on Pete's door hadn't been planned.

"I need you."

"Okay," he said. "I'm yours." Fezzi appeared next to Pete's legs. If Cici was out of town and Pete was around, Fezzi stuck to him like glue. "Let me get some pants on."

Sunny shook her head. She stepped closer, until she could feel the warmth from Pete's body against her own. He smelled like the roses that permeated Cici's room, a scent that Sunny had grown up knowing to mean her sister was nearby, and that she was safe, no matter what.

"What is it?" Pete's brows knitted.

Sunny's arms slid around his waist.

"Okay," he said. One arm went around her shoulders and pulled her against his chest. He held her tight, like she needed a hug. "It'll be okay."

Sunny nestled her face into the crook of his neck, drinking in his scents and warmth. The iron fist in her gut relaxed, but her shivers increased, changing from fear to something else, something as new as the spring wind that tried to blow the fresh scents of grass and early flowers over her burned dog quarters.

She didn't realize she'd kissed him until his body went rigid. His neck was warm and sweet. She kissed him again, closer to his ear. The arm around her shoulders tightened. After the third kiss, the hand at the small of her back balled up her shirt in his fist. She kissed along his jawline, over the short beard he'd yet to shave. By the time she reached his lips, she could feel his hardness against her. "This is what I meant," Sunny whispered, "when I said I needed you."

Pete pushed her hair from her face. "My answer hasn't changed," he whispered back. "I'm yours."

Sunny's body flooded with heat, scalp to toes. "So that means—" Sunny brushed her mouth over his "—that you'll take me back to my room and make love to me?"

Pete drew back a little. He ran his hand down her arm, to her fingertips. "Is that what you want me to do?"

Sunny nodded, her throat almost too tight to speak. "I've never done that." She wasn't sure he'd understand. She'd had sex plenty of times, and had never really thought there was anything more to it. Until the day Pete had kissed her. That kiss had been like a spotlight over every little thing Pete had ever done for her, illuminating every smile, fist bump, game played in the woods; every hour spent by her side, saving dogs, saving lives, saving her. The only other person who had ever been there for her like that was her sister.

Pete's pupils grew so big his irises almost disappeared. "I'll make love to you, Sunny Skye," he said. "But I have to warn you. I won't be coming out of that the same." There was no shame in his words. "There'll be no turning back. At least for me."

"I already can't go back." Sunny's voice cracked over her words. She'd never felt so bare in all her life. She actually felt more naked, in her see-through sleep shirt, than she ever had fully nude, in front of other men.

Pete didn't say anything. Sunny shivered and crossed her arms over her chest. He reached out and gently uncrossed them. "Don't hide, sweetheart." He drew her in again, tightly against him. "I already told you. I'm yours."

"You weren't kidding when you said you'd be here by morning." Sunny smoothed out her hair and adjusted her shirt. She didn't notice it was buttoned crooked until Constance's gaze lingered there.

Cici drew her in for a hug and held her so tight Sunny thought her spine might crack. "We got back late and slept before we came over." Constance drew back and motioned toward the Tall-Dark-and-Handsome standing inside Sunny's threshold.

Rhett waved. He looked different than he had at Christmas, when he was wearing a button-down and was freshly shaven. Now he looked like a giant beach bum, with longish hair, five-o'clock shadow and shorts that smelled like suntan lotion. Both versions were striking.

"You remember Pete." Sunny gestured to him as he suppressed a yawn.

"Yep." Rhett nodded and Pete nodded back.

"Pete's been staying with me as much as he can," Sunny explained.

Constance's eyes narrowed as she took in the scene—Pete, looking like he hadn't slept, Sunny, with her crooked blouse.

"I'm going to go check it out." Constance headed for the kitchen, which would give her access to the backyard.

Sunny followed, along with the two men, who shook hands when they passed each other. Sunny could hear them making casual talk as she trotted to keep up with her sister. Without a word, Sunny knew that Constance knew. Just from her quick assessment, Constance knew everything.

They all gathered in the back, the once serene woods with Roger's and the dogs' quarters blending in peacefully among the trees now a horror scene of wet, black wood, ash, mud and yellow crime scene tape.

"Did you lose anyone?" Constance's voice was steady and hard. "Roger's okay? You were crying too much for me to understand anything you said on the phone, and you haven't said much in your texts."

"I'm sorry. I couldn't talk about this. I couldn't text about this. But yes. Roger is okay. He's the reason things weren't worse," Sunny said. "He's staying in one of the cabins for now, with Sinbad, Willy, Calypso and Ranger. Pete took the rest." She nodded toward Pete, where he stood talking to Rhett. Her gaze lingered, her skin tingling all over despite the gruesome scene and smells.

"You're blushing," Constance said.

"What?" Sunny tore her gaze away as Pete and Rhett gestured toward the ruins and spoke in low, serious tones. "No," she said. "No, I'm not."

Constance sighed. "You slept with Pete. Sunny. How could you?" Her voice dropped. "I know you're devastated, and feeling vulnerable, but Pete's our best friend. He's not like the other guys you go for. What do you think is going to happen when you get bored this time? You can't just toss Pete out of your life. And he's not going to just fade away."

Sunny was surprised at how calm she felt, despite her sister's words. "I know that." Tears welled up behind her eyes, but she made no attempt to hide them. "I really, really know that."

Constance was quiet awhile. Her eyes narrowed as she tilted her chin up. She stepped closer and drew in a deep breath. She put her hands on Sunny's shoulders and peered closely at her face. "Oh, my God," she said. "You're not lying."

Sunny leaned her head on Cici's shoulder as tears jumped down her cheeks. She cried quietly as Constance rubbed her back. Her tears were both good and bad, a product of being overwhelmed by everything that had happened in the last few days. "You were right," she whispered. "I was arrogant. I wasn't careful. And Janice Matteri got her revenge. Even if she's arrested, the damage is done."

"You're being too hard on yourself."

"No." Sunny sniffed deeply. "You were right, as always." She pulled back and surveyed the ashes. "I've always been im-pulsive. The bratty little sister who thinks she can do what-ever she wants because she lives in the comfort of her big sister's protective shadow. Daddy was too lenient with me. I was too headstrong. You put those two things together and all you get is—" she shook her head as she surveyed her ruined dreams "—destruction. Well, I've learned my lesson." Sunny swiped under her nose with the back of her hand. "No more dog stealing. No more anything."

"Sunny, this isn't your fault," Constance said. "You didn't burn down your own rescue. Whoever did this will be caught. You're just upset right now. Nobody was hurt. That's all that matters."

"Well." Sunny's eyes filled again. "Nobody but Humphrey."

"What happened to Humphrey?" Rhett's deep voice rolled over Sunny's head. He and Pete had approached and stopped just short of the sisterly circle.

Sunny turned to face him. "He didn't get out." The words were hard to say.

"Humphrey died?" Constance took Sunny by the forearms. "You didn't tell me that."

Sunny shook her head. "He's with Dr. Winters. Pete revived him with CPR. But—" she swallowed the burning in the back of her throat "—it doesn't look good."

"The little beagle, right?" Rhett's voice changed. He had an expression on his face Sunny wouldn't have expected from such a large, imposing man. He actually looked like a little boy in a giant body.

"Yeah," Constance said. "That's him."

"The one who came out of his cage for me?" Rhett's voice was soft and high.

"That's him." Pete pressed his lips together.

Rhett turned to Sunny. Something about the expression on his face made her happy that Cici had walked so bravely into his gym one day, for no apparent reason, wearing a unicorn T-shirt and making a fool of herself while she struggled to climb a rope, and that he was now in their lives.

"Can I see him?" Rhett said. "I have to see him."

Dr. Winters let them both inside her mobile vet van, stepping out as she did. "You know I trust you, Cici," she said, pushing her glasses up her long nose. "If you say Humphrey likes this guy, then have at it. I'm willing to try anything. Just don't mess with his IVs."

"I wouldn't." Rhett shook his head. "I wouldn't do that."

Dr. Winters looked like she bit back a smile. "I'll be inside." She hitched a thumb toward her house and let the door fall closed.

Constance led Rhett to the back of the van. He let out a gush of air when they saw Humphrey. The beagle looked even smaller and thinner than he had before. His paws were bandaged, probably from the burns Dr. Winters said he got from the crate when the metal heated up. His fur was shaved where the IV lines ran. His rib cage expanded with rapid, shallow breaths. His eyes were closed.

"No," Rhett whispered. It was more of a sound than a word.

Constance clasped his hand. He squeezed it.

"Do you think he'll make it?"

"It doesn't look good."

"Can you—" Rhett lifted his free hand and made a rolling motion "—do whatever you do? To his energy? You know, where you don't touch him but you still touch him?" Rhett blinked down at her, his lashes dark and thick over his sparkling eyes. "I've seen you do it to him. I know you've done it to me." He squeezed her hand again.

It won't work, she wanted to say. *No amount of love is going to bring him back. This little guy is beyond saving.* But she kept her thoughts to herself. The sight of this large, rock-solid man, who'd done five combat tours and back-squatted more than twice his body weight, all choked up over an abused little dog was too much to bear.

"Stanzi," Rhett said. "We have to help him."

Constance's lungs grew tight. "You have to do it."

"Me?" Fear ran through Rhett's eyes, the brown and green battling it out, swimming in his emotions. "I don't know how to do that."

Constance turned him toward the beagle. "You do." She edged him closer. "Just stand near him. Think about him. Feel him, without actually touching him." She squeezed his shoulder. "I know you've done it to me."

They grew silent after that. Rhett's eyes closed as he hovered his hands just above Humphrey's battered body. "I feel his heat," he whispered after some time had passed. "It's weak. He's weak."

"True," Constance whispered. "But this goes both ways. Humphrey's feeling you, too. And you're strong. Very strong." She rubbed Rhett's back, which had grown damp with sweat, even though the van was air-conditioned.

They stood awhile longer, the silent minutes stretching into an unmeasured passage of time. Just when Constance was about to suggest they go, and give Humphrey some last peace, the little dog's right eye blinked.

Rhett gave off a quiet gasp. "Did you see that? He blinked."

"I saw it." Constance's heart swelled. "He knows you're here."

"Hey, buddy," Rhett whispered. He rolled his palms around the dog's shoulders and back, petting the air above him, without touching. "Remember me? I'm the big dork who didn't take you home, when he should've." He sniffed. "I didn't mean anything by it. I just thought you deserved better. Somebody like her." Rhett pointed at Constance. "But I changed my mind." Rhett's fingertips grazed over the fur on Humphrey's back, barely a whisper of a touch. "You definitely deserve me." He chuckled under his breath. "You stubborn little cuss."

"How's it going?" Dr. Winters's voice came tentatively from the front of the van.

Constance peered over her shoulder. Dr. Winters's brunette hair, streaked with gray, was back in a ponytail. The hard lines around her mouth were set. "He blinked," Constance said. "If that means anything."

Dr. Winters's eyes widened and she reared her head back. "Well, that's new."

"Really?" Rhett sounded like a little boy, the eagerness on his face like he anticipated bubble gum or video games.

"Hasn't looked at me once."

Constance and Rhett shared a smile.

After that, they left Humphrey in peace, securing Dr. Winters's promise to text as soon as she knew anything, whether the little beagle took a turn for better or worse. They stopped next to Rhett's Jeep.

"I'm going to head home to unpack," he said. "But I'll text you later."

Constance smiled, but it had little strength. "I'm worried about my sister," she confessed. "I've never seen her so—" she gazed up into the clear sky "—helpless. She's got no fight left. And if Humphrey dies…"

"Hey." Rhett squeezed her hands. "Don't sell her short. She's still in shock. Plus, she's got Pete to help keep her head above water. He's not going to let her go under."

"You noticed that, too, huh?" Constance thought back to the thick trail of energy the two of them had left in their wake, an invisible force as strong as a spider's web that stretched between Sunny and Pete.

"I thought they were together at the Christmas party. That's how long ago I noticed it."

"Sometimes you can't see the forest for the trees," Constance agreed. She drew a breath of spring air and noted it was tinged with ash. "Rhett." His name was barely audible as it mixed into the thoughts brewing in the back of her mind. Thoughts she couldn't believe she was even contemplating. "Part of Sunny's reaction is my fault. I've always come down hard on her for being so impulsive. Not taking more care. Now she's blaming herself for the fire, for Humphrey. Even though, without her, Humphrey wouldn't even be here."

Rhett watched her in silence.

Constance drew another deep breath. "There's this dog," she said. The more her thoughts steeped in the possibility, the stronger they got. "One we were keeping an eye on. One that

Sunny never went after. As far as I know, she never got him out. And now—" Constance pursed her lips and shook her head "—she never will. And once she quits saving dogs, she's going to quit. Saving. Dogs." Constance made a chopping motion in her palm. "And once she quits saving dogs, she's going to stop being who she is. And I can't let that happen."

Rhett nodded, waiting.

"I can't believe I'm saying this, but I was thinking that… well, the dog's on this remote property, an old farm, chained to a barn, and I was thinking… Rhett…" Constance noticed she was wringing her hands together. She shook them out. "I was wondering if you'd be willing to—"

"Yes."

Constance blinked rapidly. "What?"

"Yes," Rhett repeated. "I'll help you steal the dog."

thirty-four

It was nearly impossible to see at 13 White Fern Road at midnight. There were no streetlights, and porch lights were few and far between. On top of that, Rhett had scoped the place and found a way to go at the barn from the back, so that headlights wouldn't be spotted.

"I've got the meat." Constance held up the baggie of raw steak she'd brought to feed the poor soul that had been chained out front each time she'd come by.

With Rhett's Jeep nestled in the trees, they skirted their way out to the overgrown farmland and picked their way through the dark, one small flashlight trained on the ground. The night sky was full of the sound of tree frogs, the chirping of the Virginia peepers so loud they needn't have worried about being heard. You could smell the barn before you could see it, the rotting timbers and rusted nails thick on the humid air. Rhett's movements were easy, calculated, thorough—suggesting he was definitely in his element on a stealth mission.

"No dog," Rhett whispered, shining his light over the rustic structure. "He's either inside or out front."

"Or dead."

"No negative thoughts," Rhett ordered.

"Maybe he's around the other side." Constance's voice was hopeful. Her stomach was tight, but she otherwise felt cool and controlled, with none of the jitters or shakes she thought she'd get from trespassing.

"We'll find out in a second."

They peeked their heads around to the front of the barn. Constance spied the metal chain, connected to a stake in the ground. The chain lay in the grass and wound around to the other side of the barn. She lifted it and followed the trail, until she came to a black lump that she nearly tripped over.

Rhett squatted down next to it, but the black lump didn't move. For a second, Constance thought it was too late. Her throat tightened up and shrunk, making it hard to breathe. Rhett waved a hand near the lump.

Slowly, a head raised. Then it sank back down.

Rhett ran his pencil flashlight over the form. The yellow beam illuminated an ugly sight of dull, black pelt stretched over visible ribs and skin with open sores, ticks and infection.

"He's worse," Constance gasped. "Way worse than when I spied him months ago." Bile rose up the back of her throat. How did Sunny do this on a regular basis? New respect filled her heart for her baby sister, even though it was simultaneously breaking for the poor creature on the ground.

Rhett said nothing, his lips pressed tight, the residual light from the flashlight making his angry face look ghostly.

A cracking sound came in the distance. "Who's out there?" An older woman's voice barked out from the vicinity of the house. A screen door slammed shut. The sound of a weapon being cocked followed.

Rhett put a finger to his lips, killed the light and melted into the dark. A second later, Constance heard a long, slow creak. "Psst!"

Constance fumbled by the meager light of the stars and moon until she bumped into Rhett's back. He caught her by the arm and pulled her in front of him, into the barn. Once he'd pulled the door closed he flicked on his flashlight.

"We can't leave him out there." Constance's whisper was full of panic, her fear for herself overridden by her fear of what the old woman might do to the dog.

"We won't. We just need to bide our time. Trust me."

The yellow beam of the flashlight revealed the barn in circles of narrow, diffused light, but each dark corner was the same as the next: empty nooks of rotting wood, moldering hay, rusted chains and farm equipment. There was a wheelbarrow with no wheels, an assortment of shovels, picks and scythes, buckets, broken lanterns and even discarded horseshoes.

"I said—" the woman's voice was getting closer to the barn "—who's out here? I'm armed! And trust me, I'm not afraid to use it!"

"Wait." Rhett's light, aimed at the ground, froze. He went back a few inches. "What's that?"

Constance watched the light travel upward, until she recognized what she was looking at: a long, frayed, twisted piece of hemp. "A rope."

"It leads to a loft." Rhett looked down at her. "Looks like all your rope-climb training wasn't in vain."

"Holy shit."

"Let me go first. At the top, I'll shine the light down. Then I'll be able to pull you in." The light clicked off, and only the sounds of Rhett scaling the rope followed. Within twenty seconds the light clicked back on. "Come on," Rhett said from the ledge inside the loft.

Constance walked over and tested the integrity of the knot. It felt secure. She remembered back to the first time she'd seen the people at Semper Fit doing rope climbs and the thought that had crossed her mind: *When in real life will I ever need to climb a rope?* She hissed a laugh, then drew a deep breath and jumped onto the rope.

"Hook your feet," Rhett instructed, just like they were at the gym.

Constance flailed at first, but then grasped the hemp with her feet and stood up. She fumbled in the dark but eventually got herself to the top. There, Rhett's hand grasped her forearm, then her waist as he pulled her onto the ledge. They spilled on the floor.

Rhett made a gesture with his fist that Constance took to mean, *Be quiet.*

Then he killed the light.

They waited, watching the door of the barn. A bright circular beam ran around the gaps in the slats and between the bottom of the door and ground. The door creaked open.

Rhett hooked his arm around Stanzi's head and clamped his hand over her mouth. Her muffled cry came into his palm as a figure edged into the barn, holding a bright light. The lantern was set on the ground, and as the light shone upward Rhett could see the person was an older woman, training a shotgun around the barn.

His brain immediately assessed and categorized the scene: elderly civilian with what looked like a Sako, which would be lightweight, but accurate. The way she held the weapon told him she knew how to use it. There was only one way in and one way out of this place, and the old lady was blocking it. Options were limited.

She lowered the weapon and drew something out of her

pocket. A flashlight clicked on, which she shined around the barn. Rhett and Stanzi both ducked beneath the ledge and waited as the light passed over top of them. Stanzi's cool fingers wrapped around his wrist, just beneath his watch, and squeezed.

Another pass of bright light, before it finally went out. The barn door creaked, then banged shut. Rhett raised his head and peeked over the ledge. There was nothing but blackness, punctuated by moonlight through the many gaps and holes eating through the rotted structure.

"We're going to scale down in the dark," he whispered. "Can't risk the flashlight. I'll go first and be on the ground to catch you."

Stanzi squeezed his wrist again.

Rhett felt around in the dark until his fingers lit on the rope. He rappelled down, landed without a sound and waited. A few seconds later, the rope wiggled in his hand. Stanzi gave a series of soft, whispered grunts as she made her way down. Near the bottom, Rhett grabbed her around the waist and eased her to the wooden floor. He took her sweaty hand and led her toward the door, taking his steps slow and silent.

When he reached the door, he peered through the slats. All he saw was darkness. Just as he was about to push the door open as quietly as he could, he caught a whiff of cigarette smoke.

"Is she gone?" Stanzi's whisper filtered upward.

Rhett didn't answer. He put his finger to his lips. Stanzi hushed as he pushed her behind him, just in case. After a couple of minutes, the sounds of a rough foot in the grass, maybe stomping out a cigarette, came through the door. Another minute passed before the old woman cleared her phlegmy throat, followed by footsteps heading away from the barn.

Rhett closed his eyes, which allowed him to detect, about

twenty seconds later, the sound of a door creaking a ways off, about as far off as the house was from the barn. "C'mon." Rhett shook Stanzi's shoulder. "Let's get the dog and go."

They drove in silence. Rhett had clicked off the radio as soon as the dog was loaded in the back seat, atop an old blanket, and the wheels were rolling. The windows were down, which eased the smell of blood, piss, shit, vomit and dirt that came from the back. Everything that had happened that night rolled through Constance's mind, along with every possible feeling that could accompany those actions. Delayed fear, adrenaline drain, disbelief, even pride. The only thing she didn't feel was guilt.

Except for maybe the reaction she was betting she'd get from Dr. Winters. "Another one, Cici?" she would say. "Where do you expect me to put them all?" Then she'd sigh and say, "Bring him in."

"Oh, shit," Rhett said, his voice a low growl. "What's going on there?"

When Constance first saw the red and blue flashing lights, her pulse jacked up so fast she thought she might pass out. "Slow down."

The Jeep rolled to a crawl as it neared what had to be three or four police vehicles. Two people in handcuffs were being led toward the backs of the vehicles. One of them was a tall, skinny woman and the other a bearded man in a baseball cap.

Constance's heart slowed, the beats rough and hard with adrenaline but losing their steam. She smiled so hard a laugh escaped her lips.

"What is it?" Rhett peered at her, his eyes narrowing in confusion.

"That," Constance said, her voice giddy, "is Janice Matteri. Being arrested."

thirty-five

Daddy's gravestone was a simple marker on the side of a grassy hill in a quiet cemetery about twenty miles south of home. It read Patrick H. Morrigan. 1SG US Army. Vietnam Veteran. There was a cross between his birth and death dates, and a United States flag planted in the ground above his marker. He hadn't wanted to be buried in Arlington Cemetery or anything fancy done at his funeral.

He'd just wanted to be next to Mom. Her grave marker, adjacent to his, read Nicole S. Morrigan. Beloved Mother. *La Vie en Rose.* 7 September 1947. 28 May 1993.

Sunny settled on a bare patch of grass, next to them both, and crossed her legs at the ankles. The morning sun was already warm, promising a humid, sweaty day. Constance sank down next to her, arms at rest on her knees.

"Hey, Daddy," Sunny said. "Hey, Mom."

"Hey, Mom," Constance echoed. *Hey, Daddy.* For that, she used sign language.

A sudden, cool breeze rustled through, fluttering the leaves in the surrounding trees and giving Sunny a welcome kiss on the face. She watched Constance pluck a flower from the ground, the kind that grew like weeds in dense patches of overgrown grass. Sunny remembered that she used to make necklaces from them as a kid by knotting the stems together, and would come through the back door with sticky sap dried all over her fingers as she proudly presented Mom with her latest creation. Mom would smile, her sunny hair framing her face as she bent down to accept the gift, which she strung around her neck. The necklace hung there, awkward and messy, against one of the colorful blouses she favored. The flower necklaces were one of the few memories Sunny had of Mom.

She watched Constance start to make one of those wreaths, which she did every year on the anniversary of Mom's death. It was only in that moment that Sunny remembered it was actually Constance who had taught her how to make the wreaths. "I wish you'd had someone to mother you, too," Sunny said, breaking the silence.

Constance added another flower to her chain. She didn't look up, but smiled.

"I had you at least. All you had was Daddy. And he wasn't much on mothering."

Constance chuckled, signed something to Daddy's grave, then said, "I told him you're still sassy as ever."

A little boy, off in the distance, stared in her direction. He stood beneath a giant maple tree, clutching his mother's hand. Mother and child both wore nice clothes, like they'd come from a church service.

"I was always jealous of that," Sunny admitted. "I know you think I was the little sister that got everything easy. But I was always jealous of the things you had that I didn't. Like more time with Mom." She nodded at the grave. "And all those special ways you had to talk to Daddy that I didn't have."

Constance played with her flower chain, her bottom lip tucked thoughtfully under the upper one. She signed again to Daddy's grave. "Daddy indulged you way more than he did me."

The little boy pointed at her. He said something to his mother. The mother put her finger to her lips and pulled the little boy away, heading off in another direction.

"Maybe so, but—" Sunny traced her finger over Daddy's name on his headstone "—we only had one language. And even that was limited. You and Daddy had so many languages. And then, in the end, you were the only one he let see him suffer," Sunny said. "That was a language all by itself. I was never welcome to take him for his chemo or radiation. He shooed me away if I saw him weak or sick."

"You didn't want to see him like that," Constance said. "Trust me."

"I believe you." Sunny rested her chin on her knees. "But I was jealous of all the ways you had to talk to him, none of which had anything to do with words. Because Daddy hated words."

Constance sniffed deeply and blew it out in a sigh. "Yeah," she agreed. "But you were his little girl. The only little girl that he had." She must've seen Sunny's look of confusion, because she held up a hand. "See, you got to be his daughter." Constance offered a weak smile. "You got to be a little kid. That bright spot of sunshine who reminded him who he once was, before the war. Before Mom's death. That's why he indulged you. You were that missing piece of him. That missing piece of what he wanted his life to be. I couldn't be his little girl, after Mom died. I had to be something else. He knew he couldn't raise us alone. So I had to step up. And he hated that. You were so much like Mom—bright and shiny and everything good. I was just a symbol of his weakness."

Sunny went silent after that. She watched her sister lay the flower wreath on Mom's grave. A cool breeze rustled her hair, breaking through the humidity. "Thank you."

Constance looked up with a wrinkled brow.

"For being there," Sunny said. "For rescuing the dog," she added. She snorted a laugh. "I still can't believe you did that."

The night Constance and Rhett had shown up at her doorstep, after midnight, with the stolen rottweiler mutt from 13 White Fern Road, Sunny had thought she was hallucinating. "Am I seeing what I think I'm seeing?" she'd said. "Did my straight-nosed sister suddenly go rogue?"

Constance laughed, too, finally letting go. "I had to rescue Buddy," Constance said, using sign language at the same time she spoke. If Daddy was in the room, even if he was buried six feet under, Cici would include him. "Not just for him. I had to show you that I was wrong."

"Wait. What?" Sunny rubbed her temples. "Did my big sister just say she was wrong?"

Constance got up and settled herself behind Sunny. A moment later, Sunny felt the familiar pull of her big sister doing her hair in a French braid. She used to do it before every dance class or cheerleading meet. "I'm sorry I ever made you feel like you needed to change. You're perfect the way you are. Every impulsive, fearless, irritating little piece of you."

Sunny laughed, which quickly turned into a yelp. "Ouch. Quit pulling so hard."

"You need your hair done," Constance scolded. "You can't run with your hair loose."

Sunny's stomach squeezed. "I don't want to run."

"You're running." Constance jerked her hair a little tighter.

"People have been raising money all month for you and Pete and the dogs. Now you have to do the workout."

"Good morning, everyone. Thanks for coming out this fine Saturday morning for a heavy dose of fitness, community and hopefully some fun." Rhett paused while people variously whooped or groaned. "But seriously." Once everyone had quieted, he continued. "Today is a special day. Most of you know why you're here. But in case you live under a rock and missed the boat, today we are here to support a very important fundraiser. Many of you have worked hard to raise money to help rebuild Pittie Place, a dog rescue near and dear to one of our members' hearts. I think you all know Red." Rhett gestured to Stanzi, who waved at the community she'd become such an integral part of. He paused again while everyone cheered, clapped or called out, "Hey, Red!"

"Turns out, Red's got a sister," Rhett continued. "And her name is Sunny."

Sunny waved, and everyone whooped and clapped again.

"She works tirelessly and selflessly to rescue not just abused pit bulls, but any dog she comes across. Many of those dogs are taken in by Pete." Rhett gestured to the unassuming army vet who stood quietly with his arm around Sunny's waist. "He takes in many of the dogs Sunny rescues and rehabilitates them into service dogs for wounded veterans."

The claps and cheers again took over the gym.

"Because the cause is so important—" Rhett rubbed his hands together "—we've got a workout to match."

This is when the groans came, followed by comments, gagging sounds, good-humored threats to leave and heavy sighs.

"Today, in order to make your workout worthy of your donations, we will execute the following: a one-mile run, into the park and back, followed by fifty pull-ups, fifty push-ups, fifty sit-ups, fifty air squats, fifty wall balls, fifty lunges, fifty box jumps, fifty double unders and another one-mile run into the park and back."

Once he was finished reading the intro, Rhett surveyed the packed gym. "Most of these are deceptively simple movements. But trust me, you're going to feel it. Our one-mile route is out the bay door—" Rhett pointed "—across the street and into the park. The half-mile turnaround point is marked with white flags on either side of the path. The quarter-mile turnaround is also marked, for those of you scaling the runs to half miles. Last but not least, all of you know how I feel about whining. Multiply that times a thousand, and that's how I feel about whining during today's workout. Just do the work, remember why you're doing it and be thankful you're above ground and suffering with your friends."

After that, they all warmed up, then started gathering what they needed for the workout. Days like this always brought a special sort of chaos—a lot of bodies filling up the gym, competing for space on the rig, with everyone working together to make sure the job got done with as much flow as possible.

Stanzi and Sunny met Rhett outside at the starting point, along the wall of the building by the open bay door. Stanzi's ponytail was the longest it'd been since he'd met her and she looked confident, ready for the workout. She wore a pair of bike shorts and a tank top with a white pony on the front. The pony had a multicolored mane and tail and kicked its little hooves in the air.

"Everyone loves the new shirt."

She planted her hand over it and gave him a shove in response to the big grin he got on his face. "I couldn't resist when I saw it."

"Yeah," Sunny agreed. "The blue really brings out your eyes."

"Shut up."

Sunny giggled.

"I can't wait for you to die during the one-mile runs." Stanzi gave her a shove.

Sunny jumped up and down on her toes. "I can't believe you talked me into this."

"You'll do anything for your dogs."

"True."

"Hey, man." Pete stuck out his hand to Rhett. "Thanks again for the fundraising opportunity. Much respect."

Rhett clasped Pete's hand and squeezed. "The respect is all mine."

Pete moved off to get ready for the workout and Rhett turned his attention to the sisters. He'd sensed a new closeness and calm between them ever since the night at the barn. They'd spent all day together at the emergency vet the next morning, and when the dog had pulled through, Stanzi had named him Buddy—her father's nickname in Vietnam. Rhett had watched from the wings as Stanzi had helped the vet bathe him, her slender fingers going carefully over his filthy coat, one hand gently shading his eyes when she rinsed soap from his head.

Something funny had happened in his chest in that moment. He wasn't sure what it was, but it had both scared the hell out of him and made him feel a safeness he hadn't experienced in almost two decades.

"Hey." Stanzi took his arm. "You go on ahead when we run. Don't wait for me."

"I won't leave you," Rhett said.

"I know you won't." She offered a soft smile.

She meant more than just the run. Rhett could see it, flooding those crystal clear eyes. He reached out and tucked a loose strand of hair behind her ear. Her eyes widened and she looked around at the crowd. "I don't care who saw me do that," Rhett said.

Hobbs, Duke, Sean, James and Zoe, all waiting to run together, stared in their direction. They'd most definitely seen that, and were now whispering to each other. Rhett ignored them.

"Are you sure?"

"Yeah. They can all suck it."

"No." Stanzi giggled a little. "About running with me. You're faster. Much longer gait."

"I'll wear body armor to slow me down."

Stanzi shook her head. "Badass."

Rhett ran back inside the gym and grabbed his twenty-pound vest. As soon as he had it fastened he raised his voice. "Three…two…one… GO!"

The most competitive streaked out ahead. Rhett, Constance and Sunny fell in behind them and everyone else came after. Energy was high but the nervous chatter petered off once they clomped across the street and hit the entrance to the park. The woods were a welcome, cool relief from the hot sun and humid air. Constance practiced good breathing as much as she focused on steady, even strides with good foot strike. As much as Sunny bitched about running, all her spinning had done her good. She was able to keep up for about a quarter of a mile before she fell back and waved them on.

Just as they passed the quarter-mile flag, staked on the side of the trail, Constance reached up and touched the little flower she'd pinned in her hair, just to the left of her ponytail. She'd relied on her father all her life for guidance and strength. Just before she left the graveyard this morning, she decided this might be one time she needed her mother instead, and she'd grabbed one of the flowers from the necklace to carry with her.

"Up around this corner," Rhett said, his voice conversational and unfettered, despite the heavy vest he wore. "How you feeling?"

Constance smiled. "Good." She glanced behind her, but Sunny offered a cheerful wave. There was a good chunk of space between her and Rhett and the next set of runners. Farther off, those that were scaling to half miles were already turning around.

Next thing she knew, Constance was at the top of the hill.

"C'mon, Stanzi." Rhett motioned her to keep up. "You got this."

Something deep inside her fluttered like a bird, dying to get out. "I'm right behind you."

Constance grabbed Rhett's hand and turned in the direction of Zoe and Hobbs and the others, who were just ahead. And then she took off, at top speed, headed back to the gym to jump on that pull-up bar and attack the rest of this workout.

By the time Rhett finished the indoor portion of the workout, he looked for Stanzi and spotted her, hands on her knees, gasping for air. Sunny was next to her, flat on her back. She'd cut all the reps in half and ran just the one mile.

Rhett estimated he had time to run his mile and make it back before Stanzi was ready to go on hers.

The second mile was slower than the first, but thanks to all the running he and Stanzi had done, it wasn't as difficult as he'd anticipated. By the time he streaked back inside the gym to officially finish, Stanzi was right there, ready to go out. Rhett stripped off the weighted vest and fell in beside her. The loss of extra weight felt so glorious he wanted to cry.

"You don't have to run this with me," she gasped, her feet

shuffling more than running, or even walking. "I got nothing left. You're already done."

"Shut up." Rhett gave her a gentle shove.

She rewarded him with a weak smile.

By the time they made it to the turnaround spot in the woods the second time, Stanzi actually got her second wind and picked up her pace. Rhett ran beside her in silence all the way back to the gym.

Stanzi streaked into the bay and looked at the timer on the wall. Then she sank to the floor, next to her sister, who was still on her back. Her chest rose and fell in great gasps. Her hands covered her face. Zoe, Hobbs, Duke, Pete and a few others who were finished walked over and gave her high fives. Stanzi just stuck her hand in the air and let them slap her.

Rhett grabbed her hand and squeezed it. She squeezed back. He sank to a squat. "You did it," he said. "I'm proud of you."

Her eyes fluttered open. "Yeah?" she said between gasps. Her mouth turned up at the corners. "Thanks. I'm proud of you, too."

Rhett didn't know what to say to that, but it made his chest tight. He left her lying there so he could finish coaching the rest of the group, most of whom were not yet finished. He grabbed his phone and recorded some footage of people who were still working, utter fatigue overcoming their bodies and faces. People came back in from their second runs, drenched in sweat and cheeks on fire. Some sank against the walls and others directly to the floor. Somebody went outside to puke. When he came back inside, Rhett realized it was Callahan. He grinned. Callahan gave a rueful grin, shook his head and stood there gasping, hands on his knees. The music boomed and the ceiling fan whirred, mixing up the humid, natural air. It smelled like sweat and dirt and weak perfume.

By the time it was all over, Rhett called for everyone to

gather around for a group photo. Rhett got one of the older kids, who hadn't done the workout, to take the picture, so that he could be in it, next to Stanzi. He slipped an arm around her shoulders and hers slinked around his waist.

Once the picture was snapped, Stanzi grasped him by the biceps and stared up at him with a new kind of light in her eyes. Her hair had come loose of the barrette and ponytail, causing little flyaways to stick to the dried sweat on her cheeks, and her shirt was drenched in sweat.

He leaned down and pressed his forehead to hers. "Nice job, My Pretty Pony."

She kissed him. "Thanks."

thirty-six

By noon, most people had gone home. Constance had opened up her massage chair and given postworkout care to anyone who wanted a little relief before they left. She listened to all the exhausted chatter going on around her while she worked. Sean hung out and chatted with Sunny, and from the snippets Constance could overhear, Sunny was thanking him for helping with the arson investigation, which he'd taken the lead on. Zoe and Hobbs were last, both rising with satisfied, sleepy expressions.

"Marry me, Red," Zoe said, stretching her arms high over her head.

"She's all mine," Hobbs argued, tossing his empty beer bottle into the recycling bin. He'd popped it open about two minutes after the workout and screamed, "Carbs!" at the top of his lungs before he'd chugged half of it down in one go.

"Move over." Rhett ordered them both out of the way and plopped into the massage chair. He rested his face in the cradle with a satisfied grunt. His long, large body dwarfed the chair and Constance had to raise the face cradle to its highest level to accommodate his torso without making him hunch.

"Something tells me you get plenty of massages," Hobbs muttered, but he gave a good-natured smile on his way out. "Later, people. Enjoy the rest of your day."

"I'm going to head home, too," Sunny said. "You people are crazy and I'm going to take the longest bath of my life, then sleep until dinnertime. Plus, Buddy is waiting for me. I'm not going to lie. I'm in love."

"You better be talking about me." Pete came up behind her, slid his arms around her waist and lifted her up.

"I totally meant the dog." Sunny broke into giggles. "But only you would understand that. So—" she turned around in his arms and hugged him close "—that's why I love you, too."

"Glad you had fun, guys." Rhett stuck up a hand without lifting his face from the massage chair.

Once they were all gone, Constance pressed her palms to Rhett's back and leaned forward, giving him all her weight. She worked on him for about ten minutes before the sweet scents of his sweaty body, so close to hers, made her shiver inside. She slid her hands up under his shirt, gently caressing his back. He made a satisfied sound in the back of his throat. "Why don't we go back to your place," she said, "and do this right."

Rhett sat up with a curious grin on his face. "My place?"

"Yeah. I've never seen it. You should take me to your place."

"Oh, yeah? What're we going to do there?" He climbed out of the chair and stretched.

Constance stepped in close and arched an eyebrow at him. "For starters, you're going to let me see Humphrey. I want to know how he's doing."

"He's awesome." Rhett's voice got quiet. "Made himself right at home."

"Where'd you put his cage?"

"At the curb. For the trash."

"Are you kidding?"

"No. We did it together." Rhett swiped some residual sweat from his forehead. "Walked out to the curb with that ugly metal hunk of shit. Humphrey followed behind, no leash. I set the cage down and told Humphrey he never had to get in it again. He sat down and leaned against my leg. We stared at it awhile before he got up and went right back into my house. I am not shitting you."

Constance felt her eyes well up.

Rhett smiled, like he saw right through her. "When I went back inside I found him balled up in my recliner. We fight over it every night."

Constance giggled through her tears. "I hope you let him win."

Rhett's hand went to her hair, where he carefully removed her ponytail holder. "No need. He wins all on his own, fair and square. He may look small, but he's tougher than all of us."

"Of course he is." Constance tipped on her toes and gave Rhett a gentle kiss on the lips. "He's a dangerous breed. You better watch out."

Rhett laughed softly and kissed her back. "I'm not scared," he said. "Not with you around."

"Hey, guess what?" Constance leaned back and smiled. "I finally found your nickname."

"What?" Rhett's face spread into a big smile. "No way. What is it?"

"How would you feel—" Constance danced her fingertips around his waist, to the bare skin at his lower back "—if I called you—" she pulled him roughly against her "—sweetie?"

"Hmm," he mused. "I like where you're going. But I'm not sure it fits. We'd be living a lie."

Constance giggled. "Pumpkin?" she joked.

"Meh."

She tried a British accent. "Darling?"

Rhett grunted disapproval.

"Baby?" She winked. "Can I call you baby?"

"You're getting warmer." Rhett leaned down, his voice softening.

"How about…*querido*? Or—" Constance leaned in and whispered against his ear "—*amorcito*?"

He made a groaning sound and squeezed her so tight he lifted her off her feet. "I like it, *munequita*," he whispered back. "I knew you wouldn't let me down."

"No," she said, and slid her arms around his neck. "Never."

★ ★ ★ ★ ★

acknowledgments

One of my earliest memories is of sitting on the cold concrete stoop of my Alaskan home, just outside the back door, with a stack of books by my side. Our military quarters had a community yard that contained a large dandelion patch, a rusted-out swing set, trees that flanked the sand dunes and a long expanse of grass where my father taught me how to play football.

My mother let me take as many books as I wanted to sit on that porch, under a sunny sky, and read to my heart's content while the world bustled around me. I was only four or five years old.

That's why my first acknowledgment belongs to my mother.

I'm not saying that books wouldn't have existed in my life without her, or that I wouldn't have been an avid reader. But because of Mom I saw books as a treat, a respite, an escape, a discovery and a privilege. Mom is the one who showed me that books are *magic*.

The fact that I now have a book of my own to share with

the world is a personal triumph that I can't even describe, and I'm honored to be able to thank those who helped me realize this dream.

To my amazing, talented, brilliant literary agent, Sara Megibow, who believed in me from the start and who never, ever gave up—your endless cache of patience, optimism, knowledge and passion amazes me and I'm so fortunate to have you on my side for this journey. Thank you.

To my editor, Margot Mallinson, and to the entire team at Harlequin, thank you for taking a chance on me. You always seem to know what I'm trying to say, even if I don't nail it the first time. Thank you for shining a light and reading between the lines. You made this book stronger with your eagle eyes.

Chris Boswell, who's been reading and critiquing my stories since we were starry-eyed contest winners who met at Pikes Peak Writers Conference, thank you for your unwavering belief in my success, story after story, year after year. Sometimes I think you believed in my stories more than I did. You've most certainly earned your "coffee in a cup," my friend.

Thank you to Jennifer Sovine, the hero of my massage world. I can't believe my luck in getting such a smart, talented lady as my instructor. When I start getting frustrated or too ahead of myself, I still hear your patient voice in the back of my mind: "Slow down, Elysia. Breathe." Thank you for your "yes/no" story. Your way of teaching via storytelling went straight to my heart.

To Laurie Landers and Operation Paws for Homes, whose tireless, selfless work rescuing dogs has inspired me for years, thank you for giving me such a lovely, warm heart in which to model the heroines of this book. Without people like you, the world would truly be a sad place.

To all military service members, both active and veteran, thank you for your service. To all the wounded warriors who have entrusted themselves in my care, I am honored to have worked with you. My intention in this book is a respectful reflection of my service to you. To my favorite veteran, responsible for my determination and inability to quit: I couldn't have come this far without you. Thanks, Dad.

To my sons, Brody and Brayden, who've always cheered me on: it means the world that you are proud of me. To my daughter, Magdalena, who reads everything I write and inspires me daily with her unwavering strength—you enrich my life, and in turn, make my stories more colorful, more real and more magical.

And finally, to my husband, Mike: thank you for always being my foundation of love, support and encouragement. I'll never forget your words, the day you read the first chapter of my first novel: "Wow. Are you prepared for success? Because this is really good."

Thanks for being my best friend. We did it!